Elizabeth and Darcy

*A comic sequel to
Jane Austen's novel*

Pride and Prejudice

by

Marlene Jondal Ebert

Copyright © 2012 by Marlene Jondal Ebert

Published by MYEbert Publishing
4171 Donald Ct.
San Diego, CA 92117
Phone: 858-270-5336

E-mail: myebert@localnet.com

Published for : Marlene Yvonne (Vonne) Jondal Ebert

Book design by Marlene Ebert
Text: Optima, Headings Andale Mono

Cover photo: Helen Jondal Elliott

Cover design by Wild Woman Design, San Diego, CA

ISBN : 978-0-578-11902-1

No portion of this work may be published by any means without the express permission of the copyright holder.

Subjects: Family life, Humor, History of Contraception, Jane Austen's England, Sexuality

765432

Price: $24.95

TABLE OF CONTENTS

The Wedding	1
The Honeymoon	1
Pemberley	5
December 1, Thursday	27
Carleton	40
Lambton Church	43
The Blakeley's	47
Mrs. Flanders	55
Georgiana	66
The Gold Dress	93
Tea at Pemberley	99
December 23	103
Christmas at Pemberley	105
Dinner at the Winston's	106
London Trip	112
Sightseeing	121
Fitzwilliam	123
The Pemberley Ball	136
Tea at the Vicarage	157
Tea at the Carleton's	159
A Fair Proposal	162
Thornwood	172
Mrs. Bennet	179
The Fair	189
The Fox Hunt	197
Benjamin	207
Harrison	225
Miss Bingley	228
Lady Catherine de Bourgh	230
A Thornwood Ball	236
Christmas at Thornwood	240
Dinner at the Carleton's	240
Emiline	244

Dedicated to women
everywhere

The Wedding

Half of the young women of Meryton envied Elizabeth Bennet, and the other half of them pitied her, for the day had arrived when she would marry Fitzwilliam Darcy, a man of considerable wealth. But the community in its brief acquaintance with him had judged him proud, even arrogant.

One could well see the possibilities in the match either for happiness or misery. Darcy has attained the age of 28 without ever having to serve in the military, and Elizabeth has reached the age of 21 without being orphaned or even breaking a leg.

Though Darcy's mother died quite some years earlier, his father lived until he was 22 and his sister Georgiana 12. The elder Mr. Darcy had husbanded his extensive properties in Derbyshire carefully, and, as a result, Darcy inherited Pemberley, a large estate, and a sizeable fortune. His father had apparently educated his son well for Darcy had been managing the estate since his father's death to good effect.

Elizabeth and Darcy didn't reach this day entirely without difficulty, but the errors, frictions, and misunderstandings were now past.

Elizabeth grew up in Hertferdshire in a much less wealthy family. The wedding day was a very special one, for not only were Darcy and Elizabeth to wed, but also Darcy's best friend Bingley would marry Jane, Elizabeth's dearest sister.

A year earlier Charles Bingley had come to Hertfordshire and rented the Netherfield estate, bringing his friend Darcy with him to visit. Nearby at Longbourn the Bennet family lived, and at the village of Meryton the two gentlemen met Jane and Elizabeth.

The night before the wedding all the fond farewells were expressed between Jane, Elizabeth, their younger sisters Kitty and Mary, and their parents Mr. and Mrs. Bennet.

November 26, 1814, Saturday: The Honeymoon

After the wedding, Mr. and Mrs. Bingley repaired to Netherfield to pursue the life of happiness due to two persons so considerate, agreeable, and rich.

Darcy and Elizabeth also left immediately after the wedding, but would not reach Pemberley until the following evening. It was the last Saturday in November. The weather was cool at first and progressed to cold during the trip to Pemberley as they traveled northward.

Darcy had made arrangements for the overnight stay at an inn along the way for themselves and the servants handling the chaise and four.

On arrival at the inn the porter took Mr. and Mrs. Darcy to their comfortable, pleasant room, though it could hardly be deemed grand by Darcy, accustomed to very fine surroundings indeed.

Darcy helped Elizabeth shed her coat and removed his own. Unused to life without his valet, he then looked around to determine what to do with them. Elizabeth found the storage space for wraps, and they managed together to stow them. Before they could gather their thoughts someone rapped at the door.

"Begging your pardon, sir," the porter said, "The footman found one more small box you should have." Darcy opened it and found a bottle of sherry and two wine glasses, carefully packed.

"Apparently Selbey didn't trust the quality of the inn's cellar for our first post-wedding toast." He proceeded to open the bottle, and as he did, said, "It shouldn't be long til our supper tray arrives."

Elizabeth had moved to the fireplace and was alternately rubbing her hands and shifting her skirts to warm all sides.

Darcy filled the glasses and handed one to her. Before they could take a sip there was another rap at the door. This time Elizabeth said, "Allow me," and she opened the door, revealing the waiter standing with a large tray.

"Just as you ordered, sir," he said.

Darcy thanked him and took the tray. Elizabeth closed the door, and they made their way to a small table with two chairs flanking it. Darcy set the tray down, brought their wine glasses, and sat at the table. Elizabeth was already seated, pouring the tea.

"I hope you won't think me unladylike, Mr. Darcy, but I am ravenous."

"I thought we agreed you'd call me Darcy."

"And so I shall, but somehow 'Mr. Darcy' seemed more appropriate in this situation."

"Are you generally so casual in breaking contracts?"

"Yes, when they are of a trivial nature."

By now they were both happily devouring the sandwiches, pickles, tea, and little cakes.

"I do believe I'm finally warm again," she said, finishing the last of her wine.

"Another glass?" he asked.

"Not now, thank you." He poured another glass for himself, secured the items on the tray, and picked it up. Elizabeth opened the door, and he set the tray in the hall on a table.

They closed the door together, and, slipping an arm around her, he gently pulled her towards him. Looking up she placed her hands on his sides and waited.

"Ah, Mrs. Darcy, what fate awaits us? If only happiness could be determined by a wedding ceremony." He gently caressed her back with both hands and looked towards the window. He paused a few moments before continuing. "But I think you may have observed as I have that many a marriage is held together by grit or fear rather than by happiness."

"Are you trying to frighten me, Mr. Darcy?"

"Not at all. I think I know you well enough to realize that I couldn't even if I wanted to, which I certainly do not. However, to get back to my thought. I believe that few really good things happen by chance however we may wish that they would."

Elizabeth was listening intently, but said nothing.

"I expect that many people look forward to great happiness in marriage, but not a few are disappointed."

"You don't expect me to be unhappy, do you?"

"Not if I can prevent it. But consider how little we are taught about how to create a happy marriage. I would not be surprised to learn that you have received far more hours of instruction in embroidery than you have about married life."

Elizabeth was looking down now, her face flushed. They had moved away from the door and were standing side by side facing the fireplace.

"I can tell you in one sentence what I have been taught about intimate relations between a man and a woman," he continued.

She looked up at him in surprise.

"I'm not talking about what men say in casual conversation to each other. I'm referring to my father's instruction. He's the only person I feel I could rely on for disinterested information. No, the other comments are so wildly various that it's hard to determine if there is any truth in them at all."

"What did your father tell you?"

"He said that most respectable women don't like intimate relations with men, that nothing can change it, and I might just as well accept it."

"That certainly sounds bleak. And about as extensive as my own instruction."

"Are you going to tell me what it was?"

"I was told that I would not like sleeping with my husband, but that I should just think about England."

A grin spread over Darcy's face, and Elizabeth responded in kind. When he had composed himself, he looked around the room and said, "Lizzy, my love, it's a bit chilly. Do you suppose we could shed our outer clothing and continue our conversation under the covers?"

"You'll have to unfasten these buttons," she replied, turning around.

He released them, and they quickly undressed themselves. They both moved to the near side of the bed, and when they collided, he said, "After you, Mrs. Darcy." She climbed up onto the high bed and moved to the other side. They pulled the coverlet up to their chins and faced each other.

"So," he said, "perhaps we must conclude that in our own little universe it is generally acknowledged that you are not going to enjoy our encounter this evening."

"I don't think we should be quite that hasty."

He waited, but she said no more. "Do you suppose you could elaborate?"

"Well, I suppose there are many inconsiderate men in the world, but I cannot count you among them. And your consideration will likely determine my happiness. Even I won't know until later; therefore we must conclude at this point that no one knows what my experience will be."

"Well said, Elizabeth." He reflected for a while and continued, "I can't say that my parents were unhappy, though I only remember once seeing Father kiss Mother. He had stopped while riding in the fields where he saw some wild flowers. He picked a small bouquet, brought them home, and handed them to her as she was standing by a table. He leaned over and kissed her cheek, but she didn't respond.

"And I can't say I saw much evidence of real affection between your parents either during the times I saw them together. I thought I sensed more affection between you and your father."

"Both observations are very near the mark, Darcy. It's difficult to describe the relationship between my parents, and I don't really want to try right now. Father was on occasion affectionate to me—moreso when I was young. I always felt his love, and when it really mattered he was there for me. Indeed if he had not been, I would now be married to Mr. Collins."

"Mister Collins! Your cousin Mr. Collins?"

"The very one. He proposed to me the morning after the ball at Netherfield, and Mama was determined I should accept."

"Why was that?"

"Surely you know that Papa's estate is entailed to Mr. Collins, that none of the five of us daughters can inherit it."

"Ah, I see. So you were to be the preserver of the family fortune." He reflected for a few moments, and then frowned. "So now, it seems, I must be indebted to you for your courage in rejecting Mr. Collins." He reflected on this idea, then added mischievously, "And when you refused my proposal at Hunsford, you had already had some practice."

He brought his arm from under the covers and caressed her cheek with his thumb. Under the covers she reached across and lay her hand on his side, feeling the firmness of his body through his shirt.

He lifted his head and looked down at her through the soft candle light. Her eyes followed his as he slowly brought his lips to hers and gently kissed her. He rose again and moved his fingers over her hair. He moved his hand from her shoulders over her body to her hips and lifted her pettycoat. They helped each other remove their remaining clothing.

Sunday

A rapping at the door awakened them. Darcy grabbed his robe and went to the door. "Here's your tea, sir, just as you ordered."

"Thank you," he replied and took the tray. Elizabeth slipped out of bed, donned her robe, and tried to arrange her tousled hair into a bit of order with a couple of pins. She met him as he set the tray on the table. He slipped his arms around her. "Good morning, Mrs. Darcy." Her arms around his waist, they stood gently stroking each other's backs.

"Is it really time for breakfast already?" she asked.

"No, it's half past time for breakfast, but I asked them to wake us an hour later than I usually arise. That should give us more than enough time to get to Pemberley while it's still daylight."

They sat down, she poured the coffee, and they slowly ate their breakfast. Finished, they dressed for their day's journey. Darcy was quickly dressed, but Elizabeth was slower, having to carefully coax her hair into obedience. He folded their robes into the cases and sat down to watch her nimble fingers as she pulled and pinned her tresses into order. She was reminded of the gatherings where she had seen him when he first came to Hertfordshire. He often seemed to be watching her; even Charlotte had remarked on it.

"Will I pass muster as the new mistress of Pemberley?" she asked with a smile.

"Most assuredly," he responded, a look of contentment spreading over his countenance. He stood, took her hand to lift her, helped her with her coat, then she with his. They closed the cases and walked out the door. Farris was waiting in the hall. He took the cases and followed them to the coach, already waiting in front of the inn. Darcy settled the account and followed Elizabeth out the door. The footman handed her into the coach, and Darcy followed.

A jostling coach is hardly the place for conversation, but the scenery was varied, and they contented themselves with drinking it in. Darcy had traversed these roads more than once before, so he watched Elizabeth as much as the scenery. They did catch each other's eye countless times throughout the day, feeling their own contentment and observing the other's. Dinner at an inn along the way was satisfactory, but unremarkable.

Pemberley

They reached Pemberley well before dark. Memories engulfed Elizabeth—memories of the first time she had seen Pemberley only a few months before and seemingly a lifetime.

Tired, they alighted from the coach and made their way into the house. Fenton greeted them at the door. As he took their coats Darcy told him they were very tired and would like some supper sent up to their bedroom presently; also that he should tell Annie and Bradford that they would like water for baths.

William following with their cases, they ascended the broad, oak stairs and entered their luxuriously appointed bedroom, the middle of the suite of three rooms comprising the bedroom suite formerly occupied by the late Mr. and Mr. Darcy.

Darcy closed the door, turned towards Elizabeth, and wrapped his arms around her. They stood, entwined, swaying from side to side, luxuriating in the closeness. He pulled his head back, and bent down to kiss her. She responded with warmth and pleasure. Pulling away a bit, but with one arm on her back, he moved them towards a door at their right. He opened the door, saying, "This will be your dressing room. Mine is there," pointing to a door at the opposite side of the bedroom.

"This was my parents' suite of rooms. I've never slept here, but it should be very convenient for us. They'll bring up your trunk tomorrow, but for now, you should be able to do with the things we brought along."

Elizabeth nodded in assent. She walked to one of the two large windows and looked out at the beautiful view. He followed her, circled her with his arms and kissed her again, his flattened hand under her shoulder blades gently pulling her up to him. He drew back and basked in the contentment he saw in her countenance.

Now noises began in Darcy's dressing room and in Elizabeth's as well. He walked with her to her dressing room, and opened the door. "Annie, I don't think you met Miss Bennet when she called on us here last summer. As you know she's now Mrs. Darcy."

"I'm pleased to meet you, I'm sure, ma'am," she said, smiling.

"Annie attended my mother, Mrs. Darcy, and has had other duties since. I'm sure she'll take very good care of you."

"I'm sure she will," Elizabeth replied, smiling, first at Darcy, then at Annie.

"I'll leave you now; Bradford is waiting." Then he was gone.

"Are you tired, Mrs. Darcy?" Annie ventured.

Elizabeth nodded, "A warm bath is just what I need." She turned so Annie could unfasten her dress, and together they removed her clothing. Bathed, dried and snug in her robe, Elizabeth sat at the dressing table and watched lazily while Annie brushed her hair.

"Thank you, Annie; I'll see you in the morning."

"Goodnight, Mrs. Darcy."

In the bedroom she found Darcy waiting for her, looking out of the window. She joined him, and he put his arm around her. They stood looking out into the dusky evening.

"I don't think I've ever seen Pemberley looking more beautiful," he said.

Astonished, she looked up and said, "On such a gray day? Surely you're jesting. I saw it myself looking far finer last summer."

"Aye, but on that day we were outside, and today we are inside looking out. It makes all the difference."

"Are you flattering me?"

"Not at all; I'm just expressing the way I feel," he said, stroking her hair.

"Well, I will grant you the view from here is fine, indeed. And when I have thoroughly examined the view from all the other windows in the house I don't doubt that this will be my favorite."

"Madam, your supper awaits." He turned and moved her to the chair, adjusted it for her, and took his seat. She poured tea for them, and they set about relieving their hunger. She could see that care had been taken in selecting tasty foods for the tray, but it occurred to her that the exhaustion from the travel and the novelty of all that had surrounded her the past two days had dulled her appreciation for the efforts taken.

They enjoyed the view across the table as they savored the food. Finished, they rose and moved to the bed, larger and far more beautiful than that at the inn. He unfastened the ties of her robe and slipped it from her shoulders to fall to the floor. He assisted her up into the bed, walked around, doffed his robe, and climbed in.

She turned her back to him, and they lay together, warming each other and the bed. Without intending it, they fell asleep.

Elizabeth turned onto her back, but accustomed to sleeping alone, Darcy's form woke her, and, in moving, she woke him. She looked to the window. "What time is it?" she asked.

He looked over at the clock and said, "Almost ten." He began stroking her body in random motions, like a traveler lost in a desert without a compass. She opened her eyes, and in the soft candle light could see his eyes were closed. She closed hers again and concentrated on his touch. His breathing deepened, and hers followed.

Her thoughts flew among the varied memories of her encounters with Darcy over the past year: his refusal to dance with her when they first met, his intent observations of her in social situations, their verbal exchanges, at times even resembling sword play. Her mind darted through his first unfortunate proposal of marriage and her refusal, then her chagrin at discovering how badly she had misjudged his character. A moment seemed to be enough to flit through an entire series of exchanges with him.

As he made love to her the memories raced through her mind—memories of his enigmatic responses to her challenges. But when she came to the thought that only a few months earlier it seemed certain that she would never see him again, her entire body responded with a shudder. "Oh, Darcy, what a strange series of events has brought us together."

His head beside hers, their bodies joined, he breathed near her ear. "Yes, Elizabeth, strange indeed." He withdrew and lay on his back, looking at her. "We are lucky to have made our way through such a maze."

She reached up and caressed his cheek.

They lay relaxed, both now allowing the memories of the past year to flow over them.

"You gave me a very bad turn, you know. You altered quite remarkably my sense of myself as a gentleman. It was quite some time before I could appreciate your willingness to tell the truth as you saw it. You might have agreed to marry me in spite of your low opinion of my character if all you were concerned about was a comfortable home and a secure future. Then we would likely have had a very different kind of marriage."

He snuffed the candle by the bed and they lay in the dark, his hand over hers until sleep overtook them.

Monday

When Elizabeth awoke she found that it was almost nine, that Darcy had already requested warm water for washing, and that breakfast would be at ten in the dining room. He heard her stretch and moved from the window to lean down and lightly kiss her. "Annie's waiting for you." Elizabeth slipped out of bed and into the robe as he held it. In her slippers, she padded into the dressing room.

"I thought you'd like a little bath, Mrs. Darcy," Annie said, handing her a warm, wet washcloth. She took it, freshened her eyes and face and stepped into the warm water. The bath finished, Annie helped her dress. Then Elizabeth sat at the dressing table while Annie brushed her hair.

"You'll have to tell me how you want your hair arranged." Elizabeth guided her through the process, supplying pins to secure it.

"How do I look?"

"You look just fine, ma'am."

Elizabeth returned to the bedroom, Darcy joined her, and they walked down to the dining room. Selbey was waiting for them, the food on the buffet, their place settings at opposite ends of the long table. As Darcy held her chair, Elizabeth hesitated and quietly said, "Do I have to sit so far from you?"

"No, of course not." Then to Selbey, "Please move Mrs. Darcy's place setting next to my own." While he moved them, they went to the buffet, selected from the offerings, and returned to their chairs. Selbey adjusted her chair and poured coffee for them. Rays of sun penetrated the windows, lighting the room. They ate in silence for a few minutes. "Do you have any special requests for dinner or supper, Mrs. Darcy?"

"I'm sure your cook has everything under control, but I'd very much like to meet her."

"And so you shall, perhaps later today. After breakfast we'll take a short walk. We'd best take advantage of the sun while it is to be had. It's rather cool, but it will serve all the better to wake us up."

"Do you always walk in the mornings?"

"No, I hunt on occasion, but often I have business of some kind to attend to in the mornings. However, we'll make an exception today." Changing the subject, he continued, "I gave orders before I left that the servants should not appear after your arrival until each is called. You may want to meet with Mrs. Reynolds first. She's been a very competent housekeeper for us for as long as I can remember. After Mother died, Father relied on her to carry on, and I've seldom had to intervene to keep things running smoothly. But you're likely to want to make some changes, and I suggest you start by getting acquainted with her."

Breakfast finished, they left the table, fetched wraps, and walked through the morning room to the gravel path. The path was moist from a shower during the night, but pleasant for walking nonetheless. They strolled for several minutes and were about to turn a corner when he stopped, drew her towards him, put his arms around her, and gently caressed her back.

"Are there likely to be servants watching?" she asked.

"I would be very surprised if there were not." He looked down at her, and said, "It would be a great scandal should people discover that Mr. Darcy is in love with his young wife, would it not?" He kissed her lightly, and she rested her head against his chest. They stood for a while, embracing. They ambled further, then returned to the house.

"We'll walk again after dinner if the weather is still fine, but I need to prepare to see Woodbury tomorrow. And, you might want to collect your thoughts before you see Mrs. Reynolds."

"How do I contact her?"

"Just ring a bell. Someone will come and you can tell them to send Mrs. Reynolds to you." By now they had re-entered the morning room where they found Katie tending the fire. Darcy introduced them, and Elizabeth asked her to inform Mrs. Reynolds that she would like to meet her in the former Mrs. Darcy's study. After Katie left Darcy took Elizabeth in his arms and embraced her; then, one hand under her chin, he lifted her face and kissed her lightly. They walked to the hall and parted, he to his study, and she upstairs to hers, no longer "the former Mrs. Darcy's study."

It was nearly eleven so she just sat, closed her eyes for a few moments and decided just to let Mrs. Reynolds tell her what they should consider first. She then walked to the window and let the beauty of the landscape wash over her. Presently she heard foot steps and roused herself from her reverie. "Mrs. Reynolds."

"Mrs. Darcy, how delightful to have you here at last. What a surprise to discover that the pretty young lady who visited here last summer had captured Mr. Darcy's heart!"

Elizabeth beamed in response, touched by this lively old lady who had greeted herself and the Gardners last summer. "You could not possibly be more surprised than myself."

"Well, it's a happy state of affairs, without a doubt."

Elizabeth motioned Mrs. Reynolds towards a chair and seated herself near her. "I think it would be best to begin with if you tell me of anything you know that I should be thinking about."

"I see. Of course. There's nothing that comes to mind immediately, but I have no doubt that by tomorrow my thoughts will be organized, and I shall have something to say."

"I think until I know more about the household management, we should meet each day, except Sunday of course. Is eleven o'clock convenient? Should something interfere, I'll send word to you."

"Aye, that's a good plan. And the servants will no doubt appreciate comments and ideas when you have them."

That decided, Mrs. Reynolds left. Elizabeth glanced over the furnishings in the room—books, the desk, and its contents. She then returned to her dressing room and found her trunk had arrived. She rang for Annie, and together they stored the clothing, separating the items that needed pressing for Annie to take with her. She put her few books aside to take them later to her study. She took the piano music and went to the music room, memories of the summer visit there keen in her mind. She sat down and played a few simple melodies, relaxing into the pleasure of the familiar, after so much novelty. Now she selected a more difficult piece, concentrating on the music alone, repeating difficult passages and allowing the sound of this fine instrument to envelop her. Content that she had rendered the piece creditably, if not perfectly, she folded the music, and looked closely at one of the paintings. Then her attention was drawn to the window that Mrs. Reynolds had pointed out on that summer visit for "its fine prospect." She reflected for a few minutes on the last few days, on the past year, and the changes in her life that had begun as a result of her marriage to Darcy. A rabbit ran across the lawn and jolted her out of her musings. She found a clock and saw that it was nearly two o'clock, time for dinner. She briskly walked to her dressing room, tidied her hair, washed her hands, and went to the dining room.

As she entered the dining room, Selbey said, "Mr. Darcy's waiting for you in the morning room, ma'am."

"Oh, thank you." She returned to the hall and entered the morning room.

"Well, Mrs. Darcy, how have you enjoyed your first morning as Mistress of Pemberley?" Before she could answer, Selbey was at the door to announce dinner. They went in, took their seats, and waited as the food was served. Selbey finished serving and took his post by the wall.

"Selbey, we'll ring if we need you."

He nodded and left.

Elizabeth's eyebrow raised slightly. Darcy reached out his hand and she met it with hers. They sat like this for a few moments, until she said, "This would be a perfect arrangement if only I could eat with one hand." At that, both smiled and took up their forks and knives.

"Well, Elizabeth, did you find any skeletons at Pemberley this morning?" Her eyes flew to his and rested there. She chewed and gazed until she saw the grin appear.

"Are there skeletons?" she responded, continuing the game.

"I don't know, but I've never looked, so I'm not sure."

She took another bite and allowed herself to drink in the furnishings of the room. Seeing the still life painting of undressed game, vegetables and fruits, she said casually, "No, but I did see a rabbit." Out of the corner of her eye she caught the quick movement of his head towards her.

"...on the lawn, from the music room," she said, looking up.

"Well, then, your morning was not entirely uneventful."

"Not at all. I found many objects for my attention. I even found time at the piano, for both enjoyment and study."

"Then may I look forward to hearing the results of your study?"

"Yes, but we must keep in mind that your former enjoyment of my performance may be somewhat altered."

"How so?"

"Well, now that I am Mrs. Fitzwilliam Darcy, my performance may be held to a higher standard."

Smile wrinkles played about his face as he reflected on her challenge. He toyed with his food, chewed, and drank.

"Perhaps it will. I see many possibilities for change. You may decide you enjoy performing at a higher degree of skill than satisfies my taste. You may choose to please others than myself. You may find practicing so enjoyable on such a fine instrument that you neglect your other duties."

Now he could see in brief glances that she was getting impatient at his rambling discourse, and he also found interest in the room's fine furnishings.

At length he looked back, smiled, and she caught his teasing. By now they had finished their dinner, and they left the dining room. They found their coats, and once outdoors he led her towards the stables. "I want to introduce you to Prince."

She glanced up at him, and he added, "My horse."

"Oh," she said. Elizabeth had never become an accomplished rider, preferring walking. They entered the stable and immediately Mr. Sims was before them.

"Mrs. Darcy, let me introduce you to Mr. Sims, our stable master. He and Cook Sims are married, and their son works as a stable boy. Is Davey about?"

"I sent him on an errand, sir."

"Where's Prince?"

"He's in his stall, sir; I just brushed him down. I took him out earlier to the pasture for some fresh air. Here he is, Mrs. Darcy," he continued, "and a fine animal he is too."

Elizabeth looked up appreciatively at the dark face and soulful eyes as Darcy stroked Prince's neck. "I have to agree," she replied. He's very handsome indeed." Prince nickered, and she started a bit.

"Have you ever ridden?" Darcy asked.

"Father had horses on the farm, work animals. Jane learned to ride Nellie, but somehow I was never much interested in old Nellie. I always preferred walking."

Darcy led Elizabeth from the stables along the side of the house across the grass and down toward the lake. They strolled along the gravel path into a sunny area. At length he said, "I'd like you to learn to ride. I do ride Prince for transportation, but at times I just enjoy riding, and I'd like you with me. Do you have any objection?"

"Do you have another saddle horse?"

"Not one that would be suitable for you, but I can get one easily enough."

Elizabeth at last began, "I would like to try to learn, but I would be unhappy if you bought a horse for me and then I found I was simply unwilling to ride."

He smiled at the careful economy implicit in her response. "I don't mean to disparage your concern, but a horse purchased one week is worth almost as much the next. And, if I'm as careful in the purchase as you are in your response, I might be able to sell it for even more."

They had ambled for quite some time until, both chilled, he put his free hand on hers where it rested on his arm and looked down at her.

"Mrs. Darcy, would you mind very much if we were to take our supper in our room again this evening? I believe the servants might grant such a concession to the newlyweds."

"It would be a pleasure."

"Then let us enter via the kitchen and inform Mrs. Sims of our plan."

"Mrs. Sims, let me introduce you to Mrs. Darcy."

Plump, middle-aged Mrs. Sims looked up from her pastry board, brushed off her hands with a towel, and smoothed her apron. "Ah, Mrs. Darcy; I'm pleased to meet you."

"The pleasure is mine, Mrs. Sims. Mr. Darcy just now introduced me to Mr. Sims and told me of your son David."

Darcy intervened to say, "Mrs. Sims, we'd like to have our supper this evening in our bedroom. I'm afraid Mrs. Darcy found the trip rather tiring."

"Aye, sir," she said, with a sly smile, "and I expect it would be to your liking as well."

Darcy tried unsuccessfully to suppress a smile.

"And what time would you be liking your supper, sir?"

"At seven, I think," he said. "Thank you, Mrs. Sims." They found Fenton and asked him to tell Annie and Bradford that they wouldn't be needing them 'til morning. They removed their coats in the hall and climbed the stairs hand in hand.

Inside the bedroom, he drew her into his arms and held her closely as they rocked back and forth. "Now, Lizzy, come," he said, taking her by one hand into his dressing room. He poured water into the basin, pushed her sleeves up and his own. He took her hands and the soap and washed all their hands at once. He took the towel and tumbled them both dry. Dropping the towel, he kissed her palms.

He led her by the hand back into the bedroom to her side of the bed. He cupped his hands over her shoulders, then turned her around, unfastened the buttons of her gown, and helped her out of it. "Now it's your turn," he said and let her help him remove his jacket and vest.

He turned her around and unbuttoned her petticoat so she could remove it. He left her to finish undressing and went to his side of the bed. He lit a candle, and climbed into bed.

With only heads uncovered they lay, facing each other. He reached over and tugged at her until her back was up against him spoon fashion. He stroked back and forth over her body and limbs as if memorizing the contours.

She followed his touch in her mind. He turned her over and kneaded her back, feeling the firm flesh. "Ah, my lovely Elizabeth," he said, and the memories of the day of their engagement engulfed her consciousness, leaving her warm, and as attentive as she had ever been. Each contour of her body now memorized, he tugged at her again to turn her over. She lay on her back, and he rested his head on one arm.

As he stroked, she opened her eyes, and in the dim light saw that his were closed, his face in rapt attention. She closed her eyes again and drifted in the flow of her feelings.

"Lizzy, do you love me?"

"I do, Darcy" she said softly. "I do love you."

Thoughts of all sorts ran through her mind as he caressed her, then seemingly no thoughts of all, only delicious sensations as they floated in time. She could hear and feel his breathing by her ear in the mass of her hair.

Their motions seemed more those of one than of two, when a thought struck her so forcibly that she opened her eyes and inadvertently became still. Darcy felt the abrupt change in the feel of her body and became still himself. He lifted his head, and said, "What is it, Lizzy?"

"I just had the most disturbing thought. I just suddenly felt so ashamed."

"Ashamed of what?"

"Ashamed of myself, of wanting to be here, like this, together; ashamed of enjoying your touch."

He began gently kissing her face and neck. "Please, please, don't be ashamed of making me happy."

"Oh, Darcy, how could I feel this way, with all the love you've shown me."

"Very easily, my love. You only felt what the world has taught you to feel. What's happening here is what is coming from within you, from your make-up as a human being, a woman who is willing to expose her nature, not cover it up."

She hugged him closer and relaxed into the pleasure of lovemaking.

Tired and happy, they lay side by side. He said, "Lizzy, Lizzy. Will you ever know how much I love you?"

Her cheek against his shoulder, holding his hand in both of hers, she said, almost in a whisper, "I'm not sure I could bear more than I already know."

He turned and kissed her forehead. "If it is within my power, my love will rest on you with the weight of a summer's breeze."

"You're not going to tell me now that you're a poet, too, are you?"

"No, that's it. That's the sum total of my life's output as a poet."

"What a relief!"

He looked at her intently until she remembered the way she felt during their first several meetings when she felt she had never encountered such an acute observer. "Turn, Lizzy," he said as he tugged her body and pulled her back to his chest. They lay like that for some time, quiet, content, almost asleep.

He turned on his back, and, disturbed, she murmured, "What time is it?" He lifted his head, and said, "After six-thirty."

"Mmmm."

He lifted the covers, turned himself out of bed, and put on his slippers and robe. He ran his fingers through his hair, found Elizabeth's slippers and robe, and brought them to her. He poured a glass of water and set it on her table. Then he poured one for himself and walked to the window. He sipped the water as he looked out at the beautiful grounds in the dim light of this November evening.

Elizabeth, now out of bed, came and stood beside him. He set his glass down, put one arm around her shoulders, and guided her into her dressing room, saying, "Now, Mrs. Darcy, our supper will be here soon, and it's your turn to wash my hands." He poured water from the pitcher into the basin, immediately dunked his fingers into the water, and waited. A hint of a smile subtly altered her expression, but she pulled up his sleeves, then her own, took the bar of soap, wet it, and studiously turned it round and round in her hands. All lathered up, she set the bar in its dish and lifted his right hand. Gently she rubbed it between her palms, laid it down, and picked up the left. This she washed, looking up at him as she did, lingering over each finger. Finished, she splashed all four hands together removing the soap. She took the waiting towel and dried his hands and her own.

"Ah, Mrs. Darcy, you must have performed this service for many men," he said, playfully.

A burst of laughter escaped her as she turned away, saying, "What nonsense!"

Immediately behind her, he put his arms around her waist and exclaimed, "You mean that's the first time you've ever washed a gentleman's hands? That is difficult to believe. I apparently have found a far more precious gem than I had ever hoped for. To perform such an important task, and so expertly on the very first occasion!"

By now she was nearly doubled over with laughter, his body following. At last she turned around, panting from laughter, "Oh, Darcy, what Hertfordshire resident would believe me if I told them you had invented such nonsense. I would be declared a mad woman and excluded from all polite society. Fortunately...."

A rap at the door interrupted her and they moved back into the bedroom, their laughter subsiding. Darcy opened the door and took the tray, saying, "Thank you, William."

He bowed and left.

Darcy set the tray on the table, and Elizabeth poured. Then, freshly inventive, he took the tray and set it on the bed. He motioned for her to get into bed. She propped up the pillows. He set the tray on her lap, got in beside her, and moved the tray so they were both supporting it. They ate the sandwiches, somehow tastier and more perfectly assembled than either was accustomed to seeing. Together they examined the biscuits and sweet breads. Each seemed to be in a distinctive shape, not round or square, as usual. The biscuits seemed to be in the shape of eggs and rabbits. "These we always used to have at Easter," Darcy remarked. "And look at the breads. This one looks like a donut, and this one a finger-shaped donut." There were marzipan candies on the tray as well, with the shapes echoing those of the biscuits and sweet breads. Darcy narrowed his eyes and pursed his lips in that familiar expression of disapproval mixed with mockery. "I begin to think Mrs. Sims is getting a bit too sure of her position in this household."

"Whatever do you mean?" Elizabeth queried, puzzled.

"If I'm not mistaken, what we are viewing are refreshments prepared for a fertility festival."

At the word "fertility," Elizabeth blushed and then began to laugh. He burst out laughing as well, rocking the bed 'til they were in danger of spilling the tray. Laughter subsiding, they ate what they wanted, and Darcy set the tray on the table. He returned to bed, and they lay facing each other fondling each other's hands. At length he turned on his back, she on hers. They lay, drowsy. "Whatever shall I do about Mrs. Sims?"

After reflecting at considerable length, Elizabeth ventured, "Increase her pay?" At this they both again melted into laughter.

"Well," he said, sleepily, "I suppose initiative should be rewarded." Before long they were asleep.

Tuesday

At breakfast, Elizabeth said, "If you're serious in wanting me to learn to ride, I'll need something to wear. How soon were you thinking of buying a horse for me?"

"You're quite right, you will need proper clothing. As for the horse, I don't imagine it will take long to find a good one for you, perhaps a week or two. I'll have Woodbury begin inquiries immediately."

"I suppose it will be possible to go to London in January to arrange for some additional clothing as soon as I get a sense of what I'll need. But I can't imagine I'd find a seamstress nearby for such a task, and on short notice."

"Talk with Mrs. Reynolds and Sarah. She takes care of linens. She may have some skill at sewing or know someone who does." Looking at her, no, examining her, he said, "Mother rode, you know, though not often. She did have riding clothing, both everyday, and dress, for fox hunting. She was a little taller than you, larger actually. I wonder what became of her clothing."

They finished breakfast and took their walk. The weather was rather mild, but still refreshing. Darcy left to find Woodbury, and Elizabeth went to her study where she found Mrs. Reynolds.

"Good morning, Mrs. Reynolds. Before we get into household matters, I have a problem. Mr. Darcy wants me to learn to ride a horse, actually rather soon, but I don't have proper clothing. Do you have any idea what became of the late Mrs. Darcy's clothing? I'll be going to London in January, but we just need something to get started."

"Aye, ma'am, the quality garments she had were stored, the older ones discarded. I know exactly where they are."

"Then unless you have other pressing matters to discuss, would you find it? Not the dress set, just the everyday outfit."

"Aye, ma'am, it will take awhile, perhaps an hour."

"Then I'll spend an hour at the piano and meet you at my dressing room. And please ask Annie to meet us there also."

"Aye, ma'am."

At the piano, Elizabeth looked through the music and found some Christmas carols. "I'd better brush up on these," she mused. "And that reminds me, I'd better ask Darcy about inviting the Bingleys and Gardners for Christmas." The hour was happily spent. "Fortunately, Georgiana will be back by Christmas so we won't have to rely on me entirely for our musical pleasures."

At the dressing room she found Annie and Mrs. Reynolds with the riding habit. Annie helped her out of her day dress and into the habit.

Mrs. Reynolds commented, "It's a bit out of fashion, but it seems to be intact, and it should certainly be possible to alter it if we can find someone with enough skill with a needle."

"Yes, but who?"

"Perhaps you should ask Sarah." ventured Mrs. Reynolds.

"Would you summon her?"

"I'll find her and send her here." With that she left.

"What do you think, Annie? Can we make do?"

"I don't doubt it, ma'am, but it's a bit more than I'd care to try. There's a woman at Lambton who sews for those as has the money to pay."

"Really; who?"

"A Mrs. Flanders. Her husband is the game keeper at the Howell estate. They have three children and no doubt would be happy to have the money."

Sarah arrived and looked at Mrs. Darcy in the riding habit, obviously too large. "Well, ma'am, I do sew for myself, but alterations are more difficult, and if you please, ma'am, I'm not sure I could do a good job of it."

"Thank you, Sarah," and she left.

"Well, Annie, I suppose I must pursue the only course that is apparent, at least right now."

Once again in her day gown, she went to her study and penned a note to Mrs. Flanders, asking her if she would be willing and able to do the job. She addressed it and took it to the morning room, as it was nearly time for dinner.

Darcy was already there, reading. Before she could tell him of the morning's activities, Selbey called them to dinner. After they had been served and Selbey left, Elizabeth brought up the subject of guests for Christmas.

"Darcy, I've been thinking about the possibility of having a few guests with us at Christmas time. I realize that Georgiana will be here, but that is a very small party for the holidays."

"Of course; what do you have in mind?"

"Well, it's only a few days since the wedding, and so many things have been happening that I must admit I have not been thinking of Jane or anyone else in my family. But, by Christmas, I wouldn't be surprised to find myself getting a bit lonesome, wishing to have some old friends around me."

"The Bingleys would come, I should think."

"My thought exactly. And perhaps the Gardners?"

He reached across the table, and she put her hand in his. "The Gardners will always be welcome here. I think that is an excellent idea."

"I don't think you've met the Gardner children."

"No, but this should be a good opportunity for me to do so as we won't have children of our own this Christmas to enliven the festivities."

"Thank you, Darcy. Then, I'll write to Jane and Aunt Gardner so we can get a reply from them soon enough to make preparations."

The weather still being agreeable, after dinner Darcy and Elizabeth went again for a walk, this time on the path that rather closely followed the lake.

They had not walked far when Elizabeth said, "Darcy, I do know what causes babies to begin, but not everyone has babies right after marriage."

"You aren't suggesting that we sleep in separate bedrooms, are you?"

"Oh, no," she said and held his arm tighter. "But is that our only choice?"

"If there is any other, I'm not aware of it."

"But some people don't have children right away."

"Just a matter of chance as far as I know. Besides, would it be so bad to have a child soon?"

"No, but we're still really quite young. It seems a shame not to have a little time before children come."

He put his hand over hers where it rested on his arm. "This is one of the reasons why I want you to learn to ride now, while you're still fit. You can ride after a child is born, but while expecting...."

"Yes. Well, there will be time enough to think about that later. Perhaps I won't like riding anyway."

"I've been giving more thought to the riding. I'd like Georgiana to ride as well."

"She learned to ride, didn't she?"

"Yes, but on a pony. By now she's grown so much that I'm sure she would feel ridiculous riding Patches. If she agrees, I'll buy a horse for each of you. Then when I'm not available, you two can ride together."

"I'm beginning to think that you have mapped out for me a career as an enthusiastic horsewoman."

"I expect you to like it very well indeed."

They walked on in silence for awhile.

"Mrs. Reynolds found your mother's riding habit for me."

"Did she?"

"Yes, you're right about your mother being taller and larger than me. Not too much though. We all agreed it could be altered, but neither Betsy, Sarah nor Mrs. Reynolds knew anyone on the estate who might be able to do it. Sarah suggested a Mrs. Flanders in Lambton. She says her husband is a game keeper on the Howell estate."

"Yes, I think I know who you mean; good man. Well, that seems like a good place to start."

"I wrote a note to her, hoping you would agree; how do I send it?"

"Just leave it on the table in the front hall. If any of the servants are going to any of the nearby towns they look there for mail and take it. If it's urgent, of course, we can arrange for someone to make a special trip." Then, changing the subject, "I got a note from Morris, a neighbor who lives towards Gormley. He invited me to go shooting with him sometime soon."

"In the note to Mrs. Flanders I asked if she could see me on Tuesday."

"Then that might be a good day for me to go hunting. You'll need the carriage, of course, but I'll be riding Prince anyway. Let me know when you hear from Mrs. Flanders, and I'll send off a message to Morris. Well, we are becoming a boring old married couple."

"Hardly that."

"Already contemplating a morning apart for only a little more than a week after the wedding."

"By Tuesday it will be 10 days. Besides, if you weren't so urgent about me learning to ride, I could delay my trip. I haven't sent the note yet," she said, taunting him.

"Ah, Lizzy," taking her in his arms, "I believe that I am feeling so secure in your love that we will be able to be apart that morning."

"You're only saying that because you want to go hunting."

"Am I wrong about your love?"

"Not at all, but that doesn't mean that in six months' time I'll be content to see you off hunting any old time."

"Perhaps I shall have to teach you to shoot also so you can go with me."

By now both were basking in contentment.

Their walk ended, Darcy went into the drawing room to read, and Elizabeth went to her study to get a book, leaving the note to Mrs. Flanders on the hall table.

Once again in the drawing room, Elizabeth sat down beside Darcy on the sofa and interrupted his reading to say, "I've decided that I should meet with each of the servants alone for a few minutes to get acquainted with them. That should make it easier to fix in my mind the workings of the household."

"That sounds like an admirable plan. Where will you meet with them?"

"Oh; I hadn't gotten that far." Puzzling over it a bit, she said, "I think I'd prefer, at least for the first visit, to see Mrs. Sims in the kitchen. I'll know better then what to ask her, and she can show me around. Perhaps Sarah can take me to the linen room and show me around there. I think I should ask each of them what their usual duties are and write them down. I doubt if Beatty would mind talking with me for a few minutes when I see him outside in the flower beds."

"You'll want to talk with him about the kitchen garden, but before you get any very decided ideas about flowers or other plantings you should be aware that I have spent quite a lot of time on that part of the estate and have some very decided ideas of how things should be."

"I'm glad to hear it; I do believe my duties will keep me busy if I never have to contemplate flower beds."

He reached over and drew her near to him. "Do you think each of us can concentrate on our books if we sit like this?" he asked, putting his arm around her.

"Of course, but, if one of the servants should come in, they would surely be confirmed in the conviction that Mr. and Mrs. Darcy are very much in love."

"It's about time they witness a proper demonstration."

Both smiled and began to read.

Selbey announced supper, and they went into the dining room for their first evening meal there.

"You can stay, Selbey; we may want something," Darcy said.

"The room looks lovely in candle light, Elizabeth remarked. It looks lovely in the daylight too, of course, but different."

Selbey served them and retreated to his post by the wall.

"Darcy, where does Georgiana get her new clothing?"

"She has a dressmaker in London. She has at least one milliner that she patronizes regularly too."

"I do think we should plan for me to make the trip sometime in early January. Will it be convenient for you to go then?"

"I don't see why not. The weather can be rather unpleasant, but not usually enough to be a problem."

"Where do you stay in London?"

"I have a small town house. We'll have to find something larger later, but for the moment it will do."

"Darcy, when I do go into Lambton to see if Mrs. Flanders will alter the riding habit, is there anyone else you think I should call on?"

"It wouldn't hurt to call on the Vicar and his wife. Ford is his name. There may be many who would like to meet you, but I think we can wait for awhile. We should have some kind of gathering so you can get to know more people. I'm not sure how we should go about it. You might discuss the possibilities with Mrs. Reynolds; she should have some ideas. I'm beginning to see the advantages of a summer wedding. However, we married when we did, and we'll meet each situation as it comes. You'll meet people at church on Sunday, of course. People do tend to chat a bit after church, though at this time of year the weather isn't very conducive to conversation. Yes, call on the Vicar. He will, no doubt, invite you to take tea with him and Mrs. Ford. I wouldn't be a bit surprised if you were to be invited for tea hither and yon before long. I dare say people have just been waiting for a decent interval—giving the newlyweds a few moments of peace.

"Well, Mrs. Darcy, might this be a good time for me to hear the results of your study at the piano forte?"

"How can I refuse such an appreciative audience?"

They made their way to the music room, and Elizabeth selected a few simple melodies, likely to please anyone, and certainly Darcy. Darcy took his place on the sofa where he could watch her perform. She played the first three songs and was going to search through the music for more, when she looked up to meet his gaze. What she saw instead were closed eyes. She selected a lullaby, thinking, "I'd better get used to playing lullabies anyway, given the warmth of our relationship." Finished, she looked up, and to her astonishment saw him lying sideways, his head on the arm of the sofa. "Well, so much for my appreciative audience. Where is that prelude that gave me so much trouble?" She found it, placed her fingers carefully on the many notes and played the first chord far louder than the composer ever intended. Then, seeing him jump, she ran over to him, fearful that he would fall on the floor.

His eyes were open now, barely; she sat beside him as he groped his way back to consciousness. "Well," she said, "we now know of a good sedative for you."

"I can't imagine why I should fall asleep."

"Perhaps you've had a more strenuous week than usual," she teased. She sat, rubbing his hands. "Should we should retire early tonight?" she asked.

"Yes, perhaps."

"Who will snuff the candles?"

"Oh, you can be sure that one of the servants is lurking about, probably in the hall right now." That settled and Darcy quite awake, they made their way to their bedroom.

Wednesday: Mrs. Wilson

The next morning Darcy and Elizabeth were just finishing breakfast when Fenton entered the dining room. "Mrs. Darcy, there is a Mrs. Wilson to see you, ma'am."

"Please show her into the morning room and tell her I'll be there presently."

"Yes, ma'am."

Darcy and Elizabeth rose from the table, embraced for a moment and parted.

"Mrs. Wilson?" Elizabeth said, greeting the neat, matronly woman.

"Yes, Mrs. Darcy, I am very pleased to meet you. I do hope I'm not intruding. I was reluctant to call unannounced, but thought I must."

"Not at all. Please sit down." They both sat and Elizabeth waited, quiet.

"Mrs. Darcy, each year in December we organize a bazaar to benefit the infirmary in Lambton, and we were hoping you might participate in some way."

"I'm sure you know I've just arrived; I'm still learning how things are done here. I will have to consult Mr. Darcy, of course, but I assure you we will participate in any way we reasonably can. Perhaps you could make a few suggestions."

"Of course," she replied. "Well, Christmas breads sell very well, and dried fruits, even cured meats. Also handiwork, crafts, you know, of all kinds, rag dolls for children. We also have a sale of quality used items—clothing, especially children's clothing; but of course you wouldn't have any children's clothing to donate," she said, laughing. "And, we would especially like you and Mr. Darcy to attend the bazaar as well. You'll find some very appealing items I'm sure you'll want to buy."

"I'll have to talk with Mr. Darcy, but I dare say he'll want to be there. When is the bazaar?"

"Saturday, December 17, at the assembly room in Lambton. We usually hold it in early December, but our leader Mr. Perkins fell ill and none of the other gentlemen could step in, so they asked me to carry on, so it is late this year."

"That was very good of you. May I send you a note to let you know what we will be donating?"

"Yes, that would be fine; just send it to Mrs. Curtis Wilson, Lambton; that's me," she said, laughing. "Thank you Mrs. Darcy. I'll look forward to hearing from you."

"I'll not delay." They parted at the front entrance.

Elizabeth returned to the morning room to collect her thoughts, looked out the window, and saw Beatty and his helpers raking twigs fallen from the trees. She noted the time and realized that Mrs. Reynolds would by now be waiting for her in her study. At least she could get help from her about the bazaar. Reflecting further, she decided to consult Darcy first. This business of being mistress of Pemberley was beginning to seem rather complicated.

"Mrs. Reynolds, good morning."

"Good morning, Mrs. Darcy."

Elizabeth motioned, and they sat down. The bazaar possibilities still on her mind, she did not speak at once. At length Mrs. Reynolds said, "Mrs. Sims has been asking if you have any suggestions for meals."

"Oh, well, everything has been very satisfactory, and if she's willing to continue on her own initiative, I think that would be best for the time being. Perhaps by next week I'll have further thoughts. In fact, let us say now that on Wednesday of next week, instead of my meeting with you here, I'll meet with Mrs. Sims in the kitchen at eleven."

"Wouldn't you rather meet with her in the morning room?"

"No, I think not. I'd like to get a better sense of how the kitchen functions, and if I'm there, I'll know better what to ask, and she can show me. On later occasions the morning room will serve very well."

"That seems like a good plan. I'll tell her."

"Now that I think about it, please ask Mrs. Sims to find her bread recipes, and I'll talk with her tomorrow morning about them at eleven. So, unless you have anything else to discuss, I'll see you on Friday."

"Very good, ma'am. It appears to me that you're finding your way very nicely as the mistress of Pemberley,"

"I'm afraid it's too early to say that, but I do thank you."

"And I must say that Mr. Darcy seems very content as well."

At this, Elizabeth blushed and said, "I certainly hope you're right. I should be sorry to hear otherwise." In mutual regard, they parted.

Elizabeth took paper from the drawer, found the pen and ink, and wrote:

"Dearest Jane,

I would beg your forgiveness for spending so little time thinking of you during these past several days had I not reason to believe you to be in a similar mood.

I sincerely hope you are finding your new state as agreeable as I find mine. However, such bliss cannot last indefinitely, and I don't doubt that by Christmastime I shall be quite lonesome for you.

Darcy has more than readily agreed to guests at Christmas, and he named 'the Bingleys' before I could offer a suggestion. Do tell us you will be willing to make the trip to Pemberley and stay with us for several days, at least from the 23rd until the 28th and longer if you can manage it.

The household staff manages so well that I would not expect difficulties, but a little advance notice would make planning easier.

Please do not tell Mama and Papa that you are coming until you must. I am still not sufficiently 'Mistress of Pemberley' to be able to feel easy inviting them as yet.

Please give Darcy's love and mine to Bingley.
Affectionately,
Elizabeth"

She folded the letter, wrote the direction, and sealed it. Then with another sheet she wrote:

"Dear Aunt and Uncle Gardner,

The benefits of our Derbyshire vacation last summer continue to increase. Would that all brides could be so happy.

However, there is one thing that could add to that happiness: your presence as guests at Pemberley for Christmas. I realize that the distance might make the trip at this time of year seem onerous, but perhaps the novelty of the destination will make it worth the effort. I would like very much for you to be here with the children from the 23rd to the 26th, but I leave the dates to you.

Please let me know as soon as convenient.

When I talked to Darcy about Christmas guests, he said, 'The Gardners will always be welcome here.'
Your loving niece,
Elizabeth"

She laid the letters on the hall table and returned to the morning room. She picked up her book and read for some time before Darcy appeared, Selbey close behind. They made their way to the dining room.

"And what news do you bring me, Lizzy?"

"We have received our first appeal from the community following my arrival at Pemberley."

"And what form does the appeal take?"

"It seems the annual bazaar will be held in Lambton to raise money for the infirmary."

"Ah, a worthy cause. And what are we to do?"

"I'd rather hoped you would tell me. Mrs. Wilson made several suggestions, but I think you will know better than I how to respond. She suggested a number of things that even I know would not be within reason for us this year. However, we might be able to comply with a few of the suggestions. She suggested baked items, such as fruit cake or other breads, dried fruits, and even cured meats."

"They all sound appropriate to me. Talk to Mrs. Sims, and see what she can come up with. I wouldn't be a bit surprised to learn that she has already made rather a lot of fruit cakes. At least she did when Mother was alive, and she may have anticipated needing some this season, with a somewhat more active social life likely."

"She did make one other suggestion that we might consider. She said that they have a sale of used clothing. Perhaps we could look in the boxes of your mother's clothing. There might be something there. At the least I could determine which items I would certainly not need. Perhaps one rather nice dress in good condition."

"It's an idea worth investigating, at least. Mother's everyday gowns might do very well for finery for a number of the women in the village."

Dinner ended, they made their way to their walk, with only light wraps.

"You haven't told me yet when Georgiana will be coming home."

"When we talked about it, we tentatively set some time between December 7 and 14. That's a week or two from now. When she lived in London earlier she was in school and had little opportunity to enjoy what London has to offer. But this time, staying with the Findleys, she'll have a rather different stay. They are great theatre goers, so you can be sure if there is anything appropriate they'll take her. And, they will take her to any of the museums she is willing to trek through. Rides in the park and so forth. It shouldn't be long before we hear from her. She'll let us know."

"Do you think she will feel she should stay away the maximum period, thinking that would best accommodate us?"

"Perhaps; Georgiana is so quiet, it's often difficult to know what she's thinking."

"A family trait, perhaps?"

"You can hardly call my behavior this week quiet!"

"No, you've quite astonished me. But, I keep wondering if you might sink back into the comfort of silence, leaving me talking but with no audience," she said archly.

"I doubt if that will be a real concern."

"But back to Georgiana...."

"If you're concerned that she's following what she conceives to be our feelings rather than her own, by all means write to her; or I could if you prefer. I certainly have no objection to her coming home at her earliest convenience."

"I think I'd rather do it myself. She might be more certain of my feelings if the message comes directly from me."

"Then it's decided. You shall write to her. Send her my love."

"There is another point I'd like to discuss with you. As I told you, I plan to go to talk with Mrs. Sims tomorrow morning. I was thinking about the tray she prepared for us for Monday evening."

"Yes."

"Well, it was a rather distinctive array of food."

"It certainly was. Now that I think of it, it might be best if we go together now and thank her for her efforts," he said, looking at her fondly.

In the kitchen they found Mrs. Sims looking through recipes. "Mr. Darcy," she said, rising, "and Mrs. Darcy."

"Mrs. Sims," Darcy responded. "We wanted to thank you for the care you took in preparing the tray for us for Monday evening. You really should not go to so much trouble. You'll be spoiling us."

"Not at all, Mr. Darcy; it was a pleasure."

"Yes, I have no doubt." They all smiled, and Darcy and Elizabeth left, parting in the entry hall. Darcy went to the stables, and Elizabeth to her study to write a letter.

"Dear Georgiana,

I should not waste paper writing what you must already be certain of, but I shall anyway. Your brother and I have been spending our time forming the foundation of an enormously happy marriage and show every promise of success. We shall be quite intolerable companions for you.

Nevertheless, I want to discuss with you your return to Pemberley. I have just discovered that you and Darcy decided you would return sometime between December 7th and 14th.

Please stay as long in London as you truly want to stay. Certainly there are many pleasures there that you will not find here. But be assured that you are most welcome to return at the earliest date you wish.

Darcy sends you his love and I mine.
Your new sister,
Elizabeth"

She left the letter on the hall table and then went to the drawing room. Looking around, she thought, "I wonder if there are any games around." Near the card table she found a book shelf with a cupboard below it. She opened it and did, in fact, find some games. They were old, but in good condition: a cribbage board, a chess set, cards, backgammon, checkers, and even some puzzles. When Darcy arrived, he found her checking that the card decks were complete and that all the pieces were in fact in the boxes of checkers and chess.

"Interested in playing cards, are you?"

"I don't much care for cards, or for games in general, but Georgiana will be here soon, and I should at least display some sign of civility. Does she like to play?"

"I can't say that I know. She was too young to play the kinds of games I was interested in, and I don't know what she may have learned at school. Little about games, I imagine."

"Then we should teach her. And if we are going to do that, perhaps we should brush up ourselves."

"I hope you're prepared to lose."

"Oh, yes, I'm prepared. Why do you suppose I don't care for games?"

Just then Selbey arrived, and they went in to supper.

"I truly cannot remember seeing such wonderful weather this late in the year. Perhaps we can thank you for bringing it with you," Darcy said.

"I shall have to take your word for it that it is unseasonable, and I am happy to take the credit."

"I took Prince out for a while this afternoon. I do believe he enjoyed it almost as much as I did."

"I think you're trying to make me jealous."

"Yes, before long you will be asking me when your horse has been found and will arrive. That reminds me. We'll have to look for a saddle for you also."

"Where will you look?"

"There's a saddlery in Gormley. If we don't find what we want there, we can go to Derby or even further. We could have one made for you in Gormley. It may be more expensive, but could be more suitable."

Elizabeth reflected on the details involved with buying a horse and saddle.

After their pudding and coffee they repaired to the drawing room. "Perhaps tonight would be a good time to review the games. I'm not sure my pride could be sustained if you should fall asleep while I play the piano two nights in a row. At least this way, moment by moment I'm determining that you are staying awake."

"Yes, but last night was less strenuous."

"Are you forgetting this morning?"

"Oh, yes, I guess I am. Now you have caught me in a truly unforgivable lapse of memory." He reached over and took her hand in his. "Am I forgiven?"

"Of course; but I still don't want to play again this evening."

They played with little enthusiasm since games were not a great favorite of Darcy's either. Nevertheless they were reminding each other of the rules and getting through the games creditably. As predicted, Darcy won most of them. In the midst of a game of checkers, he looked down at the cover of the box, seeing the decorative design. "Elizabeth, I didn't think about it when we discussed the items we might give to the bazaar, but there is something you might want to know. Mother used to do that kind of thing. I remember one Christmas season going with her to deliver loaves of Christmas breads and other treats to the tenants. She tied them with ribbon with the Pemberley name woven into it. She must have ordered that ribbon specially made. There was lots of it; I can't imagine that all of it would have been used. You might ask Mrs. Reynolds. She should know where it is. I remember one time later seeing a little girl with that ribbon in her hair. Strange what one remembers."

"How extraordinary. I'm beginning to think I've had only a glimpse of what life will be like here."

"Yes, I dare say. One does get used to it though. The house, that is. I rather doubt if I shall get used to having you here facing me. The house remains the same; you are constantly changing."

"Are you flattering me?"

"It's not my intention. Lizzy, I'm becoming bored with these games. There's something that interests me much more."

"Yes?"

"It's in our bedroom."

"It's not even nine-thirty yet."

"Yes, but you have been very pointed about my difficulty staying awake last night."

She proceeded to store the games, but he said, "Just leave the games. Let the servants take care of them; we haven't been giving them enough to do."

December 1, Thursday

At breakfast, Elizabeth said to Darcy, "I don't imagine we shall always have breakfast so late."

"No, of course not. Let's see. Sunday church is at eleven. We shall have to have breakfast at nine. That would be a good time to change. But through Saturday, ten o'clock. Agreed?"

"Yes, that should work very well." Then she continued, "I haven't received any mail yet, but no doubt I shall soon. When it does come, how shall I know that it has arrived?"

"Mail is left on the hall table and often arrives by mid-day. That reminds me; I have some extra correspondence to take care of this morning; I am afraid I shall have to forgo our morning walk today."

"Then I shall practice at the piano before I go to see Mrs. Sims."

"Excellent idea. Work on that loud one; something that will keep me awake."

They stood and embraced, then parted.

"Maybe he's right; something loud. The prelude is too difficult, though." She settled on a few selections and set to mastering them. "Well, they may need more polishing later, but I think I know them better now, at least."

In the kitchen Elizabeth proceeded to quiz Mrs. Sims on the duties of the various kitchen helpers, taking notes; she looked over Mrs. Sims collection of recipes, examined the equipment in the kitchen, then asked to see the wine cellar and was shown. "If we were to have a rather large affair with many guests, how would you manage dinner and all that entailed?"

"Do you have something particular in mind?" Mrs. Sims asked.

"No, but I don't doubt that the question will arise sometime during this next year. If our invitations for Christmas are accepted we will be having eight guests for several days during the holidays; with Mr. Darcy, Georgiana, and myself that would make 11. That should not be terribly difficult for the present staff, even for several days, but a truly large event with perhaps 60 guests or 80, surely more help would have to be found."

"Yes, indeed. It's been some years since Mrs. Darcy died—the former Mrs. Darcy, I should say—so it's a bit difficult to remember. And after she died, old Mr. Darcy didn't have large parties. However, it shouldn't be too difficult to find additional help. We'd have to train them, of course, and provide proper clothing."

"It's too soon now to make inquiries; I wouldn't want people round about thinking that something is planned for very soon. However, you might keep your eyes and ears open for ideas of who might help out with such an event.

"Now, Mrs. Sims, something of a more immediate nature. A Mrs. Wilson called here from Lambton yesterday. It seems that in December each year they hold a bazaar, and she was hoping we could donate something—Christmas fruit cake or breads, perhaps, or some dried fruits."

"Aye, ma'am, this sounds very much like times past."

"It may be too late for making fruit cake...."

"Well, ma'am," Mrs. Sims interrupted, "we've been knowing for some time that Mr. Darcy would be bringing his bride here in late November, and we decided, Mrs. Reynolds and I, that is, that I should go ahead and make some fruitcake; we decided we'd rather be eating fruitcake 'til Easter than run short."

"Mr. Darcy knows you very well, I see. He suggested that you might have anticipated me. As for breads, I was hoping you might have a dark bread recipe such as we always have enjoyed at my parent's home. It has some molasses and raisins in it."

"Aye, Ma'am," I was looking through the bread recipes as Mrs. Reynolds said I should, and I saw one like that. I haven't made it for some time, but I'd be happy to make a batch."

"Do you suppose you could make some so we could have it on Sunday morning?"

"No trouble at all, ma'am. You can count on it."

"Then if it is the recipe I like, perhaps you could make some for the bazaar."

"Nothing could be simpler."

"And Mr. Darcy said bacon might be appropriate for the sale and perhaps a picnic ham?"

"Indeed. They will find a ready buyer. Some of the tenants pay part of their rent in kind. We always have plenty of such these months of the year."

"And dried fruits?"

"There was a good crop of apples for drying this year. We could send a few pounds along to the bazaar without cutting too far into our supplies."

"Then it's settled. I'll talk with you again one day next week. I'd like to meet and talk with your helpers at that time also."

"You'll be most welcome, ma'am."

"And, Mrs. Sims, I do appreciate your continuing to plan the meals for the time being. Before long I'll be more help to you."

Her head fairly swimming, Elizabeth went to her bedroom and lay down for a few minutes to absorb all that had transpired in the kitchen. Then she washed her hands and went to the morning room. She had been there for some time when Darcy appeared, and Selbey soon followed.

Elizabeth was silent as they ate, still trying to absorb the workings of the kitchen and the details of the bazaar offerings.

"You're very quiet, Elizabeth."

"Yes, well my visit with Mrs. Sims has my head fairly swimming. I tried to read for awhile, but I don't have the smallest notion of what I read."

"You didn't encounter any difficulties, I hope."

"Oh no, none whatever." It's just all so different. Our household was so small, and Mama handled most of the dealings with Cook. I'm beginning to think I was an ornament at Longbourn as much as anything."

"Perhaps it's a bit much for you; perhaps you should just let Mrs. Reynolds continue as she has...."

"Oh no, Darcy, it's not that at all. It's just going to take awhile until I get used to it."

"Perhaps you have a touch of spring fever."

"Spring fever! In December?"

"You may not have noticed what a fine day we're enjoying. Looking out the window," he continued, "I can't remember when we have ever had such a summer-like day in December at Pemberley. Let us not waste a moment of it. It's warm enough to walk dressed as we are." They left the dinner table, walked through the morning room and on outside.

As they neared the grass, Elizabeth looked up at the sky, then at Darcy and said, "Perhaps we should play a game of tag."

"Tag! Tag?"

"Surely you know how to play tag."

"Of course I do, but you aren't suggesting that you and I play tag."

"And why not?"

"It certainly would be an unfair game."

"How so?"

"You don't expect to outrun me, do you?"

"If you are so sure of winning, why do you hesitate to play?"

He looked up at the few clouds in the sky, and, as he was about to speak, she tapped his arm and ran off onto the grass, holding her skirts as she ran. Stunned, he looked after her, realizing the game had begun before a contract to play had been made. Overcoming his reserve, he sprinted after her, quickly catching and tagging her. She immediately tagged him before he could get away and headed for the nearby row of tall slender bushes. They were far enough apart to run between pairs but quite close together; she ran between two bushes, turned, passed two bushes and stood between the second and the next. By this time Darcy had passed to the opposite side of the row and looked both ways. Not seeing her, he paused to listen. At length she came out on the side they had come from and ran toward the lawn. Hearing her, he followed, sprinting after her. By this time she had reached the gravel where stood a bench. She reached the opposite side and stood several feet away, breathless and laughing. He stopped and watched her as she stood, a bit crouched, poised to go the opposite way he should approach. He couldn't jump over without slowing down. Panting for breath himself, he paused, laughing, trying to decide which side to run towards. Side to side they rocked, waiting for his move. Finally he ran to his left, and she ran the opposite way, the bench between them, avoiding him. She reached the grassy area again, but he quickly caught her. He tagged her and took off. She ran at full tilt after him more than half way down to the lake. Now far behind him, she slowed down, laughing in full voice, her arms dangling in exhaustion beside her. Finally, realizing how far behind she was, Darcy slowed, turned, and, also laughing, raised an arm in triumph. But as he did, he saw her slowly crumple to the grass.

"Elizabeth!" No response. He paused only a moment, and seeing no motion, ran towards her at full speed, stopping short, out of arm's reach.

"Elizabeth!" Still no answer. He dropped to his knees, and as he did, her eyes flashed open, and she tagged him! He immediately tagged her other wrist, and back and forth they tagged, laughing, until nearly exhausted.

"Mr. Darcy, Mrs. Darcy," came a call. They both looked toward the voice and saw Beatty, the gardener, running toward them as fast as his stolid old frame could carry him. As he came near and could see them both looking his way, he slowed, and his voice dropped as he said, "Is somethin' amiss, ma'am? Sure and you frightened me out of my wits seein' you on the grass in a heap."

"No, Beatty," Darcy replied, "she's quite all right. It seems Mrs. Darcy has a bit of a sense of humor," he added, hoping to calm the old man. Beatty had ceased talking, but stood, his gaze fixed on Elizabeth, his mouth gaping. Darcy continued, "I'm afraid I let her entice me into a game of tag, and she cheated by pretending to faint." During this exchange Darcy helped Elizabeth stand up, and she dusted her skirt with her hands.

Before Beatty could collect his thoughts to say something their attention was drawn to a figure running towards them. It was Susan, running across the grass, holding her skirts up, an agitated look on her face. As she approached and saw Elizabeth, by now breathing almost normally, Susan slowed and said, "Oh, Mrs. Darcy, are you all right?"

"Yes, Susan, I'm perfectly well."

"But I saw you lyin' on the grass, sure as I'm alive. I was dustin' the window sills in the morning room, and I saw you out the window."

"Your eyes did not deceive you, Susan; I was lying on the ground, but I'm perfectly well. I do apologize to both of you. I'm afraid I carried our game too far." Reading the disbelief in both their faces, she continued, "I had no intention of frightening anyone. Please believe me; I am well."

Subdued, Beatty and Susan both turned and walked toward the house. Darcy offered his arm to Elizabeth, and they moved slowly away from the house. They walked silently for a few minutes. Then he looked down at her and said, gently, "This isn't the end of this matter, of course." She looked up at him expectantly, and he continued. "Susan will be in the kitchen now telling all about her frightening experience. And Beatty will be shaking his head all the way to the flower bed. Before the day is over every servant on the estate will be wondering if Mrs. Darcy is really all right. Or is she just being a brave lady even now in the clutches of some dire complaint."

"Surely you exaggerate. I was perfectly plain and sincere in my explanation and apology."

Darcy looked down at her lovingly, though seriously. "No, by Saturday all the neighborhood will be wondering what ails the lovely new mistress at Pemberley."

Elizabeth looked up again, searching his face for a sign of jest. But he only continued quietly and with as loving a tone in his voice as she had yet heard. "I'm sorry to say it, dearest Elizabeth, but you're likely to be hearing about this little episode for some time to come."

"Such fantasy. You're teasing me."

"At first the story will be that you sprained your ankle. But after a great many people have seen you walking perfectly well the rumor will be that you're in the family way. It will take some time for that rumor to die away. At the Christmas Bazaar people will be searching your face and figure to determine which rumor is true." He looked up at the few clouds in a beautiful sky, turning his face away from her.

Now she was certain he was mocking her. She stopped, withdrew her arm from his and looked directly at him. He turned also, forced to face her. She noted the tenseness around his mouth, a sure sign of mendacity, she thought. "Admit it; you're teasing me."

Smiling, he conceded, "Yes, I suppose you're right. But that doesn't detract from the truth of my assertions."

Both turned again, and once again she took his arm. They slowly strolled on, he looking upward and away from her searching gaze, again serious. She waited, hoping for more, but he only moved his right hand over to cover her hand where it rested on his arm. "Ah, Elizabeth, my lovely wife. We have an interesting week ahead of us. We'd better caution

Georgiana when she arrives in case she should hear any of the servants gossiping."

"Is that really necessary?"

Now looking toward her, "Perhaps not absolutely necessary; but I wouldn't want her wondering and worrying. We've been separated a great deal, as you know, and I'm not sure how accurate her assessment of me is. And she's known you a very short time. If she did hear something, I'm not certain she'd ask me about it."

"You make this sound like a major event."

"Possibly, but what other events does one find hereabouts, besides births, marriages, and deaths?"

Elizabeth fell into silence, remembering the rumors that flew about when Lydia eloped. Then she remembered Lady Catherine's visit to her trying to track down a rumor. Others divined her marriage to Darcy even before she dared to entertain such thoughts herself. At length she said, "Are you upset with me?"

"Not at all. One pays for one's pleasures. And it was a delightful game." He smiled down at her. "You may find the price excessive, but I think it was well worth it."

Now she knew she had had enough teasing for one day. They made their way to the house. Once in the morning room, they paused; he put his arms around her for just a few moments. "Off with you, 'til supper."

She walked to the stairs, was just ready to lift her skirts to bound up the stairs, when she thought better of it and climbed deliberately.

She went to her study, hoping to calm herself with the familiar. She took pen and paper and wrote:

"Dear Mama, Papa, Mary, and Kitty,
Perhaps you will forgive my delay in writing to you to say we arrived safely when I say that my new life at Pemberley has kept me very thoroughly occupied indeed.

I do not mean to mislead you into thinking I have been spending all my hours in duties as "Mistress of Pemberley," though that has occupied part of my time.

Darcy does have business to take care of, but we have been spending a great deal of time together.

If you could see how happy we are you would readily forgive me for any lapse in writing to you.

If I did not make plain earlier my appreciation for all your efforts to create a beautiful wedding for Darcy and me, please now accept my thanks.
Affectionately,
Elizabeth
P.S. Perhaps Lydia was correct that we married ladies don't have much time for writing letters!"

She sealed the letter, and wrote the direction on it. She went to the library and found a book to her liking, left the letter on the hall table, and returned to the drawing room.

Darcy was there when she arrived. He met her, took her in his arms and kissed her warmly. They embraced, rocking from side to side. Finally he released her and directed her to the sofa where he'd been reading.

"Have I disgraced you?"

"Certainly not. I knew I was marrying a vibrant young woman. Had I wanted a different kind of wife, there are plenty to be found. And you must admit I had the resources to devote to the search."

Before she could think of a reply, Selbey was at the door. When he had served them, Darcy said, "Selbey, I don't think we'll be wanting any pudding; just bring the coffee, and we can serve ourselves."

"Aye, sir." He brought the coffee and left.

He reached his hand over and held hers just for a few moments, until he could see the smile that said, "I need two hands to eat."

They ate in silence until Elizabeth said, "I wrote to Mama and Papa."

"Excellent."

"I told them that if they could see how happy we were, they would forgive me for not writing."

"Always be sure when you write to them that you send my love."

"Of course."

"And to the Bingleys and Gardners as well."

Elizabeth nodded her assent.

Rising from the table, Darcy said, "I don't much feel like playing games tonight, do you?"

She shook her head.

"And I doubt very much that you truly want to play the piano."

Again she agreed.

"What I would really like would be a nice long conversation."

She nodded.

By now they were near the drawing room door. He looked around and saw there were no servants nearby.

"...preferably horizontal and warm."

She looked up, smiled, and nodded assent. They ascended the stairs and made their way slowly to the bedroom, pausing to look at several of the paintings, then to look out the window of the gallery in the dim light at the surrounding beauty.

As they neared the bedroom, he said, "I forgot about Bradford. He rang, Bradford came, and Darcy said, "Bradford, I won't need you tonight, nor will Mrs. Darcy need Annie. Please tell her."

"Aye, sir," and he left.

Inside the bedroom he found Elizabeth near the window. "Come," he said, directing her towards the bed. He threw back the blankets and helped her remove her clothes and get into bed. He covered her, removed his own clothing, and got into bed beside her.

He lay on his back, one forearm resting on his forehead, the other hand under the covers caressing her hand. "These have been lovely days, Elizabeth. Just you and me. Before long we're likely to be caught up in the bustle of constant activity, not daring to go to bed early for fear someone will drop in to see us." He paused for awhile, silent. "You've made me a very happy man, Elizabeth. It isn't so easy to know how to express affection when one has received so little. You've made it very easy for me." He paused, reflecting for awhile, and then continued. "I can't help wondering what is the best way to treat children, how we should treat our own, when we have them.

"As it happens, in a way, we're in a position of raising a family backwards. Instead of starting with infants and raising them to adults, we're starting with a young woman in the midst of the most difficult period of her life, in all likelihood. Georgiana is my charge, of course, but as a practical matter, we no doubt will be working together to help her through this period."

"And Colonel Fitzwilliam?"

"Legally, of course, he has equal responsibility with me, but he will rarely be available, and I can't help thinking of one other aspect of the situation. It is possible after all, for them to marry each other, even though they are cousins. From your own personal experience you know that it is not only possible, but often actually encouraged, if not coerced."

"Do you think it likely he would attempt to attach her affections?"

"Who can say. They are, of course, fond of each other. He's an attractive man." He turned and caressed her cheek. "Georgiana can't help but be affected by our relationship."

"Certainly you don't want us to hide our affection for each other from her."

"Not at all. I think she could profit from it. And our affection for her is more likely to keep her from rushing into an unsuitable alliance than the reverse. If she is valued here she won't have to go elsewhere to seek approval."

"Would you be unalterably opposed to her marrying Colonel Fitzwilliam?"

He reflected awhile as if trying to determine what his feelings actually were on the subject. "No, I suppose not, but there is a great deal of difference in their ages. She's barely 17 and he's 31. I think that's probably my greatest objection. But his career in the military is perhaps as much a concern for me. One has so little control over one's fate...subject to the whims of kings and emperors. Living here now and there another time. Georgiana has lived a settled, sheltered life. The military life, I should think, would be a difficult one for her."

He tugged at her until her back nestled into the curve of his body. They lay while he caressed her as if lost in time and thought.

Sensation, warmth, movement, closeness, words, all combined to intensify lovemaking in this relationship of mutual affection.

They lay quiet, feeling each other's warmth. She ran her fingers along the line where their bodies met, up and down as far as she could reach. Reluctantly, they untangled their bodies and lay back, exhausted and content. The fingers of their hands laced together, they fell asleep.

Friday
At breakfast Elizabeth turned to Darcy and said. "It looks as if I shall have time at the piano this morning. Do you have any particular pieces you'd like me to prepare for you?"

"I think it's variety that interests me more than any particular piece; however, if I were to choose between just piano and you singing along, I'd prefer the latter."

"Then I'll keep that in mind. On Sunday I'll have the opportunity to hear you sing."

"Yes, in a crowd I do join in."

"Then you'll be happy to hear I've been practicing Christmas carols. Perhaps you can sing along with me tonight."

"That's one way to keep me awake." He looked out the window and said, "I'm afraid I'm going to have to pass up our morning walk today. Woodbury will be here soon and we're going to make the rounds of some of the farms on the estate."

"Is that necessary?"

"Yes, I think so, if I intend to keep aware of problems as they arise and prevent them from becoming difficulties or even disasters. It's much easier to understand when I see than to listen to descriptions of problems."

With an embrace and a kiss they parted in the hall. Elizabeth went immediately to her study and penned a letter to her friend Charlotte.

"Dear Charlotte,
I was so glad you were able to attend our wedding. Since you were married only a year ago I shall not have to write a great many details.

Suffice it to say that our determination to be the happiest of couples has not yet met any significant impediment. Perhaps seven days is too soon to speak; if so, so be it. Please extend our greetings to Cousin Collins and do us the kindness of not mentioning to Lady Catherine that you have heard from us. There is no point in irritating her.
Your devoted friend,
Elizabeth."

Before she could seal the letter Mrs. Reynolds appeared.
"Mrs. Reynolds, good morning."
"Good morning, Mrs. Darcy. And how are you this morning?"
"Very well, thank you. And yourself?"
"Oh yes, very well, as always."
"Perhaps Mrs. Sims mentioned that I had rather a long meeting with her yesterday."

"Aye, that she did. And I did not note any points at which I would differ."

"There was one question relative to the donations to the bazaar."

"Yes?"

"Mr. Darcy remembers from years ago seeing some ribbon that was ordered especially—ribbon that had the name Pemberley woven into the design."

"You know, I think he's right. I think there was ribbon of that kind. Let me look around and see if I can find it."

"Also we've decided that beginning Sunday we'll have breakfast at nine. I don't think I told Mrs. Sims; be so kind as to inform her for me." Noting Mrs. Reynolds's nod, she changed the subject. "I think I might be going in to Lambton on Tuesday. If I do, I should like to have you with me to take me around and tell me what kinds of supplies we can generally get there."

"That sounds like a good plan. I'll count on it."

These things settled, Mrs. Reynolds left. Elizabeth sealed the letter to Charlotte and proceeded to the music room. She reviewed several Christmas carols and found one song for herself to sing. Fortunately it was in her register so she didn't have to strain to sing it. "Darcy should like that one. Not that I'd be able to sing anything this month that would displease him. He seems determined to be pleased by everything I do. However, that will pass, so I must do as well as I'm able. Oh, dear, the time." She left the letter in the hall and continued to the morning room.

Selbey was announcing dinner as she arrived. At table Darcy and Elizabeth shared their dinner and comments about their morning activities.

The afternoon walk was more somber than usual and infinitely more somber than that of the day before. Elizabeth reflected on how Mrs. Reynolds had asked her how she was and that Beatty seemed very still when they passed him in the garden. "Perhaps he's fearful of a repeat performance," she thought. "There's not much danger in that. After all, Darcy may be right. It is possible. Certainly he's had enough experience in being one of the most prominent people in these parts. He should know, if anyone does, what people's reactions will be. But, maybe he's wrong. That would be a welcome change."

"You're very quiet, Elizabeth."

"I should think you'd welcome some silence." He put his right hand over hers where it held his arm, but said nothing. "I wrote to Charlotte this morning."

"You've written so many letters already you should begin to receive some soon. Be sure to let me know when you hear from the Bingleys. I'll try to arrange for some friends to hunt with us while they're here."

"I should think you'd want Bingley all to yourself."

"Perhaps I would; he's very easy company. But I expect he'll want to renew acquaintance in these parts, and perhaps even meet a few others."

"I can see you're a very thoughtful host."

"Well, Woodbury takes care of the estate for the most part; I need to do something to make me feel useful."

Back in the house after the walk, on her way to the library she found a letter addressed to "Mrs. Fitzwilliam Darcy." Suddenly she felt almost light headed. She had been Mrs. Fitzwilliam Darcy for almost a week now and had had almost minute-by-minute confirmation of that fact. But, somehow, seeing it written on an envelope in someone else's hand was a fresh sensation. She could feel a tingling in her skin.

She opened the letter carefully, almost as if it were sacred and found it was from Mrs. Flanders, saying she would be pleased to see Mrs. Darcy on Tuesday morning. She added that if Mrs. Darcy would bring the riding habit along she would tell her immediately if the alteration could be made. If it could be done, she would be happy to do it.

Elizabeth found a few books in the library that looked promising, took them to the drawing room, and was reminded of the pleasures of the printed word and the many hours she had spent reading at Longbourn. "Right now it looks as if I shall never have so much time for reading again. I'll have to choose more carefully the books I do read," she thought.

Darcy also arrived early for dinner, a book in hand, "Lizzy, I have news. Woodbury thinks he's found a horse that should suit you. We can go on Monday to see it if you wish."

"I do wish it. Did he give any details?"

"Yes, he did. The horse—Midnight, they call him—is accustomed to a woman rider; she's been riding for some time and has decided she'd prefer a younger, livlier horse."

"He's not a Nellie, is he?"

"Not at all. He's young enough to serve you very well, if Woodbury has judged correctly, at least during this first learning phase. As you become more confident, we can purchase a livlier mount. I just don't want you to be thrown off or have some other unpleasant experience. That could end the whole adventure."

"Hmmm. Well, I have to trust your judgment. At least it all sounds reasonable. But is there so much difference in horses?"

"Almost as much difference as in people. With people, of course, it's easier to tell the differences; just listening to people speak tells you a lot. With horses you have to be keener to observe the differences."

At the supper table Elizabeth remembered the letter. "I quite forgot. I was so engrossed in your comments about the horse that I completely forgot—I received a reply from Mrs. Flanders. I am to see her Tuesday at eleven about the riding habit." To herself she added, "How extraordinary that I should forget the letter, when it struck me so forcibly at the time. I do think this business of being mistress of Pemberley is quite confusing me." Fortunately, through her musing she heard Darcy's brief, positive response to the comment about the letter.

"Since you are going to Lambton, I'll arrange to hunt with Morris that morning."

They finished supper quietly and repaired to the drawing room. Elizabeth began to think she might fall asleep if she read, and so challenged Darcy to a game of cribbage. "Now, as to rules; is cheating permitted or not?"

"Certainly not," he shot back. "What a thought!"

"I was just thinking about Georgiana."

"Whatever do you mean?"

"Well, if we teach her games we really should teach her to recognize cheating when it occurs."

"She won't be involved in games involving money."

"Of course not; but a game's a game, and everyone likes to win. It's a part of life. She should be made to realize that not everyone is to be trusted, not always at least."

"But surely you didn't play games in your family in such a way, did you?"

"No, but perhaps we should have. Perhaps then Lydia would not have been so trusting as to run off with Wickham."

"I'd rather not be reminded of that episode."

"Nor would I, but it is part of our past. And if one ignores history one may find oneself repeating it."

"I believe the quote runs a bit differently."

"Perhaps, but the meaning is the same."

"Well, I don't want to cheat."

"All right then, I'll cheat, and it will be your responsibility to catch me."

He agreed, reluctantly.

She shuffled the cards, fanned them out and said, "Draw for deal; aces high, high card deals."

He drew a jack and she an eight. She closed the deck and proceeded to shuffle.

"You said high card deals."

"Very good; you caught me the first time out."

He reshuffled and began to deal the cards for cribbage as she watched closely.

They picked up their cards and arranged them. She played a card, and the play followed, back and forth.

"You counted wrong," he said.

"So I did; imagine that!"

The hand ended, and it was her deal. She gathered the cards, shuffled, and dealt. The last card to herself she dealt off the bottom of the deck.

"Caught you!" he said. "Every card must be dealt off the top of the deck."

"Right again." She returned the card to the top of the deck, but he caught her again.

"That card came from the bottom of the deck and must be returned there."

"It's plain to see I'll need a lot more practice to be able to fool you."

They played out the cards and Elizabeth was pegging her score on the board, but took one hole too many.

"Elizabeth."

"It's no fun at all trying to cheat you. Shall we try another hand?" They did, but he was too sharp and caught her at every attempt. She tried again to cheat at keeping score, but he was right there to keep her honest.

"Plainly if Georgiana has your talent, she shall have mastered the art of detecting deception in games in short order."

"My dear, you have played the part of card cheat admirably, if a bit clumsily. It should certainly be an adequate demonstration to Georgiana regarding unalloyed trust. But I have to admit I don't take much pleasure in such proceedings." He rose, took her hand, and lifted her to her feet; one arm at her back he directed her to the door and upstairs. "I much prefer the pleasure of basking in the rays of a trusting relationship."

"Is this another bout of poetry coming on?"

"My dear Elizabeth, if poetry it is, I have only you to blame, or credit, whichever you prefer."

Their seventh night together and they had finally managed to stay away from the bedroom long enough to take advantage of Annie's and Bradford's services.

Undressed and fresh from washing, in their robes, they met in their bedroom. They stood by the window, Elizabeth in front of Darcy, his arms around her waist; he looked over her shoulder, laid his cheek against her head, and they gazed out at the star-lit sky. They stood like that, relaxed, until all noises from the dressing rooms had ceased, and Bradford and Annie had gone.

He directed her to her side of the bed, lifted her chin and kissed her. Then he slipped her robe off to reveal her body in the soft light. He helped her into bed, went to his side, disrobed, and climbed in. Propped on his arm, he caressed her, watching her eyes and expression. She reached up and drew his head closer. He kissed her and listened. She moved her arm past his body as he lifted himself. As he kissed her again she ran the flat surfaces of her fingernails over his torso, tracing it's contours.

Lovemaking—how often she had wondered what it would be like, and now she found it was like nothing else. His strength, breath and touch—how could she have believed she would not like sleeping with her husband, or rather, not sleeping with him.

They moved rhythmically until they were both exhausted and contented. But, there was something else, something she could feel, but not identify. She pushed it away and felt herself convulsing.

"Well, Lizzy," he said when his breathing had returned to normal. "Aren't you just full of surprises?"

"So it seems."

Untangled, they lay quietly.

"Ah, what secrets your lovely body contains."

"I suppose this is the inner nature you mentioned."

"Ah, how often we speak of things we understand not."

"Is that poetry again? Or perhaps philosophy."

"I'll leave it to you to decide.

"You are fortunate that I am not a writer, or I should surely be recording these bits of wisdom."

"I need not worry. Such scribblings are ill rewarded, and so few take the trouble to do it."

"Yes, it's good you're rich to begin with, because I should not like to live on the income of a writer."

"You may safely tease me; I'm much too tired even to respond with clever retorts, much less the merciless tickling you richly deserve."

Lying on her side, she held his hand between hers and rested her cheek on his shoulder. "Yes, no doubt I richly deserve something; I shall devote many hours to determine exactly what it is."

"A horse." Both chuckled at that.

"I've noted on a number of occasions that people choose gifts for others that they themselves would like to receive," she said.

"Perhaps now I can call you a philosopher."

"At one time or another we must all be philosophers. It's a matter of necessity. Somehow we must each of us accommodate ourselves to the circumstances we find ourselves in. For some it's easy. Like me now, for instance. It would be difficult to find a person more fortunate than I feel at this moment."

"And that is my reward," he said, sleepily.

Saturday: Carleton

Elizabeth and Darcy were about to enter the dining room for breakfast when they heard noise outside the front entry. "I'll see what it is, Lizzy; you go on in."

Darcy opened the door. "Carleton, old friend, what brings you here?"

"Darcy, good to see you. I've been hunting and decided to share my good fortune with you."

"That is a handsome brace of birds. Tommy, take them to the kitchen. Come in, come in, I'll introduce you to Mrs. Darcy. We were just now on our way to breakfast. You will join us, won't you?"

"So late?"

Faintly smiling, Darcy said, "Yes, at least for our first week of marriage we've been indulging in a late breakfast."

They entered the dining room and found Elizabeth standing by a window. "I have a surprise for you this morning, Mrs. Darcy. My old friend Carleton has come bearing a gift of game, a wedding gift, I daresay," looking toward him. "Carleton, Mrs. Darcy."

"I'm very pleased to meet you, Mr. Carleton."

"The pleasure is all mine, I assure you."

Darcy said, "Selbey, tell Mrs. Sims Mr. Carleton is staying to breakfast."

"Aye, sir," and he left.

"Let me get you some coffee; here, sit next to me." He poured coffee, and they all sat down.

"And how is Mrs. Carleton," Darcy asked.

"She's very well, thank you. And I'm delighted to see you looking so well, Mrs. Darcy."

"Thank you, I have been fortunate always to enjoy good health, as I do now."

"Then the rumor is untrue?"

Darcy and Elizabeth exchanged glances. "What rumor is that, Carleton?"

"Well, that Mrs. Darcy has some dire and mysterious ailment."

"Yes, Carleton, the rumor is untrue. Did the rumor include any details?"

"Indeed," looking towards Elizabeth, "I heard that she collapsed on the grounds and had to be carried into the house."

At that Darcy and Elizabeth smiled broadly. "She did collapse on the grass, Carleton, but was not carried into the house. She collapsed deliberately and not as a result of illness. Mrs. Darcy, it seems, has a lively sense of humor. She was, unfortunately, successful in enticing me into a game of tag."

Carleton, appearing incredulous, looked from one to the other, trying to understand the situation.

"When she could see that she couldn't win, she deliberately collapsed on the grass to trick me. You can guess the rest. The servants, seeing her crumpled on the grass believed her to be taken ill. By now, no doubt, all Derbyshire has heard that the lovely new mistress of Pemberley is the victim of some unknown malady."

Grinning, not entirely satisfied, Carleton said, "So she pulled you into a game of tag, Darcy. The rest of the story sounds plausible, but I've known you a very long time. I can only conclude that this young lady has a very powerful effect on you."

Darcy knitted his eyebrows and busied himself with his food. Elizabeth ate intently, glancing from time to time at one or the other.

In an attempt to change the subject, Darcy said, "So, you have been enjoying good hunting."

"Indeed; perhaps you'd care to join us Monday."

"I'd like to, but Mrs. Darcy...."

Carleton interrupted with, "Of course, perhaps later in the week then."

"Let me send a note when I see some time available."

Carleton looked from one to the other and said, "Perhaps January would be convenient." Neither Darcy nor Elizabeth could suppress their laughter at this comment.

"I will contact you, Carleton, have no fear. And thank you for the birds. They will provide a welcome change at table."

They finished their breakfast, walked to the entry, and said their goodbyes, Carleton still with a lingering trace of puzzlement on his countenance.

At supper, Selbey had served the pudding and left. Darcy looked at Elizabeth and, seeing her looking alert and far from tired, said, "I would like to hear some of the music you've been practicing this week."

"And I would like you to hear it, preferably early."

"Then we'll go directly to the music room. Let's get our books and just stay there for awhile to read after you play."

She nodded assent. Entering the hall, Elizabeth went to get the books while Darcy found Fenton. "Fenton, please tell Bradford and Annie we'll be retiring at 9:30."

"Aye, sir."

Hand in hand they made their way to the music room and Darcy seated himself where he could look into Elizabeth's face as she played. First she played a short, easy piece, then one of the first pieces she had memorized as a child. Looking at him and thinking he seemed a bit sleepy, she played a rollicking sailor song. Then she said, "Come, Darcy, and sing along with me. Let's practice some carols. Sit beside me so you can see the words." He drew up a chair and sang with her, at first methodically, dutifully, but as they went along, with more enthusiasm and involvement in the feeling of the music.

"I think that's enough for this evening," she said.

"Yes. You do play well, Elizabeth. You make light of your skill, but you do play well."

"Thank you, sir."

Now, rather than read separately, I would like to read you a short story.

"Ah, a treat," she said, moving towards the sofa.

"I came upon this story not long ago and think you might like it."

"He was right...as usual," she thought. "And he reads very acceptably. Bed time stories will be his specialty, no doubt. At least he's prepared for what seems our fate." As he finished, she said, "I did like it. You're right, as usual. I'm beginning to think I shall truly wear out those words."

"Isn't it a bit late to be mocking me—when I'm tired and quite incapable of defending myself?"

"I'm sorry," she said. They were now heading toward their bedroom suite, and she took his arm and said, "I know it sounded like teasing, but I truly did like the story."

Annie and Elizabeth must have been unusually quick or Bradford and Darcy slow, for Elizabeth arrived in the bedroom first. Quickly she slipped off her robe and climbed into bed, adjusted herself, and proceeded to feign sleep, intending to tease him. He slowly padded his way to the bed, lifted the covers, and noted her closed eyes and deep, rhythmic breathing. Gingerly he got into bed and found a comfortable position. Before he could consider whether to snuff the candle immediately or later, he was asleep.

It all happened so fast that Elizabeth didn't have time to consider that he might immediately go to sleep before he actually had. "Apparently he also is full of surprises," she thought. Not quite that tired, she closed her eyes, and memories of the past week flooded over her, carried her flying through the events and feelings in rapid succession. The dominant force, of course, was Darcy, but her own lively response to every new situation had played an important role in the events as well. In fact, if Carleton's reaction to the gossip was any indication, it could turn out that she was the most active force—for good, or more likely, she thought, evil. She thought of Darcy's statement that if it was within his power, his love would rest on her like a summer's breeze. "Perhaps poetry does have its place." On that thought, she drifted into slumber.

Sunday: Lambton Church

She woke to the dusky light of an early December day. Stirring, she realized that Darcy had already awakened.

"Wife," he said, lazily, "a good morning to you."

"Hmmm. And a good morning to you as well, husband."

Slowly, deliberately he said, "Eight nights we have passed together—let us say one week. And I have a quiz for you."

"And what might that be, sir?"

"A quiz consisting of one question. I think an essay question would be best." He paused, reading her face to confirm her attention.

"Yes, sir."

"In twenty-five words or less, what do you think about England?"

"At first puzzled, then understanding, she said, "Oh dear, I completely forgot to think about England."

He burst out laughing, reached for her middle with both hands, drew her to him, and embraced her in a bear hug. Laughing uproariously, they tumbled about the bed, until they were exhausted. Lying back and holding her hand, he said, "Well, I see that I passed the test."

"Oh, yes, Darcy, you did indeed, with flying colors."

They made love until, exhausted, they lay back in each other's arms.

"Elizabeth, I have come to a decision. Today I shall begin a diary." Alert, she listened. He could feel that firmness in her body that told him she was attuned to his words. "And the first words in the diary will be, "She completely forgot to think about England."

"Darcy!" She freed herself from his embrace and bounded out of bed. As she stood nude, he watched her search for her robe.

"Is this what you're looking for?" he asked, holding it up.

Chilled, she climbed back onto the bed. "You are dreadful! Incorrigible!" She pounded him with her pillow. Her anger subsided, she said, "You wouldn't write down anything about us, would you, you know, about our intimate relations?"

"Of course not!"

"And you wouldn't talk about me to your men friends, would you?"

"Never," he said, gently pulling her to him. "You are mine alone; I couldn't expose our love in such a fashion; it wouldn't be ours alone then."

"Well," she said, sighing, "I'm glad I can trust you implicitly. I know if you say it, you mean it."

"Am I imagining it, or did I tell you once that I would all too soon become predictable? Married just one week and you know me backwards and forwards."

"Hardly that."

Relaxing, eyes closed, it seemed only too soon it was time to arise. They could hear bustle in both dressing rooms, and when it quieted, they rose, took robes, and parted to enjoy warm baths and pampering. Dressed for church, they went to breakfast, looking very contented indeed.

"Hmmm, Darcy purred, "Very good bread. Haven't had this kind for a long time—makes a nice change."

"And that is my first effort in the kitchen."

"You made it?"

She smiled broadly. "No, dear, I suggested that Mrs. Sims make it for today."

"Well, it couldn't be better if you had made it yourself."

"You can be very sure of that!"

"Selbey, more bread."

Selbey wasn't there, of course, so Elizabeth replied, "Darcy!" Now both were engulfed in mirth. "If that is all it takes on my part to please you, it's obvious I'm going to be a very successful mistress of Pemberley."

"Without a doubt, you shall."

The carriage was waiting for them as they donned their coats. As soon as they noted that one of the footmen had supplied blankets for this chilly morning they left for church.

Elizabeth drank in the freshness of the fields, the grass dusted with frost. She looked for signs of rabbits and watched for birds flying. But she was more than rewarded for her attention by a glimpse of a doe deer near a large clump of trees. It sensed the carriage and was gone before Elizabeth's alert could draw Darcy's attention.

"Yes, there are quite a lot of deer here. And when I find time to hunt, you may be rewarded with venison at table."

"Is that a hint?"

A faint smile warmed his countenance.

On such a chilly day people were entering the church as soon as they arrived, and Darcy and Elizabeth did likewise. He directed her to their pew and they sat on the hard bench, silent. She looked around, everything at once so new and still so familiar. Everyone was bundled in their coats, waiting for the service to begin, nodding when eyes chanced to meet. The simple stone structure enveloped them in a simplicity that seemed a welcome contrast to the elegant finery she had been surrounded with all week, inducing in her a sense of perspective, a calmness.

The organ music began, the congregation rose and they were embarked on a routine so familiar that her mind tended to wander. She thought of the likelihood that before a year or two had passed she would not be arriving at church in so carefree a manner; that her thoughts would be at home with an infant. She thought of the remarkable fact that she was here at all—that only four months earlier in this very village she had seen Darcy walking out the door at the inn, certain that she would never see him again, and beginning to realize that she was falling in love with him.

She shook herself back to consciousness. The singing was over, and she had not even noted Darcy's singing. The minister was preaching now: words, phrases, injunctions she had heard so often that only the features of his face brought variety to the experience.

A young boy of perhaps eight years was seated next to her. She could sense him looking up at her. She stared at her gloved hands, not wanting to meet his gaze, fearful of lapsing into a silent communication with him. "I've caused quite enough uproar for one week," she thought.

Only two pews ahead a boy of perhaps four years, on his knees in the pew beside his father who was trying to control him, looked back alternately at her and the boy beside her. It was more difficult to avoid his gaze, but she looked up, now at the minister, then to the organ, then up at the only stained glass window in the church, straight ahead of them.

They were singing again, and this time she attended to Darcy's singing—clear, strong, but far from overpowering. "Very creditable," she thought. She was glad to have him standing so close, sharing the hymn book, his shoulder behind hers.

Then the familiar ending to the service, organ music accompanying their exit. Freed from the constraints of the service, she smiled both at the boy next to her and at the boy two pews ahead. The press of people moved them on.

At the door the Vicar greeted the parishioners, including the Darcys. "Good morning, Mr. Darcy, and welcome to you, Mrs. Darcy. We're so pleased to have you with us this morning."

Few people lingered in front of the church; it was too cold for that. They scurried off, no doubt thinking of the warmer surroundings of their homes. A number of people did exchange nods with Darcy. Mrs. Wilson greeted Elizabeth, "Good morning, Mrs. Darcy; so glad to see you here."

"Good morning, Mrs. Wilson."

As Farris handed her into the coach, she heard Darcy say, "Good day, Morris; G'day, Winston!" Then he joined her and they covered themselves with the blankets. She decided not to ask for a longer trip home, feeling thoroughly chilled.

"Would you care to take a little walk before dinner, Mrs. Darcy?"

"All I want is to stand by the fireplace and thaw out my body."

"Quite right; I'll join you."

Warmed, each sought the quiet of their books until Selbey called them to dinner.

"You said you'd like us to go tomorrow to see Midnight."

"Yes, morning would be best, early, I should think. If we leave soon after breakfast we should be back well before dinner."

"I'll send word to Mrs. Reynolds that I can't meet with her tomorrow then."

"Let Fenton tell her." Taking his time eating, he looked at Elizabeth appreciatively. "And did you have any share in planning this meal?"

"None, whatever; indeed, if you are to depend on my efforts, you are likely to go hungry, at least for another week. My husband keeps drawing my attention elsewhere," she said archly.

"Yes, well...." Then in a more lively manner, "I did send a note to Morris that he can expect me Tuesday about nine for some hunting."

"But we don't eat breakfast until nine."

"Just ask Mrs. Sims to have coffee and some of that bread for me at eight o'clock. That will serve until we've finished hunting. You can be sure Morris will demand I stay to dinner. If I'm lucky, he won't have a party of ten, prepared to quiz me about your mysterious ailment."

"...or about how you like married life?"

Soberly he responded, "Whatever the number there, you can be sure I won't escape that question."

"So I shall breakfast and dine alone Tuesday."

"Yes, but I believe the principle danger lies in leaving a lady with such a lively imagination to her own devices." He waited with obvious anticipation for her reply.

"Then, I believe I shall breakfast with Mrs. Reynolds in Lambton at the inn. I daresay they have a nice variety of breads and other delicacies to choose from."

"Excellent idea. You might keep in mind though, that if you do call on the Vicar, they will likely press you to stay for tea. And, you just might find Mrs. Wilson there as well."

"Why do you say that?"

"Well, you're going to see Mrs. Flanders. Surely you don't expect her to keep that information secret, do you? And, if you're in the village, would you fail to call on the Vicar? As for Mrs. Wilson, I have do doubt that she's part of a very lively network for gossip. Her work on the bazaar will put her in contact with several people every day."

"What an imagination! If father were here, he'd say, 'With such lively company, who would read novels?'"

"Would he, indeed? Then perhaps you come by your philosophy legitimately."

Elizabeth subsided into contemplation. "Perhaps he's right. After all, Darcy predicted the gossip about the tag incident. Carleton heard about it; and he doesn't even live close by."

Looking out the window, he said, "It's warmer now; shall we walk?"

Elizabeth mused, "Sometimes at home on Sunday afternoon Aunt and Uncle Phillips would drop in to visit with Mama and Papa." They rose and left the table, got their coats, and exited the house. "Do you think we might have visitors this afternoon?"

"It's entirely possible. It's been so many years since Mother died, I've quite forgotten what Sunday afternoons were like."

"Perhaps we should walk near the house then, and keep a watch on the road."

"I agree."

"It's so much easier to get acquainted with people a few at a time. I wouldn't want to miss such opportunities." They walked in silence. Her mind racing ahead, Elizabeth asked, "When I go into London in January about clothing, you will go also, won't you?"

"Absolutely. The theatre season is at its best then, and I wouldn't miss the opportunity to display my lovely wife to the world."

"And Georgiana also?"

"You sound as if you'd like her with us, and I'd be reluctant to leave her here."

"Yes, and she may need some new gowns herself."

"I wouldn't be a bit surprised if this were to be the liveliest social season of her life. She will need plenty of clothing to keep up with it." They walked on, enjoying the bracing air. Elizabeth saw a large gray perfect feather on the ground and picked it up.

"So now you're going to be a collector."

"Yes, of beautiful things; offerings from the universe."

"We seem to be showered with poetry this week!"

"You are right...as usual."

They were facing the house now, and their attention was drawn to an approaching chaise. "It looks like Blakely," Darcy said. They walked briskly to the carriage where the passengers were disembarking at the entrance. "Blakely," Darcy said, "Welcome." By now the four were facing each other. "Mr. and Mrs. Blakely, I want you to meet Mrs. Darcy." They all made their greetings and Darcy ushered them into the front hall. Fenton took their wraps and they all proceeded to the drawing room. The ladies moved immediately to the fireplace, and the gentlemen stood nearby.

Mrs. Blakely looked around the room appreciatively and then at Elizabeth. Before she could speak, their attention was drawn to Blakely,

"So, Darcy, you've found a Mistress for Pemberley at last." Then looking at Elizabeth, he continued, "I'm sure I was not the only one who was beginning to think this might never happen." Elizabeth smiled, looked up at Darcy, a smile lighting up his face. Nevertheless, she thought she could see him casting around for some subject more to his liking.

"We're very glad to have you here," Mrs. Blakely intervened. "Not just so Mr. Darcy will have company. We're a bit selfish, hoping that perhaps we might have a somewhat livelier social environment," she said, with a question in her tone.

"You'll find Mrs. Darcy enjoys company a great deal, Mrs. Blakely," he responded. "It's a bit too soon to tell, but I wouldn't be surprised if by spring I shall be wishing for some peace and solitude." They all smiled at this. Now warmer, Elizabeth walked to a sofa, motioning to Mrs. Blakely that she'd like her to come also.

"Everything is so new here, it's difficult even to know what to say when I meet someone."

"I don't doubt it in the least," Mrs. Blakely responded warmly. She and Mr. Blakely appeared to be in their late twenties. "I'm not fond of large gatherings, myself," she continued. "One must go when the opportunity offers, of course, but I prefer smaller groups. We're hoping you and Mr. Darcy will join Mr. Blakely and myself at our home for dinner on Tuesday week." She waited for a reply, and Elizabeth, at first in confusion, then having decided, turned towards Darcy. He was looking at her, listening as Blakely spoke.

As Blakely finished, Elizabeth said, "Darcy, Mrs. Blakely has asked if we could join them for dinner Tuesday week."

Roused, he thought a bit and said, "Georgiana should be back by then."

Mrs. Blakely interrupted to say, "She's invited as well, of course."

"Then, with pleasure," he answered and turned again to Blakely.

"I'm so glad," Mrs. Blakely said. There will be perhaps another couple, two at most."

"You will stay for a light supper, won't you?" Elizabeth asked. "We dine at two o'clock here, but a six o'clock supper would be convenient."

"Actually, we dine at three o'clock, so it's a bit early. We usually have supper at eight-thirty. Mr. Blakely is quite a night owl."

"Tea, then?" Elizabeth asked.

"That sounds delightful."

Elizabeth excused herself, stepped into the hall, found Fenton, and requested that tea and some light refreshments be prepared and brought. "And be sure some of the raisin bread is on the tray."

"Yes, ma'am."

She returned to find Mrs. Blakely at a window. "Lovely grounds; absolutely lovely."

"Yes, Mr. Darcy tells me he's put rather a lot of effort into it these past several years, and his father and grandfather did far more over several decades."

"I don't doubt it in the least. It's pleasing to see that you have, apparently, already a deep appreciation for it."

Looking out, Elizabeth said, "One can never begin to pay back in appreciation for such beauty."

"Yes, well, my dear," she said, turning and moving toward the sofa, "I expect you have a very lively year ahead of you."

"I can see that already, and we've been here only a week. Georgiana will arrive soon, so I expect she will help me put it all into perspective."

"Yes, she seems to be a very steady girl. And an excellent musician, too. We've heard her play the piano forte; lovely. And do you play?"

"I do, but not well." Nevertheless, Darcy insists that I play, so, no doubt, eventually you'll be able to judge for yourself."

The tea arrived, and Elizabeth directed that it be served at the game table, where they sat down to enjoy it. Mr. Blakely looked at Elizabeth as she poured and said, "You're looking very well, Mrs. Darcy."

Elizabeth set the cup and saucer down before him and said, "Yes, as always, thank you." Then, considering a second possible meaning and seeing an expectant look on Mr. Blakely's countenance, she looked at Darcy, who was looking at her with a suppressed smile playing over his features.

"Yes," he said, looking up at a painting behind Mrs. Blakely, "I think I shall have to place an advertisement in all the newspapers: 'No, Mrs. Darcy does not have a mysterious ailment. She tricked me while we were playing a game of 'tag' by deliberately collapsing on the lawn.'"

Gasps of laughter escaped their guests as Elizabeth tried in vain to suppress her smile.

"Well," Mr. Blakely said, regaining his composure, "I've seen remarkable thinks in my time, but I've never before seen marriage turn a man into a humorist."

Now even Elizabeth had to join in the laughter.

Mr. Blakely took a bite, chewed the raisin bread and said, "Very tasty."

"Yes, this is Elizabeth's first contribution to our gustatory pleasure."

"Indeed," Mr. Blakely responded, "the Mistress of Pemberley baking bread?"

"No, Mr. Blakely," Elizabeth interjected. "I asked Cook to bake the bread. I'm not certain whether Mr. Darcy is determined to exaggerate my virtues out of all proportion or if he is pressing me to expose the meagerness of my contribution to the elegance of Pemberley." They relaxed into delight over those possibilities and the pleasures of Cook's offerings.

At length, Blakely ventured, "Darcy, hunting has been good of late; we've missed you."

Looking at Elizabeth, he obviously was casting about for a response. Elizabeth looked back at him, giving him no assistance. Now Mrs. Blakely was looking back and forth between them, "Something's going on; what is it?"

At length, Darcy replied, "Let us aim for January." Smiles all round. "But if I do have a morning sooner, I'll send a messenger."

"Fair enough."

"We're hoping the Bingleys will join us for Christmas and a few days after."

"Have I met Bingley?"

"I'm not sure," Darcy answered, searching his memory. "We were together at college my last three years. He was a year behind me, but at the same college. He visited here a number of times during those years; you must have met him. If they can stay for some shooting, I'll send a message to you. His wife is Mrs. Darcy's sister, so she will have company while we hunt."

They finished their tea, and Mrs. Blakely said, "I would enjoy a longer visit, but Mr. Blakely promised we'd be home before it gets dark." They parted amid good wishes on both sides and expectation of dinner together at the Blakely's.

Monday: Midnight and the Pettigrews

Darcy went down early to order the carriage for nine-thirty.

On her way to breakfast, Elizabeth asked Fenton to tell Mrs. Reynolds she would not be able to meet with her this morning. Then, on the hall table she found a letter. She entered the dining room to find Darcy drinking his coffee. "A letter from Lydia," she said. "Well, here's where we learn if *a* letter is better than *no* letter."

"What does she say?" Darcy asked.

"She's asking for assistance that I have no intention of giving."

"Are you being a bit hasty?"

"I don't think so; you're welcome to read it yourself." She handed it to him, and added, "It may be that someday I'll be willing to extend some help, but she'll have to offer a better reason than that she needs a new bonnet. Lydia will get along just fine; she always does."

"Returning the letter," Darcy said only, "Hmmm. Well, I trust your judgment."

"Now, on to more urgent matters," she said. "Where do we go to see Midnight?"

"The owners—the Pettigrews—live not far beyond Chipping Burnside. We should be back in time for dinner."

"Perhaps we could stop to look at shops in Chipping Burnside."

"There's not much there, but as long as we're there, why not? Their market day is Wednesday, I believe, so another time for that, perhaps."

Breakfast finished and coats donned, they left in the coach. Most of the road was different than the road to Lambton, so Elizabeth watched the scenery go by, making sure Darcy showed her the limits of the Pemberley estate.

The day was somewhat warmer than Sunday, crisp, but sunny. As Darcy had said, Chipping Burnside was a quiet little village. Arrived at the Pettigrews, they were warmly greeted by Mr. and Mrs. Pettigrew, and at the stable, by Mrs. Pettigrew's brother, Stuart Harrison. Elizabeth judged him to be about 22 and Mrs. Pettigrew perhaps 24, though her husband must be in his late 20s.

"I'm not exactly happy to part with Midnight, Mrs. Pettigrew said, but we really can't keep two horses for me, and I've become fond of a livelier style of riding."

Midnight looked sleek and healthy. Elizabeth had no idea how old he might be, but Darcy opened the horse's mouth and made his own appraisal.

"Is he gentle?" Elizabeth ventured.

"Oh, yes, I've never been thrown off, if that's what you mean; but he has a lot of life in him yet; the family we got him from had good experience with him. And Mr. Pettigrew's sister has made it a point of taking him out whenever possible on her visits here—enjoyed him enormously. Would you join us for tea?"

Elizabeth looked toward Darcy, and he nodded assent.

"Let's go on into the house, then, Mrs. Darcy, and the others will follow us shortly, I'm sure."

Inside the house, very attractive and obviously comfortable, if far less grand than Pemberley, Mrs. Pettigrew asked the maid to bring tea. Once in the sitting room Mrs. Pettigrew commented, "I understand you live beyond Chipping Burnside, towards Lambton."

"Yes."

"There's a very fine house over that way—Pemberley, I think it's called."

"Yes, that's Mr. Darcy's estate."

"Your home?"

"Yes."

"Really?"

Elizabeth began to feel rather uncomfortable, looked around and said, "You have a very comfortable house here. It reminds me somewhat of my parent's home in Hertfordshire."

"Indeed?"

"Yes, well, the Bennet home is rather close to a church, but the area is rural, with only a few tenants nearby. It's about 2 miles from Meryton. My sisters and I used to walk there often."

"I rather doubt that the mistress of Pemberley will be walking to Lambton. Oh, I hope you don't think me impertinent," she added hastily.

"Not at all. You're quite right. I'm finding being married to Mr. Darcy is not as easy as it appeared."

Looking sympathetically towards Elizabeth, Mrs. Pettigrew said, in a lower voice, rather hesitantly, "He's not unkind...?"

"Oh, no, I didn't mean that. It's just that, well, apparently everything I do seems somehow very important."

"Ah, I see, well, and if you're not feeling well...."

"I don't think I know what you mean."

"Well, I'd heard that the new mistress of Pemberley was not at all well."

By this time the maid had arrived with the tea tray, and was serving it as the gentlemen came in and found places to sit.

By now Elizabeth realized that news of the "tag" incident had penetrated this far, and while Mrs. Pettigrew was pouring, Elizabeth, now in rather good control of herself, said, "Mr. Darcy, I'm afraid the news of my 'mysterious malady' has preceded us."

"Indeed," Darcy said, smiling broadly. "And have you let Mrs. Pettigrew in on the secret?"

"No, we were interrupted by your arrival."

"What malady is that?" inquired Mr. Pettigrew.

"Dear," Mrs. Pettigrew said to her husband, "Mr. Darcy is the owner of Pemberley over towards Lambton."

"Is that right? Well, I'm sorry I didn't ask a higher price for Midnight."

"Does that mean you've bought him?" Elizabeth asked Darcy.

"Yes, unless you say 'no' now; he seems a fine horse, exactly what you need. And the price is right."

"Then of course I want him."

"Then it's agreed," Darcy said to Mr. Pettigrew.

Now threading his way back through the conversation, Mr. Pettigrew said, "Well, Mrs. Darcy, you look to me as if you enjoy fine health."

"I do, sir."

Then looking at Darcy for explanation, Darcy responded with, "I'm afraid that I've had to explain only too often that Mrs. Darcy is in excellent health. She is only the victim of her own sense of humor and determination to win a game at all costs, even if it means deliberately collapsing on the lawn during a game of tag, pretending to faint. I'm beginning to think we need to stage a grand ball to demonstrate that Mrs. Darcy is very well, indeed."

At this suggestion they all straightened up as if ready to accept the invitation. He looked in turn at each of the others, wondering what he had said that was so startling.

At length, Elizabeth said, "Do you realize what you just said?"

"What do you mean?"

"About having a ball."

"It was just a figure of speech, a wild attempt to find a way out of a dilemma."

"Mr. Darcy," said Mrs. Pettigrew, is it such a wild idea?" It might be just the thing to quash a silly rumor."

Appearing bewildered, Darcy looked around and at length smiled and said, "You may be right."

Elizabeth looked over at Harrison and said, "Mr. Harrison, are you a riding enthusiast as well?"

"I'm afraid not, Mrs. Darcy; I mean, I like to ride, but I don't usually have the opportunity. I'm just here for a few days' break from my studies at Oxford."

"Indeed, and what are you studying?"

I haven't decided on my life's work yet so I'm following a liberal course. I'd like to be a professor of literature or humanities, but I might have to follow the law instead, or perhaps teach in a boy's school."

"What a variety of possibilities!"

"Harrison usually spends his vacation in Somersetshire with our parents, but for such a short break, he decided to come here. He'll be leaving tomorrow."

"You've been very hospitable, but I think we should complete our business and be on our way," Darcy said.

"Of course." Mrs. Pettigrew and Mr. Harrison walked with Elizabeth to the hall and chatted while Darcy and Pettigrew completed arrangements for payment and delivery of Midnight.

At departure, thanks and best wishes were extended all around.

Settled in the carriage, Elizabeth sighed and said, "That was a rather more exciting visit than I anticipated."

"Yes, I wonder what we've gotten ourselves into?"

"For one thing, in an attempt to quash one rumor, we may have started another."

"How so?"

"Do you imagine that the prospect of a ball at Pemberley is not a welcome addition to the local supply of gossip?"

He reflected awhile and said, "Then let's convert rumor into reality. Let us set a date, say late February, and spread the word that invitations for a ball will go out by mid-February. The Pemberley staff hasn't had a good work-out in a long time."

"I should hate to attempt to quash the "malady" rumor by converting it to reality!" Elizabeth noted Darcy's grin.

The sudden prospect of a ball was so startling that Elizabeth completely forgot their intention to stop in Chipping Burnside, until they were far past the village. Upon their return home, a letter was waiting for them addressed to Mr. and Mrs. Fitzwilliam Darcy. Darcy opened it as Fenton took Elizabeth's coat.

"Who is it from?"

"Colonel Fitzwilliam."

"What does he say?"

"He has leave during the holidays and is wondering if the newlyweds might welcome him for a few days."

"And shall we?"

"I don't see why not. Having won the fair lady," he said, looking playfully at her, "I believe I can be magnanimous to one of the vanquished."

"Darcy!" she said, shaking her head.

Before she could say more, Selbey called them to dinner.

After Selbey left, she said, "If both the Bingleys and Gardners accept, with Fitzwilliam there will be twelve of us during the holidays, at least for a few days."

"Yes, that will round out the numbers nicely."

For their walk, Darcy and Elizabeth seemed content to enjoy the fresh air and allow the events of the day to settle into order in their minds without conversation.

In the drawing room before supper they read quietly, but Elizabeth's mind wandered. She noted that Darcy appeared to have no difficulty concentrating. "Perhaps the expenditures related to a ball are of less import to him than whether or not he would take pleasure in the evening's amusement," she thought. She found herself longing for a letter from Jane or the Gardners responding to the Christmas invitations, or a letter from Georgiana telling when she would return. She even found herself wishing for a letter from her mother, though she had no better expectation of its contents than complaints about her nerves or urgings that Elizabeth and Darcy help Lydia further.

At last the call to supper released her from her ruminations. Even the dining room served as a fresh environment, and she could make trivial comments to Darcy without interrupting his reading.

"If Fitzwilliam comes at Christmas, he might enjoy going out with you, riding Midnight."

"Perhaps. Pettigrew is bringing Midnight on Thursday. I rather think Fitzwilliam prefers walking or shooting, but we shall see. I doubt if you will want to ride while Jane is here."

"Not at this time of year, and as a novice still. I expect we shall be content to amuse ourselves with conversation. Oh, I do hope they come!"

"You sound almost desperate."

"It's just that so many things have been happening; I just long for something familiar."

"Something familiar; like an assembly ball, for instance?"

"Yes, even that would seem familiar."

"There's going to be one in Gormley on Friday."

"And can we go?"

"Certainly."

"And will you dance?"

"With my wife, you can be sure."

"Oh, Darcy, thank you." She reached her hand over and he met it with his.

Now, somehow calmer, she said, "I did like Mrs. Pettigrew."

"Did you? Yes. They seem a sound family. I don't think they've been married more than a year or two, from what Woodbury said."

"It seemed easy to talk with her." Now reminded of Darcy's comments about the ball, she asked, "Were you serious about having a ball? You seemed to make the comments so casually. Were you serious or just having sport?"

"Only the date needs to be settled on, I believe, except for the actual arrangements, of course. Perhaps it is a rather large undertaking, but if the date is at the end of February, that leaves almost three months for preparation. I doubt if it will take anywhere near that long. I can begin working on a list of guests on Wednesday. Surely you can begin planning next week with Mrs. Reynolds and Mrs. Sims. You may be surprised at how easily it can be managed with so much help."

Dinner over, they retired to the drawing room. She picked up her book and at last was able to concentrate.

In bed that night, Darcy took Elizabeth in his arms, and she thought, "Oh, the comfort of familiarity," and then, "What a marvel that such intimacy should so soon become familiar when it was so recently the utmost of novelties."

Tuesday: Mrs. Flanders

Morning arrived, and Darcy was out of bed not long after seven and on his way to a morning of hunting.

Elizabeth was still snuggled under the covers when the sound of his footsteps ceased. She had not spent a great deal of time praying over the past several years. It always seemed so much more sensible to concentrate on doing those things that are likely to lead to an agreeable life than to beg for assistance out of avoidable difficulties.

But the interior of the church on Sunday had struck a chord within her, and it seemed to be resonating now. Her eyes closed, she sent a prayer to forces she knew not where, "Oh God, please don't give me a baby soon. You know I want babies, but not yet. Please give me a year at least alone with Darcy. That's not too much to ask for, is it?" She felt tears welling up in her eyes, her chest constricted. "I promise to be a good mother, but not right away, please." She took in several deep, deliberate breaths and dried her eyes on the corner of the pillow case.

She sat up, looked out the window, and noticed on a table the feather she had picked up outdoors. She held it in one hand and drew it between the fingers of her other hand, noting its softness and the beauty of the coloring. She set it back on the table, took her robe, and went to the dressing room.

Annie had arrived so quietly that Elizabeth hadn't heard her. Bathed, dressed, brushed, and coiffed, she went to the dining room. Her breakfast soon finished, she met Mrs. Reynolds in the hall, carrying the package containing the riding habit.

In the carriage, she disclosed to Mrs. Reynolds that she intended to stop at the vicarage before proceeding to see Mrs. Flanders. "I hope you'll join me."

"If it pleases you, ma'am, I'd be happy to do so."

"You don't think ten o'clock is too early, do you?"

"I rather doubt it. I expect he finds it necessary to keep early hours."

That estimate proved correct. They were greeted by the Vicar very cordially.

"I don't really have anything in particular to say," Elizabeth said, "just that I'm very pleased to be here in Derbyshire and that if there's any way I can appropriately share in the life of the congregation, I want to do so."

"You're very welcome in Derbyshire, Mrs. Darcy, I'm sure."

Before he could say more, Elizabeth continued, "Mrs. Wilson called on me last week to invite our participation in the bazaar fund raiser for the infirmary."

"Yes, that's not a direct part of the church's activities, but we do encourage our parishioners to participate. Mrs. Wilson is a member of the congregation."

"Yes, I saw her on Sunday."

"We are always on the alert for new members of the choir, as you can imagine. As you saw, we have a very small group of regulars."

"Yes. I do enjoy singing, and eventually, I have no doubt that I will want to join in, at least for a time."

"I begin my day rather early, Mrs. Darcy. It's almost time for Mrs. Ford to bring my tea. Would you and Mrs. Reynolds join us?"

"With pleasure."

"It's rather a coincidence that you should stop in just now; Mrs. Ford is expecting Mrs. Wilson at any moment." As he was speaking, a rap was heard at the door, then Mrs. Ford's footsteps, and finally an exchange of greetings. Apparently Mrs. Wilson had brought something for Mrs. Ford.

Both ladies entered the room, and greetings were made all around.

"I've invited Mrs. Darcy and Mrs. Reynolds to stay to tea, Mrs. Ford."

They were still discussing the weather when Mrs. Ford returned followed by a maid carrying a tea tray.

While taking tea Elizabeth assured Mrs. Wilson that decisions had been made concerning contributions from Pemberley for the bazaar. It was agreed that they would be delivered to the assembly room by nine on the morning of the sale. Elizabeth assured her that she and Mr. Darcy would attend, and Mrs. Reynolds mentioned that she would be there, as she was every year.

"I can see, Mrs. Ford, that you get ample experience serving tea," Elizabeth said. Mrs. Ford smiled, but before she could say anything, Elizabeth continued, "These biscuits are, I should say, a favorite?"

"Indeed they are. I intend to donate some for the bazaar."

"Then I shall look for them." Turning to the Vicar, she said, "Mrs. Reynolds and I are on our way to see a Mrs. Miles Flanders. Do you suppose you could direct us to her home?"

Before he could answer, Mrs. Wilson said, "The Flanders live not far beyond my house. I'd be very pleased to show you the way."

"Then if you are on your way home, we can take you there."

"I am indeed. I'd be happy to go along."

The three ladies took their leave and were handed into the coach by the footman. As they proceeded through the village, Mrs. Wilson sat very straight, looking to both sides alternately, waving to everyone she knew as they passed—which was apparently everyone—to Elizabeth's amusement. When they arrived at Mrs. Wilson's house she pointed out the Flanders house and left them.

Mrs. Flanders met them at the door and invited them in, smiling, but appearing a bit shy. She was a plain woman of perhaps 40 years, neatly but inexpensively dressed and wearing a large apron. Her hair was pinned into a bun at the nape of her neck. She appeared tired, but held her body erect. She invited Mrs. Darcy and Mrs. Reynolds into their small parlor where two young children looked at them expectantly, obviously interrupted in their play. The girl appeared to be about eight, not unattractive, but not really pretty either. Her wide eyes and alert expression, though, lent an appeal to her appearance. The boy was perhaps five, chubbier, pink-cheeked, eyes wide and lips parted, alert to a new object in his environment.

Their greetings complete, Elizabeth opened the package and together they laid the riding habit out on the dining table.

They looked it over, noting that the fabric was sound and clean. Mrs. Flanders suggested she try it on so she could assess what needed to be done.

She parted the curtains separating the adjoining bedroom, and Elizabeth went in. With Mrs. Reynolds's assistance she removed her own dress and put on the habit. They could hear that the children had resumed their play, tumbling and giggling.

Mrs. Reynolds and Elizabeth came out of the small, neat bedroom into Mrs. Flander's view. Elizabeth stood very straight, feeling a bit strange in this excessively large dress and jacket. Mrs. Flanders said, "Yes, of course, it can be done. It will take rather a lot of time; I shall have to charge you 12 shillings."

Elizabeth's eyes opened wider. "That seems more than reasonable; are you sure?"

"Yes, ma'am. I like better to sew from scratch, but I have done enough alterations to know what needs to be done."

"Then, by all means, you shall do it."

Mrs. Flanders took her pins and began pinning all the seams that needed to be adjusted. As she did, Elizabeth began to feel that it might fit her very nicely. Finally, the skirt hem pinned, Mrs. Flanders said, "I can have it for you by Friday morning."

"Thank you."

"It would be best if you could try it on after my stitching, so we're sure of the fit. The skirt hem is no problem, but I am concerned about the shoulders and bodice."

"Would Thursday afternoon at four o'clock be a good time to try it on?"

"Yes, ma'am."

"Then I'll be here."

Mrs. Reynolds then showed Elizabeth around Lambton. The village was small, but seeing the actual locations of businesses that might supply goods and services of one kind or another seemed to fix them in her mind and provided a bit of stability very welcome to Elizabeth.

On their return ride to Pemberley Elizabeth reviewed in her mind the morning. Tea at the vicarage had passed without untoward incident, and the riding habit would serve very nicely.

When they arrived at Pemberley she found letters—one from Jane, one from Georgiana, and a third from Charlotte. She was still in the morning room eagerly reading the letters when Selbey announced dinner. She took the letters with her and read as she ate. Yes, the Bingleys would join them for Christmas. Jane apologized for not having written and reported her own happiness.

The letter from Georgiana informed them that she would be arriving in Lambton in the coach on Thursday with Mr. and Mrs. Findley, and she requested that they meet her at the Inn at four p.m.

"Ah;" Elizabeth thought, "we shall be in the village anyway; what luck!"

The third letter was from Charlotte. She opened it greedily, and discovered it had been written before her own was received. She wished Darcy and herself well and expressed pleasure at having been able to attend the wedding. "Dear, dear Charlotte," she thought. "Were it not for you, it is highly unlikely that I would now be here at Pemberley. The memory of Darcy's first disastrous proposal in the Collins' parlor flooded over her. "Well," she thought, "anything that is worth doing is worth doing badly, at least the first time."

After dinner she decided that even with Darcy gone she should take her walk. Fresh air would do her good. She put the letters in her coat pocket and headed toward the lake. She followed the path around the lake, observing the reflections of the vegetation at the opposite side as she moved. She took out Jane's letter again and re-read it. Only 11 days since the wedding, but what an age it seemed. Then she re-read the letter from Charlotte and considered what service had been rendered to herself by Charlotte's willingness to enter a marriage she herself thought so unsuitable, then and still. Because Charlotte had invited her to Hunsford she had been thrown once again into Darcy's company. Without those meetings it would be difficult to imagine how she ever could have come to marry Darcy.

At least no one pressured Charlotte into the marriage as Mama had been willing to pressure herself. Dear, dear Charlotte, somehow making a satisfactory life for herself in circumstances that seem so unpromising. A great deal of the credit could be attributed to Charlotte's own sense of self-worth and calm, her sense of herself as a person, and not just as an appendage to the ridiculous Mr. Collins.

Elizabeth returned to the house to find Darcy had returned from hunting. "Shall we be having variety on our table tomorrow?"

"Indeed we shall," Darcy said, taking her into his arms, lifting her up, and twirling around on the marble hall floor.

When he had released her, Elizabeth said, "Well, perhaps you should go hunting more often."

"Excellent idea." They retreated to the drawing room, with Elizabeth querying, "And did the gentlemen have their share of merriment at the expense of the new groom?"

"Actually, they were very good about it," Darcy said, slyly, watching her and waiting for her response. "They were quite sympathetic."

She burst out laughing at his characterization of their behavior. "I don't believe a word of it. They were seething with envy."

"Not at all; they commiserated at considerable length over all the good hunting I've been missing. Only news that Carleton had dropped in with some birds seemed to raise their spirits."

"Oh, Darcy," she said, taking her place beside him on the sofa. "I love your nonsense. How did I ever get along without it?" Then, remembering Jane's letter, she told him that the Bingleys had accepted the Christmas invitation.

"I'm glad to hear it." He reflected awhile, and continued, "Elizabeth, I've been thinking about the ball."

"Yes?"

"I think Mother used to keep some records—not a daily diary, but notes about more important events. They just might still be in her study."

"An excellent idea! I shall look for them tomorrow. Oh, more news!"

"Yes?"

"Georgiana is arriving Thursday afternoon at Lambton. She wrote asking that we meet her after four at the coach stop at the inn."

"Good. If I find it inconvenient to go with you, perhaps you can take Mrs. Reynolds or Annie along with you?"

"Certainly. Is there a problem? I must go, of course because Mrs. Flanders is going to check the fit on the riding habit at four."

"Midnight is going to be delivered Thursday, and I want to be here when he arrives."

"Yes, of course you must. A letter from Charlotte came as well."

"Indeed, and how is your former suitor?"

"You mean the vanquished swain?"

"Yes, I like that," he said, drawing her into his arms. "Ah, Elizabeth, how I missed you today. No one to torment me about my rivals!"

"You haven't mentioned whether news of my 'mysterious ailment' had reached them."

"Oh, yes, definitely. Perhaps that had something to do with their sympathetic behavior."

She was smiling and shaking her head when Selbey called them to supper.

"Perhaps we should have a theme for the ball."

"Hmmm. I'm not much good at that kind of thing. "Give me some suggestions, though, and I can comment."

"Yes, there is a certain ease in the critic's role."

That evening while leaving the dining room, Darcy looked to make sure no servants were around and said, "Would you be interested in a long conversation someplace warm?"

"...preferably horizontal?" she added.

"Excellent idea." He found Fenton, asked him to tell Bradford and Annie they would not be needed 'til morning and followed Elizabeth up the stairs. In the dim light of the gallery, he found her looking out the window at the starlit sky. He took her in his arms, and kissed her, each losing self in the other.

They walked, each with an arm about the other to their bedroom.

In the bedroom, Darcy lit the candle by the bed and led Elizabeth to the window. He moved her in front of him, wrapped his arms around her and covered her hands with his. They stood, looking out the window, his head nuzzling down on hers.

The cold, dark night revealed only traces of the landscape.

"I can't see the moon," she said.

"No, but we can see the effects of its light. Look at that tree. See how the light plays on the leaves. The breeze gives them a shimmering effect."

"Poetry?"

"Yes, I suppose so."

She turned around, put her arms around his middle, looked up at him. He held his hands lightly together behind her. "Now that you have me for your own, your eyes are free to roam elsewhere, and you've rediscovered the rest of the world."

"I suppose there is truth in that statement. Surely the rest of the world exists, but you're the most important part of it."

"Such nonsense."

"Lizzy, there's something I want you to do."

"Yes?"

"Undress yourself, just as you would have at your parent's house, and let me watch."

"You'll have to unbutton me." She turned around, and he unbuttoned her dress and pettycoat. He lay on the bed, fully clothed, head propped up on pillows. She sat on the chair by the window, unfastened each shoe and removed it, then the stockings, setting them neatly by her chair. She stood up, removed the pins from her hair, and put them on the table.

She lifted her dress, pulled it over head, and released her arms; then her underclothes, carefully shaking each garment and laying it carefully over the chair back.

He threw back the covers for her and she slipped under them.

"Now it's your turn," she said.

He bounded off the bed, sat on the same chair and removed his boots, placing them neatly beside hers. Then he removed his socks; more playful now, he flung each into the air, and let them land where they would.

A gust of laughter escaped her. "It's obvious you've always had somone to tidy up after you!"

"Actually, no," he said, "I was always required to be very neat in my habits." Standing now, he took off his jacket and dropped it where he stood. He took a step toward the foot of the bed and stood unfastening the vest buttons, looking at her. She met his gaze and then followed the actions of his fingers. The vest came off, and landed where he was. Another step forward and he unfastened the shirt, which he also dropped. By the time he got to the point of lifting the covers, he was bare.

She flung the covers down on his side, and he climbed into bed. He lay down, pulled her to him, and caressed her body, while concentrating on the sensations of her hands on him. Eyes closed, their breathing became deeper.

"What are you thinking about, Lizzy?"

"Please don't ask me that."

He paused and put his hand at the side of her head and caressed her cheek with his thumb.

"Is something wrong? What's the matter?"

"I can't tell you while we're making love."

He lay back on the pillow and waited. Nothing. He turned on his side, looking at her, waiting. "I have to know."

"Oh, Darcy; I'm afraid."

"What are you afraid of?"

"I'm afraid we're going to have a baby, and I'm not ready for that."

"But we already talked about that. You seemed to accept it."

"Oh, Darcy, don't you see. I want you to myself for just a little while. Not forever, just for awhile. Of course, I want babies, but not just yet."

"Well, I guess you're asking for one of the few things I can't give you...or at least don't want to if it means separate bedrooms."

"I didn't want to tell you, and I don't want separate bedrooms."

"But it's important."

"Just don't ask me when we're making love. And don't force me to say something I don't want to say." She took a breath, but the sound was of sniffles.

"You're crying," he said, putting his thumb under her eye and feeling the tears.

"Elizabeth, close your eyes." He got up, walked around the bed and from the table took the feather. He went back to his side and got into bed again.

"Keep your eyes closed." He lifted the covers to reveal her torso, and brushed the feather over her breast. Her eyes flashed open, and seeing the feather, she closed them again. He played the feather all over her torso, gently, slowly, saying "I promise you, Elizabeth, that I will not ask you what you're thinking when we're making love; I'll wait for you to tell me. And I promise I'll never force you to tell me something before you're ready to tell me." He kept playing the feather over her, circling her breasts. "I promise on my word of honor and on the feather."

"Oh, Darcy," she said, sniffling, "such nonsense."

"It is not nonsense," he said steadily. He put the feather on his bedside table, snuffed the candle, and pulled the covers over them. "Elizabeth, tell me you love me."

"I do love you, Darcy, more than words can say. That goes without saying."

"But it goes much better with saying."

"Aren't my actions enough?"

"Your actions are the words of a sentence. The words "I love you" are the punctuation at the end of the sentence, and very necessary."

"Your poetry is becoming more obscure and a lot more difficult to understand."

"Perhaps that means I'm moving from amateur to professional status."
At this she could contain her laughter no longer. They embraced and tusseled, kissed, caressed and laughed, and brought each other to exhaustion and contentment.

Wednesday

They woke, sleepy, happy, and reluctant to leave the snug warmth of the bed. However, each was propelled by the demands of the day and rose to meet them.

After breakfast, Elizabeth went directly to her study and began searching for any records that Darcy's mother might have kept. First she scanned the book cases, carefully, making sure all were books and not journals.

Then she rummaged through the desk. There wasn't much there, but she did find some notebooks of varying sizes and some calendars, all rather disorganized and not very promising. She did, however, try to organize them into chronological order. First she would consult Darcy and Mrs. Reynolds as to which of the years would be the latest likely to contain anything she wanted. Then she would work her way back from that date looking for significant information.

Not long after she finished Mrs. Reynolds arrived. They greeted each other warmly and took adjacent chairs. Watching her face carefully for reaction, Elizabeth said, "Mrs. Reynolds, Mr. Darcy has decided that it would be a good idea for us to hold a rather large ball in February—possibly toward the end of February, but earlier if that is convenient."

"Mrs. Darcy," she replied, smiling, "What a delight it will be to see such a merry gathering again at Pemberley. It's been a good many years, you know."

"And you don't see any difficulty?"

"Oh, the preparations are quite a lot of work, and it will be necessary to take on additional employees for several days, but that's just work, not difficulty. Even if it were as early as the second week in February, that should still give us plenty of time."

"Remembering the letter from Jane," she added, "We received a reply from my sister; she and Mr. Bingley will be spending Christmas with us from the 23rd to the 28th. And there may be several others, as well."

"As soon as you know how many there will be, let me know, and we'll make all the arrangements."

"Oh. Georgiana is returning tomorrow afternoon. We'll be meeting her in Lambton at the four o'clock stage."

"That's excellent news. It's a delight to have her here."

"It's a relief to see you so sanguine at these coming events."

"You'll get used to it, ma'am. With so many to do the work, everything goes easily. However, you might consider hiring an extra hand for the kitchen for several days at Christmas and an extra upstairs maid."

"Could you make inquiries for me?"

"I surely will."

"By the way, Mr. Darcy says he thinks his mother kept some records of balls and such events held at Pemberley."

Looking at the stack of calenders and journals on the desk, Mrs. Reynolds replied, "Yes, I believe she did keep some information of that kind; but keep in mind that Mrs. Sims keeps a journal of all meals served at Pemberley as well."

"Does she? That just might be even more valuable than these records."

"In better order, at least."

"Do you remember which was the most recent year Mr. Darcy's parents actually entertained visitors?"

"She was not well her last few years...I think Mr. Darcy may have been about 16 the last year they had a ball here; but he'll be able to remember that better than I."

"Of course."

She told Mrs. Reynolds to tell Sarah that she'd like her to ride into Lambton Thursday afternoon if Mr. Darcy could not go and to be ready at two-thirty.

She went to the music room and had practiced again most of the pieces she would be playing during the Christmas season when Susan came with a message. A visitor had arrived, and Mr. Darcy wanted her to go to the morning room. She stopped at a mirror along the way to make sure her hair still looked acceptable and entered the morning room to find Darcy standing next to a distinguished looking, though not exactly handsome, older man, perhaps 50 or 55 years old, short enough to appear somewhat odd standing next to Darcy. They both turned as she entered.

"Mrs. Darcy, I want you to meet Sir Humphrey Winston, a long-time friend of my father's, and mine as well."

They greeted each other warmly, and Elizabeth waited.

"What a pleasure to see Darcy with a bride at last, and a very handsome one too, I see." Turning to Darcy he added, "Waited for the best, eh, Darcy?"

Both Darcy and Elizabeth smiled at this comment.

"Sir Humphrey brought us some game. Thought surely I would not have had a chance to go out hunting."

"You will stay and dine with us, won't you, Sir Humphrey?" Elizabeth inquired. "We dine at two, so it won't be long, now."

"That's a tempting offer, Mrs. Darcy, and I'm happy to accept. I don't have the opportunity of young companions every day."

Elizabeth went to ask Fenton to arrange for a guest at dinner and then returned.

"As it happens, Sir Humphrey," Darcy continued, "I did manage to go out yesterday for my first post-wedding shooting party. We're having those birds today, and we'll enjoy yours tomorrow."

"Then my gift is immediately repaid!" Elizabeth now returned, he said, "I understand you come from Hertfordshire, Mrs. Darcy."

"Yes, my family has long lived there."

"And how do you like Derbyshire," he asked, with a twinkle in his eye.

"Very well indeed," she replied, looking at Darcy.

"Yes, it was a foolish question, wasn't it? And, yet, Darcy does seem different somehow. I suspect you may have used a bit of witchcraft on him, eh?"

"She's bewitching, Sir Humphrey; it's true."

Elizabeth's eyebrows raised at that, but they were saved by Selbey's call to dinner.

"And how is your mother, Sir Humphrey?"

"Exceptionally well for a woman her age. Goes to church every Sunday; walks in the garden almost every day, with a servant not far behind, just in case; supervises the household. Mind you, all the servants are old hands and know what they are to do; doesn't take a lot to keep things going. I told her, of course, that I was coming to see you. She very particularly asked me to invite you to join us for dinner soon."

"Thank you; your invitation is welcome, though taking advantage of it might present a problem. It seems that marrying this late in the year is pressing us to fulfill the obligations we already have."

"Well, right after Christmas then, say the 27th?"

"My good friend Bingley and his bride, Mrs. Darcy's sister, will be visiting us for several days at that time."

"Bring them along! The party will be all the merrier."

"In that case," Darcy said," looking to Elizabeth and reading assent, "we shall be there."

"Two o'clock, then, but don't be late," said Sir Humphrey. "My mother is a very kind lady, but she doesn't like to keep good food waiting."

With this happy thought they finished their dinner, and he took his leave.

Darcy and Elizabeth went for just a brief walk, cloudy and chill as the day was, knowing that all too soon they would be glad to stay by the fire rather than venture outdoors. Quiet reading in the drawing room for a couple of hours before supper was a welcome period of calm for Elizabeth to prepare herself for Georgiana's arrival.

During supper Darcy seemed to be musing over Sir Humphrey's visit and content to be quiet. As Selbey was serving the pudding, Darcy broke out of his solitude, and said, "Eliza, I was...."

Before he could say any more, she interrupted him, "I know you aren't trying to be unpleasant, but I'd really rather you didn't use that name."

"Of course, if you wish, but why not?"

"One person in particular called me by that name, and she seemed determined to torment me at every opportunity."

"And who was that?"

"Miss Bingley."

"Indeed! I don't remember that."

"She tried to belittle me in your eyes at every turn."

"Did she?"

"You must have been aware of it."

"I can't say that I was, except perhaps when you visited at Pemberley last summer. It didn't work, though, did it? Somehow when the two of you were in the same room, you always looked better than when you stood alone. Certainly you didn't think of her as your rival!"

She lifted her chin and responded. "I didn't consider myself to be seeking your favor, but I don't like to be diminished in anyone's eyes, save by my own virtue or lack of it."

"But you don't think she was interested in me, surely?"

"And why not?"

"Well, it's just so absurd."

She waited for further explanation, but none came.

"Miss Caroline Bingley?"

"And what is so absurd?"

"I can't say, really. I just always thought of her as Bingley's sister and nothing more."

"Then her efforts, apparently, were in vain."

"This puts a new light on matters, though I'm not sure exactly how. But to get back to my thought; might I hear you play again this evening?"

"If you will practice the carols with me."

"And why not?"

They enjoyed the music and went to bed, to pleasure, and to rest.

Thursday: Georgiana

Thursday morning was a time of lively anticipation for Darcy and mild uneasiness for Elizabeth. Midnight would be delivered sometime during the morning.

Though Darcy seemed distracted at breakfast, Elizabeth took the occasion to ask him if he remembered what year his parents had held their last ball at Pemberley. He seemed thoughtful, and when he didn't answer, she mentioned that Mrs. Reynolds thought it had been when he was about 16.

"Yes," he replied, absently, "that could have been it."

After breakfast Darcy went to his study to wait, and Elizabeth went to talk with Mrs. Sims.

"Oh, yes," Mrs. Sims said, "I've always kept a record of what is served for meals at Pemberley and how many were served. The records were kept before I took them over too." They found the two books that covered the six years before Darcy was eighteen to take with her.

She thanked Mrs. Sims for the excellent fashion in which the game had been prepared the day before and the ready compliance with the needs of an extra guest at short notice.

"Mrs. Darcy, in the old days, we always had to be on the alert for extra guests, and I have no doubt the coming months will seem much the same."

Elizabeth also remarked on how both she and Mr. Darcy had enjoyed the raisin bread and mentioned that Miss Georgiana would be returning that very afternoon. At that, Mrs. Sims ventured, "Perhaps you'd like me to make another batch Saturday."

"I know it would be greatly appreciated."

"Mrs. Darcy," Susan interrupted, coming in the kitchen door. "Mr. Darcy asked me to tell you to come to the entry hall right away."

She took her leave of Mrs. Sims and found Darcy in the hall holding her coat, waiting with Mr. Pettigrew. She left the record books on the hall table, and all three went outdoors where Midnight and Mr. Pettigrew's horse were tied up.

They untied the horses, and Mr. Pettigrew, anticipating another long ride home prepared to depart immediately. "Won't you take tea?" Elizabeth asked.

"Thank you, ma'am, but I have some errands to attend to, and I'd best be on my way."

With thanks all around, he left, and Darcy led Midnight to the stables, Elizabeth walking along. "You bought the saddle as well," Elizabeth said.

"Yes, didn't I mention it? You were in the house talking with Mrs. Pettigrew when the subject arose. It seems she bought a different saddle when she got her new horse and no longer needs this one. You seemed so uncertain about the prospect of learning to ride that it just seemed sensible to follow the easiest path. As you gain experience with this horse and saddle we can decide if you need something different. Until then, how would you know?"

"Is there so much difference in saddles?"

"There certainly is...in size, style, and comfort, to say nothing of workmanship and appearance."

Mr. Sims met them at the stables and looked thoughtfully at Midnight. He took Midnight to the stall that was to be his, and Darcy and Elizabeth stood outside the stall reaching over the wall to stroke his neck.

"He's had quite a walk; we won't ride him today."

They returned to the house, where a letter was waiting from Longbourn. To Elizabeth's surprise it was from Mr. rather than Mrs. Bennet.

"My dear Elizabeth,

I have for some time sensed that you believed me to be a laggard at correspondence, so it pleases me to reply almost as soon as your letter arrived.

You are surely missed at Longbourn, but the expression of happiness in your letter is a very welcome compensation. You well know my early misgivings about your marrying Darcy, and I am delighted to be proved wrong.

Your mother, Mary, and Kitty are very much as always and send their love.

My love to both you and Darcy.
Your Papa"

With Midnight settled in the stable, Darcy was free to go with Elizabeth to meet Georgiana at the stage. As Elizabeth had planned, he left her at Mrs. Flanders shortly before four o'clock, and he proceeded to the inn. When the stage arrived he greeted Georgiana and thanked the Findleys who were continuing beyond Lambton to their son's home.

Darcy returned to the Flanders house with Georgiana where she asked to go to the door, pleading too long confinement in the coach from London. Darcy stood on the street by the coach, pacing. Georgiana knocked on the door, was admitted, and found that Elizabeth had already tried on the riding habit and was again wearing her day gown. The alterations were complete, and Elizabeth was just paying Mrs. Flanders. Georgiana, standing near the door, was being closely observed by the two young children. A clattering on the stairs drew the attention of all as a young man of about 18 years ran down the stairs at full speed, almost bumping into Georgiana.

"Excuse me, miss," he said. Then, to his mother, "I'll be back at six," and was out the door. Elizabeth finished counting the coins and gave them to Mrs. Flanders. Thanks and farewells were exchanged, and they left.

"I'm glad he didn't knock you down," Elizabeth said.

"Who is he?" Georgiana asked.

"Their son, apparently," Elizabeth replied. "He wasn't here Tuesday when we came, but Annie did say they have three children."

Darcy handed them into the carriage as they were completing this conversation.

"Well...?" Darcy queried.

"Elizabeth held up the package. "It's all done, and very nicely, too."

"Is it a secret?" asked Georgiana.

"Not at all. But first, let me greet you. I rather feel as if I've been through a hailstorm." They were sitting side by side, facing forward. They exchanged greetings, experiencing the pleasure of being together, now both at Pemberley.

Georgiana glanced at the package, and before Elizabeth could speak, Darcy said, "Elizabeth has agreed to learn to ride, and we've already bought a horse. The package contains an old riding habit, now made new. I'm hoping you'll want to ride again also. I'd like to buy a horse for you as well, one more suitable than Patches, so you can ride with Elizabeth when I'm not available. No doubt we'll often want to ride all together."

The smile on her face signaled her approval of the plan. "Yes, I'd like that. I've never really had anyone to ride with."

The conversation then turned to Georgiana's stay in London. She assured them she had had a most enjoyable stay with the Findleys. They had taken her twice to see plays, they had gone for rides in the parks almost every day, and Mrs. Findley had taken her shopping and to an art gallery. One day they all strolled along the Thames watching the boats.

"Well," Elizabeth said, "Life at Pemberley may seem rather dull after such pleasures!"

"Oh, no, I love life at Pemberley—pleasant walks, the piano, reading."

"It may be a bit more lively than that," Darcy suggested.

Elizabeth then told Georgiana that they were planning to attend an assembly in Gormley the following night. "And, we'll be having guests at Christmastime. The Bingleys have already accepted our invitation. And...it seems there is to be a ball at Pemberley in February."

At this, Georgiana's eyes lit up. "A ball! My first ball at Pemberley." Then realizing what she had said, she looked to Darcy for assistance.

Darcy had been following the conversation carefully and said, "Yes, Georgiana, I wouldn't be surprised if the February Ball were to become an annual event, but we must first have one ball before we declare we shall have a second."

Another thought occurred to Georgiana, and she said, "You wouldn't expect me to play for the guests, would you?"

"Perhaps not 'expect,' but we hope you'll want to play."

"Will there by very many people?"

Now Elizabeth was attentive as well.

"Fifty, perhaps sixty, maybe more," Darcy replied.

She seemed thoughtful now.

"You have plenty of time to decide," Elizabeth added, "more than two months." This seemed to reassure her. By this time they had reached Pemberley.

At supper Elizabeth told Georgiana she needed a dressmaker and milliner in London.

"Yes, of course; I think you might like mine. And if there is to be a ball, I'll want a new gown too."

Darcy intervened to say, "You will do well to have plenty of gowns for this next year, Georgiana; it looks to be a lively season."

Georgiana looked back and forth between Darcy and Elizabeth attempting to divine more than had been said.

"Actually," Elizabeth said, "We already have an invitation for dinner next Tuesday. It may not be the highlight of your season, but it's at the Blakelys, and they seem a very pleasant couple. At the very least, it should be a fine dinner.

"And something of a more casual nature," Elizabeth continued. "We've been asked to make donations to the bazaar in Lambton on Saturday, the 17th, and to attend. That should give us a glimpse of some of the residents as we all shop for some Christmas gifts."

Darcy added, "And Colonel Fitzwilliam will be here for Christmas Eve and Day as well." Both Elizabeth and Darcy were looking at Georgiana to gauge her response, but it revealed little.

"I'm glad he's coming," she said. "I saw him at the wedding, of course, and later on the ride to London, but we really didn't have much time to talk. I never did see him later in London."

Suddenly remembering, Elizabeth added, "In all the confusion of our arrival, I forgot to tell you that a letter came from the Gardners accepting our invitation. They expect to arrive on the 24th and leave on the 26th." To Georgiana, she added. "They'll be bringing all four children along."

Georgiana looked pleased, but a bit overpowered by all these plans. Elizabeth decided to wait until later to tell her of the Winston's invitation to dinner. She turned her attention to Darcy. "I suppose you'll want me to try to ride tomorrow."

"I think it might be better if we just get acquainted with Midnight, walk him around a bit, let him into the pasture for a run. It's rather cold out for a long outing, but it will give him some time to get acquainted with all of us, the stables, and the pasture." Looking toward Georgiana, "I hope you'll join us after breakfast, Georgiana."

"Should I wear the riding habit?" Elizabeth asked.

"Yes, it's rather dirty around the stables; no sense in soiling your other clothing. You have a riding outfit, don't you, Georgiana?"

"Yes, though it may be rather small now. I'll try it on. I can get a new one in January."

"So, is it agreed we all arrive at breakfast ready to ride?"

"Yes," Elizabeth and Georgiana answered together.

They adjourned to the drawing room, but it wasn't long before Georgiana said, "I am very sleepy; if you don't mind, I think I'll just walk for a few minutes in the picture gallery and then go to bed."

"We'll see you in the morning."

"Good night, Georgiana," Darcy replied. "Oh, by the way, we're using Mother and Father's bedroom suite, just so you'll know where we are."

Once alone, Darcy commented, "She didn't mention meeting any young men in London."

"I would be surprised if she didn't though. If you're willing to write to Mrs. Findley to ask, she might have something to say."

"Let's just wait until January. We may see them then in London. We can arrange to go to the theatre together."

"I agree," Elizabeth said. "Besides, I think I'd enjoy a play." Then more seriously, "She didn't seem to have any special response to the news that Colonel Fitzwilliam will be here."

"That was my observation, too."

"I was so surprised when the Flanders boy bounded down the stairs and out the door. I was glad he didn't knock Georgiana down."

"Yes, he fairly flew down the street; looked at me, but didn't say a word. Such vitality would place him on any of the teams at Cambridge. I recognized him from shooting parties at the Howells when they've used beaters."

His voice now in a tone almost conspiratorial, "Come here," he said to Elizabeth, who was sitting in a chair.

She got up and approached him. "What is it?"

He took her hand and pulled her down to sit beside him on the sofa, "You're not going to let my little sister ruin our love life, are you?"

"I doubt that I could if I wanted to."

He reached up and caressed her cheek with his thumb. "We've had rather a lot of excitement for one day, wouldn't you say?"

"I certainly would."

"It's a bit early, but we could tell Bradford and Annie we won't be needing them tonight."

"Yes, with Georgiana here we might not feel so free to go to bed early; we might as well take advantage of this one last opportunity."

Their lovemaking was less exuberant than it had sometimes been, but more pleasurable than Elizabeth had ever imagined such intimacy could be.

Friday

In the morning, Darcy was startlingly wide awake, shaking Elizabeth and rubbing her hands and shoulders to waken her.

"One would think you were 12 years old and getting your first pony," Elizabeth drawled, sleepily.

At length, she got up, washed the sleep out of her eyes, and let Annie help her into the riding habit. She asked her to have a bath ready at three o'clock and water for washing her hair. "If we're going to the Assembly, I might as well look my best," she thought.

In the dining room she found Darcy and Georgiana already enjoying their coffee and conversation, Georgiana telling more about her stay in London. When they arrived at the stable they found Sims walking Midnight around the yard.

"Sims, good morning."

"Good morning, Sir, Ma'am, Miss."

Georgiana and Elizabeth returned his greeting.

"Midnight seems content."

"Aye sir. Eating proper. Quiet. No fuss."

"I'll walk him around the yard," Darcy said, taking the halter rope from Sims. He walked toward the pasture fence and back, talking to Midnight along the way, pausing to look him in the eyes and pat his face and neck, then walking again.

"Georgiana, would you walk him for awhile?"

"Yes, gladly." She followed the same path as Darcy had walked, also talking, pausing, and petting Midnight as Darcy and Elizabeth watched.

Darcy, standing close to Elizabeth said, "He's rather good looking, don't you think?"

"Yes, perhaps not as handsome as Prince, but a very good looking horse."

"You shouldn't be ashamed at the way you'll look riding him, do you think?"

"My mind will be so occupied with the thought of not falling off, I doubt that I'll be thinking about how I look."

"You're too modest, Elizabeth. You're very graceful. You're going to have no difficulty whatever."

By now Georgiana had nearly completed another circuit, and Darcy said, "Now it's your turn, Elizabeth."

She took the rope, held it and led Midnight as Darcy and Georgiana had done.

"I hope he's not too large for Elizabeth. What do you think, Georgiana?"

"I shouldn't think so. He seems a fine animal—calm, easy."

"We'll let her take a couple more rounds of the yard and then perhaps you'll mount Midnight; give Elizabeth an idea of how she'll look."

"Don't you think we should let Elizabeth ride first?"

"No; you've had experience riding, but Elizabeth hasn't. She's very skittish about this whole idea. I want her to be completely confident of what she's doing as she learns."

As Elizabeth completed a circuit, Darcy said, "Just wait here, Elizabeth, and watch as I help Georgiana mount." With his assistance at the mounting block Georgiana mounted and shifted around until she had her skirt arranged and had made herself as comfortable as possible in the saddle. "You look comfortable, Georgiana. Would you like to take him for a little walk?"

She smiled, nodded, and he backed away; she held the reins to the side to direct Midnight and clicked her tongue. He moved away and they followed the circuit he had already walked several times.

Elizabeth and Darcy watched the horse and his rider. "Are you ready to ride, Elizabeth?"

"Yes, I think so; as ready as I shall ever be."

Georgiana took Midnight several circuits and returned to dismount. Darcy stood ready to assist, but Georgiana slid off easily, gave him the reins, shook her skirt, and stood back to watch.

With Darcy's assistance, Elizabeth mounted as she had seen Georgiana do, though she didn't seem quite so much at ease on her high perch.

"Do you want to walk him, Elizabeth?"

She nodded.

"Click like this when you want to start," he said, as he clicked with his tongue. "To turn just pull the reins towards the side you want to go, and when you want him to stop, just pull back on the reins. He'll be sensitive to the bit in his mouth, so just pull back enough to make him do what you want."

Nodding in response to his instructions, Elizabeth clicked, and Midnight began walking. The scene was not quite so elegant as Georgiana had presented, but horse and rider did manage. Darcy and Georgiana looked on encouragingly as they chatted.

"Do we still have Patches?" Georgiana asked.

"Yes, but as long as you don't want to ride him, I think we can let him go."

"But the Gardner children will be coming at Christmas. Perhaps we'll have a day then that's warm enough for riding. Or maybe they'll come back next summer."

"Quite right. I didn't think of that. No need to rush to sell him."

"I don't think the saddle I used for Patches will fit a full-sized horse."

"You're right. I'll ask Woodbury to keep his eyes open. He'll find one."

By now Midnight and Elizabeth had taken several circuits, and Elizabeth looked as if she had had enough riding for one day.

Elizabeth pulled back on the reins, and Midnight stopped. Darcy approached and as Georgiana held the bridle, Darcy helped Elizabeth dismount. Sims came forward to lead Midnight away.

"After you've taken the saddle off, Sims, let him out in the pasture for awhile. We're going into the kitchen to ask Mrs. Sims to make some hot chocolate for us, and we'll return."

They went in, found Mrs. Sims, glad to prepare chocolate; they enjoyed the warmth of the kitchen for a few minutes and returned to the stable yard. Sims was just letting Midnight into the pasture. All three stood by the fence and watched him. He trotted a short distance, paused, searched for edible grasses, and began grazing.

"Makes a pretty picture, even on a rather cold day," Darcy offered.

"Yes," Elizabeth agreed, holding her gloved hands over her cheeks. Into the house they went to find the chocolate waiting for them in the morning room.

Sitting quietly, at length, Elizabeth said, "I just remembered, Darcy; we talked about donating one of your mother's gowns to the bazaar clothing sale, but I never did select one. Georgiana, would you be willing to look them over with me and choose one to give?"

"Yes, I would."

"Then let's send word to Mrs. Reynolds, change our clothes, and go do it. If we help each other with buttons, we should be able to leave Annie and Fiona to their other duties."

They told Fenton to ask Mrs. Reynolds to meet them in the entry hall. Clothes changed, they returned to find Mrs. Reynolds, who took them to the store room to see the chests of clothes. Before they made a final choice, they had looked at all the gowns. The one they chose was of a rose color, not terribly bright, and much less fancy than most of the others. It was clean and apparently in perfect condition, possibly never worn.

"It may not fit any of the ladies in the village perfectly as it is, but I dare say many of them have enough sewing skill to make the necessary alterations."

As they were folding the others back into the chests, Elizabeth took one and examined it more closely. "Golds and yellows have always been my favorite colors," she said. "Look at the quality of the fabric: velvet. It must have been very expensive. And the lace around the neck and shoulder area—how fine. It's rather surprising to see a dress that old look so appealing."

"You look as if you wouldn't mind wearing it yourself," Georgiana said, a trace of jesting in her voice.

Elizabeth looked up, startled by the suggestion. "I have rather run on about it, haven't I? None of my gowns are so lovely. They all look rather plain in the elegance of this house. I'll be getting new gowns in London in

January, but I don't think I shall feel comfortable ordering anything so fine as this."

"Perhaps Mrs. Flanders would like another alteration job."

"Let's take it to Darcy and see what he says." They left Mrs. Reynolds to tidy the mess and wrap up the gown for the bazaar.

Georgiana waited in the morning room while Elizabeth went to fetch Darcy from his study. "Darcy, you must come," she said, taking him by the hand. "You must see what we've found."

Puzzled, he followed her into the morning room. Elizabeth took the gown and held it up against herself. Georgiana stood behind her holding up the shoulders of the gown as they looked at Darcy expectantly.

"Is that one of Mother's gowns?"

"Don't you recognize it?" Georgiana asked.

"I can't say that I do. She had a lot of gowns; and it is hard to tell, just seeing it hanging there."

"It's very beautiful, Darcy. If Mrs. Flanders will alter it I could wear it at Christmas when Jane and Aunt Gardner are here."

"I wouldn't want people to think I'm not willing to buy my bride new clothes of her own."

"I'd only wear it here at home; only family will be here."

"Of course you can, Lizzy; but I shall have to get used to the idea of clothing my wife for shillings rather than pounds."

Elizabeth and Georgiana rushed to Elizabeth's dressing room to confirm that it would fit well enough to make alterations possible.

"Oh, Elizabeth, it looks very elegant. I shall have to select my own dress with care for the day you wear it or look very plain indeed."

They undressed and dressed Elizabeth again, and only the memory of the "tag" incident kept Elizabeth from running as she went to her study to write a note to Mrs. Flanders.

Georgiana went to the music room and renewed acquaintance with the instrument she commanded so well.

At dinner Elizabeth again commented on the quality of the gold velvet gown with the elegant lace, "The lace must have come from Belgium."

"I hope you don't make Mrs. Gardner and Jane look shabby," Darcy said.

"I should be more concerned for the contrary. Jane is always the handsomest lady in the room," Elizabeth responded, "as I once heard a certain gentleman point out," pausing to look directly at Darcy until he met her gaze. "And I have never seen Aunt Gardner looking anything but elegant."

"Well, then, we shall have a roomful of grand ladies," he said, reaching across the table to both Elizabeth and Georgiana. "We gentlemen shall feel quite drab."

"Hardly, in your elegant black and white," Elizabeth said. "You will look stunning. And, as I've noted, some of the gentlemen favor rather colorful dress themselves."

Elizabeth retrieved Cook's journals from the hall table and went to her dressing room. She bathed first, and then let Annie wash her hair. She sat before the fire as Annie brushed and dried her hair and opened the journal that held the dates most likely to contain a record of the most recent balls. The most recent one was the year Darcy was 16. Eighty people were served that evening.

Elizabeth had seen the ballroom the previous summer on the day Mrs. Reynolds showed her and the Gardners through the house. Now, she decided, she would look at it again tomorrow. She tried to remember its size and thought, "Eighty people should fit into it very easily. Perhaps in earlier years when Mrs. Darcy's health was better they had even larger balls when they were more active socially."

She looked back farther and found that four years earlier 105 were served the night of the ball.

"We're not likely to have nearly so many people attending our first ball. Few of his parents' friends would have become close friends of Darcy's, and no one in Derbyshire knows me yet; well, almost no one: Carleton, Sir Humphrey, the Blakelys, the Pettigrews, Mrs. Wilson, and the Fords. Well, maybe the guest list will be longer than I can now imagine."

"I will surely want Jane and Bingley to attend if they can, and Kitty, and possibly Mary.

"Nevertheless, Darcy may be close to the mark when he suggests there will be 50 or 60 at our ball."

The warmth of the fire was delightful, as were Annie's hair drying efforts. "Such pampering," she thought. "And how easy to get used to it. I shall be spoiled in no time at all."

They dressed her in the gown she would wear to the assembly in Gormley. Elizabeth loved to dance and had attended many assemblies in Meryton over the past few years, and others in nearby villages. But she had to think back to her first assembly to find excitement such as she felt this night. Always there had been a hope of seeing a particular gentleman, or meeting one for the first time. But this would be the first she would attend with her handsome husband. Even had he not been rich, it would have been a very special occasion. But to have stolen the heart of one of the most eligible bachelors in all Derbyshire—this lent an added excitement to the event. "I can only hope that Cousin Collins was exaggerating when he called Darcy one of the most prominent men in all England. Surely there were sons of Earls, and Baronets enough to hold those places of distinction."

Still, many eyes would be upon her, and she would have to be alert to the possibilities of disaster as well as enjoyment. She could not forget that this was an important night for Georgiana as well.

She could hear sounds now from Darcy's dressing room. "How easy it is for men, she thought. Well, perhaps not. I would not like to scrape my face with a razor."

She walked through the bedroom to knock on Darcy's door to tell him she would wait in the gallery. But as she went to knock on the door, she saw he had already arrived and had stationed himself at their favorite window.

"Ah, there you are," he said, and they walked together to supper.

Georgiana was already in the drawing room, looking lovely. They ate their supper, the ladies particularly too excited for much conversation, clever or otherwise. The carriage was waiting as Darcy had arranged; they carefully buttoned up their wraps for this chilly night ride. In the coach they wrapped blankets around themselves and were on their way.

Georgiana sat facing forward, with Darcy and Elizabeth opposite. Georgiana might see something in the dim light, but the lovers were not likely to see much anyway. The most interesting sight for Georgiana along the way was the contentment in the faces of her brother and his bride.

Quiet contemplation suits better than conversation in a moving coach. Elizabeth could imagine herself in the carefully altered gold velvet gown, descending the stairs on Christmas Eve on the arm of her handsome husband. Georgiana could imagine herself dancing with all the handsome young men at the assembly, and even those not so handsome, if they danced well. And Darcy could imagine himself riding in the fields on a spring day with his wife beside him, riding confidently on her sleek, handsome horse. He could, but perhaps he would rather contemplate his next hunting outing.

At last they arrived, not the first, but likely not the last either. They handed their coats to an attendant and walked into the hall where music was already playing, and people were dancing.

They looked around in the hopes of seeing a familiar face, or even a friendly one. Elizabeth was trying to find a vantage point from which she could watch the dancers should Georgiana be dancing when she was not. In quickly scanning faces, to her surprise, she found one that was familiar—Mrs. Pettigrew. She saw her nudge Mr. Pettigrew, standing beside her. He looked their way and immediately approached them.

"Mr. and Mrs. Darcy, please join us," he said, motioning them toward his wife. They followed, happy to see anyone they knew, and doubly happy to see someone as agreeable as the Pettigrews.

"Mrs. Darcy, how pleasant to see you again so soon."

"And you. All of us, apparently, have been willing to endure the cold for an evening of dance and company."

"Yes, Mr. Pettigrew and I go to several villages for assemblies. I'm very fond of dancing, and he's very fond of pleasing me."

Elizabeth smiled at this, thinking of Darcy's lack of enthusiasm for dancing and his suggesting this outing.

"Let me introduce Mr. Darcy's sister to you. Mr. and Mrs. Pettigrew, Miss Darcy."

"Miss Darcy, welcome; stand here beside me. I think we will find a partner for you before long."

Georgiana complied and was casting about for something to say when a young man walked up and said, "Good Evening, Mrs. Pettigrew."

"Mr. Feldman, good evening. Let me introduce you to Mr. and Mrs. Darcy and Mr. Darcy's sister, Miss Darcy. This is Mr. Feldman, a neighbor of ours."

Greetings were made all around, and Mr. Feldman immediately took the opportunity to request that Miss Darcy dance the next with him, then just forming. She agreed and he led her into position for the dance.

"Very clever young man. He would not have been quite so quick to greet me had there not been a lovely young lady by my side." Then, to Elizabeth, "And how do you like Midnight, Mrs. Darcy? Have you ridden him? Are you already an expert rider?"

"I did ride today, but I believe it will be some time until I deserve compliments for horsemanship. I found the saddle somewhat difficult to get used to."

By now Darcy and Pettigrew were engrossed in conversation about horses and hunting, and Elizabeth continued her attention to Mrs. Pettigrew.

"Yes, I eventually did get accustomed to it, but finally determined I would try a man's saddle, and, I can tell you, I infinitely prefer it."

Elizabeth was unprepared for such a disclosure, and the surprise was evident in her expression. Before she could gather her thoughts, Mrs. Pettigrew continued; "Yes, you might well be surprised. It took all my powers of persuasion over a period of months before I could get Mr. Pettigrew accustomed to the idea. Even now, I believe, he would be greatly relieved if I would go back to using the side saddle. But I am determined to enjoy riding, and my enjoyment seems to be persuading him as well as my words."

"But the habit—it has to be awkward."

"True; I found it necessary to design an outfit for myself, and it took rather a lot of persuasion to convince my dressmaker to make it. But it's worth it.

"Mrs. Darcy, if we are not careful, our husbands will escape dancing with us." She took her husband's arm, looked up at him expectantly, and Elizabeth followed her cue. Mr. Pettigrew, no doubt, had played this scene many times before because, as soon as he completed his comment to Darcy, he said, "My dear, may I have the honor of the next?"

"You may, sir, and it is almost ready to begin."

Elizabeth was not pleased at the thought of leaving Georgiana alone, should she not have a partner for the dance, but the question was decided when Darcy said, "Would you do me the honor, Mrs. Darcy?"

"With pleasure," she answered, and they moved into the line of dancers. It was now just over a year since they had first danced together. How much had happened since and with what different feelings did she now face her partner, as handsome as then, but less solemn, more approachable.

"An easy, but pleasant dance," he remarked.

"And so many couples," she responded with a smile.

They both noticed that Georgiana was dancing again with young Feldman.

At the end of the dance they returned to the post they had left and found the Pettigrews returning also. Before they could resume conversation, they noticed an older gentleman approaching them.

"Darcy, Mrs. Darcy, what a delight to see you here!"

"Sir Humphrey," Darcy said, "You've come rather a long distance, haven't you?"

"Yes, but I do so enjoy watching the young folks dance; it's well worth the trip. "And on occasion, one of the ladies favors me with a dance," he said, looking toward Elizabeth.

Elizabeth looked to Darcy who said, "He's a fine dancer, Elizabeth, you should not pass up the opportunity if he asks you."

Sir Humphrey followed Darcy's comment and, looking again to Elizabeth, "Would you dance the next with me, Mrs. Darcy?"

"I'd be delighted."

By then Georgiana had returned to the group and accepted Darcy's request to dance. They moved to join the dance, then forming, and the Pettigrews joined as well.

By the time the evening had passed, Mr. Pettigrew had danced with Mrs. Darcy, Darcy with Mrs. Pettigrew, Darcy and Elizabeth again with each other, and Georgiana had danced all but one dance, with two additional partners.

It was a happy threesome that rode home on that cold December night under a waning moon. Fenton greeted them and went to get the hot chocolate they had requested to be prepared for them. When he returned to the drawing room they were warming themselves by the fireplace.

Georgiana seemed to glow with the pleasure of the evening, and Elizabeth could not count herself less fortunate. Even Darcy seemed pleased with the overall success of the evening. Warmed by the chocolate and contented, Georgiana went to bed.

Elizabeth joined Darcy where he stood by the fire and slipped her arms around his middle.

"Elizabeth, you seem very contented. Does this mean you're going to be ready to ride again in the morning?" he asked, circling his arms around her.

"I don't see why not. I shall write letters to the dressmaker and milliner in London, but there's time enough for that later."

Bradford and Annie had been told not to wait up since it would be a late evening. Retired to their bedroom, Darcy unbuttoned Elizabeth, they undressed, and cuddled in bed, each silently reviewing the pleasures of the evening. Before long comfort and sleep overcame them.

Saturday

Elizabeth dressed in her riding habit and joined Darcy in the dining room, already enjoying his coffee. As soon as they finished breakfast they went to the stables. Sims saddled Midnight and, and Darcy helped Davy with Prince.

"We didn't see you here yesterday, Davy," Darcy said.

"No, sir; I had some errands to take care of for Father."

Darcy helped Elizabeth onto Midnight. "Now, Elizabeth, remember that when you want to slow him down, you just pull back on the reins until he slows. To stop, pull even more."

He mounted Prince, got him started, and beckoned to Elizabeth to follow at his side. She urged Midnight into motion, and he continued with little direction.

"Rather cold for riding today, Lizzy, but refreshing."

"Yes," she answered soberly, trying to balance over the jogging motion of the horse's gait.

"It's much more pleasant in the warmer months."

"I dare say it is."

"By spring you'll be riding so well we'll be able to go much farther than we would consider today."

"No doubt we shall."

Looking up at the overcast sky, he said, "I don't think I've ever heard you use so few words, Elizabeth."

"Yes." This spare response brought smiles to both faces.

They walked on, feeling the freshness of the morning, noting birds overhead and among the bushes and trees.

"In spite of all my good intentions," Darcy said, "I was quite unaware of who Georgiana was dancing with last night. I wonder who that young Feldman is."

"His manners may not be perfect, but we must grant that he was very alert to notice so quickly a pretty girl and immediately devise a means of meeting her. Whoever these young men were, perhaps the most important thing was that it was a lively evening."

"You seemed to have a lot to discuss with Mrs. Pettigrew."

"And you with Mr. Pettigrew."

"When all else fails, hunting and horses provide an endless source of conversation. Pettigrew said he might know someone who has a horse we could buy for Georgiana. Said he'd inquire about it."

"And Sir Humphrey once again proved he is entertaining company."

"Yes, he really seems to enjoy watching the young folks dance. Also said he picks up bits of information never available in the newspapers."

"Gossip."

"Yes."

"Like news about young brides with "mysterious maladies?"

"He didn't say so specifically, but I believe we can safely draw that conclusion."

They rode on for awhile, until Darcy said, "I think we had better turn back. I don't want you to get too tired." Elizabeth appeared relieved, and they turned back.

"Pity that Sir Humphrey's wife died so young; must be five years ago already. He's a very vital man. He must miss her company. His mother is too old to be much company, I should think."

"Does he stay at home always?"

"Oh, no; I expect that he spends time in London or Bath each winter, a few weeks, at least. And perhaps some weeks in Brighton each summer."

They rode on quietly until they reached the stable. Darcy dismounted, tied Prince and Midnight, and helped Elizabeth dismount. By this time Sims had come to unsaddle the horses. They petted the horses in appreciation and went into the house via the kitchen.

"Mrs. Sims," Darcy said, "after a pleasant ride on a very chilly day, we'd like some tea sent up to the morning room for us."

"Mrs. Darcy, your cheeks are bright red. Are you sure you wouldn't prefer chocolate?"

"No, thank you, Mrs. Sims, I think tea would be best."

"Right away then."

They found a fire burning in the morning room and stood before it spreading hands and arms to get the maximum exposure to the warmth. Then Darcy, standing behind Elizabeth drew her back close to him, his arms around her.

"Ooh, you feel toasty warm," she said. She turned around and they embraced, swaying side to side.

Susan came with the tea and they proceeded to warm their insides as well. They relaxed in the warmth of the occasion until at last Elizabeth said, "Now I must change my clothes."

On the way, she asked Fenton to tell Annie to prepare a bath for her. She then went to her bedroom, opened the door to the dressing room, and went to lie on the bed to rest until Annie arrived.

Rested, bathed, coiffed, and dressed again, she went to the morning room where Darcy and Georgiana were waiting. She listened as Darcy related to Georgiana the events of the morning ride, both of them expressing satisfaction at her performance.

When called to dinner and seated at the table, Elizabeth began to think the entire meal would be devoted to conversation about her success as a rider. Instead, Georgiana said, "You are well, aren't you, Elizabeth?"

"Yes, of course; why do you ask?"

"At the assembly last night I heard a remark about someone with a mysterious complaint, and I rather fancied they were looking at you."

Darcy and Elizabeth looked at each other and melted into chuckles and head shaking. "I told you we should tell her, Elizabeth. But we've been so busy, I completely forgot."

"What is it?" Georgiana asked, looking alarmed.

Darcy then told Georgiana about Elizabeth's fainting trick and all the interest it apparently had caused in the surrounding community.

"Oh, Elizabeth, I'm so relieved. I was having such a good time last night that I forgot about it. Then when I awoke this morning, I was thinking about everything that happened last night and I remembered."

Elizabeth continued, "There's just one good thing that has come out of the incident. Your brother got so tired of explaining to everyone he decided we should have a ball and demonstrate to everyone that I am, indeed, well!"

At this, Georgiana's eyes lit up. "Perhaps you can teach me how to faint, Elizabeth."

"No, no," Darcy said, "No fainting lessons, I beg you."

With so much excitement over the past days, all agreed to an afternoon and evening of reading. Elizabeth went to the library and searched for books that might contain information on horses, riding, and saddles. She found two that looked promising, and set them aside. She also looked for books on balls, games, parties, clothing and costume, without success. "Perhaps I'll find them in my study," she thought.

She took the books to the drawing room and broused through them until Selbey's announcement of supper. At table she suggested that Georgiana might ask Mrs. Sims to prepare some of her favorite dishes, explaining that she had been relying on Mrs. Sims own ingenuity as she herself tried to find her way through her other duties. Georgiana agreed to give it some thought.

In the drawing room after supper, Elizabeth found herself nodding over her books. Darcy noticed also and asked Georgiana if she would read a story aloud for all to hear, which she agreed to do. Darcy found one of his favorites, and Georgiana read while Darcy tried to keep Elizabeth propped up and awake.

The story finished, Darcy said, "It's been a tiring day after a late night. I'd better take her to bed. I'll take a book along and read for awhile in our room."

"That sounds like a good idea. I think I'll do the same." They told Fenton on the way to tell Bradford and Annie they would not be needed, and that Fiona should go to Georgiana's room right away. They then made their way to their bedrooms.

Darcy helped Elizabeth undress herself and tucked her in.

"I'm so cold, Darcy, I need my nightie." He got it, and helped her into it.

He then undressed, got into bed, and could feel her shivering. He tucked the blankets close around her, snuffed the candle, and lay with his arm around her. He felt her forehead: cool, but certainly of normal temperature.

He lay, allowing the memories of the past two weeks to flow through his consciousness until they drifted into sleep.

December 11, Sunday

Before dawn he was wakened by Elizabeth's rapid jump out of bed. Still groggy, he sensed her scurrying across the room. Before he was fully awake, she had returned from her dressing room and was gingerly trying to get back into bed without him noticing.

"What is it, Elizabeth. Are you all right?"

"I'm sorry, Darcy; I didn't mean to waken you. Yes, I'm all right. I just started my period."

"Your period?"

"You do know about menstruation, don't you?"

"Yes, of course."

"Mine almost always seems to start early in the morning. I didn't want to stain the linens."

He put his arm around her under the covers and pulled her into the curve of his body.

"I said I was all right, Darcy, but I don't think it would be wise for me to go to church today. That building is so cold; I'm afraid that no matter how I bundle up, I'm sure to be a shivering mass. It's always this way; especially in the winter. I wouldn't want to cause a scene."

"Of course. We can stay home today."

"But Georgiana should get out to see people."

"If we go and you stay home, people are going to decide the rumour is true."

"And if I do go, my appearance will confirm it."

"If none of us go, they'll think you're near death."

Now both could see the humor in the dilemma.

"Oh, Darcy, there's something else. I noticed last night that my note to Mrs. Flanders was still on the table."

"Apparently no one went into town."

"I thought we could leave the note at their house after church if we didn't see them at church."

"It's really important to you, isn't it?"

"It's a lovely dress, Darcy. I'd so much like to wear it."

"Perhaps you could just go to their house next week and ask."

"I don't like to act the part of a grand dame who commands the services of all at will."

"Of course not. Well, it would do us good to get out. Will you feel better tomorrow?"

"Yes, of course; but don't expect me to ride for a few days."

"Perhaps after church I could find some hunting partners for tomorrow."

"That's an excellent idea. And be sure to invite them to stay for dinner as well. I'll feel better later so you can expect me to join you both for dinner. When Annie comes, we can send her to bring tea and porridge for me."

Once all these details had been sorted out, they went back to sleep until it was time for Darcy to get ready for breakfast and church. Dressed, he kissed her lightly, tucked the blankets around her once again, and left.

Elizabeth took her breakfast in bed and spent the morning drifting in and out of sleep.

Georgiana was accustomed to attending church with Darcy, so today seemed much the same as formerly. After church, while handing her into the carriage, Darcy saw Paul Flanders run away from the church. Before he could think, the young man was out of hearing, beginning to run down the street.

"That was young Flanders. I might have given him the note." Before Georgiana and Darcy entered the carriage, the coachman had been given directions to the Flanders home, so they were now following Paul. They were soon behind him and then a bit ahead.

"If we could only get far enough ahead, we could stop and wait for him, then give him the note." But Flanders was a good runner and during church, apparently, had been storing up his enthusiasm for running.

Georgiana began to observe other people on the street and even glanced at windows of houses for signs of life.

If the village had been larger, the plan of catching Flanders might have worked, but it was a small village. Even though the Flanders house was at the far edge of the village the carriage arrived just shortly before Flanders did.

Darcy alighted from the carriage and was standing on the street just before Flanders slowed down in front of his house.

"You're quite a runner, Flanders."

"Mr. Darcy."

"Mrs. Darcy asked me to bring this note to Mrs. Flanders. Perhaps you will be so kind as to give it to her."

"Yes, sir. Thank you, sir."

Darcy got back into the coach, and as he did, Georgiana and Flanders were exchanging shy looks and smiles.

"You have a very satisfied look on your face, Miss Darcy; I might even suspect you of being satirical."

"Darcy, the thought of us in the carriage chasing him down the street was very amusing; you must see that."

"Must I?" He reflected a bit and then grinned. "You're right, of course. What a pity Elizabeth wasn't here. The humor would not have been lost on her!"

They found Elizabeth in the drawing room. "Oh, Elizabeth, I'm so sorry you weren't with us."

"Well, Mr. Ford must have preached a fine sermon, indeed, to occasion such enthusiasm."

Eyebrows furrowed, Georgiana responded, "Perhaps he did, but the race after church was the highlight of the morning."

Darcy, standing by the fire, seemed decidedly less amused.

"We were just ready to drive to the Flanders house when their son bounded out of church, got ahead of us, and we were chasing him half the way to his house, and he chased us the rest of the way. One old man was walking with his dog, and when he saw us coming he stopped dead in his tracks to watch us. I was looking at the windows of the houses and saw more than one curtain parted with a face peering out from behind it."

"Georgiana, I don't think I have ever seen you so merry."

"Elizabeth, it was so funny. I'm only sorry you weren't there."

"And, Mr. Darcy, did you also enjoy the spectacle?"

"Rather less I should say; but she does have a point. There's no doubt that the Darcys are providing more than their share of the community's amusement for this month."

"Once again Father is proved right," Elizabeth said.

Darcy's look begged for more.

"I heard him say more than once, 'What do we live for but to provide amusement for our neighbors and laugh at them in our turn?'"

"I can see I need to get better acquainted with your father. I could profit from some of that philosophy."

At dinner Georgiana said, "Elizabeth, you look as if you're feeling better."

"Yes, Georgiana, I am. Thank you. And did you both get sorrowful looks from the other parishioners?"

"Yes, Lizzy, I feel thoroughly smothered in sympathy," Darcy replied.

"Poor baby."

Turning her attention to a new subject, Elizabeth asked, "Did you find hunting partners for tomorrow?"

"Yes, two: Howell and Morris. They'll be here about nine."

"Georgiana, perhaps you could talk to Mrs. Sims and ask her to have some breakfast ready for your brother and the others at eight-thirty."

"Yes, I shall."

"And can we expect them to join us for dinner?"

"Yes, if that's convenient, though one o'clock dinner would be better. We'll likely be back well before then."

"Georgiana?"

"Yes, I'll tell her. Mrs. Sims always seems ready to oblige."

After dinner all declined interest in walking on such a cold day, and Georgiana decided she'd like to play the piano forte for a while. She agreed to let Darcy and Elizabeth listen, and they all went to the music room. She played a variety of short pieces, generous in melody, but quite lacking in bombast—a very pleasant afternoon concert. Darcy and Elizabeth returned to the drawing room, but Georgiana decided to walk for awhile in the picture gallery. "It's not nearly so cold as outside, but I can look out and see what's happening—the sky and birds."

She joined them at supper, rather a subdued meal. Darcy told Georgiana of the visitors they had already had: Carleton, Sir Humphrey, and the Blakelys.

"Darcy told me you want to teach me some games, Elizabeth."

"Yes, I do. I suppose it's possible to go through life never playing games, but they can come in very handy as one tries to get through the social scene. Perhaps we could start with cribbage. The rules are not terribly complicated, and it provides an interesting mix of luck and skill."

They agreed that Darcy would explain the rules while playing with Georgiana, and Elizabeth would offer suggestions to Georgiana as the play moved along. Georgiana learned fast and soon knew the rules of play and scoring on the peg board.

Darcy was shuffling the cards while they tried to decide on another game. "Whist is good," Elizabeth said, but you need four players. Perhaps checkers is the best game to try next."

"I know how to play checkers," Georgiana said. Papa used to play with me when I was quite young."

"Perhaps then we can increase your skill," Darcy suggested.

"Yes, I'd like that."

Darcy won rather consistently, and Georgiana seemed to be getting discouraged.

Elizabeth reminded her that at Christmastime the Gardner children would be coming and that perhaps she could play with them, or teach them if they did not know how. "It's always easier to win when you're playing with beginners, a situation your brother is now enjoying."

"I wonder if they know how to play Authors."

"Let's play a few hands just so we are sure we remember how. Then we can teach them if they don't."

Finally, tired of games, they each found quiet in a book until bedtime.

Elizabeth and Darcy cuddled under the covers until both they and the bed were warm, and they fell asleep.

Monday: Mr. Morris and Mr. Howell

On Monday morning, Darcy was dressed and ready to leave before Elizabeth was even fully awake. He kissed her and left the bedroom.

At breakfast Elizabeth and Georgiana discussed possibilities for the day. "It looks as if it might rain," Elizabeth said. "If it does, your brother and his friends are not going to have very good hunting. I thing I'd like nothing better than to sit all day by the fire and embroider."

"Then why not? I've been neglecting mine for some time now."

"You do embroidery too?"

"At school it was considered of high importance that all the young ladies embroider well."

"I know I brought a pillow cover with me that I had started. I'll send Annie to find it for me."

"And I'll get mine."

Stitchery in hand, they were sitting by the fire, quietly embroidering when they heard a commotion. They were rising to see what the cause of the noise was when the door opened, and Darcy came in, Morris and Howell following.

"Mrs. Darcy, Miss Darcy," Darcy said, "Allow me to introduce my rather wet fellow hunters: Mr. Morris and Mr. Howell. Greetings were made and the guests shown seats.

"It looks to me as if tea is in order," Elizabeth offered.

"Excellent idea," Darcy responded, and the others readily assented.

Elizabeth and Georgiana's silent communication resulted in Georgiana's departure and, in a few minutes, her return.

General commiseration about the rain's interference with their sport led Elizabeth to the thought of their card playing of the past few days. "We've been indulging in playing cards and other games recently; perhaps you'd be interested in a dryer substitute for hunting?" Before long the men had seated themselves around the card table and were playing scat.

Tea arrived; Georgiana poured, and all were served. Seeing that they were no longer needed, Elizabeth and Georgiana excused themselves and went to the music room.

A fire was burning, and Elizabeth contented herself in embroidery while Georgiana practiced. Finally, Georgiana looked up and said, "That's enough practice for today. What have you been playing, Elizabeth?"

"I've been reviewing the Christmas carols so we can all sing together during the holidays. I've even managed to get Darcy to sing with me."

"Really!" Georgiana exclaimed, "You do have him under a spell, don't you? He seems so different, Elizabeth, even funny."

"Yes, I believe you're right. He seems to be taking himself somewhat less seriously. I'm only hoping the spell doesn't break," she whispered, conspiratorially.

Georgiana and Elizabeth returned to the morning room to find the card playing ended and the men trading hunting stories: the largest bird; the bird downed, but never found; a dog swimming to retrieve a duck in the water only to return with a piece of drift wood.

"Confused, that one was!"

"To say nothing of the waiting hunter."

At dinner the men, while trying to include the ladies in the conversation, time and again lapsed into one adventure or another.

"No doubt this day of card playing will enter the lore as the day the fewest birds were bagged, the most points scored?" Elizabeth ventured.

"We really don't much like to talk about the less successful hunts, Mrs. Darcy," Howell said. "It's only if someone else finds out about it and they remind us. By the way, Darcy, I understand your coach horses had a race with Paul Flanders on Sunday after church."

"Did you witness it, Mr. Howell?" Elizabeth queried.

"No, Mrs. Darcy; I went back into the church to talk with Mr. Ford for a few minutes, but I heard about it later. It must have been some relief to you that the horses won, Darcy."

"Yes, Mr. Howell, the ladies have been careful not to let me forget the incident. They have been enjoying it enormously. Before long we shall feel the community is quite indebted to us for all the amusement we've been providing."

"At least your team had a worthy opponent. I don't think there's a lad in the village that could beat Flanders in a fair race. I use him as a beater, you may remember, when I organize larger hunting parties. Bright young lad. Ambitious too. Hopes to be a game keeper, like his father. Too bad he can't afford further education. He'd give some of your Cambridge friends a run for their money."

"Indeed?"

"Top scholar in his class in school; small class, but he was at the top; studious; picks up odd jobs in the village and on surrounding farms whenever he can—at lambing and sheep shearing, harvest and the like."

"Sounds like a hard worker."

"Yes, very conscientious; truly a worthy opponent for your horses."

The dinner finished, Morris and Howell begged to be excused, saying their wives would be waiting. They thanked their hosts and departed.

Georgiana left to go to practice the piano, and in retiring to the drawing room, Elizabeth said to Darcy, "Well, what a relief not to have to explain about my 'mysterious ailment.'"

"Yes, perhaps word of the ball has already circulated. But now, how are we going to survive the taunting over the 'race?'"

"My love, I think you did admirably today; just letting everyone enjoy it may be the best way." Turning to another subject, Elizabeth said, "I was truly surprised at all the comments Mr. Howell had to say about young Flanders. If it's true, it really is sad that he cannot continue his education."

"It's hard to say what value it would be for him."

"It seems to me that the people who have more education do manage to lead more agreeable lives—like Uncle Phillips, for instance. As an attorney he earns more than most people in Meryton."

"Don't you think there are attorneys enough as it is?"

"And clergymen have more education and lead more agreeable lives."

"But rarely earn much money."

"What do people do with degrees from Cambridge and Oxford and other colleges?"

"Some of them become university instructors and professors."

"There; surely that is a more agreeable life than that of a game keeper. And government; what about government?"

"Many such positions fall to younger sons of the nobility."

"But surely not all. Surely some government officials come from families of common ancestry."

"Some, to be sure. Functionaries, especially in the colonies."

"And what of architects and ship builders?"

"Yes, I believe some of them attend university. Not all of them make their way through apprenticeships."

Having at least partially won her point, Elizabeth took up a book and began reading. The thought of a bright young man sinking into a life as a game keeper kept intruding into her thoughts though, and she was relieved when Georgiana returned and Selbey appeared.

"Georgiana, did you enjoy our guests at dinner today?"

"Yes, I did. Mr. Morris and Mr. Howell were truly interesting to listen to, and you too, Darcy, of course. You can't imagine how dull conversation in a girl's school is. We had interesting times in London at the Findley's too, of course. We seemed always to be with some of their friends. Men do live more interesting lives, don't you think, Elizabeth?"

"Yes, Georgiana, I do. Perhaps I shall think differently after a few weeks in London, or after a few more of these escapades we seem fated to get into. Some people call the country boring, but we seem determined to prove them wrong."

Darcy now intervened to say, "Mrs. Darcy, might you be induced to play the piano this evening?"

"If Georgiana will play as well, and if you both will sing carols with me."

All agreed, and spent most of the evening in singing and listening to music.

Tuesday

Tuesday brought a note from Mrs. Flanders saying she'd be happy to see Elizabeth on Thursday at eleven.

After breakfast, Elizabeth went to her study, wrote letters to the dressmaker and milliner whose names and addresses Georgiana had provided. She asked for appointments for the first Thursday and Friday in January respectively. Before leaving the letters on the hall table, she went to Darcy's study to get his approval on the January dates.

"Yes, I think we can leave here the first Tuesday in January; two days will make an easy, agreeable trip to London. I'll notify Mrs. Jones, the housekeeper at my town house, that we'll be there for a week or more."

Seeing papers scattered on his desk, Elizabeth asked what he was doing.

"Just looking over some of the detritus of my college years: what courses were offered and so forth, and looking for possible information on scholarships. There must be some way young Flanders can get assistance for further education."

"And remove him from the neighborhood?"

"Yes, well...I did find some odd items; here's one relating astronomical instruments and time pieces to the practical problems of navigation something very important to government and trade. And recently I read an article telling of advances in understanding the structure and processes of the human body, with possibilities for treating disease. Glasgow is becoming a great center of learning in many areas.

"Even eyeglasses show promise of improving lives: making it possible for people to continue reading into later life, or even improving the vision of people who never could see very well. Just being able to read makes life a lot more enjoyable for many people."

"Hmmm," Elizabeth murmured. Then coming back to the present moment, "You haven't forgotten that we are invited today to the Blakelys for dinner, have you?"

"No, I remembered; we probably should leave at two o'clock to make an easy ride and arrive well before three."

Bundled into the carriage, the three enjoyed the ride to the Blakely's as much as could be expected on a cold, overcast day. They arrived well before the appointed hour and were warmly greeted by the Blakelys. They found that the Morrises had already arrived, along with Mr. Morris's young brother Stephen.

"He's home for a few days from university in Glasgow," Morris explained.

Everyone was introduced and had exhausted the topic of the weather when dinner was announced.

Mrs. Blakely seated young Morris on her right and Georgiana next to him. She bid Darcy to her left, Mrs. Morris beside him and then Elizabeth. That left Elizabeth with Mr. Blakely on her left and Mr. Morris opposite. Elizabeth immediately noted the happy arrangement of Georgiana sitting next to the only person at all near her own age.

The food and service were excellent, which may have been part of the reason for the quiet progress of the conversation. At length, Elizabeth said to Mrs. Morris, "I know Mr. Morris hunts because he came to hunt with Mr. Darcy yesterday. Does he hunt often?"

"Yes," she replied, "About as often as time permits. They usually have better luck than yesterday, though, so we often enjoy game at table. I understand you come from Hertfordshire. Does your father hunt?"

"Yes, and I suppose he hunted more often in his earlier years, but he's really more fond of reading."

"Indeed; and are you a reader too?"

"I always have been, though I'm beginning to wonder how much time I shall have for reading now that I'm married."

"You two took us quite by surprise. We began to think Mr. Darcy rather liked the bachelor life."

At a loss for how to continue this line of conversation, Elizabeth noted that Georgiana was in conversation with young Morris and turned to Mr. Blakely. Before she could speak, he asked, "Mrs. Darcy, are you becoming accustomed to life in Derbyshire? Have you been enjoying the countryside in the most enjoyable manner—on horseback?"

"Is there a rumour that I've been riding?"

"Not that I'm aware of; I just assumed that such a lively young lady would be an avid horsewoman."

"Actually, I have not been accustomed to riding, but Mr. Darcy was determined that I should learn and has already bought me a horse."

"And have you ridden?"

"Just once, but I expect to be urged to ride almost daily."

"Mrs. Blakely rides, you know, and I believe you do also, don't you, Mrs. Morris?"

"Yes, I do ride; I learned to ride when younger, but have ridden frequently only since we were married." Returning to the earlier subject, Mrs. Morris said, "So Pemberley is keeping you busy. It is an enormous house."

"Yes, I haven't even seen all the rooms yet; it seemed more sensible to see them as I need to know. I'm planning to look at the ballroom tomorrow."

"Might that mean you are planning a ball?"

"Yes, about the end of February, we think. We hope to send the invitations about the middle of February."

"That is something to look forward to."

Dinner complete, the ladies adjourned to the drawing room, leaving the gentlemen to enjoy their brandy and conversation.

"Mrs. Blakely, did you know the Darcys are planning a ball?"

"Really, when?"

"We haven't set the date, but we think it will be late February."

"That's quite an undertaking."

"Yes, but our housekeeper assures me the servants will be easily able to manage."

Mrs. Blakely and Mrs. Morris covered a variety of subjects, allowing Elizabeth and Georgiana to listen and observe the beautiful appointments of the room.

The gentlemen had returned from the dining room only a short time when Elizabeth observed Stephen Morris say something quietly to Georgiana and then approach Darcy. "I'd like to take Miss Darcy outdoors for a short walk." His expression asked permission. Darcy, looking at Georgiana and seeing assent, replied, "Yes, of course."

Conversation continued enjoyably but, wanting to return home before dark, not long after Georgiana and Stephen returned the Darcys left, as did the Morrises, amid expressions of appreciation and hopes of future meetings.

Returned to Pemberley, Elizabeth asked Georgiana about Stephen.

"He came home to talk with his father. He isn't happy at college. His father wants him to become an attorney, but it doesn't interest him. One of his friends had to leave university because he didn't have enough money. He went to America and has been writing letters to Stephen, urging him to do the same."

"Well, you learned a great deal in a short time."

"He does talk rather a lot. He told me most of this when we went outside. He's hunted with the Blakely's and knows their dogs. The stable keeper let him take them out with us."

Now Darcy's interest was engaged. "Took the dogs out, did he?"

"Yes, he found a stick and threw it for the dogs to retrieve. They seemed to love it. Each time they brought it back, he threw it again. I'm not sure who enjoyed it more, Mr. Morris or the dogs."

"And do you think he will go to America?" Elizabeth asked.

"I don't know; his father is against it."

"At any rate, you didn't have to spend the entire afternoon listening to all the older people."

"Yes, I suppose you're right."

Once in bed that night, Elizabeth said, "Georgiana didn't seem terribly impressed with Mr. Morris."

"Really? I thought she rather liked him." He paused, then said, "I do hope we won't always have three of us in bed."

"Sir?"

"You, me, and Georgiana."

"I can assure you we are very much alone."

"Then, cuddle up and concentrate on me."

"With pleasure."

Wednesday

At breakfast, Georgiana greeted Elizabeth saying "I see you're dressed for riding again today."

"Yes, it's cold, but at least the rain has stopped, and if I'm going to learn, we'd better take advantage of that while we can. I wouldn't be surprised to see snow soon."

"Nor I," Darcy offered. "We've been lucky not to have snow before this."

After breakfast, Georgiana left for a morning of practicing, and Darcy and Elizabeth went to the stable. The men saddled the horses, Darcy helped Elizabeth mount, and they followed the road that led toward Lambton.

They had not ridden long when Darcy moved Prince side by side with Midnight, and, looking directly at her, asked, "Have I told you this morning, Elizabeth, that I love you?"

She closed her eyes only for a moment, took a short breath, and looked back at him. "Yes, Darcy, you have; I feel truly enveloped in your love."

They rode on silently until their cheeks were thoroughly chilled.

"We'd best return, Lizzy."

They turned, returned to the stable, and dismounted. Hand in hand, they walked to the kitchen.

"Mrs. Sims, this is getting to be a habit, but the day is chill and tea is what we need."

"You surely do, Mr. Darcy, and you shall have it. When Mr. Sims told me you went out, I put the kettle on right away."

They were standing in the morning room by the fire embracing when Georgiana walked in. They parted, but Georgiana said, "Please, don't let me interfere; you make a very pretty picture."

Before they could respond Susan came in with the tea tray.

Georgiana poured, saying, "You look stiff with cold."

"Yes, I am."

Warmed by the hot tea, Elizabeth left to meet with Mrs. Sims about menus for Christmas and with Mrs. Reynolds about the ball. They went to look at the ballroom and discussed what cleaning and waxing would need to be done and how many extra employees would have to be hired and how to get them.

After dinner, Elizabeth wrote letters to Jane and Bingley to confirm she had received the Christmas invitation acceptance; then she wrote to her father and mother, and to Charlotte.

The evening was spent with games and conversation.

"Georgiana," Elizabeth said, "I have some questions for you: What are you going to wear to the bazaar Saturday morning? Have you been in the Lambton assembly room? Is it heated or as cold as all outdoors?"

"I suppose I have been there, but I really don't remember it. Darcy?"

"Yes, I've been there; they do have a fireplace, which they use, but usually there are so many people entering and leaving that it doesn't do much good; the principle source of heat is the people themselves. I suggest that we dress warmly, all of us. Speaking of the sale, I'll have to see that you both have enough money; if there are appealing gifts, you will want to buy them."

"And you?" countered Elizabeth, "will you buy anything?"

"Possibly, but I'm better at buying horses and saddles. I'll be looking for anyone I think might be interested in selling a horse or saddle, or who knows someone who would. After all, all horses become one year older on January 1. So selling late in the year, the owner is selling a horse that is technically one year younger than a short time later."

"And so the supply of horses for sale should be plentiful," Elizabeth said.

"Exactly."

By the time they got into bed that night, Elizabeth was as eager as Darcy for a long, leisurely session of lovemaking. Perhaps it was rather late when they actually calmed down into a warm, delicious slumber. And perhaps Bradford and Annie did have to wait in the morning for awhile as the lovers rested following an early morning experiment with closeness.

Such is the luxury of a well-matched pair fortunate enough to enjoy the world's wealth.

Thursday: The Gold Dress

At breakfast Elizabeth asked, "Will you go with me to Lambton this morning, Georgiana?"

"Yes, I'd like that. It's cold out, but it is something different to do."

"Then we'll leave at ten."

Darcy cautioned, "You're not due at Mrs. Flanders until eleven, but you're likely to arrive in Lambton about ten-thirty.

"Yes, but I want to go into a couple of the shops Mrs. Sims showed me and look more closely at stock so I know better what's available.

Georgiana was ready, and they left as planned. It did not snow, but looked as if it might at any time. They browsed in two of the stores and bought a few skeins of embroidery yarn and some candies.

When they arrived at the Flanders, Mrs. Flanders greeted them as before, and the two small children, noisy when they arrived, became quiet upon the entrance of the two ladies.

They opened the package, laid the dress on the table to look at it.

"Yes," Mrs. Flanders said, "it's a very fine dress, well worth altering if the fit allows."

Georgiana and Elizabeth went into the little bedroom and got Elizabeth into the dress.

Looking at it, Mrs. Flanders very quickly determined that the alterations were very reasonable and said that she certainly could do it. "It will cost 15 shillings," she said. "The finer fabric will take more care in handling."

The price agreed upon, she took her pins and set about drawing in the several seams that would have to be restitched. She only had a small mirror, but Elizabeth turned it this way and that so she could see that it would fit very attractively.

That done, they all three carefully extracted her from the dress so as not to dislodge the pins.

Again in her own dress, she put on her coat and hat. Purse in hand and following Georgiana, she exited the house. They were nearing the carriage, when Paul Flanders came running down the street. When he saw them, he slowed down, stopped, and said, "Good morning."

Each replied, "Good morning." Farris handed them into the coach, and they looked out to see the young man still standing, looking at them; Georgiana smiled at him and then looked down at her gloved hands.

"What remarkable energy," Elizabeth said. "He almost seems to be in constant motion."

"He is rather nice looking," Georgiana said.

"Georgiana!"

"Well, he is. Does it change matters to pretend not to notice?"

"You wouldn't talk that way if your brother were here," she said playfully.

"No. Oh, Elizabeth; it's so wonderful having a sister! Just being able to say some of the things I'm thinking."

"I've never known what it is like not having someone I could talk with. Jane was always there with me. Almost two years older than me, I've never known life without a sister. And with three younger sisters as well, we were fairly brimming over with sisters."

At dinner, all agreed that the weather had improved; perhaps a short walk would be refreshing. Their first objective was the stable, to see how Prince and Midnight were getting along after the previous night's rain.

"I walked them in the yard," Sims said. The pasture is wet, and on such a cold day I thought just fresh air would be best. They were back in their stalls and seemed contented.

They all petted the horses. Darcy wanted to see his dogs, so they went to the kennels. "You were good sports in the rain, weren't you," Darcy said to the dogs, petting and playing with them. "You've had to spend a lot of time alone while I've been keeping Mrs. Darcy company, haven't you?"

"They seem like children to you," Elizabeth said, watching.

"They've been good companions and good hunters, too. It doesn't do much good to shoot a bird down if you can't retrieve it. They don't miss finding many."

They took a short turn around the grounds, and, Georgiana and Elizabeth pleading chill, they returned to the house. On the way they stopped in the kitchen and asked Mrs. Sims to send tea.

Friday

Darcy and Elizabeth rode again on Friday, though not far; it was too cold. She found Annie, changed out of her habit, and arranged with Annie for a bath and her hair to be washed at three.

Mrs. Reynolds took Elizabeth through the various rooms that might be used by the guests at the Christmas holiday, and they selected the most suitable ones.

Then Elizabeth made final decisions with Mrs. Sims for meals that would be served during the several days guests would be with them. It was agreed that breakfast should be ready in warming pans on the sideboard at eight with so many people to serve, and that the children would take their dinners and suppers in the nursery, except on Christmas Day, when they would join the others for dinner.

They compared notes once again on the contributions for the bazaar the next day, examining those already assembled. Fenton would supervise the loading of the packages into the carriage, which was to be ready for departure at eight-thirty the next day.

At dinner, Darcy and Elizabeth decided that he, Bingley and Uncle Gardner would go hunting on the 26th, weather permitting, and the ladies would take gifts to the tenants.

Elizabeth relaxed in the tub before the fire as Annie dried her hair, allowing the events of her new life to wander through her mind. When she was dressed and her hair arranged, she selected the clothes she would wear to the bazaar, remembering Darcy's caution to dress warmly. "It should be subdued in style and color. There will be enough people watching me without drawing additional attention."

She found herself looking out the windows, wishing for more agreeable weather. "And winter hasn't even begun," she thought.

After supper, restless, she shuffled through the books on horses and saddles, trying to find something meaningful. At last she selected a novel and read until the characters compelled her full attention.

December 17, Saturday: The Lambton Bazaar

Saturday was crisp and gray as they rode into Lambton.

"I'll wait with the coach while you and Georgiana shop at the bazaar."

"Oh, no, Darcy; you must come in; people won't understand my arriving without you; I need you to introduce me to people."

He hesitated, but conceded the point.

"And don't forget the horse for Georgiana. You may see someone who can help you find one."

The footman carried in the donated items, and while those and other offerings were being arranged, Darcy introduced Elizabeth to a few people and Georgiana as well, since she had been away at school so much recently that to some she was a stranger also.

Once the sale was underway, Elizabeth took Darcy's arm and applied gentle pressure to move him toward the tables.

Quietly he said to her, "I'll just wait here for you."

"No, please; just look at the things; pretend you're interested."

"I'm better at buying horses."

"Then just move around the room looking at everything quietly and then go back to the horse hunting."

"Agreed."

He left her at a table examining stuffed dolls as he slowly, but surely, walked around looking at everything superficially. He spotted a white rabbit-fur muff, glanced toward Georgiana and saw that she was absorbed with Elizabeth comparing dolls. He quickly paid for it and the attendant wrapped it in newsprint.

At another table he selected some marzipan, paid for it, and pocketed it, again noting that he was not observed. As he made the purchase, a toddler gazed up at him with big eyes, watching his every move. His transaction complete, he reached into his pocket for another coin, paid for more candy and handed it to the child. He looked up again to find Elizabeth observing them.

Her expression said, "Softie."

"Have you finished shopping?" he asked.

"Not quite. I see you found something."

"Just a harness for Prince. Imagine finding such an item here."

They moved in opposite directions, each noting where Georgiana was.

Darcy spotted a finely-woven woolen scarf, decided it was just the thing for Elizabeth, and quickly paid for it. Looking further he was amazed to find some carefully crafted and novel fishing lures. He selected four likely ones with Bingley and Fitzwilliam in mind. As he was paying, he felt a hand on his shoulder.

"For me?"

"Sir Humphrey, good morning."

"Christmas shopping?"

"Yes." he said, glancing toward Elizabeth. "Marriage is bringing various little changes into my life."

"Sir Humphrey," Elizabeth greeted him. "How delightful."

"Mrs. Darcy; and Georgiana too. I hope you'll be coming to dinner after Christmas with your brother and his bride."

"We hadn't told her about it yet," Elizabeth intervened. "So much has been happening we were holding that as a surprise."

"You will be there, won't you?" he repeated.

"Of course; I wouldn't miss it."

Before they could continue their visit, a friend of Sir Winston's drew his attention away.

"Darcy, would you mind taking my packages to the coach? I would like to look awhile longer."

"Gladly," he responded, and Georgiana and Elizabeth piled their purchases into his arms.

He was just opening the door when young Flanders burst in, pressing two young charges ahead of him. They all three looked up, wide-eyed to see their impressive doorman.

He hesitated, then said, "Good morning, Mr. Darcy; thank you."

"You're welcome, Flanders," he said, a bit flustered. Then, recovering, "Enjoy the sale."

Outdoors he found the coach and deposited the packages. He strolled back towards the assembly building and paced back and forth in front of the building, waiting expectantly for Elizabeth and Georgiana. Several people he knew passed and he greeted each and chatted with some.

"When are they coming?" he muttered to himself. Finally, chilled, he opened the door and just as it swung wide, he found before him the Flanders children about to exit, Paul's hand on the door handle, the children close behind him, each clutching small packages.

Giving in to the inevitability of the occasion, Darcy said, "Allow me," and held the door as they all exited. Looking up, he saw several people looking at him, smiling or turning away quickly.

"Darcy, that was sweet," Elizabeth said, as she followed, with Georgiana directly behind her.

In the carriage Elizabeth asked, "Did you find a horse for Georgiana?"

"Not exactly, but I told at least five people that I was looking for one. By tomorrow morning everyone in Derbyshire should know about it, and by nightfall on Monday we should have a new mount for Georgiana bedded down in the stable—especially since the news can be embellished with the story of my new position as doorman at the assembly."

"You'll not help us forget the event by your own embellishment!" Elizabeth chided.

"So, did you buy something for me?" he asked, hoping to change the subject.

"Oh, dear, we shall have to return!"

Now the laughter Georgiana had been stifling burst forth.

"I shall be content with a lump of coal in my stocking," he retorted.

Georgiana and Elizabeth glanced knowingly at each other.

"I see; you're ganging up on me."

"Did Mrs. Wilson thank you for your contributions?" Elizabeth queried.

"Profusely."

"She's only trying to be nice."

"Still, it does make one appreciate the biblical injunction to give without others knowing."

"So wise," Elizabeth said quietly to Georgiana.

"And he's not even old."

"I mentioned to Sir Humphrey that he could look forward to our ball in February," Elizabeth said. "He seemed delighted."

"Yes, I expect so. He'll ask you to dance with him, Elizabeth. Maybe even you, Georgiana...if he sees you aren't standing up for every dance."

"Is this a warning?" Georgiana asked.

"Not at all; he's quite a good dancer. I remember seeing him dance with Mrs. Winston, and it's some years since she died. He never seems to lose hope though that he'll find a new wife."

"Surely he wouldn't pursue me!"

"Certainly not. But he's not above showing the young men that a wallflower can blossom into a fine dancer. Some of the young men might be afraid of looking foolish with a clumsy dancer."

"Do you speak from personal experience?" Elizabeth inquired.

"Not at all. Mother insisted that I take dancing lessons for years when I was too young to know what a wallflower was."

"Where did you take your lessons?"

"In our ballroom. She organized lessons every summer. Sometimes she played the piano herself, and sometimes a neighbor or a servant played a fiddle. And each summer she held at least one party dance for all the young people who came to classes, with several musicians to play."

"And you, Georgiana; were you in those classes too?"

"Yes, but I was very young, and then Mama died; I learned most of the dances I know at school."

"I think we should have lessons for young people next summer in our ballroom," Elizabeth proposed.

"For whom?" Darcy queried. "We don't have any young people."

"Georgiana isn't exactly old."

"But she knows how to dance."

"Then she can help me teach the others. Or she can play the piano and I'll teach." She paused, searching his countenance for his response. "You seem doubtful."

"Who would attend?"

Then Georgiana joined in, "Oh, Darcy, let us do it. I know the children will come."

"Well, why not? I won't have to participate...will I?"

"Only at the party dance...as chaperone," Elizabeth concluded.

"There seems no end to the messes I can get into. It's a good thing we're home. I'm not sure I could withstand another scheme. One just concluded, another already planned."

Katie brought tea to the morning room as Darcy was asking, "Well, what did you buy that isn't a secret?"

"Lots," Elizabeth retorted, opening the packages. What fun to spend money as if I would never run out! Stuffed dolls for Mary and Ellie Gardner, wooden toys for the boys, beautifully embroidered pillowcases for Aunt and Uncle Gardner, and a crewel stool cover, cakes, including some of Mrs. Ford's, fishing lures for Fitzwilliam...."

"Indeed. Then he'll have plenty of lures."

"You bought some too?"

"I was surprised to find such an item, and I didn't hesitate. And you, Georgiana?"

"I'm afraid most of mine are secrets."

"Well, that sounds promising."

Katie handed Elizabeth her cup of tea.

"Ah, the tea is just what I need! What a cold day!" Elizabeth exclaimed.

"Surely Derbyshire isn't a great deal colder than Hertfordshire," he suggested.

"Not a lot, I suppose; but we've been staying out longer here, I guess, so I feel it more. I do so wish we'd get some warmer weather. Then maybe I'd want to go out."

"Then I suggest we stay indoors and let others make the trip to us. I propose we ask some people after church tomorrow to stop in for tea at four."

Georgiana and Elizabeth grinned at each other. Elizabeth said, "I'm pleased, of course, but a bit perplexed. You always seem so content with your books."

Shrugging his shoulders he replied, "I wouldn't want you to get bored with my company. Perhaps closer acquaintance with some of the local citizens will make you appreciate me even more."

"That's not at all likely; but I heartily endorse the idea whatever the motives. Whom should we invite?"

"Morris and Howell perhaps and their wives."

"But they were just here Monday."

"Not the wives."

"True."

"And perhaps Mrs. Wilson and her husband, and the Vicar and his wife. Sometimes it's agreeable to invite several people so they can help by entertaining each other."

"You're quite right. Mrs. Wilson must be delighted with the success of the bazaar and would likely enjoy telling about it." Elizabeth savored her tea and looked thoughtfully at Darcy. "Thank you, Darcy."

"For what?"

"For everything. For going to the bazaar with us, for the idea of inviting guests to tea, for buying the candy for that child, and especially for opening the door for the Flanders children. You've been very generous, as always. I just don't usually remember to thank you."

Looking towards Georgiana, he said, "What is Georgiana going to think about all this?"

"Well, she might suspect that I'm in love with my husband."

"She's right, Darcy, I do suspect it." Georgiana said. Fortunately, I'm good at keeping secrets."

Sunday: Tea at Pemberley

Sunday was still chill, with only a hint that the sun might peek through the clouds later. Darcy reached Howell and Morris after church, and Elizabeth asked Mrs. Wilson and Mrs. Ford to come to tea with their husbands. The Blakely's also agreed to come.

The guests arrived at very much the same time, and soon after they arrived Darcy took the men to the stable to see Midnight and to the kennels as well to see the dogs.

They returned, rubbing their hands to warm them, and found the ladies already in the drawing room taking their tea. They received glasses of wine and settled together to converse.

Mrs. Ford was quiet, alert, listening attentively to Mrs. Wilson telling about the bazaar. Elizabeth thought that Mrs. Ford recognized her cakes from the bazaar on the serving tray. She seemed a bit shy, perhaps a bit too willing to please, but apparently pleased to be included in the party.

"Mrs. Morris," have you heard from Mr. Morris's brother in Glasgow?" Elizabeth asked.

"Stephen...." she said thoughtfully, as if trying to decide what to say. "He's well, I hope."

"Oh yes, well enough, I think. He'll be with us for a few days at the holidays. He just seems so unhappy. I only wish he could resolve on a course for his future."

"Georgiana said he might go to America."

"I don't think that's likely. His father is determined he should be an attorney. But if there were something else Stephen really wanted to do, I think his father would continue to help him. He just doesn't seem to have a better idea himself."

She paused, and as she did, Mrs. Howell spoke, "You seem content to be at Pemberley again, Georgiana."

"Yes, quite a lot has been happening. And in January we plan to go to London for a week or more."

"That should be pleasant. Sally told me she saw you after church today."

"Yes, I invited her, but she said she had other plans."

Before Mrs. Howell could pursue the subject, Mrs. Wilson said to Elizabeth, "You seem very much at ease as mistress of Pemberley; one might think you had been here a year...."

A bit surprised by so personal a comment, Elizabeth said, "Thank you, but I'm not quite so much at ease. After musing a few moments, she added, "I didn't really realize how much I had learned growing up with mother and father and four sisters until suddenly I found myself in an entirely new home with all the people about me strangers, except for Mr. Darcy, of course. It's not that I do so much; the servants take care of almost everything. It's just that almost everything seems just a bit different, and some things are quite different.

"Mr. Darcy has been wonderful, though, and now Georgiana too. I'm in very good hands indeed. I'm sorry. I'm afraid I've been running on."

"Not at all," Mrs. Blakely countered. "You know, you've done something that many of us must have dreamed about as children—leave our families to marry a handsome prince and live in a beautiful castle in a far country. It's very pleasant to hear the princess tell what it's really like," she added, in a quieter, almost conspiratorial voice.

The guests having departed, Darcy said, "Did I hear you talking about the Morris boy?"

"Yes," Elizabeth replied. He's having difficulty deciding what he wants to do."

"Well, those professors at Glasgow will try to stuff him with literature and Greek...."

Georgiana broke in, "Last week at the Blakelys he told me he's studying science."

"Indeed."

"He said he might become an animal doctor."

"Doesn't sound very promising as a way to earn a living."

"And he talked about building roads and bridges."

"He does seem determined to follow a difficult path."

"He even talked about designing ships or military weapons."

"Now there's an idea. The government always finds money for weapons and ships."

"Do you know Stephen, Darcy?" Elizabeth asked

"Yes, a little. He's hunted with us on occasion."

"What is he like?"

"Good shot, for a boy that young."

"He's hardly a boy," Georgiana objected.

"...young man; yes, for such a young man. Keeps his mind on the hunt; good with the dogs, doesn't treat them like pets."

"That seems an odd comment from you, Darcy," Georgiana said. "By the way, I haven't seen your dogs in the house lately."

"No, I thought it might be easier for Elizabeth to get used to Pemberley if she didn't have that distraction."

To Elizabeth Georgiana said, "He used to take them to bed with him."

"Are you going to give away all my secrets?"

"Oh, I'm sorry; I didn't realize it was a secret," she replied, a bit chastened.

"It's not a secret, exactly; I just hadn't mentioned it." Seeing her chagrin, Darcy moved from where he had been standing by the fireplace to sit down next to Georgiana. "Besides, I don't intend to keep any secrets from Elizabeth. There's a lot to be said for secrecy, but not among family."

"Have you told her my secret?"

"What secret is that?"

"You know...Ramsgate."

"Yes, I'm afraid I had to tell her about that." By now Elizabeth had joined them on the sofa, also beside Georgiana.

"But why?"

"Georgiana, you did not do anything wrong. Elizabeth knows that. But Wickham had deceived not only you and me, but Elizabeth as well. Elizabeth would never have married me if I hadn't told her the whole story. Wickham told her that I treated him very shabbily, and she believed him."

Thoroughly confused, Georgiana looked to Elizabeth for denial.

"It's true, Georgiana."

"But you did marry Darcy."

"But she refused me the first time I proposed."

"Then Darcy wrote me a letter telling me the whole story of Wickham's connection with your family."

"But how could you have believed bad things about Darcy?"

"I didn't know him then. He came to Meryton as a stranger. Wickham was friendly and pleasant, and everyone thought he was wonderful. He deceived everyone."

"But your own sister married him."

"They eloped. Had we known his true character, Papa would never have consented to the marriage. Darcy found Lydia and Wickham living together in London and insisted he marry Lydia."

"Finding a husband...or wife...is beginning to seem like a very tricky business."

"And you have one problem I did not have," Elizabeth said. "You have to determine that the man who seeks your hand is not just after your fortune. I had to find a man who would take me even though I had almost no money."

"That sounds easier."

"I can assure you I and all my sisters were convinced that we would be happy to trade places with any young woman of fortune."

"I shall find someone, though, don't you think?"

"Without a doubt. Finding someone will not be too difficult. Finding someone you can be happy with could be more of a problem."

"You're not alone," Darcy joined in. "We'll help. And you'll be looking. And, of course, the young men will be looking for you."

Georgiana was now thoughtful, but relaxed. Darcy said, "It's been a long day. I wouldn't be surprised to hear you've already forgotten the sermon."

"No, I haven't. It was the prodigal son. It reminded me of Mr. Wickham."

Monday

The next few days were a flurry of Christmas preparations, checking rooms for guests, revising menus, and making certain all the servants knew what they were to do. Mrs. Reynolds had arranged for extra helpers for Mrs. Sims in the kitchen and for Sarah upstairs.

Gift stockings were found and hung.

The night before the first guests arrived, Elizabeth tried on the gold velvet dress just before retiring for the night. She came into their bedroom to find Darcy standing by the window in his robe. He turned around expecting to find her in her night gown, and she could see the surprise on his countenance. "Lizzy, you look positively elegant."

"Thank you," she said and turned toward the dressing room.

"Wait."

She turned again and waited as he walked to his bedside table and took a box from the drawer. "After you took the dress to be altered, I found this necklace among Mother's jewelry. I want you to have it."

Her eyes widened as he removed the necklace from the box. They moved to the mirror, and he fastened it for her. "These must be emeralds."

"Yes, they are."

She turned around and put her arms around him, her head against his chest. He returned her embrace, and they stood silent for a moment. They parted, and she returned to the dressing room.

Even Darcy could hear Annie gasp.

Once in bed, lying spoon fashion, they both were quiet, reflecting on their love, their marriage, their relationship, this environment.

Elizabeth turned around to face him, and said, "I don't want you to think I love you just because you give me beautiful gifts."

"I know, Lizzy. I learned before we were married that I couldn't buy your love."

Less than a month had passed since they all had assembled for the double wedding, but to Elizabeth the flurry of events had made it seem much longer.

December 23, Friday

Jane and Bingley completed their two-day trip from Netherfield in their chaise and four arriving on the 23rd in time for afternoon tea. This was Jane's first visit to Pemberley, so Elizabeth guided Jane through part of the house after tea, to have time alone to compare notes on their new lives. Jane confessed that she and Bingley had already considered leaving Netherfield if they could find a suitable place in the north of England.

Her mother was only too often visiting at Netherfield or writing to ask for an invitation, and as often offering advice. Even the sweet-tempered Bingley seemed to be losing patience. In fact, Bingley was probably at that moment asking Darcy to be on the lookout for a suitable estate he could purchase.

While Elizabeth lamented the reasons for such a move, she expressed delight at the possibility of Jane and Bingley living nearby.

The Gardners arrived from London the next day, children bursting out of the carriage after the long ride, pleased they had arrived just in time for tea and cakes.

Later that same day, William and Farris brought Colonel Fitzwilliam home from the four o'clock stage at Lampton, arriving just after tea. He explained that they had stopped for dinner and that he was not hungry. Elizabeth explained that Darcy and Bingley had taken the dogs out for exercise, and when she offered to go with him to look for them he readily accepted. They soon spotted them some distance from the house. They waved to them and they started back, repeatedly throwing the stick for the dogs to retrieve as they walked toward the house. While waiting for them to approach, Elizabeth took the opportunity to thank Fitzwilliam for his part in bringing her and Darcy together.

"But I did nothing."

"No, you did do something; I'm not sure exactly what. I believe that somehow seeing your attentions to me at Rosings revealed me to Darcy in a different light. I don't think he would ever have proposed to me had we not spent those hours together at Lady Catherine's."

"But he didn't propose there," Fitzwilliam objected, "...or did he?"

"Someday I'll tell you more about it. For now I just want you to know I'm grateful to you and consider you a dear friend."

Together they took the dogs back to the kennels and rejoined the others for supper. There Georgiana mentioned that Darcy and Elizabeth had been teaching her several card games.

"Fitzwilliam," Darcy said, "Soldiers must often play cards."

"Indeed we do. All too often we find time hanging heavy on our hands; most soldiers become expert at cards. A deck of cards is small and can be carried almost anywhere."

"And do you ever encounter anyone who tries to cheat?"

"I'm sorry to say we do. Play is often for money, and cheating is only too common. One could almost say that spotting cheating is an important part of military training."

"Have you observed incidents of cheating?"

"Rarely, but I've heard of many instances. I'm fairly good at spotting cheaters, and I could try to give a demonstration, but I'm afraid I'd be very clumsy, and you'd unmask me at every turn."

Dinner finished, they all moved to the drawing room.

"I suggest we all try to cheat each other and each try to catch the others," Elizabeth said.

Uncle Gardner proposed that the men should play and the ladies watch. This was readily agreed to. Bingley suggested that only players should expose cheating during play, and that observers should wait until the hand was completed. Much laughter attended the formulation of the rules, but these things settled, the group settled down to the serious business of the game.

The Gardner children had come in during the rulemaking, dressed for bed, to share in the festivities for awhile. The three youngest were playing on the floor, but Henry, the oldest stood, watching with the ladies.

Whist was the game selected, and Fitzwilliam began as dealer. The first hand passed uneventfully, with everyone watching the others closely.

"I'm afraid we have a rather timid crowd here," ventured Uncle Gardner. "I sense that no one is trying to cheat. Let's screw up our courage. We may never get another chance to cheat with the approval of the group."

This time it was Bingley's deal. He shuffled and let Fitzwilliam cut the deck. As he rejoined the two stacks of cards, Darcy spoke up: "Stop! You returned the deck to the same way it was."

"Right you are," Bingley responded. He let Darcy cut them, and this time recombined the deck correctly. He dealt out the cards, and the play proceeded, though no cheaters were caught during this hand.

"I'm beginning to think that whist is not an easy game to cheat at," Uncle Gardner said, "or the cheaters are expert beginners."

On the next hand Darcy shuffled and dealt the cards, taking one card for himself from the bottom of the deck. This time Gardner noticed him and called a halt. Conceding, and returning the card to the deck, Bingley caught him replacing it on the top of the deck. Once again caught, he replaced it on the bottom and dealt his card from the top.

Play proceeded, and if anyone cheated during the rest of the hand no one was caught.

Now it was Gardner's turn to deal. They were halfway through play on the hand when they were distracted by the youngest Gardner child, Charles, tugging violently at his mother's skirt. "Mama, Mama, there's a card down here."

The ladies looked under the table quickly enough to see Fitzwilliam removing an ace from between his knees.

All laughed uproariously, including Fitzwilliam.

Uncle Gardner declared those present were failures at cheating and that they had best stick to honesty.

December 25, Sunday: Christmas at Pemberley

Christmas day provided all the delight one could hope for in congenial company, good food and drink, and the wide-eyed looks of children who received gifts that pleased. At dinner Elizabeth felt like a queen in her gold velvet gown and emeralds. Jane and Aunt Gardner were suitably impressed, she thought.

Darcy had informed Georgiana earlier of his presentation, so she could take pleasure in the gift, as well. She realized that she would ultimately possess most of her mother's jewelry, but heartily concurred in the appropriateness of this gift, and her pleasure was apparent.

The day passed only too rapidly.

Immediately after breakfast the next morning the Gardners left, and Fitzwilliam also, not long after. All assured their hosts that they would return for the ball if it was at all possible.

Bingley and Darcy then left for a morning's hunt, while Elizabeth, Georgiana, Jane, and Mrs. Reynolds went to the tenants' cottages with gift baskets that had been prepared for them: breads, candies, fruitcake, dried fruits, and a pound note for each family. Mrs. Reynolds introduced Elizabeth to the families at each cottage since this was Elizabeth's first opportunity to meet them. Returning home she made notes about each family, resolving the following year to visit earlier in the fall so she would know what gifts would be most appropriate for each.

Along the way where they had stopped at a cottage, Paul Flanders passed by on the road, carrying a gun, a dog dancing around him. Elizabeth observed that Georgiana followed his moves and smiled when he looked their way. He doffed his hat in recognition, but said nothing.

For dinner on the 26th, their number was reduced to five. Holiday preparations had disclosed that the long dining table could be separated, so one half was removed to the wall at one end of the room. Now at the smaller table, Darcy sat at the head and Elizabeth at the foot. Georgiana sat on one side and on the other Jane and Bingley.

The warmth of all the relationships made wit unnecessary, if not unwelcome. The event might be remembered years later by the participants, without remembering any morsel of conversation.

Elizabeth did try to get suggestions for the ball from Bingley, but Bingley was too agreeable a person to offer advice. Indeed, Bingley seemed intent on one subject only: finding a home for Jane and himself in one of the northern counties.

Later, Georgiana played the piano as she had the night before, and Elizabeth played and sang just one song she was sure Darcy would enjoy.

Tuesday: Dinner at the Winston's

After breakfast on Tuesday Elizabeth took Jane for a tour of the rest of the house they had not visited earlier, including the ballroom and the kitchen, where they both thanked the kitchen staff for their holiday efforts. In the portrait gallery they lingered, walking and puzzling over one visage after another, particularly examining those of Darcy and Georgiana, the only persons they knew.

They looked out the windows, longing for a sunny day that would permit a pleasant walk in the gardens. Elizabeth considered telling Jane about the tag incident, but decided to wait for a more leisurely occasion. Instead she asked for news about Longbourn and Meryton residents and listened to Jane's responses.

This was the day of the invitation to dinner at the home of the Winstons. Elizabeth was only too happy to enjoy an elegant dinner in the home of friends, with hostess responsibilities in the hands of another. Jane seemed at least as eager, and Bingley and Darcy, enjoying each other's company, readily fell into the spirit of a gathering of congenial company.

The trip to Sir Humphrey's was ten miles, but the weather tolerable for this time of year. Nevertheless, they allowed plenty of time, remembering Sir Humphrey's injunction not to be late.

On roads new to them Jane and Elizabeth observed the scenery attentively. Bingley had spent his youth in the north of England and had seen a great deal of these parts over the years, so his interest was more casual. Elizabeth thought Darcy seemed more interested in observing the herds and flocks they passed and the dwellings and grounds.

At last they arrived at Sir Humphrey's estate. The butler took them into the drawing room where they were warmly greeted by Sir Humphrey and his mother. To their surprise, another couple was present to enjoy the festivities as well—Carleton and his wife Theresa. Introductions were made all round, and to all appearances, a pleasant evening lay before them.

Sir Humphrey explained that he and Carleton had been very lucky hunting the day before. The decision was made to enjoy the birds the following evening with the Darcys and Bingleys who had been invited earlier. All delighted in the happy coincidence.

Sir Humphrey was seated at one end of the table, his mother at the other. Darcy and Elizabeth flanked Mrs. Winston, with Carleton next to Elizabeth.

Dinner was fine, and the conversation enjoyable, though Mrs. Winston seemed to occupy her thoughts more with the smooth progress of the dinner and the convenience of her guests than with attempting much to engage in conversation. Nevertheless she obviously enjoyed the happy combination of guests and seemed well pleased with the success of the event.

They had been discussing various other enjoyable gatherings of the recent past, including anecdotes and bits of politics. Theresa had not said a great deal, but when they all were recovering from laughter over a particularly enjoyable political anecdote Sir Humphrey had related, Theresa said, "I have noticed in various groups, regardless of the topic of conversation or the persons present, that when I make a statement the response is much more likely to be one of opposition than support."

Mr. Winston immediately responded, "I think you're right!"

General laughter engulfed the group.

Mrs. Winston had not heard the exchange, but with such general merriment, insisted that Theresa repeat her statement.

Immediately she finished, Mrs. Winston replied, "Why, I don't agree with that at all."

This brought fresh gales of laughter.

Carleton smiled at his wife and said, "So, my dear, you have here both refutation and proof of your contention."

The laughter subsided, and, in an effort to become better acquainted, Elizabeth said, "Tell me about your family, Mr. Carleton." Before he could answer, Darcy interrupted in a voice rather louder than usual, "Elizabeth, would you please pass me the butter; I need a tag more." He emphasized the word "tag."

Thinking that she might be facing a bit of local vernacular, Elizabeth asked, "You mean "tad," don't you?"

"No," he replied, looking at her intently, "I mean 'tag.'"

Passing the butter to him, it struck Elizabeth that he must be referring to her "tag" fiasco.

Mrs. Winston and Carleton seemed as perplexed as Elizabeth was, but as Darcy launched into a new line of conversation with Carleton, it occurred to her that she might be enmeshing herself in a new brouhaha on the order of the "game of tag" incident—that her question to Carleton might actually have been a path to a quagmire.

That settled in her mind, her attention once more focused on the conversation.

They did discover one bit of news: the Carletons were to be in London also in early January. Darcy and Elizabeth agreed to meet them at the Carletons' hotel for supper on the evening of their arrival.

The rest of the engagement passed very agreeably and without incident, including the ride home.

That evening in their bedroom after Annie and Bradford had gone, Darcy took Elizabeth loosely in his arms and said, "Lizzy, Lizzy. You almost got yourself into a very tricky business this evening."

"What do you mean?"

"I mean by asking Carleton to tell you about his family. You do not ask about a person's family unless you know them. Carleton had a sister who ran away some years ago. They haven't heard from her since. If they have something to report, they will. Until they do, we say nothing. Carleton is a good friend and I don't want to offend him."

"Why didn't you warn me?"

"I didn't expect him to be there. Besides, there are a great many skeletons in the closets of any community. You can't possibly expect me to warn you about all of them."

Elizabeth reflected, remembering Lydia and Wickham's elopement.

"Would you like someone to ask that question of you? If someone did ask, what would you say about Lydia? Even if his only sibling had been James, would you have felt comfortable with him explaining how his brother died of a fatal fever and that due to his death Carleton has become inheritor?"

"I see," she said, chastened. "I hadn't thought of it that way."

"You always lived at Longbourn, and over a lifetime learned who had difficulties, as I have lived and learned here in Derbyshire. I'm afraid my interference was a bit crude, but it was the only thing I could think of at the time to keep you from unpleasantness."

"Yes, Mr. Carleton and Mrs. Winston looked even more puzzled than I felt. Oh, Darcy, I am sorry; will you forgive me?"

"Of course; not that there's a great deal to forgive. I just want people to love you as I do."

"I'm afraid that is not at all likely," she said archly.

"You know what I mean. I know you wouldn't knowingly offend anyone, but I don't want little slip-ups to diminish you in their regard in any way."

"It seems there is a great deal for me to learn as mistress of Pemberley."

"People who live in very fine houses are expected, perhaps, to be more perfect than is possible. We're not going to let things like this destroy our happiness. However, we might be able to arrange a more subtle cue. We wouldn't want people to think of us as that mad couple from Pemberley who are continually making unintelligible remarks." At this, they dissolved into chuckles, hugging each other.

Wednesday

The Bingleys left on Wednesday morning. The gray, chill character of the weather reflected their moods at parting. Bingley and Darcy seemed quieter, more accepting of the separation, but Jane and Elizabeth couldn't completely stifle the tears. Only the prospect that they would return for the February ball relieved the sadness of the departure.

Elizabeth and Darcy returned to the house, shivering. Before they could even be seated in the morning room, Elizabeth was quizzing Darcy about invitations for the ball.

"If the ball were scheduled for Friday, February 24, the invitations should go out by the third of February. You said we might be inviting as many as 60 persons."

"Yes, I've started on the list. It's 40 already, and I haven't finished it yet. It could be as many as 60."

"That would be a great many invitations for me to write by hand. Do you think we could have them printed?"

"Certainly."

"Then our next problem is, Who should print them?"

"There's a printer in Gormley."

"Should I write to him?"

"I propose an outing...tomorrow. Woodbury tells me there's a family near there that has a horse we should look at for Georgiana; not too promising, but a possibility."

"Might we also stop at the Pettigrews, as well?"

"Certainly."

"Perhaps Mr. Harrison will be visiting there."

He approached her chair from his post by the fireplace and gently kissed her. "I can see our thoughts are beginning to follow the same paths. I doubt that Harrison would be a suitable partner for Georgiana, but meeting so few people she has little basis for comparison."

Elizabeth proceeded to compose an invitation. Completed, she handed it to Darcy. He read it twice, trying to find things to correct or change.

"I wonder if Saturday night might be better. In the summer there's no problem because all the young men are home from schools and colleges. But during the winter, a Saturday night might make it easier for some of them to attend."

"But think of all the weary people trying to wake up for church the next morning."

"Perhaps you're right. But if we have a second ball the following year, I think it should be in the summer."

"Exactly what Jane said when she saw the terrace next to the ballroom!"

"Friday it is then—this time."

Georgiana had just come in from her morning at the piano, and they explained the pros and cons of timing for balls.

"Georgiana," Elizabeth said. "We're planning an outing tomorrow with several purposes, and we'd like you to accompany us.

"Of course."

"But we didn't say where we're going."

"Wherever it is, I want to go."

"You do have an adventurous spirit!"

"I've always been that way. When I was little, whenever the carriage was hitched up I wanted to go along."

"It's true. On those rare occasions when we had to leave her at home she would cry bitterly," Darcy said.

"Aren't you curious about where we're going?"

"I'd be happy to know."

"There's a horse we'd like to look at."

"Excellent."

"Actually we don't expect it to be suitable, but sometimes it's necessary to look, anyway."

"Then I won't get my hopes up."

"Then we're going to the print shop in Gormley about ball invitations," Elizabeth added.

"I see."

"And as long as we're that far, we're going to stop at the Pettigrew's, the people we bought the horse from."

"The couple we met at the assembly."

"Yes."

"It should be a pleasant outing."

Darcy took this as his cue and said, "Agreed. Now I must attend to some correspondence," and he left.

Elizabeth went to find Mrs. Reynolds to begin making more specific plans for the ball.

After breakfast the next morning, the carriage was waiting for the threesome. The sun failed to break through the clouds, but at least there was no rain.

The horse proved unsuitable, as feared: too old, not lively enough. But the owners were interesting: conversation revealed that the Waterfords, a couple of perhaps 50 years, had a son who had just left to apprentice as a sailor, an older son who had preceded him, and a married daughter living nearby.

Regrets were expressed, and the Darcy's departed with thanks for being allowed to see the horse.

The visit to the print shop was more successful. Yes, he could do the job. The invitations would be finished easily by January 16th. Suitable paper and typeface were selected, and the order was completed.

By the time they arrived at the Pettigrews it was eleven-thirty. They were invited to tea and chatted very enjoyably. They were told of the date for the ball and assured they would receive an invitation.

"Perhaps even Harrison will be able to attend," Elizabeth ventured.

"We'll certainly let him know. It is easier sometimes to get away from school for a day or two than at others."

Friday and Saturday were spent packing and planning for the trip to London. Mrs. Jones was expecting them at Darcy's townhouse in London late in the afternoon Wednesday. They would stay overnight at an inn along the way on Tuesday night.

They went to church on Sunday, New Year's Day, but once home, Elizabeth had difficulty remembering what had transpired. She kept remembering their Christmas festivities and thinking ahead to the week in London and preparations for the ball. "What am I forgetting?" was the question that kept running through her mind.

January 2, Monday

Monday after breakfast she met with Mrs. Reynolds and Mrs. Sims together, going over the menu, accommodations for overnight guests to the ball. Then she remembered. "The music, that's what I forgot."

Once they had settled on what Sims and Mrs. Reynolds could do while they were in London, she went directly to Darcy in his study. "Darcy, my love, guess what we forgot!"

"I've no idea."

"The orchestra...music for the ball."

"Of course; how foolish of me. Well, that's easily remedied. I'll send a note to Sir Humphrey. He attends every assembly for miles around; he'll know exactly how we should proceed. I'll tell him to send me a note here, and that we'll return at least by January 16th. We'll act on his recommendations immediately upon our return."

"You make it sound so simple." Then, turning her attention to the papers spread out on his desk, she asked, "What's all this?"

"I've been doing a little research."

"About what?"

He rose and closed the door. Then he propelled her to a chair.

"You remember that you said you didn't want babies right away."

"Yes," she said, coloring slightly.

"Do you remember the day you came in here and I was looking for scholarship possibilities for Flanders?"

"Yes."

"Well, somehow an envelope of papers that had belonged to my father got mixed up in that stack of papers from college, and I found it that day. I set it aside to look at it later. Since then we've been so busy that I haven't had a chance to look at them until today."

"And what are they?"

"Most of them are clearly useless, and I've been discarding them, but here is one that is very curious."

"It's dated 1776—that's 38 years ago."

"Yes, amazing isn't it that father should have kept in his papers a handbill that was 32 years old when he died. See how the paper is discolored and the edges are frayed."

"'Implements of safety for sale that will secure the health of its users.' Whatever can it mean?"

"I don't know, but I'm going to try to find out."

"How strange to be distributing health information in a handbill. Are there other papers in the envelope that old?"

"Nowhere near it. Here's one for 1799. It was nine years old at Father's death. This health flyer is 23 years older than any other paper in the envelope."

"Strange...but I must get busy packing for our trip to London." She stood up, bent over, and placed her hands on both sides of his head and kissed him, slowly, deliberately.

"Maybe I'll go and pack now too."

"You will not. You will clean up this mess...and solve the mystery!"

Tuesday: London Trip

Georgiana joined Elizabeth and Darcy the next morning, packed, dressed, and ready for the trip. Blankets were stowed in the carriage, and by nine o'clock they were on their way. The morning was not only cold, but heavily overcast. Just past midday they reached a suitable inn for dinner. Their food ordered, the conversation spilled forth after a morning of riding in the carriage. The subdued spirits that had lingered since their Christmas guests departed were dissipated. Elizabeth in particular enjoyed examining the interior of the dining room, observing discreetly the patrons of this country inn.

Elizabeth queried Darcy on how he intended to spend the mornings of Thursday and Friday while they were at the dressmaker's and the milliner's.

"I plan to go to the library at the British Museum Thursday."

"You won't forget to get theatre tickets."

"Not a chance. I expect the Carleton's will want to go with us."

"And a concert, perhaps?"

"That should present no difficulty."

"An operetta?" Georgiana queried.

"If you like."

"I'd enjoy visiting some art galleries," Elizabeth said.

"Then I suggest we go Saturday. And the Tower of London?"

She nodded her assent, her eyes dancing.

"Georgiana?"

"It sounds perfect to me."

"What will we do about meals?" Elizabeth asked.

"Mrs. Jones provides a very creditable breakfast, but usually I prefer to take dinner at a restaurant."

Georgiana and Elizabeth exchanged glances. "That sounds delightful," Elizabeth responded.

"As for supper, it will depend on how we plan to spend the evening. Mrs. Jones can prepare something for us if we want to take supper at home."

They returned to the carriage and a rapid ride to their overnight stay.

Georgiana's room was next to theirs and, once settled, they rapped at her door and took her to supper with them in the Inn dining room. They conversed quietly after supper for awhile, but the day had been tiring, and they returned early to their rooms. They agreed that Darcy and Elizabeth would knock on Georgiana's door at eight o'clock to go to breakfast.

The door closed, Darcy took Elizabeth in his arms and held her, rubbing her back. "It's only about 5 weeks since we were in a similar situation."

"But how different it seems. I love you, Darcy."

"I know. Almost as much as I love you."

"Is it a contest?"

"If it is, I'll surely win, unless you cheat, of course."

"I suppose when I'm seventy years old, you'll be reminding me of how I cheated at a game of tag."

"I hope to have such a good memory at that age," he said, releasing her. "Last one in bed has to snuff the candles."

"Unbutton me then."

"I'm sure you can do that yourself," he said, busily unbuttoning his vest."

She took off her shoes and removed her stockings and hair pins as she said, "If you don't unbutton me, I shall forever accuse you of cheating."

"Oh, all right," he said. He unbuttoned her dress and petticoat and quickly resumed undressing.

She struggled with the rest of her clothes, but he did win, and he slid under the covers. He flung those on her side back for her. She snuffed all the candles but one and jumped into bed beside him.

"I hope these are nice thick walls," she whispered.

"If they aren't, Georgiana is no longer going to suspect we are in love. She is going to be certain of it."

She snuggled up to him, and they proceeded to warm each other physically and mentally.

Darcy, her lover, her husband, warm, funny Darcy, kissing her, loving her, imperfect and yet perfect, returning her affection with play, humor, inventiveness; challenging her to love him and leading her to do so, emotionally, physically, in every way until the mutuality was complete and their beings exhausted.

They untangled their bodies and lay relaxing in the dimly-lit, unfamiliar room.

At length Darcy broke the silence, "You know, Elizabeth, that if I say I will do something, you can depend on it."

"Yes, I know."

"Well, I promised I would never reveal to anyone anything about our intimacies."

"Yes."

"Now I'm going to ask you to modify that agreement. But whatever you decide will rule."

She withdrew a bit and asked, "What do you mean?"

"I mean that I intend to learn what I can to see if there's any way we can have babies only when we want them."

"How can we do that?"

"That is the question. We don't know, and if we don't ask questions, we may never find out."

"I see. What do you propose?"

"First, I'm going to the library at the British Museum. I'm not hopeful of learning any more there than I could from my own library, which, I assure you, I have thoroughly searched. Then I'm going to go to bookstores, and possibly even to the University. But I think I should inquire among a few friends as well. Not all knowledge is in books."

"Who would you ask?"

"That's the problem, and that's where I expect your objection. I want to ask some of my closest friends."

"Who?"

"Bingley, Sir Humphrey, and Fitzwilliam to begin with."

She withdrew and lay on her back, holding the covers up to her chin. At length she said, "You're right; it does make me feel uncomfortable. But what would you say?"

"I could say that I'd like to delay having children."

"Would they believe you?"

"I doubt it. I can just hear them: 'You, Darcy? Delaying children? That huge house and all your money? you're 28 years old; what are you waiting for—old age?'"

"I see; and if you tell them it's me, they'll think I'm selfish and heartless, an unworthy wife for such a fine husband. They'll wonder what I'm waiting for? I'm older than most women when they have their first child." She reflected for a few minutes. "Can I think about this for awhile?"

"Of course, but there's a possibility of seeing Fitzwilliam while we're in town, and it's the kind of thing I wouldn't trust to a letter. When he comes for the ball, we probably won't have a minute alone. I could arrange to see him in London. Soldiers have such a different life from the rest of us. They're likely to encounter things we don't."

She snuggled up to him again, and he kissed her forehead.

They lay awake this night much longer than usual. Elizabeth heard the lobby clock chime midnight before she fell asleep.

Daylight and purpose enlivened all three travelers. Prompt at table, they climbed into the carriage before nine.

Elizabeth had a great deal to think about during the day and took advantage of the opportunity. Georgiana had traveled this route several times over the years, but did not tire of it. Going through villages she looked closely at the people, and in the countryside she scanned the fields for birds and small game, anything moving, creating variety in the passing scene. She seemed oblivious to Elizabeth's detachment.

They arrived at the townhouse before four o'clock. Darcy introduced Elizabeth to Mrs. Jones and asked for tea. Georgiana showed Elizabeth their room while Darcy went out for a newspaper. As they enjoyed tea, they scanned the newspaper for entertainment ideas.

Darcy was content to read, but after such a long trip, Georgiana and Elizabeth decided to rest in their bedrooms before dressing to meet the Carletons.

Darcy rapped on Georgiana's door at seven and found her ready for the evening. He roused Elizabeth from her nap, refreshed, and they prepared for their departure.

The coachmen had supped with Mrs. Jones and now took the threesome to the Carleton's hotel, where Darcy directed them to return by eleven. The Carleton's were waiting for them in the hotel lobby, and they proceeded to the hotel dining room.

During a pleasant meal, they decided which entertainments they would try to get tickets for and that the Darcys would call for the Carletons the next evening at their hotel. The Carletons had come into town the preceding week and had already seen a number of people they knew. When invited by the Campbells to a ball on Saturday night, they told the hostess the Darcys would be in town as well. Mrs. Campbell said she would send an invitation to Darcy's townhome.

Thursday

Mrs. Jones served them a substantial breakfast, and Darcy left immediately for the British Museum. While waiting for the carriage to return to take them to their appointment with the dressmaker Georgiana showed Elizabeth around the rest of the house.

At the dressmaker's, Elizabeth and Georgiana viewed the styles and fabrics and made their selections and decisions on alterations to the design. They were led to separate rooms where measurements were taken. Statements for garments ordered were then prepared, with their prices. Appointments were made for the first fitting on the following Tuesday and the second on Thursday.

Elizabeth was shocked when she saw the final bill and decided to show it to Darcy immediately in case it would be necessary to cancel any of the items.

The morning's task completed, they found a tearoom in the neighborhood. Following a leisurely chat, the waiting carriage took them to a nearby park. There they strolled until it was time to meet Darcy at three for dinner at the restaurant he had selected. When they arrived Darcy was already enjoying a glass of wine.

Their order taken, Darcy asked about their foray into the world of fashion. Elizabeth showed him the dressmaker's statement. He handed it back to her without comment, and she waited, staring at him. Puzzled, he looked at Georgiana for help.

"Oh," he said; "I see; I'm supposed to say that's a great bargain. My dear, you obviously have had a very successful morning; I'm very proud of you. But you'll never match the success of the gold velvet dress!"

Content with the ladies amused response, Darcy changed the subject. "I did get tickets for the Carleton's and us for the theatre for tonight. Also for a concert tomorrow night. Then there's the ball Saturday night."

"Thank you, Darcy," Georgiana said.

From Pemberley Darcy had arranged an appointment with a portrait artist for Elizabeth. Their dinner finished, they left in their carriage for the first appointment. There they discussed with the artist—the same one who had painted Georgiana's portrait only a year earlier—what they would like the portrait to be: Elizabeth in her wedding dress, standing, the portrait intended to be a mate for Darcy's own full-length portrait. Further appointments for following days set, they turned their attention to the evening and theatre with the Carleton's.

Friday

On Friday Darcy again left early, the carriage returning to take the ladies to their appointment at the milliner's and afterward to the restaurant Darcy had selected.

They had brought snippets of fabric from the dressmaker and they needed few bonnets so their visit to the milliner's was uncomplicated. That appointment complete, the coach took them to the artist's studio for Elizabeth's first sitting, a misnomer since she would have to stand. Fortunately, Georgiana had brought a book and read while occasionally noting the artist's sketching.

When they arrived at the restaurant and were seated with Darcy, who had arrived before them, Elizabeth showed him the bill for the hats.

"Outrageous, simply outrageous." Their response gave him no assistance, and he said, "I know that if I just keep trying, I'm going to get this game right."

Their food came, and they savored it along with the views of the other diners.

"With so many people on all sides, one would expect eventually to encounter a familiar face," Georgiana mused.

"Oh, we will; I've frequented the same restaurants for some time, as have a number of my acquaintants, and I do indeed see people I know on occasion."

They returned to the townhouse, read the day's newspaper and relaxed and chatted until it was time to prepare for supper and the theatre.

The evening with the Carleton's was enjoyable, lacking only one thing: no handsome, suitably rich young men attractive to Georgiana were encountered.

At supper the conversation had been revolving about occasions visiting friends when Theresa began telling a story: "It started with a game—someone chose the name of a book, a song, or a play, and the others had to guess what the name was. A dispute arose between a husband and wife. As they kept arguing, the others listening, they revealed more and more details about their spouses. It all got more and more embar..."

At this, Carleton broke in impatiently, saying, "What is the point, dear?"

"Well, it just suddenly struck me: ordinarily, we get acquainted with people a little at a time, rather like removing the layers of an onion. But as they argued, the image of a knife slicing through an onion popped into my head, revealing all the layers at once. I even thought I felt the onion juices stinging my eyes."

Silence ruled as everyone reflected on her story. At length Elizabeth said, "I see I shall have to be very cautious in revealing myself to you. I wouldn't want to make you cry."

"Mrs. Carleton does like to tell stories," Carleton said. "And you, Miss Darcy, do you like to relate anecdotes?"

"I'm afraid very little happens in a girl's school. Maybe by next year I'll have more to say."

Now Darcy, looking at Elizabeth, said, "And we shall have to be very careful not to supply her with amusing stories."

Home again, Georgiana retired for the night after a brief review of the evening.

Alone with Darcy, Elizabeth said, "Darcy, I've been thinking about what you said—that if we're going to learn anything, that we should take someone into our confidence."

"Yes?"

"I think you're right. But I don't think you should talk with Sir Humphrey. He never had children, though he may have wanted them, and he might not be sympathetic. Besides—he's so sociable, even teasing, I don't feel I could trust him to keep a confidence. And Bingley...well, I think you can be sure he'd tell Jane."

"Would that be so bad?"

"Perhaps not, but they're both so accepting of what life offers them, I doubt if they'd be much help. I once teased Jane about having ten children, and she didn't protest.

"And, remember the way he accepted your arguments against Jane. Despite his feelings for her, he was all too willing to give her up. No, I'm afraid we'll have to confide in Fitzwilliam. I can't imagine that he would disclose a confidence that could expose me to censure. And, I think you're right about the military life; they go more places and have opportunities for information that most of us do not. But, if you do talk with him, you must make it plain that I do want babies, but just not right now. I feel sure he'd accept that."

"This hasn't been easy for you, has it?"

"I've barely been able to think of anything else since you suggested it. You do promise me that you won't write about it, won't you...that you'll arrange to see him?"

"Yes, I promise. His unit is encamped at Portsmouth. I'll write to him in the morning, asking if he can meet me in London next week. He can stay here; there's plenty of room. I'll search the bookstores Monday, but I'm not hopeful."

After some quiet moments Darcy said, "I'm not ready to give up this search, but I confess I don't completely understand your reluctance to have a child soon. You seem determined, though I don't see why."

"It isn't entirely a matter of having a child immediately, though that's an important part of it. It's also a matter of how many children we will have. I'm young. We could easily have 10 children. It's not unheard of. One of our neighbors in Meryton had eleven. How many children do we really want? Five children were a handful for my parents."

"But they didn't have the resources we do."

"But what are our resources? Do you have a Pemberley for more than one son? Do you have fortunes for several daughters, even half as large as Georgiania's? For eight? Or 10? You haven't spoken with high regard for military careers. Where would you direct several sons?"

They reflected on her comments for several minutes. In a lighter vein Elizabeth continued, "There is another matter. I'm quite confident the gown they are making for me for the ball will be suitable. But if you would come to see it, I should rest easy that it will be truly appropriate. I'd like you to come Tuesday with me to the dressmaker's to see what you think."

"That sounds reasonable, except that I probably won't be of much help. Nevertheless, if you want me, I'll be there."

Saturday

Darcy awakened early the next morning and wrote to Fitzwilliam. He offered the note to Elizabeth when she awoke.

"My Dear Fitzwilliam,

I have a matter of some importance that I'd like to discuss with you. While not extremely urgent in character, an early meeting would be most advantageous. We will be in London until late next week. Might you be able to meet with me in London on Wednesday? Or perhaps you could find an hour to see me Wednesday in Portsmouth, where I could travel to meet you.

Please reply by return messenger.
Faithfully yours,
F. Darcy"

Elizabeth returned the letter to Darcy, saying, "If you are to see Fitzwilliam on Wednesday, Georgiana and I will be alone."

"Yes, but for just one day I dare say you could find ways to amuse yourselves."

"That might be a good day to call on Aunt Gardner. I'll send a note to her today that that is my intention."

"Excellent."

The threesome sought out some art galleries as planned, a special treat for Elizabeth, but enjoyed as well by Darcy and Georgiana who, having made such outings before, followed Elizabeth's lead, learning from her comments and offering theirs.

They enjoyed a substantial tea at seven, uncertain what refreshments might be offered at the Campbell's ball.

"Yes," Darcy said, "I'm well acquainted with the Campbells, but I have never attended a ball arranged by them. They have a daughter I saw on more than one occasion when we all attended the same social events."

"One of the possible Mrs. Darcys?" Elizabeth asked.

"Some may have considered the possibility though I never did."

"And do they have any sons?"

"It's possible. Sons are often off somewhere—college, trips, and so forth."

On Friday evening Elizabeth entered Georgiana's bedroom when it was nearly time for the ball. Elizabeth helped her arrange her hair and noted with approval her choice of gown for the evening.

"Perhaps there will be some attractive young men at the ball this evening." Elizabeth said.

"Yes, I suppose so."

"You don't seem very interested."

"It's not that. It's just that beginnings always seem so promising, but then it ends...rather like playing the first bar or two of each piece in a music book and then having to go on to the next without completing any one of them. No resolution, no sense of completion or accomplishment."

"That seems rather dreary. We'll see what we can do to improve that situation."

"I'm not so sure that doing anything would help...and it might make matters worse."

"Well, at least the music will be enjoyable this evening, and I don't expect you'll lack partners."

"I rarely do."

As they met Darcy in the sitting room he looked impressive, and Elizabeth basked in Darcy's approving response to her appearance.

The music was floating out of the ballroom already when they arrived, and Darcy was soon engaged by people who approached one after another to greet him and his sister and to meet his bride.

Georgiana did not have to wait long for a partner, and indeed danced most of the dances during the evening.

Elizabeth also had partners, the first being Mr. Campbell, who reminded her of Sir Humphrey. When he swept her off with him, Darcy asked their daughter Ellen to dance.

Mr. Campbell was a good dancer and conversationalist as well, but far from the handsomest man in the room. For Elizabeth, that was Darcy, and she made sure he danced two dances with her during the course of the evening.

A Mr. Grace also asked Elizabeth to dance and proved an acceptable dancer as well. It occurred to her that the less attractive the man, the more likely he was to be a good dancer...excepting Darcy, of course.

At home following the dance, Elizabeth queried, "Georgiana, who was that young man you danced the third dance with?

Georgiana smiled and slowly, teasingly, doled out her reply, "Well...he is James Price...and...he is a student at Cambridge...visiting his parents here in London for the weekend."

Elizabeth and Darcy waited for more details as Georgiana sipped her hot chocolate, but none came.

"I believe you sat out the fourth dance with him also."

"Yes."

"Are you going to keep us in suspense? Surely you learned his whole life's story during that dance."

"Well, he is quite a talker, but hardly his whole life. Mainly he talked about his plan to become an engineer or perhaps an astronomer."

"Astronomer?" Darcy repeated.

"Yes, he's very interested in lenses and telescopes; microscopes too." She paused and then asked, "What is a microscope?"

"Well, they're for looking at very small things—makes them look larger and easier to see."

"But did he tell you about his parents?" Elizabeth probed.

"Not really. I think they live here in London."

Darcy intervened, "His father works in the City—financial work of some kind."

"How did you know that?" Elizabeth asked.

"I was talking with Mr. Grace, and he told me," Darcy replied.

Elizabeth now turned to Darcy and said, "You seemed to enjoy your dance with Miss Campbell."

"When Mr. Campbell engaged you for that dance I had the choice of inviting Mrs. Campbell or her daughter. I suppose you could say I made the less gallant choice."

"I noticed her more than once searching the dance floor as if she were looking for someone else."

"Really? I was so busy looking for you that I didn't notice."

"Now you are being gallant."

"Perhaps it's time I was."

Sunday: London Sightseeing

Sunday might be expected to be a more leisurely day, but all had agreed they should go to St. Paul's for Sunday services. The music resonates in such a large stone sanctuary with arresting beauty, so, not wanting to miss it, they were up early, breakfasted, and present for services.

The afternoon they spent at the Tower of London, wandering through the complex of structures. Upon their return, they found a message from Fitzwilliam saying that he would come to London on Wednesday and would stay that night at the officer's club. He invited Darcy to take supper with him there.

Darcy in turn sent a message to Fitzwilliam at the club that he would meet him as suggested.

Immediately after Colonel Fitzwilliam's message came, Elizabeth sent a message to Aunt Gardner that she intended to call on her on Wednesday. By return message the Gardners invited her and Georgiana to supper on Wednesday, expressing regret that Darcy would not be able to join them.

Monday was to be the last day for Darcy at the British Museum and Library. Elizabeth and Georgiana went first to Elizabeth's appointment with the artist and then went also to the British Museum where they browsed the museum, viewing the sculptures and examining rare manuscripts before joining Darcy at the carriage as arranged.

That afternoon they were guests of the Findleys for dinner, but, in private moments, could not learn that any young men had been particularly attentive to Georgiana during her stay with them in early December though she never seemed to lack dance partners.

Tuesday Darcy went with Elizabeth and Georgiana to the dressmaker and gave his approval to the ball gown choice.

"You didn't seem very enthusiastic about the ball gown," Elizabeth commented later when they were in the carriage.

"Well, it's a bit difficult to say, with the pieces barely hanging together and your hair straggling," he said, stifling a grin. "I'm sure it will be just fine."

Elizabeth was not entirely satisfied, but decided she would get no better response until it was in fact completed, by which time it would be too late to do anything to remedy the situation should it prove a disappointment.

He left the ladies at the artist's studio and set out to search through book shops, not especially hopeful, but still determined.

Wednesday Darcy left to search through more book shops and then to see Fitzwilliam. Georgiana and Elizabeth went again to the artist's studio, investigated shops for accessories and gifts, then returned home to refresh themselves before leaving for the Gardner's. When they arrived, the Gardner children were waiting for them for a brief visit before they were sent to bed, and the adults sat down to enjoy their supper.

Georgiana and Elizabeth returned home after a pleasant evening and were barely settled to read when Darcy arrived from his supper with Fitzwilliam. "I took the liberty of inviting Fitzwilliam to breakfast tomorrow morning before he returns to Portsmouth."

"I'm so glad," said Elizabeth, as she rose to tell Mrs. Jones.

"I've already alerted Mrs. Jones," said Darcy, divining her purpose.

She sat down again and asked, "Is he well?"

"Very well."

"Why did he come into London for such a brief stay?" Georgiana asked.

"Some business he had to conduct in person," Darcy replied.

Alone together in their bedroom, Elizabeth asked pointedly, "Well?"

"He wasn't sure what the handbill meant, but he did have one interesting comment. He said Napoleon distributed to his troops some things called "condoms." They are used to prevent transmission of disease, but also resulted in fewer pregnancies."

"But...what exactly are they?"

"It seems they are a kind of sheath for the penis and are made from sheep's gut."

Elizabeth's countenance revealed disbelief and disgust.

Darcy sat down beside her on the chaise, put his arm around her, and said, "What were you expecting?"

"I don't know. I didn't really have any idea; but sheep's gut—it sounds so repulsive."

"Do you know how sausages are made?"

"Yes, but I don't spend a lot of time thinking about it."

"And if we gain some knowledge on the current topic under discussion, and do the right things, we may not have to spend a lot of time thinking about it either." He paused, waiting for some response, but she just seemed to be puzzling over the newly acquired information. "We could drop the subject, if you're no longer interested."

"Oh, no, Darcy. I'm interested. And I don't mean to seem uncooperative. It just takes a bit of getting used to."

"Anyway, Fitzwilliam agreed to make a few discreet inquiries. If he learns anything that he can safely convey to me by letter he will. Otherwise I'll talk with him when he comes to the ball."

"And did he say anything about me...critical, I mean?"

"Not at all. Not even any questions. He acted as if my request was entirely understandable."

"Thank you, Darcy. I love you."

"And I love you."

Later they embraced as they lay in bed contemplating the possibility that seemed to lie before them.

Thursday : Fitzwilliam

Morning found them awake early and ready for Fitzwilliam when he arrived for breakfast.

"Two of my loveliest lady friends," Fitzwilliam said as he was admitted.

"Welcome, Colonel Fitzwilliam," Elizabeth said.

"Good morning, Cousin Fitz," Georgiana said.

"Good morning, Georgie," he replied, kissing her forehead.

They sat down to breakfast, and Fitzwilliam asked, "So how have you been enjoying your stay in town?"

Elizabeth and Georgiana alternated in spilling out the week's activities with obvious glee.

"Well, Darcy, I feel quite envious; seeing you in the company of two delightful ladies, so obviously pleased with your company and their situation altogether."

"Perhaps you'll make an extra effort then to attend our February ball."

"Yes, Colonel Fitzwilliam, it's going to be on the 24th, and we do so want you there with us," Georgiana added.

"Only a breakout of war will keep me away!"

After Fitzwilliam departed, they first drove to a book store where they left Darcy, and the ladies continued to their dressmaker, milliner's, and portrait appointments. They met Darcy at the appointed restaurant, Darcy again arriving first.

While being seated, Elizabeth recognized the young man from the ball—James Price, seated at another table. Georgiana was seated with her back to that party, and during the dinner Elizabeth noted several times that Mr. Price was glancing towards Georgiana. As the Prices were leaving, they stopped at the Darcy's table, and Mr. Price introduced his parents to them. He seemed uncomfortable, but delighted to see Georgiana and expressed a hope that their paths would cross again.

"Well, finally, we did see someone we already know," Georgiana said. "But we're not likely to see them ever again."

"Perhaps the next time we're in London we could invite them to dinner," Elizabeth suggested.

"An excellent idea," Darcy agreed.

"And perhaps we could invite the Campbells as well," Georgiana offered.

"Not quite such a good idea," Darcy responded, "unless you know of some young gentleman we could invite who might enjoy Miss Campbell's company."

"I see. Well, perhaps Cousin Fitzwilliam could come. He might like her."

"I think he is already acquainted with her."

"What kind of person is she?" Elizabeth intervened.

"A very quiet young lady," Darcy responded.

"And…"

"That's all I know."

"Perhaps she thought you were a very quiet young man."

Darcy reflected on this for awhile and replied, "That's quite possible."

"I guess it's not so easy for two young people to get acquainted if both are very quiet."

Georgiana seemed to be listening very intently to this comment. Then she returned to the previous subject. "Perhaps the Pettigrews will come to London and might bring Mr. Harrison."

"Are you really ready to throw Mr. Harrison at Miss Campbell?"

Georgiana wrinkled her brow. "It does get complicated, doesn't it?"

Friday was spent seeing sights that didn't demand a whole day each. After dinner they stopped at the dressmaker's and milliner's to get the completed purchases, Darcy accompanying them to pay the bills.

At the artist's studio they viewed the work in progress and made arrangements for payment and delivery to Pemberley upon completion.

They spent a leisurely evening at home, except for the necessary packing.

The two-day trip home had its discomforts as well as pleasures the rain seeming to follow them most of the way. All three were happy to be returning to Pemberley, long Darcy's and Georgiana's home and now Elizabeth's as well.

January 16, Monday

Monday was a day of reorganizing, checking with the servants to see what had transpired while they were gone, and planning the days to come, with the coming ball always in mind.

After dinner Georgiana went to practice for awhile and Darcy and Elizabeth settled down in the drawing room. Both had been reading for some time when Darcy looked up and commented, "One of the things I was searching for in the library concerned animals, their fertility and the bearing of young."

"But people aren't animals."

"No, but there are a great many similarities, you must admit."

"Like what?"

"Eyes, ears, nose, legs...."

"Animals have 4 legs."

"Have you seen drawings of monkeys?"

"Of course."

"Other similarities include live birth, eating, and defecating."

"I think you've made your point."

"It's well known among farmers and others who raise animals that the females are only receptive to the male's advances at one time during the year."

"But people...."

"Yes, humans are different. There's the problem. Animals only conceive at one time of the year, and their young are born in the spring...when survival is most likely."

Both reflected on these things for awhile.

"But with humans, every act of..." Elizabeth began.

"...togetherness?" Darcy offered.

"Yes, togetherness. With humans every act of...togetherness...does not result in pregnancy."

"As we can readily testify. He paused and thought for awhile. I'm afraid we have a very complicated problem on our hands. We know so little of the experience of other people, and our own experience is also limited. I once heard a professor use the expression, 'the tyranny of the limited sample.' I think I'll call it the 'curse of the limited sample.'"

They were reflecting on this conversation when Georgiana came in.

"You both look so serious; is something wrong?" Georgiana asked.

"No, not at all," Darcy replied. "I was just thinking of how hard it is for the tenants to get enough help in the spring when the ewes are lambing."

"Perhaps you could ask the Flanders boy." Georgiana suggested.

"Actually, I'd already thought of that. Woodbury tells me Flanders has already agreed to help Howell. He's helped them for the past few years whenever they need him."

"Perhaps I could help."

"And you, Elizabeth, would you like to help too?"

Laughing, she replied, "No, thank you, those lambs like to be born in the early hours when I'm very fond of sleeping. That much I remember hearing father discuss about farming."

"It's very generous of you, Georgiana, but our tenants will need rather stronger assistants. I'm sure we'll find the help they need. Even I don't offer to serve as midwife for the ewes," Darcy said.

"I do feel so useless," Georgiana said.

"Perhaps Mrs. Sims will let us help one or two days in the kitchen during the days just before the ball," Elizabeth suggested.

"That may be precisely the time when they do not want to be training assistants," Darcy countered.

"Then perhaps I can go to the kitchen each morning during the coming weeks so they can train me. Then when the ball nears, I'll already be trained."

"And perhaps the scullery maid can sit in your place at table."

"That seems unfair," Georgiana argued, "Why shouldn't I be allowed to learn something just because I'm rich!"

"You're really serious, aren't you?"

"I've been trained to be serious. Why should it be such a surprise?"

"But kitchen work!"

"Why should it be so disgusting. We eat the food that comes out of that kitchen. There should be nothing disgusting about it."

Elizabeth had been listening and watching the discussion closely, but was not prepared for what came next.

Georgiana continued. "I feel like a China doll in a glass case...so confined."

Darcy's expression was of incredulity, but shortly resolved into acceptance, ready to concede. But Georgiana had become so enmeshed in her own exploding emotions that she didn't notice.

"I have a brain and hands, and I'd like to do something other than play the piano. Besides, if I can learn to play the piano, I should be capable of doing other things."

Now Darcy lost track of his own intention to agree to her plan and protested, "But you ride, and sing, and dance."

"I mean something useful," she said, almost shaking.

"Then do it."

Surprised, she looked at him and said, "Do you mean it?"

"Yes, but only one hour a day, and not on Sundays."

Georgiana had not expected to win the battle and was somewhat at a loss as to how a winner should behave. She wiped a tear from her eye as she sat down, trying to compose herself. She looked at Darcy, then at Elizabeth. "Have I been behaving badly?" she appealed.

"No, not at all. I am surprised at the passion behind your wishes, but I'd much rather you tell me than complain to one of the servants about your 'confinement.'" I had no idea you felt that way. No doubt I have had a great deal more freedom than you have, and I suppose we just take for granted that what is is what should be.

"I do hope you don't intend to hire out as a cook to one of the neighbors," he added.

"Of course not. It's not that I expect it to be great fun; I'd just like to try it."

Elizabeth looked up from her needlework and asked, "Have you decided whether you will play for us at the ball?"

"Yes, I have. There are two rather short pieces that I've chosen. I can play them for you whenever you're ready to listen."

Darcy responded, "I believe we're ready now...before you become chief assistant cook."

Tuesday arrived, the day to go to Gormley to get the announcements. At breakfast, Georgiana confirmed that she wanted to accompany Elizabeth and Darcy even though the trip was expected to be solely for the purpose of fetching the invitations, and therefore likely to be uneventful. They decided to leave at ten.

After breakfast Darcy gave the invitation list to Elizabeth, and she quickly read through it. "Miss Bingley is on the list."

"That's not a problem, is it?"

"She is certainly not one of my favorite people. Where would she stay? We already have quite a lot of guests staying at Pemberley: Colonel Fitzwilliam, Jane and Bingley, Kitty and Mary and the Gardners. And with all the ball preparations, we'll have quite enough to do without her. And would she come without the Hursts?"

"They're on the list too."

"Where do you propose they stay?"

Darcy reflected for a moment and replied, "I suggest the inn at Lambton. It's not terribly elegant, but should suffice for a couple days."

Elizabeth paused to digest this suggestion and imagine how it would be received by Miss Bingley.

"I was a guest for quite a long time at Bingley's when she was managing his household." he continued. "I'm quite indebted to her for their hospitality at Netherfield and in London as well. We should be able to manage somehow."

"You're right, of course," she said, approaching him and putting her arms around him, resting her head against his shoulder.

"She always did reveal how handsome you are when the two of you were together, you know."

"So you've told me, though I didn't feel it at the time. I shall have to be content to be elegant," she replied, "and very diplomatic, as well."

Seated at her desk, she wrote:

"Dear Miss Bingley:

Jane informs me that you've been staying in London lately, so I hope this invitation reaches you directly. Because you would be coming from rather a long distance should you decide to attend our ball, I thought I should mention that we will be happy to arrange rooms for you and the Hursts (if they also come) at the inn at Lambton. Just let us know how many and which days you will stay.

If you do come, we would be honored if you and the Hursts would also join us for dinner at two o'clock p.m. on the Saturday after the ball.

We look forward to seeing you.
Elizabeth Darcy"

Just to be sure, she showed the note to Darcy who approved, saying simply, "Excellent."

As expected, the trip to Gormley was uneventful, though they did take time to investigate the other shops. Darcy, happily, found a gun that suited him and bought it.

At dinner Darcy asked, "What are your plans for this afternoon, Elizabeth?"

"I was hoping you might go for a walk with me. It's as fine a day as I've seen since early December."

"Much as I would enjoy a walk, I have some business with Woodbury that I'm afraid cannot wait."

"Georgiana, would you care to join me?"

"I'm not so sure I like playing second fiddle."

"You would have been welcome to go along even if Darcy were coming."

"In that case, I accept with pleasure."

Wrapped in warm coats they walked for a while in silence, enjoying the fresh air, watching wispy clouds cross the sky and birds rising to fly off as they approached.

"Wouldn't it be wonderful to be able to fly?" Georgiana exclaimed.

"Not quite so wonderful to eat worms."

"How practical you are!"

"I do know what you mean, though. I've often thought myself of how carefree it looks to be able to fly. And I see what you mean about being practical, too. Even about love. I remember that every ball I went to in Hertfordshire seemed like a new possibility for meeting a suitable husband. Dancing was not just a great pleasure, it was a very serious part of finding a life partner.

"I noticed at the assembly in Gormley and at the Campbell's ball in London, you seemed to have a very different attitude about it...rather as if finding a husband is of little concern—that at the proper moment one will just appear...perhaps fall out of the sky."

"It's not that...."

Elizabeth waited, expecting more of a response, but none came.

"What, then?"

"It's just that I'm not sure I should marry."

"Why ever not?"

They walked on, but Georgiana did not offer any explanation.

"Surely you enjoy the company of young men."

"Yes, of course, well, there has not been a lot of opportunity, but that's not what I mean."

"Surely you aren't concerned about finding someone you could care for."

"I suppose I shall, but I'm afraid it might be unfair to the young man."

"Unfair! You can't be serious. A lovely young lady like you—intelligent, accomplished, and rich, as well!"

"There is something else."

"What?"

"I've read and heard people talking too. Many men—maybe all of them—want an heir, a child."

"And why should that be a problem?"

Georgiana looked away, not wanting to answer. "I don't think I can have children."

"What nonsense. Whatever makes you think that?" They had reached a bench, and they sat down. Elizabeth took Georgiana's hands in hers and, looking directly at her, said, "What makes you say such a thing?"

Georgiana looked up at her and said, "I get these pains."

"What kind of pains?"

"Quite sharp pains, or at least definite, if not sharp. Here," she said, laying her finger tips on her lower abdomen near the side, "and here," pointing to the other side.

"How long do they last?"

"Not very long, less than a minute surely; but they keep coming back."

"How often?"

"Every month...well, almost every month. At first I didn't think much about it, but after it had happened many times I started making a mark in my diary."

"How long has this been going on."

"Since I was 14; that is, I started keeping a record of it when I was about 14."

"Maybe it is just part of menstruation."

"Oh, no; it never happens then. When I started, the matron at school suggested that I keep a record in my diary. So I did, right away. But the pains happened many times before I decided I should write it down."

"How many times do you think they happened before you wrote them down?"

"Eight times, ten, maybe even 12 or 14. I really don't know. Is it important?"

"I don't think so. I just wanted to make sure it wasn't happening when you were a young child."

"Oh, no, I'm very sure of that."

"Well, I have to admit I haven't heard this kind of story before. But you have always seemed well since I've known you."

"I am well. I've always had good health. Well, almost always, anyway. I had measles and chicken pox as a child; everyone has them, I suppose; and a cold sometimes, though not every year even that."

"You have been fortunate. And I doubt very much if these pains are serious either. If they lasted longer they might be. I think you should forget entirely about the idea that you may not be able to have children. You'll probably be like a neighbor of ours in Meryton and have eleven!"

"Oh, I hope not. That would be dreadful."

"Dreadful?"

"When would one find time to go to the theatre?"

"Perhaps the servants could take care of them."

"Still, eleven seems like a lot even for servants to care for."

"Then perhaps you'll be lucky and only have five like my parents."

"That sounds better."

"All girls!"

Her face clouded up at that idea. "Having children does seem a chancy business, doesn't it? But five boys might even be worse. I noticed the Gardner boys were a very active lot."

"Yes, it's a chancy business all right. But this bench is getting cold; we'd better get back to the house before we get chilled and have some real worries about our health."

Georgiana did try her hand in the kitchen. Elizabeth went with her to talk to Mrs. Sims, assuring her that Darcy had agreed to Georgiana's "adventure" but that she was to stay each day for only an hour, and not on Sundays.

Mrs. Sims and Georgiana set a schedule, and at dinner each day Georgiana reported which vegetables she had pared, chopped or sliced, which breads she had helped shape and which seasonings she had watched Mrs. Sims add to the soups and meats.

After several days of such reports, Darcy got into the game and, if not told, would ask, "And did you peel the potatoes, Georgiana?" He had not asked such questions many times before he could see she no longer appreciated it.

Nevertheless, she continued "the duty" and arranged to help on the second and third days before the ball for three hours each morning; having already received her training, she therefore would be a help rather than a hindrance.

The day of the ball she would spend preparing herself for the ball: her hair washed and dried by her maid, nails cared for and spending the afternoon with guests to be ready to dance all the dances.

The weeks before the ball flew by, each day full of activities. The portrait had been due to arrive ten days before the ball, but days went by and, in fact, it only arrived on Tuesday, three days before the ball. Everyone watched as the servants hung the portrait in the ballroom, a temporary arrangement, since it would later be hung beside Darcy's portrait in the gallery.

February 22, Wednesday

Two days before the ball, on Wednesday, William and Farris met Colonel Fitzwilliam at the stage in Lambton. They arrived just after tea. Greetings completed all around, Darcy and Fitzwilliam went to see the dogs and horses and to renew acquaintance. Darcy also showed Fitzwilliam his new hunting gun.

Supper for the four of them and the evening following, though enjoyable, held suspense for Elizabeth more than anything else.

Alone with Darcy at last in their bedroom, Elizabeth asked, "What did he say; has he learned anything?"

"Actually yes, he has. He said he hasn't been able yet to find a supplier for the condoms in London, but believes there is one. But he was able to import some and brought them with him. He left most of them in his traveling case, but gave me just this one. We'll find a way to transfer the rest tomorrow."

"You look hesitant," Elizabeth said.

"There is just one thing."

"What is that?"

"Maybe we can't have children. I mean, maybe we simply aren't able. I know more than one couple that never had children."

"Who, for instance?"

"Sir Humphrey...and Carleton and Theresa have been married for more than two years and she still isn't pregnant, or at least not apparently so. Consider this: we've been married for almost three months and you still aren't pregnant...are you?"

"No, I'm not; at least not as far as I know."

They reflected on this discussion for a while until at last Elizabeth said, "Are you worried about not being able to have children?"

"It's a little early to be worried."

"But are you worried...early or not?"

By now he was comfortably settled in bed and took his time thinking it over. "I don't know. I've heard about women getting pregnant immediately after marriage. I guess I've always considered the possibility that pregnancy could result from the first intimacy. It's not that I think it's important to have a child right away. I guess it's just that it's important to have children eventually...eventually not being in the distant future."

"I agree. I don't want to wait indefinitely for a child either, but I'd like a little time for just the two of us together."

"And Georgiana."

A gasp of laughter escaped her. "Yes, and Georgiana. But Georgiana is really not the constant care that a baby is."

"Sometimes it feels as if she is. I worry about her."

"She's going to be fine. She's a very dear girl. She has a fine character—very like her brother—and made of stronger stuff than we suspected, as this kitchen duty is showing us."

"Yes, but I worry about her in the kitchen, preparing tea for the stable hands."

"Davy."

"Yes. I worry she'll take a fancy to some penniless lad like Davy."

"I do care about Georgiana, and I do want to discuss any problem that may arise about her, but right now I'd like to talk about us and the prospects of a baby. Have you ever really been around a baby?"

"Only Georgiana."

"But did you help care for her? Did you really spend time with her?"

"I was 10 years old when she was born. I was away most of the time at school. And when I was at home I had plenty to do: riding, fishing, lots of things."

"There. You really don't know what it is like caring for a child. But I do. I remember the Gardner children when they were infants, and others as well. An infant requires an enormous amount of care and attention."

"But the servants can take care of them—a nanny."

"Not for the first 9 months."

At this he looked at her intently.

"I'm referring to the months before birth. It's my body we're talking about. Pregnancy makes drastic changes in a woman's life, Darcy. I want some time just for the two of us—just a year. We've been lucky so far...."

"Do you think it is luck?"

"Yes, I do. And I'd just like to stretch that luck to a year."

She snuggled up to him.

"It's very important to me that you should be happy," he said softly.

"I know."

"It's late."

"Not very."

"Aren't you tired?"

"Actually, no. Most of the preparations for the ball were settled weeks ago, and with the extra help trained and working and with Georgiana in the kitchen, I had a very easy day of it today.

"Then perhaps we should try out this "modern inconvenience."

"I was hoping you'd suggest it."

Thursday after breakfast Darcy and Fitzwilliam took the horses out for a ride. Darcy found his father's old saddle in the stable loft for Fitzwilliam to use on Midnight.

Even having endured Cousin Fitzwilliam's skeptical comments about her kitchen duties, Georgiana was prompt in arriving at the kitchen at nine and continued until noon, as arranged. Then she took off her apron to join Elizabeth in the morning room. Elizabeth had spent the morning reviewing the guest list and final preparations for the ball with Mrs. Reynolds, who assured her that everything was indeed under control.

All the servants had pitched in to clean and wax the ballroom floor in January while the Darcys were in London. The windows were cleaned this week, and everything in the entire house that needed cleaning, dusting, or polishing had indeed been cleaned, dusted, or polished. The regular and extra servants were all thoroughly instructed and ready for all possibilities.

Mrs. Reynolds reassured Elizabeth, "My dear, it's going to be a great success. Don't you worry one little bit. Mrs. Sims has done parties like this many times before. She has all the help she needs. It's going to be fine."

Elizabeth began to see Mrs. Reynolds in the role she usually had performed for her mother—tending nerves. When Georgiana found her awaiting dinner in the morning room, Elizabeth started as the door opened.

"Is anything wrong?" Georgiana asked.

"No, nothing at all. I'm just trying to calm my nerves. I can assure you that this ball is something unlike anything I've ever been involved with before. I mean, I've attended balls, of course, but I've just never been hostess."

"Well, when the music begins, you'll calm down."

"The music! Oh dear. I completely forgot." Before Georgiana could ask for an explanation, Elizabeth had left the room. Elizabeth grabbed her wrap in the hall and nearly ran towards the exit to the stables. Just outside the door she almost collided with Sims, who was on his way to the kitchen.

"Oh, Mr. Sims, have you seen Mr. Darcy?"

"Yes, ma'am. He went with Colonel Fitzwilliam just now into the house."

Elizabeth thanked him as she turned and rushed to Darcy's study. Finding it empty, she ran to the billiard room and flung open the door, startling both gentlemen as they were concentrating on Darcy's next shot.

"What is it, Elizabeth?" Darcy asked.

"Darcy, I just remembered: the music for the ball."

"And what of it?"

"Did you make arrangements for it?"

"Yes, I did, as I said I would. They'll be here an hour before the ball begins."

"Oh, thank goodness. I completely forgot about it until just now as Georgiana and I were sitting waiting for dinner. You didn't say anything about it...."

"I didn't? Well, it must have slipped my mind. Sir Humphrey had his suggestions on my desk when we returned from London, and I took care of it immediately."

"Well," Fitzwilliam said, returning his stick to the rack, "The mistress of Pemberley isn't quite as calm as I had supposed."

"I'm so sorry, Darcy, Fitzwilliam; I didn't mean to interrupt. I just felt disaster descending on me and forgot everything else."

By now Darcy and Fitzwilliam had taken Elizabeth by her arms and were gently escorting her to the morning room. They removed her wrap, and left it in the hall. They had barely explained to Georgiana what the fracas was about when Selbey announced dinner.

Colonel Fitzwilliam's comments about Georgiana's culinary talents distracted Elizabeth's thoughts from the ball. Georgiana, in turn, suggested to Colonel Fitzwilliam that he really should see the play *She Stoops to Conquer* in London, which the Darcys had so recently seen and enjoyed.

"Actually, I've already seen it," he said. Portsmouth is not so far from London as Pemberley is, so I go in as often as I can manage." Turning to Elizabeth, he said, "I think this afternoon is a good time for backgammon. It should calm your nerves."

They retired to the drawing room and set up the backgammon board. Fitzwilliam taught Elizabeth as she had never played, with Darcy and Georgiana watching. The game is not difficult but demands concentration and thought. Before long she had caught on and was playing competently.

Then it was Georgiana's turn, and Fitzwilliam continued as teacher while Darcy and Elizabeth watched.

Selbey interrupted them to say that tea was ready, surprising them all that the afternoon had passed so quickly. He was just bringing the tea tray in when a commotion at the entry announced additional guests.

"It's Jane," Elizabeth exclaimed, moving toward the door. Before anyone could comment she was gone, and before Jane could get her cloak off Elizabeth was waiting to embrace her.

"Oh, Jane, I'm so glad to see you!"

"Is anything wrong?"

"Nothing at all," she replied, wiping tears from her eyes."

"Are you sure?"

"Absolutely. Kitty, Mary. I'm so glad to see you. Thank you for coming."

Their cloaks off and taken by Fenton, Kitty and Mary stood, perplexed by this flow of emotion. Elizabeth greeted each and then noticed and greeted Bingley as well. She turned around to take them with her to the drawing room and found the others in the hall awaiting the visitors.

She directed Fenton to have the footmen take the traveling cases to the bedrooms.

All the adventures of the two-day trip had to be related as they drank their tea: some rain on the way, delicious dinners at inns, and the overnight stay at an inn next door to a tavern. "That village has some very enthusiastic singers, if not admirable for the quality of their voices," Jane said.

Kitty had found it all very amusing, but Mary quite the opposite. "Music is the province of angels, and should not be so mistreated," she said.

"We did get some sleep," Bingley conceded, "and it has provided us plenty of amusement today. Nevertheless, I think we'll look for another place to stay on the way home."

"But everything is all right?" Jane queried.

"Decidedly all right," Elizabeth replied. I'm just so glad to see you all."

"Has Darcy been mistreating you?" Bingley asked.

"Certainly not. What a thing to say! And from his best friend."

"Mrs. Darcy is still recovering from a fright," Fitzwilliam explained. "She was startled this noon to discover that there just might not be any music for the ball."

"No music!" Jane exclaimed.

"There will be music," Darcy defended himself. "I had simply forgotten to tell her it was all arranged."

Now Georgiana found her voice. "We've all spent the afternoon calming her nerves by playing backgammon!"

"Calming her nerves," Jane said. "I hope you are not taking after Mama."

"Not at all," Darcy explained. "She's usually the calmest person around. "Well, almost. She is generally very calm, I assure you."

"Enough of my nerves. Let's show you to your rooms and get you settled."

Elizabeth and Georgiana went with the ladies, leaving Darcy, Bingley and Fitzwilliam to assure each other that ladies' nerves are no great problem.

Georgiana showed Kitty and Mary to the room they would be sharing, and Elizabeth took Jane to the room she and Bingley would occupy during their stay.

"Oh, Elizabeth, I'm so glad to see you," Jane said when they were alone.

"Is anything wrong?"

"Nothing at all." At this, they heard this echo of their first words upon arriving and laughed and hugged.

"Well, almost nothing. Bingley seems more determined than ever that we should find a different place to live. Caroline has spent quite a lot of time with us, and the Hursts as well. You know how it was. Caroline had managed Bingley's household for quite some time. It hasn't been easy for me to take control or responsibility or whatever you want to call it. And Mama has been only too eager to offer advice. Her ideas are not usually very helpful, and when I do take her advice she is sure to say, 'Didn't I tell you so?'"

"I think you really do need a vacation, Jane, and you've come to the right place. Mrs. Reynolds, Mrs. Sims and all the other regular servants and extra help are wonderful. We should be able to just relax and enjoy ourselves for the next several days."

"It sounds delightful."

"I was surprised that Mary decided to come. She's usually so scornful of balls."

"Oh, she didn't come for the ball. No, she intends to make very good use of your library while we're here."

"Then I'll show it to her in the morning."

"She does, however, have a very pretty dress for the ball. She will attend though I do think that you should talk to her to make sure she doesn't repeat her Netherfield performance at the piano."

"I'll talk to her as politely as I can, and still make myself perfectly clear."

"It was Mama that made certain Mary had a nice dress."

"Dear Mama."

"She can be very aggravating, but she does have our interests at heart."

"Yes, no doubt you're right. I'm not going to ask about Lydia now. I'll ask after the ball. I have enough on my mind for now. But Papa—he is well, isn't he?"

"Yes, he's well. Still spends most of his time in his study, but he is well, and he sends his love."

She mused over these comments for awhile and then said, "We'd better rejoin the others, or we'll miss supper."

Georgiana, Kitty, and Mary had arrived in the drawing room, and Darcy informed Elizabeth that Selby had already announced supper.

"Then let us go in," Elizabeth said, taking his arm. Georgiana with Fitzwilliam followed, then Jane with Bingley, and Kitty and Mary trailed.

Elizabeth seated Jane at her right and Fitzwilliam beside her; then Kitty, next to Darcy at the opposite end. On Darcy's right was Bingley, with Georgiana at his right, then Mary, also next to Elizabeth.

"In the morning, Mary, right after breakfast, I'd like to show you the library, on condition, of course, that you promise not to spend all of your visit there. We do want to visit with you and to hear what's been happening in Meryton."

By the time Mary and Elizabeth had settled this question, she could see that this was going to be one of those meals where there were constantly three conversations going at one time, and no one would ever remember anything that was said. But, everyone was enjoying themselves, and that was the important thing.

Jane remarked to Elizabeth that the food was delicious.

"You know, Jane, we wouldn't tell just anyone, but Georgiana has been helping in the kitchen for an hour each day."

"Georgiana? In the kitchen!"

"Yes, she put up quite a battle before Darcy agreed to it, but I do believe the food has been better lately. Perhaps Mrs. Sims is taking a bit more pride in her efforts. She won't stay with it indefinitely, I'm sure, but she seems to take real satisfaction in it. She worked three hours today and yesterday as well. She's not as fragile as she looks. Real character lurks behind that shy exterior."

"Amazing."

After dinner they adjourned to the music room where Elizabeth prevailed on Mary to play for them. Then Georgiana played several tunes. But when Bingley suggested that Elizabeth might favor them with a song, Darcy said, "I suggest we wait for Saturday evening for that pleasure. In fact, it might be best if we each take a book and retire to our bedrooms. It's been a long, busy day, and tomorrow promises to be even more exciting."

He met with no resistance, except that most passed up the suggestion of the books.

Already in bed when Elizabeth came from her dressing room, Darcy watched as she slipped under the quilts and nestled in. He snuffed the last candle and took her hand under the covers. They no doubt intended to say good night, but sleep overtook them first.

February 24, Friday: The Pemberley Ball

Elizabeth awoke with a start, realizing that the long-awaited day had arrived. As she sat bolt-upright, she awakened Darcy. She was ready to get out of bed, but he pulled her back.

"I should get up...the guests."

"It's barely seven o'clock. You won't see any of them before eight, more likely nine. Just relax."

She lay down again and moved into the curve of his body, closing her eyes.

"As usual, you're right."

"You planned perfectly," he said quietly, almost whispering. "The servants will take care of everything. All you have to do is let matters take their course."

She concentrated on her breathing and almost went back to sleep. She turned and looked at him. She ran her fingers over his face, feeling each feature, then ran her fingers through his mop of hair and drew near and kissed him. She turned around again and let his body surround hers. She listened for people moving in the halls, but heard nothing.

"Now you can get up if you want to" he said, turning over on his back."

"Now I don't want to."

"Are you being perverse?"

"No, just attempting humor," she said, as she rolled out of bed. She got to her dressing room and found that Annie had arrived unheard.

Dressed and ready for breakfast, as she left she told Annie, "I'll return about ten so I can bathe, and you can wash my hair,"

"Yes, ma'am."

She arrived at the dining room not long before Darcy and found he was correct. Their guests straggled in, giving her an opportunity to talk with each. Last of all, Jane and Bingley arrived about nine. Breakfast finished, she left with Mary to explore the library.

"What we usually do," she explained, "is to select a few books and bring them into the drawing room. Then later you can go again to get others. We don't want you to miss out entirely on the chance to visit with the others."

"Of course."

"And you will be there with us at the ball. I mean, not just your body, but your mind as well."

"You can rely on me."

"Thank you, Mary. Annie will help you with a bath right after dinner. We'll be gathering in the morning room before dinner, perhaps about noon. Do not, for certain, be late for dinner, which will be at 1:00 today."

"How do I find the morning room?"

"Ask Fenton. His little office is just off the entry hall. You'll see it. He always leaves the door open."

She returned to the morning room and suggested to Jane that she accept Fiona's assistance with her bath and hair.

Kitty and Georgiana were already off on a walk around the grounds. So Elizabeth retreated to the bath with a book of poems. "Something to think about while she fusses with my hair," she thought.

Not long after noon she entered the morning room and found Kitty and Georgiana in quiet conversation. Jane arrived, and they settled in for a quiet chat. One by one the others arrived, but even with all gathered, it was a quiet crowd.

Dinner also passed quietly but enjoyably.

To Jane Elizabeth said, "I'm beginning to feel as if we're in the eye of a hurricane. I've read that once the first terrible blasts of wind die down, it is deathly still before the winds begin again."

"Perhaps everyone is concerned about your nerves," Jane suggested.

The men played cards, and Georgiana, Kitty, and Mary watched, trying to learn by observing. They then left for baths and pampering. It was nearly time for tea when Aunt and Uncle Gardner arrived. Greetings made, the footmen took them to their room, and they returned to join the others.

Elizabeth began to think she had never lived through such a long day, but at last it was time to dress for the ball.

They heard the familiar tapping on the dressing room door. Annie interrupted her work with Elizabeth's hair to open the door, looked towards Mrs. Darcy and, seeing her nod, left the room.

Darcy approached Elizabeth's dressing table and stood, gazing down at her. Elizabeth searched his countenance, but could not interpret the meaning and said nothing. His attention passed to the carpet and he stared, apparently examining something.

"What's wrong, Darcy? Are you worried about something?"

"Worried, why should I be worried?"

"I can think of nothing at all, but...." Still searching his countenance, she reached out and took his hand. Still he said nothing, and slowly she stood up in front of him. She slipped her two arms loosely around his middle, eyes still fixed on his, and said, "Perhaps you're concerned that I might embarrass you tonight, that I might not do everything as perfectly as you would like?"

He placed his hands on her shoulders, and she could see the tenseness in his countenance melt into complacence. "Oh, Lizzy, why do I worry about what people will think of you? You play the piano imperfectly and they love it. You too readily reveal your thoughts, and they still love you. Why they love you is the mystery."

"Could it be possible that they like me *because* I am not perfect, because I am very much like themselves?"

He smiled and enclosed her in his arms; there they stood quietly rocking from side to side.

Presently she looked up and said, "Perhaps we should let Annie finish my hair, or I shall be a great deal less perfect than I intended!"

"Of course," he said, releasing her. He left through the hall door, and Annie returned.

When Elizabeth entered the upper hall she found Darcy, Bingley, and Jane standing at a window.

"Mrs. Darcy," Bingley said, "How lovely you look. Am I too late to ask you to dance the third with me tonight?"

"I'm afraid so," Elizabeth responded, turning to Darcy.

"The fourth, then?"

"With pleasure."

As the four walked to the head of the stairs, Darcy turned toward Jane and said, "Mrs. Bingley, since you will be the handsomest lady in the room..." Elizabeth's head turned reflexively to face him, "...save one, I must insist that you dance the fourth with me."

"How could I refuse?"

They descended the stairs to the sounds of the first guests being admitted at the front door.

Fenton approached and in a low voice said to Mr. Darcy, "The first dance is more than half finished, sir."

"Thank you, Fenton. Well, Mrs. Darcy, I believe any guests who arrive this late will have to be greeted by Fenton." Elizabeth took his arm, and they walked slowly into the ballroom. When the second dance began, they took their place at the head of the dance. As the music began, Darcy said, "I do believe this dance is my favorite."

"And judging by the others joining in, apparently many agree with you."

One might think this dance would be less tense than the first time they danced together in Hertfordshire. Elizabeth had not really wanted to dance with Darcy, but unable to quickly think of a polite way of refusing him, she had at first taunted him into conversation, then asked a number of questions that made him very uneasy indeed.

There was no need for either to instigate conversation now. After three months of marriage, they knew each other very well for such a short time.

But other forces were at work. For many of the guests this was the first occasion to meet the new mistress of Pemberley, and many Derbyshire residents felt that one of their most eligible bachelors had been spirited away by a Hertfordshire girl. This was a cause for great interest if not for personal pique. In addition, few had failed to hear the rumour that some mysterious malady had her in its grip. Perhaps it had been only a sprained ankle, but she did seem to be walking without difficulty, even soon after the incident. Her healthy appearance discounted the possibility of delicate health. Not a few would have been pleased to credit pregnancy as the cause, but that would have indicated a very early reaction to pregnancy indeed, hardly likely in the case of Fitzwilliam Darcy's wife.

A year earlier in Hertfordshire many had noticed Darcy and Elizabeth dancing, since it was the first occasion when he had deigned to dance with any Hertfordshire lady. But the interest dissipated quickly when he and Bingley left Meryton soon after the ball.

Not everyone had noticed. Even Elizabeth's father had, apparently, not seen his daughter dancing with the impressive Mr. Darcy.

The situations there and here were very different, though each had its share of tensions. However, even though carefully observed at this first Pemberley ball by many of those not dancing, Elizabeth and Darcy were now so secure in their love for each other that they glided their way through it from beginning to end. If their dancing was not perfect, it would have been an intrepid observer who would have dared to point out any fault.

With many thanks for a lovely evening, the Gardners pleaded the late hour and went to bed just before the last dance began.

The last of the guests departed, and Darcy escorted Elizabeth to the drawing room where the overnight guests were already gathered.

"Let me tell Selbey to order tea," Elizabeth said.

"I already did. It's on its way."

Actually it had just arrived; Jane was busy serving the others, and Fitzwilliam handed Darcy a glass of wine as they entered. Bingley had settled down with his glass in a comfortable chair where he could see Jane. Georgiana, Kitty, and Mary took their cups and plates of delicacies to the game table and were exchanging comments on the ball.

Elizabeth took a cup from Jane and seated herself. Darcy stood by the fireplace near her, sipping his wine. "You look stunned, Elizabeth."

"You mean stunning, don't you?" Bingley interrupted.

"No, I mean stunned."

"Do I? I suppose I'm still trying to assimilate that the ball is over. This event that I've focused on for almost three months is really over—and with no calamity."

"Calamity?" Fitzwilliam protested. "It was a resounding success. I can't remember seeing a happier gathering of revelers."

"The music was excellent," Jane said, offering Elizabeth a plate of treats. "Perhaps you're dizzy from so much dancing."

"I do believe I missed only the first, while we were still greeting guests."

"Yes, it's a good thing I claimed the second and third before anyone arrived, because I only found you for one other after that," Darcy remarked.

"You danced three with Elizabeth? I only managed to claim Jane for two. I guess that proves who was the loveliest lady at the ball," Bingley declared.

"Not so fast," Fitzwilliam said. Looking to Georgiana he asked, "Did you dance two dances with anyone?"

The three young ladies rose and joined the others. Georgiana replied, "No, I didn't."

"And did you lack a partner for any dance?"

"No, I danced every dance."

Fitzwilliam declared, "I present to you the loveliest lady at the ball."

"That's certainly convincing proof," Darcy said as the laughter subsided, "but what of your partners, Fitzwilliam?"

"A gentleman must be very discreet in commenting about his partners."

"I danced with him," Mary rushed to say.

"And I," Kitty added.

"So did I," Georgiana revealed.

"And you, Jane?" Bingley asked.

"Yes, I did; Colonel Fitzwilliam is a fine dancer."

"Elizabeth?"

"Of course."

Were there any ladies you didn't dance with?"

"Alas, the music ended before I ran out of partners."

"Did you dance with Caroline?" Bingley asked.

"Miss Bingley is a fine dancer and a very handsome lady. I confess it; I surveyed the room and danced with all the lovliest ladies, and one who wasn't so lovely."

"Mrs. Wilson," Elizabeth said.

"The very one. She's quite a talker. I didn't realize one could talk so much during a dance."

"That's right, you were not present for the Bingley ball at Netherfield, were you, Fitzwilliam," Darcy said, looking from Fitzwilliam to Elizabeth.

She met his gaze, but, smiling, turned intently to finish her biscuit.

"No," Fitzwilliam replied, "But speaking of conversation, did I hear you talking politics with Sir Humphrey? He appeared quite intense."

"Actually, Sir Humphrey was talking politics, but he seemed much more interested in Miss Bingley; he kept watching her dance all the while he was cajoling me to stand for parliament."

"Parliament?" Bingley repeated.

"Yes, a lot of nonsense. We have a perfectly acceptable MP.

"Miss Bingley?" Jane asked. "Sir Humphrey pursuing Miss Bingley? The older gentleman she was dancing with?"

"Yes," Georgiana said. "That's him. I noticed it too. Every time I saw him dancing he was dancing with her."

Jane looked incredulous. "But he must be almost twice her age."

"It wouldn't be the first time an older man set his sights on a much younger woman," Fitzwilliam pointed out.

Hearing this Elizabeth and Darcy turned from him to each other.

Mary now found her place in the conversation. "Just look at Henry VIII. He married several women much younger than himself."

Kitty protested, "But he only wanted an heir."

"Would that be so strange?" Bingley asked. "We dined with Sir Humphrey just after Christmas. He seems a very lively man for his age. And his estate is certainly comfortable."

"But she's your sister!" Jane said. "How could you contemplate her marrying someone so old."

"I'm not. She doesn't have to consult me whether she should marry him or anyone else or no one. But she hasn't found a younger man."

Again Elizabeth and Darcy looked to each other.

"And she hasn't exactly been hidden in a remote county," Bingley added.

The room fell silent as everyone reflected on these comments.

Jane now turned to Georgiana. "Who was that young man you danced the first with?"

"Mr. Harrison. He's Mrs. Pettigrew's brother."

"And...."

"Darcy bought Midnight from the Pettigrews."

"I mean Mr. Harrison," Jane cajoled. "What does he do? Where does he live? Is he married? He's really very attractive, you know."

"He's at Oxford. He wants to be a professor of literature."

"Is he poor?"

"I don't know."

"Didn't he ask you to dance again later?"

Now Mary interrupted, "Yes, he did, but she was already spoken for, so he danced with me."

"Very nice leftovers," Elizabeth commented.

"He's a good dancer," Mary added, "and has fine manners too."

"I'm beginning to think this conversation could continue all night," Darcy broke in. "I suggest we continue it at breakfast."

Elizabeth instructed, "I've told the kitchen staff that no one is likely to appear for breakfast before nine."

"You expect us for breakfast at nine?" Kitty complained. "It's already two-thirty."

"No, Kitty, sleep as long as you like. Just don't expect to find breakfast before nine. Even at eleven you'll be served."

Contented, they all dispersed to their rooms.

Annie and Bradford had been told not to wait for them after the ball, so Darcy unbuttoned Elizabeth and helped her remove her ball gown.

They slipped into bed. "Darcy, it was a grand evening, wasn't it?"

"It certainly was," he said, smoothing her hair away from her face.

Saturday: Mr. Bennet

Elizabeth awoke to find a stream of bright light escaping the folds of the draperies. She looked at Darcy and saw his eyes closed. She started to slip out of bed, but he reached over and held her arm.

"Where are you going?"

"Just let me relieve myself; my bladder is bursting."

"Only if you promise to come back."

"I promise." She left and returned.

"It's nine o'clock," she said, as she climbed back into bed.

"I know."

"Our guests...."

"They'll be well cared for by the servants. And they entertain each other very handsomely, as you must have noticed last night."

"It does feel good just to stretch out and relax."

They lay quietly, listening to each other's breathing.

Elizabeth heard a tiny shuffling noise. "What was that?"

"What?"

"Didn't you hear it?"

"No."

She started to get out of bed, but he held her arm. "Where are you going?"

"Just let me open the draperies."

"Promise to come back?"

"I promise." She opened the draperies and as she turned, her eye was caught by something white on the floor at the door. She moved towards it.

"Where are you going?"

"I'll be right back."

"You promised."

She picked up the envelope and returned to the bed. Under the quilts and propped up on her pillows, she opened it and read silently.

"My Dear Lizzy:

By now you are, no doubt, basking in the triumph of your first Pemberley Ball. I have to admit that I was a bit disappointed that Mary decided to go since I would have enjoyed viewing your triumph.

However, I have decided on the next best possibility.

Mary has assured me she will not present this letter to you until the morning following the ball.

And, in order that I may, in fact, share in the excitement, please set an extra place for me for dinner on Saturday, the 25th.

Your loving Papa"

"He's coming, Darcy; he's coming."

"Who?" he asked, opening his eyes and pulling himself up to sit beside her.

"Papa, he's coming."

"When?"

"Today, for dinner."

"You must be mistaken."

"No; read it." She handed him the letter and bolted out of bed. She pulled on her robe and dashed to her dressing room door. She opened its door to the hall and found Annie staring out of a window.

"Annie, quick, help me."

They quickly went through the routines, Elizabeth doing for herself whatever she could. Washed, dressed, and coiffed, she returned to the bedroom. She approached the bed and was just going to kiss his sleeping face when he reached out again and took her arm.

"Where are you going?"

"To breakfast."

"What's the rush?"

"I don't know. Papa's coming has so startled me I'm not sure what to think. I just feel I should be doing something."

"The servants will take care of everything."

"You're right, of course. But I'm beginning to understand what Georgiana meant about feeling useless."

"You're not useless. It was all your efforts that ensured that the ball went so well. We all know that. Just relax and let the others do their jobs."

"I am hungry; aren't you?"

"Yes, I do believe I am," he said, rolling his legs out of bed. "I'll join you shortly."

She picked up the letter and walked out the door. It was after nine-thirty, but Mary was the only one in the dining room. Elizabeth selected food for her plate and sat down beside Mary, placing the letter between them. Selbey poured coffee into her cup, refilled Mary's, and returned to his post by the sideboard.

"Do you know what's in this letter, Mary?"

"No, I don't."

"Mama and Papa are well, aren't they?"

"Yes, of course. At least as far as I know. What did Papa say in the letter? He insisted I should not give you the letter until this morning, so I slipped it under your door as I came to breakfast. What did he say?"

"He's coming. Today, in time for dinner."

Mary looked dumbfounded.

Kitty and Darcy were entering the dining room. Kitty sat down with her plate and, at length, asked, "What's wrong?"

"Papa is coming. Today. He'll be here in time for dinner."

"You're joking."

Elizabeth handed her the letter, and she read it. "It's his hand writing. But when did Papa ever leave Meryton when he didn't have to?"

"Exactly."

The Gardners, Georgiana, and Fitzwilliam arrived, followed by Jane and Bingley. They filled their plates, and found places at the table.

"This is a quiet crowd," Jane said. "Surely there is some merriment left over from last night."

Elizabeth handed her the letter. She read it silently and handed it to Bingley. "What does it mean?" Jane queried.

"Only what it says, I sincerely hope. Did he say nothing to you?"

"Nothing at all. He seemed quite pleased at the idea of a few days with no children in the house."

"Pleased," Elizabeth repeated.

"Yes, almost merry."

"Merry."

"Yes, now that you say it that way, it does seem a bit odd. But I really didn't think about it at the time."

Now Darcy spoke. "I think we should take him precisely at his word. I propose that we say no more about it, that we enjoy our breakfast and the hours until he arrives. Then we'll soon learn if there was any hidden meaning in the letter. Besides, I did feel last night that I broke up our little gathering before everyone had finished their comments about the ball."

"You wouldn't just be changing the subject so you could bask for awhile longer in the triumph of the first ball at Pemberley since you became its master?" Colonel Fitzwilliam needled.

"Not at all," Darcy replied. "I was just thinking about a comment you made about Miss Bingley—what a fine dancer she is and how handsome."

"Yes," Georgiana said, "and she likes you too. I saw her moving in your direction several times."

"It's true," Kitty confirmed. "But Sir Humphrey interrupted her once. And when she was dancing with Mr. Pettigrew, I saw her watching the Colonel wherever she was."

"Well, don't we have a watchful group of young ladies," Fitzwilliam responded. "Perhaps there were not enough interesting young men to hold your attention."

Breakfast finished, they all adjourned to the morning room.

"The young ladies were not the only ones observing events last night," Colonel Fitzwilliam continued. "I saw you, Georgiana, dancing with a handsome young man as well—perhaps the third dance. Are you going to tell us who he is?"

"His name is Morris. He's Mr. Morris's brother."

"And what is his story?" Jane inquired.

"He's a student at Glasgow University. He's studying science, but his father wants him to be an attorney."

By this time Elizabeth decided Georgiana had undergone enough interrogation. She turned to Jane and said, "That dress Caroline was wearing last night—she did look very attractive in it."

"Just what I told her. We were quite alone at the time, soon after they arrived—a most remarkable story. I don't think she'll mind if I tell you. She and the Hursts arrived in Lambton Wednesday evening, planning to take drives in the country Thursday and Friday, and, in fact, did. But as they were leaving the inn Thursday morning, they discovered that Thursday is Market Day in Lambton. Stalls were set up and tradesmen were selling goods of every description. They decided to browse for an hour or so, just for amusement.

"Caroline usually has her clothes made to order in London, but to their amazement, they found that dress in one of the stalls. It seemed perfectly new, though obviously it was being resold.

"It appeared it would fit, so Caroline bought it, thinking she'd have it altered in London. But that evening at the inn, she tried it on and found the alterations needed were so slight that she and Louisa got needle and thread from the chambermaid and made the alterations themselves. She decided it was prettier than the one she had brought and so she wore it to the ball."

"Remarkable indeed," Elizabeth commented.

"Uncommon luck, I'd say," Kitty added.

"Can we stay until next Thursday?" Mary asked.

"I'm hoping you will, but don't expect to repeat that stroke of luck," Elizabeth replied.

"Someone else noticed Miss Bingley's dress also," Darcy said.

"Who was that?" Elizabeth asked.

"Mrs. Winston. She told me Miss Bingley reminded her of my late mother, particularly the dress. She was very impressed with her appearance. She even asked if Miss Bingley was some relation of mine."

The group contemplated these remarks in silence until Fitzwilliam suggested a game of cards, and the men, apparently tired of comments on the ball, assembled around the card table to play.

Georgiana approached Elizabeth and said, "Kitty and Mary have asked if they could see the rest of the house."

"Of course, how thoughtless of me," Elizabeth responded, putting her cup down and beginning to rise.

"I'd very much like to show them, if you don't mind."

"Mind! That's a very thoughtful offer. Thank you, Georgiana. And, please, do introduce then to any of the servants you meet."

"I will."

Before she could finish, Kitty and Mary were at the door, Georgiana following.

Elizabeth sat back and closed her eyes.

"It's been a very busy time for you," Jane said.

"Yes, it all started so innocently with Darcy saying, "Perhaps we should have a ball.""

"Darcy suggested the ball? I thought he wasn't even fond of dancing!"

Elizabeth opened her eyes. "It's a very long story. And quite amusing when I think of it now, though it didn't seem so at the time. Let's go for a walk. I'll tell you about it."

"It looks rather chilly out."

"Good; it will wake us up. Aunt Gardner, will you join us?"

"No, thank you, I believe I shall just sit and read awhile."

They were opening the door to the hall when they encountered Fenton pushing the door open from the hall. "I am sorry, Mrs. Darcy. I was just coming to tell you there's an elderly gentleman at the door to see you. Says his name is...."

Jane and Elizabeth looked at each other. "Papa!" they exclaimed at once. They rushed to the entry and together helped him remove his cape.

"Papa! you're all right, aren't you? Mama is well, isn't she? You're early. It's only noon. We didn't expect you until closer to two o'clock." Comments tumbled from both daughters at once.

"Yes, I'm fine; Mama is fine; I arrived at Lambton last evening and stayed at the inn."

"The inn? You should have come here."

"No; I was tired, in no mood to watch a lot of silly girls chasing beaux."

By now they were ushering him into the drawing room.

"How did you get here?"

"The inn keeper found a farmer who was willing to bring me for a small fee. Well," he continued, "was the ball a great success?"

Elizabeth began to speak, but Jane interrupted, "It was an enormous success, Papa."

"Then who are the young gentlemen Kitty and Mary will be marrying?"

"Not that much of a success, Papa," Elizabeth replied. "But everyone had a grand time. Indeed, I considered it a great...."

By this time the men had left their card table to greet Mr. Bennet. Darcy introduced Mr. Bennet to Colonel Fitzwilliam.

"So you are Darcy's cousin."

"Yes, I am."

"Lady Catherine's nephew."

"Yes. We did meet at the wedding."

"Of course; now I remember."

"Elizabeth and I were just about to take a walk; would you care to join us?" Jane asked.

"Thank you, but what I'd really like is a cup of tea and a comfortable chair near the fire."

"Perhaps you'd like to join our card game."

"No, no, thank you. You continue. I'm not terribly fond of cards. I discovered as a young man that cards pave one of the roads to misfortune. If I can just have my book, I'll be content."

Mr. Gardner now intervened. "And is it possible that novels pave another of those roads?"

"For the novelist, perhaps."

"Then we'll stay here and tell you about the ball."

"No, I'd really prefer it if you'd go for your walk. We'll talk when you return. If I could just get my book from my traveling case."

Elizabeth left Mr. Bennet with the footman to take him to his room with the traveling case, saying, "We'll stop in the kitchen on our way out and order tea. Selbey will bring it to you in the morning room."

"Mistress of Pemberley! My daughter! Imagine that," he mumbled as he climbed the stairs.

They ordered the tea and at the same time complimented Mrs. Sims and the other kitchen staff on the excellent food prepared for the ball supper and informed them that Mr. Bennet had arrived and would be staying for a few days.

They walked along the garden paths as Elizabeth related the episode of the game of tag and "her mysterious ailment," pointing out the bench and bushes, and the grassy area towards the lake where she and Darcy had run.

Jane, incredulous, interjected: "Darcy run? You faint? Darcy propose a ball?" It was all too hard to believe. "And all these things have been happening, and you wrote nothing to me!"

"How could I possibly write it in a letter? It was much too complicated. And, while it was troublesome in some ways, it was hardly earthshaking."

"But you said nothing when I was here at Christmas."

"There wasn't time; the visit was too short."

"Of course."

"Jane, I must tell you. Remember the dress Miss Bingley was wearing last night? And how you told me last night that she found it in Lambton? Jane nodded.

"That was Darcy's mother's dress that we gave to the Bazaar."

"Oh, no. She would be mortified if she knew."

"One more secret we must keep."

As they entered the drawing room, Mr. Bennet looked up and put down his book. "Now, my dears, I'm ready to hear every detail." They were just settling in when the three young ladies arrived. Greetings were made and Kitty and Mary were assured that all was well, Mama was well, actually visiting sister Phillips for a few days.

Kitty reported that she had danced all but two dances and that Mary had danced two.

"No, I danced three!" Mary corrected her.

Kitty named them: "Colonel Fitzwilliam and Mr. Harrison."

"And Mr. Ford," Mary added.

"The Vicar?" Elizabeth questioned.

"Yes, I guess he was."

"Did you enjoy your tour of the house?" Elizabeth asked.

"The portrait gallery is magnificent," Kitty replied.

"And Georgiana let me play the piano again," Mary said.

"Again?" Mr. Bennet queried, his eyebrows rising.

"Mary played for us on Thursday, just us, family, the night before the ball."

"Ah; good."

"Well, it is delightful to be surrounded by such a crowd of lovely young ladies, especially when they've just enjoyed a ball."

"There are two more coming as well," Jane said. "Miss Bingley and Mrs. Hurst."

"With Mr. Hurst?"

"Yes."

"They had a few minutes to inform Mr. Bennet of the fine music and food of the night before and some anecdotes as well. But time had flown, and the Hursts arrived with Miss Bingley just in time to organize themselves and greet the others before Selbey announced that dinner was served.

Elizabeth seated Fitzwilliam at her right, and Mrs. Gardner beside him; then Mr. Hurst, Georgiana, Mary and Bingley next to Darcy at the head of the table. Kitty she seated at Darcy's right, then Mrs. Hurst, Mr. Gardner, Jane, Mr. Bennet, and Miss Bingley beside him and at her own left.

"Well, Lizzy," Mr. Bennet commented, "It's fortunate indeed that I arrived when I did or you should have had 13 at table. Fortunate indeed."

"You arrived unexpectedly?" Miss Bingley asked.

"Indeed; I wouldn't want Elizabeth to go to any trouble on my account."

"No trouble!" Elizabeth retorted, "You gave me a terrible fright. I was certain something dreadful had happened."

"Nonsense!" Then turning to Miss Bingley, "There is something I must do before I forget." All eyes were on him as they were eating. "I found it necessary to disclose to someone besides Mrs. Bennet that I was making this trip. The servants will take care of everything, of course, but, since the Lucases live so close, I told Sir William where I was going. He immediately jumped to the conclusion that you would be here for the ball, Miss Bingley, and demanded that I convey a message to you."

Miss Bingley appeared incredulous, but listened carefully.

"Sir William, it seems, is determined to introduce you to some of his most admirable acquaintances when he is in London. He considers it shocking that such a fine looking woman should be unmarried still." This said, he sat back and waited for her reply.

The entire group was still following this conversation, and Miss Bingley, beginning to sting from what she perceived to be an affront, replied, "I'm rather surprised that you would feel it necessary to carry a message for Sir William."

"He was very insistent. And I try at all times to be particularly courteous to Sir William."

"Indeed!"

"Yes, you see, while I shall not suffer while I'm alive, his daughter Charlotte's husband is heir to my estate, Mr. Collins being my cousin."

"How remarkable."

"Yes; well, now that I have delivered the message, we can all enjoy the rest of the party."

Elizabeth was beginning to think that was not at all likely and was most anxious to change the subject. Unfortunately, her father's disclosure had nearly paralized her mind, and she seized on the only subject that came to mind.

"Miss Bingley," she said, "I was struck with the elegance of your appearance last night. I think I have never seen you look quite so well."

"Really?"

Everyone had been so transfixed by the inelegance of Mr. Bennet's story that they were still following the conversation, even Darcy at the opposite end of the table. He began, "You know, Sir Humphrey was talking with me about some little matter, but he couldn't keep his eyes from you, Miss Bingley. I do believe Elizabeth is right. I really thought he seemed quite enchanted with you."

"Sir Humphrey? That old man?"

"He's not so very old," Bingley interjected. "Darcy tells me he thinks Sir Humphrey is only about 50."

"The two of you looked very elegant on the dance floor together," Fitzwilliam added.

At this Miss Bingley's face flushed, and she focused all her attention on her food.

Aunt Gardner now came to the rescue. "How long do the girls expect to stay, Elizabeth?"

"I'm not sure; I'm hoping a week. Why do you ask?"

"I've just been thinking it might do Mrs. Bennet a world of good to spend a few days with us in London."

By this time other conversations had sprung up around the table and Elizabeth could relax and enjoy the meal as well.

The rest of the afternoon continued without incident. The group was too large for conveniently gathering in the music room, so it was easy to avoid Mary's efforts at entertaining at the piano. And the group was large enough that Elizabeth did not have the sole burden of entertaining Miss Bingley. She and the Hursts left early enough to get back to the inn before dark. Elizabeth did not bother to remind them that the sky was clear and there would be a full moon that evening.

Still, it was Elizabeth and Darcy who waited until the carriage departed after the others had returned to the drawing room. Back in the entry hall, Darcy closed the door and took Elizabeth in his arms. "Lizzy; I am proud of you. You handled yourself magnificently." They stood in the hall swaying from side to side as they embraced.

"They'll be wondering where we are."

"Yes," he said, and walked with her to the drawing room, his arm at her back.

Now the Gardners revealed that they were serious in their resolve to leave the next morning.

"But so soon," Elizabeth protested.

"Business requires that I return, Elizabeth," Uncle Gardner replied. "But we promise to make a longer stay the next time we come. Just let us know what will be a good time, and we'll come."

"It's been a great pleasure to be here," Aunt Gardner said, "and I'll convey all the details to your Mama and to Aunt Phillips."

"And I have decided to accompany them," Mr. Bennet announced.

"But you just arrived!" Elizabeth protested.

"Yes, but I was here for the best part; and surely you would not deny me company on the return trip. Besides, I consider the Gardner's offer of inviting Mrs. Bennet to town for a few days to be most agreeable. A few evenings at the theatre should suit your mother admirably. I'm likely to have a year of happy remembrances following it. If Kitty and Mary are here we shall not have to worry about them."

"You had this all arranged very carefully, didn't you?" Elizabeth charged.

"I did not. Just because a plan is quickly made does not mean it cannot be admirable."

They agreed that if the Bingleys should return to Netherfield before the Bennets, Kitty and Mary would stay at Netherfield until the Bennets returned.

That settled, Elizabeth offered to show her father the house.

"Just the ballroom, my dear; your mother will ask about it. The rest can wait until next summer or spring or perhaps even the fall."

"When will you come?"

"When you least expect me."

"But we may not be here."

"I'll consult my spies!"

She did take him to the ballroom. The light was already fading, but she lit a few candles, and it was still easy to see what a grand room it was.

"You're happy, my dear?"

"Yes, very. Very, very happy."

He embraced her, gently patting her back, then released her.

"There is one thing."

"What is it?"

"I really shouldn't ask. Darcy should ask you, but I'm sure he wouldn't. Or I should ask Mama, but I'm sure she couldn't help."

He led her to some chairs and motioned for her to sit, as he did.

"Darcy and I are very happy together, but I'm so worried that we'll have a baby before we're ready."

"Ah, yes." He paused and reflected for awhile on the conundrum. "I'm afraid the only thing I could offer would interfere with your happiness."

"Separate bedrooms?"

"Quite so."

"Well, maybe we'll just be lucky."

"Perhaps; some are; it might as well be you; I do hope it is you."

"I don't want Mary to play for us this evening; you're here such a short time, but I would like you to see the music room."

"I think I can manage that."

It was still light enough to see how beautiful the countryside appeared from the music room.

"It's a lovely home, Elizabeth. I am happy for you."

"You're only going to be here tonight, Papa, and I want you to see me in the dress I wore on Christmas with the emerald necklace Darcy gave me. I'll wear it to supper."

"As you wish," he said, fondly.

At supper Elizabeth seated her father at her right and Jane at her left. All others were asked to find places of their own choosing, except Darcy, who sat at the opposite end. Conversation tumbled from one topic to the next and supper was over all too soon. In the drawing room, Mr. Bennet sat observing, listening to the conversation, but offering mainly smiles and raised eyebrows.

They had known since his arrival that Fitzwilliam would leave Sunday morning. When the Gardners learned this, they suggested that he travel with them, an invitation he gladly accepted.

Departure had been set for nine, and breakfast was subdued. Conversation centered on assurances of visits during the more agreeable months to come. Tears, hugs, and waves, and then the four were gone.

Kitty and Mary rode to church with Elizabeth and Darcy, and Georgiana with the Bingleys. The weather was warmer than usual so it was possible to greet some of the other parishioners after church. Many of the greetings included "thank yous" for the lovely evening at the ball. Twice notes were slipped into Elizabeth's hand. She and Darcy introduced their guests as well as they were able, given the speed of dispersal following services on a chilly morning.

At home, warming herself before the fire, Elizabeth read the missives, which proved to be invitations to tea the following week, worded "with your sisters, of course."

Warmed, she invited Jane to take a walk in the portrait gallery, seeing that the younger women were deep in confidences and that Bingley and Darcy had left.

They walked, alternately looking out the windows and gazing at the impressive faces of the portraits.

"You're very quiet, Jane," Elizabeth commented. They walked further, but Jane didn't reply.

"There's something wrong."

"No," she said first, then, "Yes," then, "I don't know."

"Well, that gives me the entire range to choose from."

Still no explanation.

"You're pregnant."

Jane's head whipped around to face Elizabeth. "How did you know?"

"I didn't; I mean, you just told me."

"I didn't."

"What else could cause such a variety of responses? Besides, remember that we did marry on the same day."

"You mean that you're pregnant too?"

"No, meaning that if I were pregnant I should probably have answered in the same way."

They walked along, again in silence.

"I do want babies, Lizzy. I just hoped it wouldn't happen quite so soon."

"I know. I mean, that's the way I feel too. Does anyone else know?"

"Bingley."

"Mama?"

"No."

"Caroline?"

"No, only Bingley. And now you."

"It might be better if you could keep it secret awhile longer."

"Why?"

"Do you know what the due date will be?"

"Early October."

"That's a long time. People fuss over a pregnant woman so; it must get tiresome. Do you feel all right?"

"Perfectly. Well, physically, that is. It's just that I'm not entirely happy about it."

"Mama is likely to notice; and Aunt Phillips—your temperament, that is. You've always been so sweet-tempered. If there is a change, they'll notice. They're like mother hens, always cluck-clucking."

"Surely you're too harsh."

"Perhaps; but if I were pregnant, I should be very happy not to be living in Meryton."

"Do you think we'd better go back? It must be nearly time for dinner."

"Yes, but first let's get onto another subject. Might Bingley be willing to go with Darcy this week to look for a house for you in this area?"

"Yes, I think so."

"Then let us suggest it. You can stay with me, and we'll have a good visit."

At dinner, however, neither Jane nor Elizabeth had the opportunity to suggest a house-hunting trip because Darcy and Bingley had already set out a plan: they would travel together in Bingley's coach since it was smaller than Darcy's, leaving Monday morning and returning Friday evening if they didn't find something sooner.

Meeting no resistance, the gathering settled into subjects of less import but greater amusement. When given the opportunity, Elizabeth asked Georgiana, "Is your adventure in the kitchen ended now that the ball is over?"

"I hadn't really thought about it. For this week, while Kitty and Mary are here, I shall do as they wish, and when they leave, I'll decide what to do."

Kitty and Mary looked at each other in puzzlement. At this, Georgiana explained "her adventure in the kitchen."

Kitty replied, "Cook doesn't usually like us in the kitchen at home."

"Just an hour each morning?" Mary asked.

Both agreed they'd like to try it, so that was settled.

With so many guests gone, all agreed to a brief concert. Mary began, Elizabeth followed, and Georgiana completed the concert, all warmly applauded by the listeners.

Supper was subdued but pleasant, and later in the drawing room Bingley and Darcy settled into conversation. The three young ladies gathered around the game table, and Jane told Elizabeth all the news from Meryton.

That night in bed Darcy said, "Lizzy, I have been thinking about something you said the other night: you said that you think it's just luck that you're not already pregnant. You seemed so decided on the point. How can you feel so sure?"

Facing him, she replied, "Do you remember that first Sunday I did not go to church with you and Georgiana?"

"Yes, I do."

"My period that time—I mean, it's always difficult in the winter; I feel so cold. But that time it was different."

He waited for her to continue.

"First of all, it was late."

"Late."

"Yes."

"You didn't tell me."

"I didn't want to worry you. But there was something else."

He waited for further explanation.

"It was different; I bled more profusely. It just seemed different than any other period I had ever had."

"But what does it mean?"

"I'm not sure, but I suspect that I actually was pregnant."

"You mean that it is possible for you to get pregnant, but that in this case it just didn't continue?"

"I don't know; how can I know? I just suspect I was pregnant."

"I begin to feel that we're working on a giant picture puzzle; we just put one tiny piece into place, and it still does nothing to tell us what the whole picture will look like."

"Yes."

"Well, I'm tired of puzzles. Perhaps we should just try another of those modern inconveniences."

"I agree."

Monday: Bingley and Darcy at Thornwood

Breakfast complete, in the entry before leaving the gentlemen embraced their wives warmly. Then off they went, all the ladies waving from the door.

The three girls left for their activities, and Elizabeth turned to Jane.

"Come, let's take another walk in the portrait gallery." They strolled arm-in-arm, musing over the flurry of activity during the past few days and over Jane's disclosure about her pregnancy.

When at last Elizabeth did speak, she said, "Well, at least you and Bingley can make love now without fear of getting pregnant."

"A gasp of laughter escaped her before Jane realized the seriousness of the statement. "You do think it's all right, don't you?"

"Why wouldn't it be?"

"What if I miscarry?"

"And what if you do?"

"Wouldn't that be terrible?"

"I don't know. It might, but you didn't seem so very happy about the pregnancy yesterday."

Just then Kitty and Georgiana came walking rapidly towards them. Kitty was ready to blurt out a request, but paused and said, "What are you two so gloomy about?"

"We look gloomy?"

"I thought you did." Deterred, she switched back to her original objective. "Lizzy, can Georgiana and I go horseback riding?"

"But you don't know how."

"What's so difficult about it? Get on the horse and ride."

"It's not that easy."

"Georgiana can teach me."

"Besides, we don't have a suitable horse for you."

"You have two. Georgiana can ride Darcy's and I can ride yours."

"I'm sorry, Kitty. If Darcy were here..."

"But we'll probably leave soon after they get back. You have everything, and you won't even let me ride."

"Not quite everything."

"Well, what good does it do to visit Pemberly if we can't even go riding?"

Exasperated, Elizabeth turned to Jane and said, "Will you keep Georgiana company for awhile? I think Kitty and I need to have a talk. We'll meet you in the morning room later."

Still flustered, Kitty allowed Elizabeth to take her arm and propel her to Elizabeth's study, where she closed the door.

"Kitty, I can't let you go riding."

"But why?"

"Because Darcy wouldn't like it."

"He wouldn't have to know."

"Kitty, as we were on our way here, did you see anyone?"

"Yes."

"Who?"

"The maid. I think her name is Sarah."

"And how did you find Jane and me?"

"Fenton told us where you were."

"And if you went riding, would anyone see you?"

"Davy and Mr. Sims, I suppose."

"Kitty, I can't go anywhere in the house or on the grounds without someone seeing me. Now, do you suppose any of the servants keep any secrets at all from Darcy?"

"But you can do anything you want!"

"Can I really? Suppose I were to play a game of tag outdoors with Darcy."

"Huh," Kitty gasped. "Why not?"

"Because within a week, everyone in Derbyshire would know about it."

Kitty reflected for awhile on the possible implications of Elizabeth's statements. At length she said, "Did you?"

"Did I what?"

"Play a game of tag with Darcy."

"That was just an example! I'm just trying to get you to understand that I don't do anything I feel Darcy wouldn't like."

"Is he mean to you?"

"Kitty, how can you say such a thing?"

"You seem afraid of him."

"I'm not afraid of Darcy. Kitty, you had many opportunities to see Darcy before we were married, and you've spent almost a week in his own house."

"Four days."

"All right, four days. Has he treated you or anyone else other than with the greatest kindness and courtesy?"

"No, but he always was very proud, even arrogant."

"Kitty, we were all blinded by his pride, to the point where we couldn't see beyond it. But there's solid character beneath that pride, and enormous generosity besides. We are all indebted to him. Even just for this visit, don't you owe him something?"

Finally Kitty recognized her behavior for what it was. Tears flooded her eyes. "Lizzy, I'm sorry. I just wasn't thinking."

Elizabeth put her arm around her and offered her a handkerchief. They sat down together on the window seat.

"Besides, you need an excuse to come back next summer—so you can learn to ride. Believe me, it's not as easy as it looks. Tell mama you need a riding habit. That will give her something to do to take her mind off her nerves."

They looked out the window. "I believe I see a glimmer of sun through the clouds. Perhaps we can all go out for a walk after dinner. But now I believe it's time for a cup of tea."

Kitty had recovered her composure as they sat.

"The notes I was handed on Sunday invite me *and* my sisters to tea tomorrow and Thursday. You do want to go, don't you?"

"Of course."

"Even if you have to be on your extra good behavior as the sister of that elegant Mrs. Darcy, the mistress of Pemberley?"

At that, Kitty laughed, and then clouded up. "Are you joking, or are you serious?"

"Both, I suppose."

Tea had arrived, and Jane proceeded to serve as they entered the morning room.

"I think Kitty has an apology, Georgiana."

"I'm sorry, Georgiana, I behaved badly. I hope you'll forgive me."

"It was nothing."

"I suggest we all take a walk after dinner if it isn't raining. Right now it looks as if the sun is trying to shine." Meeting with only murmurs of assent, she continued. "Kitty, did you ever learn anything about chess?"

"Papa taught me the basic moves, but I was never able to beat him at a game."

"Then here is your chance to win. I suggest you teach Georgiana what you know." And, looking to Mary, nose in her book, she added, "Mary, you might watch. It wouldn't hurt you to know how to play chess, either."

"You're beginning to sound just like Mama," Jane teased.

Georgiana brought the set to the game table, and Kitty arranged the pieces on the board. Jane and Elizabeth finished their tea and excused themselves, saying they were going to go to the gallery to finish their walk.

They walked in silence. Elizabeth puzzled over whether she should tell Jane about the condoms, but decided that since Jane was already pregnant, she should wait. After all, if they weren't effective for Darcy and herself, why get Jane's hopes up for later unnecessarily?

February 28, Tuesday: Tea at the Vicarage

The five ladies fit into the carriage comfortably enough and were delivered to the vicarage just before three-thirty. Mrs. Morris was there and Mrs. Howell as well as Mrs. Wilson. The company was congenial, and compliments on the ball continued until Elizabeth was wishing for a change of subject. Casting about, she asked Mrs. Howell if there were a subscription library in the area.

"There is indeed. In addition, there has been quite a lot of discussion about the possibility of founding a public library. Money is always the sticking point, of course. But we have many people in the area who enjoy reading and would like access to a greater selection of books."

"Yes, the money is the problem," confirmed Mrs. Morris.

"There is a real possibility, of course," Mrs. Wilson said. When all eyes were focused on her she continued, "Some of the men have been discussing the idea of holding a fund raiser: a country fair, with games and stalls for selling food and donated merchandise."

"A fair," Mrs. Ford repeated, "You mean an outdoor event?"

"Exactly," Mrs. Wilson responded.

"But where could a fair be held?" Mrs. Howell asked.

"Yes, where?" Mrs. Morris echoed.

"Quite a large space might be needed," Mrs. Wilson suggested, looking at Elizabeth. The others followed her gaze until all except Mary and Kitty were looking at Elizabeth.

"Yes, where...." Elizabeth began, until she caught their meaning. Everyone waited for her to continue, but she could think of nothing to say.

"You must admit," Mrs. Ford interposed quietly, "that Pemberley would be the ideal site."

"Isn't it rather far from town?" Elizabeth replied.

"I don't think so," Mrs. Morris countered. "For an event of this kind people like to make a day of it—get out into the country—particularly if the countryside is very beautiful, as Pemberley is."

"In any event, it's not for me to say yes or no; it's Mr. Darcy's estate," Elizabeth added.

"But perhaps you could talk with him," Mrs. Wilson proposed.

"I don't think so," Elizabeth replied, "especially so soon after the ball."

"But you wouldn't oppose the idea?" Mrs. Ford queried.

"No, not at all. I consider a library to be a very worthy cause."

The group scattered into several separate conversations, most relating to the possibilities posed by the prospect of such an event as nearly as Elizabeth could tell by the snatches of conversation she did hear.

Attempting to escape the snarl that might lay ahead, she went to the piano and leafed through some of the music books lying there.

"Do you play, Mrs. Darcy?" Mrs. Ford asked.

"A little, but very ill," Elizabeth answered, "but Georgiana plays beautifully."

"I know," Mrs. Ford said, looking towards Georgiana. "Would you honor us by playing for us?"

Looking to Elizabeth for encouragement and reading assent, she went to the piano and played an Irish ballad. She didn't sing, but the song was well known, and some in the group "sang the words in their heads."

All applauded as she finished. Mrs. Ford looked then to Kitty and said, "Do you play?"

Kitty declined, but Mary broke in and said, "I do."

Before Mrs. Ford could request that she play, she was at the piano, playing and singing in her thoroughly confident manner, however lacking it might be in musical excellence. Amazingly, the ladies seemed to enjoy it and applauded her effort as well.

The party broke up shortly after Mr. Ford came in to pay his respects to the assembled ladies.

In the carriage on the way home, under Jane's watchful gaze, Elizabeth had ample opportunity to contemplate the frequency of her mother's headaches.

That evening and Wednesday passed uneventfully. Elizabeth did, however, discuss privately with Georgiana the possibility of another piano fiasco at the Carleton's. Elizabeth knew that the Carletons had a piano. Since some of the local ladies now were aware of Mary's eagerness to play, Elizabeth conspired with Georgiana to see that Mary would play before Georgiana. Perhaps they would remember best what they heard last.

March 2, Thursday: Tea at the Carleton's

They arrived at the Carleton's for tea in time to observe Mrs. Winston being escorted in and seated in the most comfortable chair. There she could see everyone, and others could bring her tea and the choicest offerings from the table.

Mrs. Darcy," she said in a voice rather too loud, "The ball was lovely."

"I'm glad you enjoyed it."

"Indeed I did. I haven't danced for years, of course, but it brings back delightful memories to see all the young people dancing."

Several of the ladies murmured their concurrence.

"And my son has scarcely spoken of anything but the lovely Miss Bingley since."

This prompted exchanges of glances between the ladies in the Pemberley party.

"She is charming," Jane responded.

"And where does she reside?" Mrs. Winston asked.

"She's been in London recently, but spends much of her time with us at my husband's estate in Hertfordshire."

"And has he lived there long?"

"No, not at all. They grew up in the north of England."

"Indeed. How very interesting."

"Now, what is this I hear about a fair at Pemberley?"

All hesitated to respond, but Mrs. Wilson finally took it upon herself to answer. "That is just a rumour, Mrs. Winston."

"A rumour, is it? Well, it seems to be on everyone's lips."

"Nevertheless," Elizabeth added, "it is only a rumour."

"I see," she said somewhat quizzically. "Well, it will no doubt be sorted out soon enough." She turned then to Theresa and said, "My dear, are you going to play for us today?"

Theresa looked at each of the Pemberley ladies in turn and said, "I'm told that one of the Miss Bennets plays."

Kitty looked at Mary, and Mary did not wait for further encouragement. She sang a song even longer than that at the vicarage, with no improvement in quality. Elizabeth suffered, while Jane endured with her usual sweetness. Mrs. Winston raised her eyebrows a few times at particularly sour notes, but applauded politely with the others.

"Now, Mrs. Darcy," Theresa said, "I have it on very good authority that you do play. Please don't disappoint us."

Elizabeth thought, "It couldn't possibly be worse." She played and sang a comic song known as "The Riddle" to an appreciative audience. She then gladly surrendered her place at the piano to Georgiana who completed the program with a beautiful piece by Mozart.

In the carriage on the way home, the five ladies entertained each other with comments on Mrs. Winston's imperious control of the tea party's conversation and her comments about Sir Humphrey's interest in Miss Bingley. All except Elizabeth, that is. She couldn't shake from her mind Mrs. Winston's reference to the rumour about a fair at Pemberley.

On their return to Pemberley they found Darcy and Bingley chatting in the drawing room.

"Back already?" Kitty said.

They rose to greet the ladies, and the conversation tumbled from comments about Mrs. Winston and Miss Bingley to the prospects of finding an estate for the Bingleys in the vicinity.

Following greetings, Darcy had stood listening to the conversation until Elizabeth said, "You seem quiet, Darcy."

"I've just been trying to think of how to break the news."

"What news?" came from three quarters at once.

"Bingley may not have found a house, but I found a horse...or rather two horses."

Georgiana sat up even straighter and smiled, but Elizabeth said, "Two?"

"We were, of course, looking for an estate for Bingley, but as you can imagine, on such a long trip, we did see some horses for sale. By last night we had made inquiries and placed advertisements in countless local newspapers and advertising circulars that there is a certain gentleman residing in Hertfordshire who would like to purchase an estate in this part of the country. That part of our journey was complete.

"Then at the inn we discovered that a horse auction was scheduled for this morning in that village. We attended, and I found two horses that I decided I must have. In short, I purchased them, we tied them to the carriage, and they are now in Sims' care in the stable."

News of the week's events were exchanged, and Kitty's prediction proved accurate: The Bingleys would depart the next day to arrive home by Saturday afternoon.

March 3, Friday

After breakfast the next morning, amid tears, hugs, and farewells, the guests departed.

Georgiana had not yet decided to terminate her kitchen experiment, so after she had practiced at the piano, she proceeded to the kitchen. Elizabeth and Darcy returned to the morning room where the silence seemed almost palpable following ten days so filled with people and activity.

They had sat in silence only awhile when Elizabeth remembered, "Darcy, there is something you should know."

"Yes?"

"That tea party on Tuesday at the vicarage was not quite so innocent as you might think."

He set down his newspaper, fully attentive.

"I expect that one of your friends will approach you soon to suggest that a country fair be held on the grounds here at Pemberley."

"Whatever for?"

"As a fund raiser for a library. Mrs. Wilson was the one who mentioned it first. Apparently a number of the men have been discussing it."

He appeared puzzled, but reflected for awhile before responding, "Probably just idle gossip."

"Perhaps, but yesterday at the Carleton's Mrs. Winston asked about it too."

"Did she? And what did you say?"

"That it was just a rumour. It is just a rumour, isn't it?"

"This is the first I've heard of it," he said as he picked up his newspaper.

"He seems quite unconcerned," Elizabeth thought. "Well, if it doesn't concern him, why should I worry about it?" So she put it out of her thoughts and returned to the moment.

The days passed. The weather was warmer, and they resumed riding the very next day.

As time was available, Elizabeth browsed through the records left by the previous Mrs. Darcy: records of balls, dinners and teas. She studied Mrs. Sims recipes and selected ones that would add variety to their meals. She consulted with Beatty about herbs and flowers that would be planted in the kitchen garden in the coming weeks. She conferred with Mrs. Reynolds to get a more thorough understanding of the patterns of maintaining the house. In sum, in every way possible way she was increasing her grasp of the complexities of her position as mistress of Pemberley.

But most of all she continued her study of her husband, his tastes and preferences, each day discovering idiosyncrasies and strengths of his character and the depth of his love for her, his sister, and Pemberley.

March 10, Friday

Only a week had passed following the departure of their guests when an invitation came in the post from the Morrises: dinner on the following Wednesday. With nothing to prevent their attendance, and with Darcy's assent, Elizabeth wrote a note of acceptance and sent it, because they could not be certain of seeing the Morrises at church on Sunday.

Bradford had found a saddle for Georgiana, and now the threesome rode together every sunny and cloudy day except Sundays, leaving the rainy days for concentrating on indoor activities.

Georiana persisted in the kitchen duties, leaving her music study to don the large apron Mrs. Sims provided. However, Georgiana was no longer content with the simplest tasks. She asked to learn how to make scones and met no resistance from Mrs. Sims. She had made them only three times before she had mastered the technique. The first rainy day following, she left breakfast for kitchen duty. Mrs. Sims agreed to Georgiana's suggestion that this morning her scones should be served at eleven to herself, Elizabeth and Darcy. She selected the jam that was to be served with them, made the scones, and put them into the oven, timed to be warm still for their tea. She told Fenton to tell Darcy and Elizabeth that she had ordered tea for eleven in the morning room. The scones, removed from the oven, she went to the morning room to await Katie's arrival with the tea tray.

"Georgiana," Elizabeth said, "you look a bit flustered. Is anything wrong?"

"Nothing at all."

"There's no difficulty in the kitchen, is there?" Darcy asked.

"No, nothing." She picked up a magazine, but only leafed through it, unable to settle down to read.

Katie came in with the tea, and Elizabeth poured.

"You're alert as a bunny rabbit," Elizabeth observed.

"Really?"

"She's quite right," Darcy added. "One would think your new horse had just arrived today rather than a week ago." He bit into the warm scone appreciatively as Georgiana observed him. Then she turned to Elizabeth who had just spread jam on hers and was about to bite into it. Seeing Georgiana's expectant look, she withdrew the scone, looked at it, felt its warmth, and guessed the truth, "You baked them, didn't you?"

"Yes, I did," she responded shyly. "Are they good?"

Elizabeth took the bite, chewed, and revealed her opinion by the satisfaction on her face.

First Darcy shook his head. Then he took another bite and nodded approval. Then he shrugged his shoulders. "What can I say," he said. He set his cup down, went to Georgiana, and kissed her forehead. "Congratulations, They're excellent. So, is this the crowning achievement of your kitchen adventure, or just the beginning?"

"I don't know," she replied.

"Then we shall just have to be patient," Elizabeth said.

March 15, Wednesday: A Fair Proposed

Wednesday quickly came, and on a gray day the threesome departed in the carriage for dinner at the Morrises. The other guests were gathering as they arrived: the Howells, Sir Humphrey, the Carletons, and the Wilsons. Mrs. Winston had declined the invitation, sending regrets.

Elizabeth noted that Mrs. Morris seated Georgiana and Sally together. The Darcys received many compliments on the ball, but during most of the dinner, several conversations were in progress at any one time. Elizabeth tried to keep foremost in her mind the indifference with which Darcy had responded to the idea of a fair at Pemberley, while trying to avoid saying anything that could result in later difficulties. She couldn't help wondering if perhaps the dinner had been staged in order to get Darcy's approval to the country fair scheme. Then her mind wandered to the hope that someday she would be able to enjoy a dinner such as this without the uneasiness she felt on this occasion.

The dinner finished, Sally and Georgiana bundled up and went outside for a walk, the ladies returned to the drawing room for coffee, and the gentlemen remained at the table for another glass of wine or a brandy.

Still more compliments on the ball, and questions about her sisters and the Bingley's stay and departure. All the while Elizabeth maintained her vigilance against an unguarded comment or question. Still no comment about the fair idea. If "everyone was talking" about it, at least they weren't talking here.

The young ladies returned from their walk, cheeks pink. The gentlemen arrived from the dining room, and inevitably, Sally was asked to play the piano and then Georgiana. Both complied and were rewarded with applause.

In the larger group, several conversations were in progress at once, and by the time they had departed, Elizabeth was eager for the relative quiet of Pemberley.

In the carriage on the way home, Darcy seemed quieter than usual, even somber. The drawing room drew all three on their return home.

Georgiana picked up a book, but Elizabeth merely sat down and closed her eyes, allowing the confusion of the afternoon to sort itself out in her mind.

Darcy sat down and stared at the flames in the fireplace. At last he broke the silence. "Well, Elizabeth, what do you have to say about the country fair idea?"

"They asked you?"

"Yes, all of them. Apparently they've been discussing the idea for some time. They seem to have many of the details worked out already. What do you think?"

"But it's your decision, surely. Of what value is my opinion?"

"Yes, it is my decision; and they all are pledging their own time and effort, but I would not be at all surprised to see the ladies performing many of the tasks. And if it's held at Pemberley, you might find yourself fully involved. Didn't you say Mrs. Wilson was the first to mention it at the vicarage? She's probably knee deep in it already."

Elizabeth reflected on his comments and on Mrs. Wilson's central role in the Christmas bazaar. "But the ladies seemed to think it would be an outdoor event entirely."

"Oh, yes; they assured me of that," he said as he got up and began pacing the room. "But think about it: Who was the one who organized our donations to the Christmas bazaar? And the Christmas gifts for the tenants? No, Elizabeth, if there is a fair at Pemberley, you can be sure every effort will be made to involve you. What would be your response?"

She thought for awhile and then asked, "When would the fair take place?"

"They're talking about August. I'd say the end of August would be best; there's less likely to be rain then."

"What did you tell them?"

"I tried as much as possible to avoid commitment."

"But you didn't refuse."

"No, I didn't refuse. They didn't press me for an answer, but it's less than six months; I think we should give them a definite answer within two weeks. That would give them enough time to find another place if we refuse."

Georgiana had been listening as the conversation progressed and now approached and sat down, waiting for further comment. Sensing their hesitation, Georgiana offered, "If you don't want to have it here you could say we're going to be at Brighton at that time."

"Are you telling us you'd like to go to Brighton?" Darcy responded, smiling.

"I wouldn't mind. I've heard it's very pleasant there in August."

"I don't think that would work," Elizabeth said. "They could just hold it at another time. No, if we refuse, we must be clear in our response." She reflected further and then said, "Has such an event ever been held at Pemberley before or at any of the other estates nearby?"

"Not at Pemberley," Darcy replied. "And I don't remember such an event at any other estate nearby either."

"If we agreed," Elizabeth said, "and if the event is successful, we might be asked each year following."

"Lord, I hadn't thought of that."

"Would it be so bad?" Georgiana asked. "It sounds like fun to me."

"Yes, I dare say you would enjoy it."

"Let's just think about it for a few days," Elizabeth suggested. "Perhaps thoughts will occur to us that will help us decide."

"I hope so. Yes, I think you're right."

They each sought refuge in a book and welcomed the announcement for supper when Selby came.

March 16, Thursday

Thursday morning while riding, Georgiana pushed ahead on her frisky Dancer, while Darcy and Elizabeth followed at a walk.

"In all the discussion about the fair, I forgot to mention that there was also discussion about a fox hunt in September."

"Do they often have fox hunts in this country?" Elizabeth asked.

"Rarely. They have, on occasion in years past, but not every year."

"Who would host the event?"

"Probably Morris. At any rate, they didn't ask me to do so."

"Do you like fox hunting?"

"Yes, it can be very enjoyable; great sport, in fact. I've only participated in a few hunts, but they tend to be memorable." He grinned, remembering. "One I remember started at Sir Humphrey's. Yes, very memorable. That reminds me. We need to check that my dress riding suit is in good condition. It's probably time for a new one. You, too. We'll need to go to London sometime in the spring; you can arrange for yours then. Why are you looking at me that way?"

"I was hoping you'd let me have your mother's dress riding habit altered for me."

"Elizabeth, this really is carrying economy too far, don't you think? You do enjoy riding, don't you?"

"Yes, I do. But I can't help thinking...."

"What is it?"

"Did Bingley tell you anything while they were here...anything of a personal nature?"

"Like what?"

She searched his countenance, but could find no hint. "Did he tell you Jane is pregnant?"

"No, he didn't. He said something that made me suspect...but not in so many words."

"The baby is due in early October."

"So how does that affect us?"

"We still can't be certain I won't be pregnant by September. If they don't have fox hunts often, it could be years until I have the opportunity to use a dress habit."

"Is that all?"

"No...I've been thinking a great deal...Bingley seems so determined to find an estate in the North. You two spent three days spreading the word of his interest. I just feel it entirely likely that Jane and he will be removed by September."

"That would be a rapid resolution of the situation. I'd say it would more likely be the following year, in the fall or winter. Such things do take an interminable length of time."

"But if Jane is nearby and needs my assistance, I want to be able to help her."

"You're serious, aren't you?"

"Very serious. You have to remember that Jane and I were not only sisters, but constant companions our entire lives until we married."

"Yes, I see. You're not just talking about the fox hunt; you're talking about the fair as well, aren't you?"

"Yes, I am."

They had completed their circuit and waved to Georgiana to rejoin them, and they returned to the stable.

That evening when Elizabeth entered their bedroom from her dressing room Darcy was waiting for her. He took her in his arms and held her closely. Then he said, "I want to forget about the fair, the fox hunt, and everything else but you." He helped her into bed and they let lovemaking remove the world from their existence.

The days passed, full of tasks and pleasures. A letter arrived from Mama. She had gone to London with Mr. Bennet and Mr. and Mrs. Gardner. The two couples had enjoyed plays, concerts, and gossip as their rightful share of life's offerings. Kitty and Mary did stay at Netherfield for several days until their parents returned.

A note came from Mr. Collins announcing the birth of a daughter. Charlotte was well and all were content.

March 25, Saturday

Only ten days had passed since the dinner at the Morrises when a letter arrived from Bingley. He had received information about an estate that was for sale—one that seemed suitable for him. Would Darcy mind visiting it to make a first-hand evaluation and write to Bingley giving his opinion of it?

"Are you going to do it?" Elizabeth asked.

"Certainly. It's a very reasonable request. You and Georgiana can come along. We need a change of scenery—something to clear our heads."

Georgiana brightened as she listened to the conversation. Elizabeth remarked, "It looks as if we won't have to persuade you to make the trip."

"Certainly not."

"But what about the fair, Darcy; what are you going to tell them?"

"I think we should agree, only making it plain that you and I will be observers, not central to the planning; that we'll lay out boundaries of the space to be used, and that we must see plans before they are decided and announced."

"I know you won't be sorry, Darcy," Georgiana said.

"I wish I could be so sure," he replied.

The following day after church he talked with Sir Humphrey, Morris, and Howell, asking that they and the other gentlemen present at the Morris dinner gather at Pemberley Tuesday at eleven.

The Darcys would leave Wednesday morning to inspect Bingley's prospective estate and return Thursday evening. Elizabeth conferred with Mrs. Reynolds about their trip, and she and Georgiana made decisions about what they would take with them.

Georgiana and Mrs. Sims conspired to allow Georgiana to make the scones that would be served to the gentlemen as they met concerning the fair.

The gentlemen arrived and were taken to the morning room where Selbey served them tea and the scones. Elizabeth and Georgiana had retreated to the music room with their embroidery. The gentlemen left about one o'clock, and Katie brought a message to the ladies that Darcy was waiting for them in the morning room.

"Well?" Elizabeth appealed.

"The deed is done. They expressed gratitude at the offer of the use of the estate for the fair—part of it, that is—and disappointment that we have determined not to play a central role in the planning."

"Did they ask for explanation?"

"Not in so many words. I think they would have welcomed explanation, but I didn't offer, and they didn't pursue the matter."

"Then we can make our little trip with no concern lingering on that score."

"True."

"Maybe I could make scones for the fair," Georgiana ventured.

"I think you've been rather assiduous on that front already," Darcy countered.

Georgiana raised her eyebrow waiting for further comment.

"They were very good. I noticed there were none remaining on the tray when Katie removed it. Our guests seemed very appreciative."

"You didn't tell them...."

"Oh no. You'll have to do your own advertising," he assured her.

Wednesday

Wednesday after breakfast the threesome gathered for their departure, their cases already installed in the carriage by the footmen. There was some mist in the morning as they proceeded, and overcast sky persisted almost until they arrived at Huntington, the village near the estate in question—Thornwood being its name. Darcy secured rooms for the night and from the innkeeper got directions to Thornwood. After dinner at the inn they re-entered the carriage and rode to Thornwood. The owner agreed that Darcy could tour the estate with his steward beginning at nine the following morning.

They returned to the inn, noting what details they could of the surrounding countryside in the waning light.

They ordered supper, ate, and chatted, musing on the possibility that this area might soon become home to the Bingleys, observing advantages and disadvantages.

During a lull in the conversation, Georgiana said, "Just think, every time we go to a new place we see more and more people we've never seen before. We hardly ever encounter anyone we've already met. Then think about the globe and maps and all the places on it. What a great number of people there must be in the world!"

Darcy and Elizabeth exchanged glances.

"Did I say something wrong?" Georgiana asked.

"Not at all," Darcy said. It's just that what you said reminded me of Theresa Carleton. She often seems to make profound comments too."

"Profound?"

"I think Darcy means a statement about larger ideas rather than about personal matters."

They agreed to rap on Georgiana's door when ready for breakfast and retired to their bedroom. "We're getting to be old hands at this inn routine," Darcy said.

"Yes," Elizabeth replied. "It does give one a rather carefree feeling, doesn't it?"

They took advantage of that carefree feeling to express their feelings for each other and appreciation for the closeness that marriage and their relationship afforded.

March 30, Thursday

Breakfast finished, the inn bill paid, and travel cases stowed, the travelers boarded the carriage and rode to Thornwood where Darcy rapped on the door. A maid admitted them and led them to a sitting room where Mr. Lonsdale greeted them and introduced Morgan, the steward.

Morgan then left with Darcy to show him around the estate, leaving the ladies with Mr. Lonsdale, who proceeded to show them the likeness of his son in his officer's uniform. "Killed, you know, in the war," he said. "Such a waste. So sure the military was the life he wanted. Cavalry. Wouldn't listen to me...or his mother."

Elizabeth wanted to ask if he had other children, but instead asked, "When you leave Thornwood, where will you go?"

"Mrs. Lonsdale wants to live in Bath...at least for a few months. Maybe we'll settle there, but I'm determined to spend summers in Brighton. Our daughter lives near Bristol, so we'll see. First I must find a buyer for this estate."

He settled into a chair, and the old dog that had been following him around settled at his feet.

"You must excuse Mrs. Lonsdale," he continued. "She hasn't been well lately. I'd show you around the house, but it has become very difficult for me to walk in recent years."

He sat quietly for a few minutes, then roused and said, "The maid could show you around. Would you like to see the house?"

"I'd like that," Elizabeth answered.

He got up and rang for the maid. When she arrived, he gave her instructions to show the ladies around the house, except for Mrs. Lonsdale's room, of course.

They followed the maid, Elizabeth particularly trying to imagine the Bingleys in this house and the changes they might make to suit their own taste. She tried to imagine Darcy and herself visiting the Bingleys. "Which bedroom would they assign to us?" she wondered.

They returned to the sitting room and sat quietly, waiting for Darcy to return. Finally the maid reappeared, this time with tea. She served them and left. At length Mr. Lonsdale asked, "Do you think you'd like to live here?"

Elizabeth replied, "Didn't Mr. Darcy tell you that it is his friend who is interested in Thornwood?"

"Oh yes, of course. They must be very good friends."

"Yes, they've been friends for many years, since college days."

"The old friends are the best friends," he mused. "Most of mine are gone now. The ones that haven't died have moved to Bath. Too crowded, I say. Nothing like the country, eh Sport?" he said, petting his dog.

"Nothing like the country." He paused, absorbed in his own thoughts, then continued, "So you two are sisters."

"No," Elizabeth replied, "Miss Darcy is Mr. Darcy's sister."

"Of course."

"Live in Leicestershire, do you?"

"No," Georgiana answered, "Derbyshire."

"I see. Please help yourself to more tea. Perhaps you could pour some for me as well."

Elizabeth refilled the cups; he drank his and set the cup down.

"A girl I knew as a child married a man from Derbyshire, name of Winston."

The name brought Elizabeth and Georgiana to attention, and they looked at each other.

"I don't think I ever saw her again. Strange. It's not so very far. But when people here go somewhere it is to Leicester or London, or Bath. I don't suppose you'd know her. Pointless to ask."

"Actually, we do know a lady by that name; she might be near your age. We know her son better: Sir Humphrey."

"Yes, that's the one. I heard she had a son who was knighted for some fool thing. Damned nonsense, all those titles."

Georgiana maintained her composure, but Elizabeth had to strain to suppress a smile.

"Lively little girl she was. Married rather well, I believe."

"She lives with Sir Humphrey. His wife died some years ago."

"It's not so sad when an old fool like me dies, but I hate to see the young ones go."

Elizabeth wondered if he would talk so openly to one of his neighbors. "You have a rather large library," she said.

"Yes; I expect I'll have to sell the books separately. The buyer for Thornwood is likely to have his own tastes. Too much to buy all in one bite anyway. I'll take some of the books with me, of course: the old favorites and some I still intend to read but never have. The eyes fail me, though. I only read during daylight now."

The door opened admitting Morgan and Darcy, with the maid following with more hot tea. She served Darcy and Morgan, then offered more to the others, but they declined.

Darcy explained to Mr. Lonsdale that he would write a letter the following day to Bingley describing the property in detail including his own evaluation.

"But do you think the property will suit him?" Mr. Lonsdale asked.

"He'll have to decide for himself, of course, but I don't see any serious obstacle," Darcy replied.

The Darcys expressed their thanks for the opportunity to see the property and left.

They boarded the carriage and rode until almost two o'clock before they found an inn where they could stop for dinner. Their food ordered, Elizabeth said, "I heard what you told Mr. Lonsdale, but is that the whole story?"

"Not quite. I intend to tell Bingley that if he does purchase the property, I recommend that the wood and painted surfaces throughout the entire house be refinished and painted before they move in. The dwelling is to all appearance structurally sound, but it needs that kind of attention to preserve the materials."

"And to brighten it up as well," Elizabeth added.

"I see you agree with me."

"And so do I," Georgiana added.

"But is it the right property for Bingley?"

"I think so. It will take some work initially, but the price is very reasonable. If he is willing to make the effort, he will in the end have a far finer property than if everything were already in top condition. In that case, the price would be much higher."

"But will he do it?"

Darcy looked at Elizabeth, puzzled. "You haven't seen Bingley as I have. He's really very enterprising. He may decide to look elsewhere, of course, but...well, we shall see."

The sun followed them the rest of the way to Pemberley, where they arrived well before dark.

Friday

The following afternoon all three Darcys were in the drawing room when Georgiana presented a sketch to Elizabeth.

"What is it?"

"An apron. I plan to have one made for me in London." Actually, I think two would be better, so I'll always have one clean to wear."

When he heard the word "apron" Darcy looked up from his book and said, "Haven't you just about finished your kitchen adventure?"

"No, I haven't."

"You sound very definite," Elizabeth said.

"I suppose I do. And Darcy, most of the time one hour is enough, but there is one thing I'd like to do...I need to spend four hours—I mean from start to finish. I won't have to work the whole time. I can read part of the time."

"What do you propose to do?"

"I'd rather not say."

"But it is cooking."

"Yes, of course. Mrs. Sims won't let me scrub pots and pans."

"So it's a secret."

"Yes, in a way."

"And when will you tell us?"

"After you've eaten it."

He looked to Elizabeth for support, but she kept her eyes on her needlework.

"Don't you think you've carried this experiment far enough? It must be two months since you started."

"But why shouldn't I continue? I practice the piano almost three hours every day, except when we're on trips, of course. And I haven't missed riding one day since Woodbury brought home the saddle for Dancer, except for rainy days."

He looked again to Elizabeth for support, but she refused to meet his gaze.

"I will have to miss riding that one morning."

"Perhaps you could do this project on a rainy day."

"It might not be so easy to schedule."

"I see. Perhaps I should be happy that you don't want to spend your days sitting on a satin cushion."

"Yes, you should. That's a very good thought. I'll remember that the next time I want to do something. But, you don't object to my project."

"Yes, I do object, but I won't stop you. I'm confident you'll soon come to your senses."

"Thank you, Darcy; you won't be sorry."

"Isn't that what she said about the fair?" he asked, again appealing to Elizabeth.

"I think it is; but she hasn't been proved wrong yet," Elizabeth replied, looking up at him.

The days and weeks flew by. The grass greened to brilliance, and the fruit trees blossomed. Morning rides were no longer so crisply cool. Mid-April had arrived. For Elizabeth, the dominant theme for her days had become routine rather than the constant newness of everything.

Occasionally the Darcys mentioned the Bingleys, wondering what their thinking might be in response to Darcy's letter about Thornwood.

The 19th was a rainy day as they arose and had not cleared up as they left the breakfast table, Darcy to his study, Elizabeth to hers, and Georgiana to her own activities.

When they gathered to wait for dinner, Darcy brought a letter from Bingley. He read through it quickly and then shared its contents with the ladies. "He's going to look at Thornwood for himself. He's interested, but not so convinced of its appropriateness as to bring Jane along for a first inspection."

The letter concluded, "Don't be surprised if you see me at your door one day soon. I may need a couple days to think over this scheme before deciding. It might prove convenient to spend that thinking time at Pemberley."

They followed Selbey to the dining room, and Darcy handed Elizabeth the letter. She read it carefully and handed it to Georgiana.

They mused over the various aspects of the situation. Why wasn't Jane coming along? Perhaps he really wasn't impressed with the property on the basis of Darcy's description and evaluation. Certainly the weather wasn't so disagreeable for a trip. Could one of the elder Bennets be ill?

The more they discussed the question, the more possibilities seemed to present themselves: If he likes it, perhaps he'll send for Jane. But, will he want her to travel alone? Oh, dear, perhaps Mama would come along. Would that be so bad? Well, perhaps she could now be welcomed with some degree of equanimity.

They had nearly finished eating, but the topic seemed still full of fresh possibilities.

About to take the last bite of her steak and kidney pie, Georgiana remarked, "It does sometimes seem that often we are so occupied with our thoughts and conversation that we eat our food almost absentmindedly."

"Another profound thought," Darcy said, looking to Elizabeth.

Elizabeth looked at him and then to Georgiana where she detected a faint smile. "Yes, Mrs. Sims could have spent the whole morning cooking our dinner, and we eat it scarcely noticing how well it tastes."

"Yes, something like that."

"Or perhaps it was Miss Darcy who spent the whole morning cooking and has mastered the steak and kidney pie recipe."

"Perhaps."

"Congratulations, Georgiana, but you're mistaken. I was aware that it was very good," Darcy said.

April 28, Friday: Thornwood

More than a week passed following the letter from Bingley. Elizabeth found herself calculating which day Bingley might leave Netherfield, how long he might stay in the vicinity of Thornwood, and if he might, in fact, appear at their door.

The threesome were gathered in the drawing room that Friday evening about six o'clock when Fenton announced that Mr. Bingley had arrived.

Darcy bounded from his chair and met Bingley in the hall. "Here, Fenton, take his coat. Come, Bingley, join us in the drawing room. Welcome."

Elizabeth and Georgiana rose and greeted him. Before Fenton could leave, Darcy told him to ask Selbey to set another place for supper, and to see that the carriage and horses were attended to.

Bingley approached the fireplace and warmed his hands.

"Jane...." Elizabeth began.

"She's well," Bingley responded. "Very well. There just seemed so many points about the property to consider from the letter that I didn't think she should make the trip. If the property doesn't suit me, there seemed no point in troubling her about it."

"You've seen it?" Darcy asked.

"Yes, I arrived in Huntington Tuesday evening and spent Wednesday examining the house and riding over all the fields with the steward—almost all, that is."

"What do you think of it?" Darcy pressed.

"I quite agree with your evaluation. And in talking with Lonsdale, it seems that the sale should take place about September first or October first with respect to the rents."

"That wouldn't be very convenient if you decide to have the house redecorated."

"True, but, as it happens, Mr. and Mrs. Lonsdale are eager to leave and would be happy to vacate the house by July first or possibly as early as June first. It seems they want to spend the summer in Brighton. Morgan can continue his stewardship through the end of the rent period, but the house itself would be available. Actually, at least at this time I'm inclined to ask him to remain as steward. That could ease the transition a great deal."

"Would you be willing to take the house with all that painting and wood refinishing to be done?" Elizabeth asked.

"I made inquiries yesterday, and it seems I should have little difficulty finding men to do the work."

They waited as he paused to think it over. Selbey arrived with a bottle of wine and some glasses. Darcy filled a glass, handed it to Bingley and poured some for himself.

"Your travel case...." Elizabeth began.

"William took it. It's in the entry."

"We prepared a room for you. I suggest you go with William now and come back directly. Supper will be served shortly."

He left and returned as they were about to go to the dining room. Seated at the table Elizabeth began, "Jane...what did she think about Darcy's letter?"

"She seemed very favorably impressed. She considered coming, but as I said...."

"Might Jane come now that you've seen the house?"

"That's what I need to decide. Darcy, how are those horses working out?"

"Very well."

"Perhaps we could go riding tomorrow. I find that riding clears my thinking."

"Capital idea," Darcy replied.

"I must say your cook does very well for you," Bingley remarked.

"Yes," Darcy replied. "She seems to get better all the time."

Saturday

Bingley and Darcy did go riding in the morning, and the ladies went to their separate activities.

Even though no decision had been made concerning Thornwood, somehow Elizabeth's thinking was freed. She decided to review her correspondence and found to her dismay that she still had not responded to Cousin Collins' note announcing their baby. First she resolved to begin a correspondence log, then she wrote to Charlotte.

"Dear Charlotte,

Please forgive me for not writing sooner. What a joy to hear about the birth of your Martha. Please thank your husband for his letter and accept our most heartfelt congratulations and best wishes.

We seem always to be in the midst of a great deal of activity, most of it agreeable. Rather than write of the various events, I'll discuss them with you when I see you.
Affectionately,
Elizabeth"

She then set up the log in a journal book listing the letters she could remember receiving and sending since her arrival at Pemberley.

She went to the music room, found that Georgiana had left, and set herself to playing and practicing "...just in case Darcy asks for some music while Bingley is here."

She arrived in the morning room shortly before two o'clock. Georgiana was already there, but the gentlemen didn't arrive until Selbey was at the door announcing dinner.

"You did make a long ride of it, didn't you?"

"Yes," Darcy replied, "though we walked here and there as well, talking with some of the tenants and listening to some of their problems."

Elizabeth wanted to quiz Bingley, but instead waited for him to disclose whether he had made any decisions. Maddeningly, he and Darcy seemed to find no end of other topics to discuss: the vagaries of tenants, which crops one should encourage them to raise, the price of wool. "Is there no end?" she thought.

They adjourned to the drawing room, but before Darcy and Bingley could raise additional agricultural topics, she asked, "Did the riding help to clarify your thoughts about Thornwood?"

"In a way, yes; though I was surprised when I awoke this morning how clear everything seemed to me. I could have told you at breakfast, but it's been some time since Darcy and I have had the pleasure of a long ride. And, in fact, I feel even more secure in my decisions now. I shall make an offer for Thornwood, but only after talking with Jane, and if she agrees. If she wants, I'll take her to see Thornwood before she decides. I'll leave for Netherfield Monday morning."

"But what if someone else makes an offer to Mr. Lonsdale first?" Elizabeth queried.

"I've thought of that. That's a risk I'm willing to take. I don't think it likely though. It's very early in the year for land transfers."

Elizabeth looked at the faces of her three companions. Darcy and Georgiana looked as anxious as she felt. But Bingley appeared perfectly serene. She thought, "He's the one in a milieu of change, while we are perfectly settled. Yet he is the one who appears perfectly calm. Strange."

In their bedroom that night, Elizabeth said, "Darcy, you know how I feel about Jane and the changes they're going through. Please understand that, for my part, I want to do whatever we can to assist Bingley and Jane."

"I was hoping you'd feel that way. That's exactly the way I feel."

"Then talk with him tomorrow after church and make him understand that. If they were to spend the entire summer here, I would be content. But, what you want must govern."

He took her in his arms and held her, his eyes moist.

Monday

Bingley did leave Monday morning. Georgiana left for her morning of music and cooking, and Elizabeth and Darcy retreated to the morning room.

Elizabeth decided that if her thoughts were not to be constantly in speculation about what Jane and Bingley might be doing as the days passed, she would have to make some plans of her own.

The weather was so pleasant that she got Darcy to agree that they should attend any assembly within reasonable distance during the coming weeks. Also, she determined to get better acquainted with some of the ladies she had already met.

"I think I'll invite a few ladies to tea."

"Who do you have in mind?"

"Mrs. Blakely."

"Of course."

"And Mrs. Pettigrew."

"Doesn't eight miles seem rather far to go for a cup of tea?"

"I can't command her attendance, but I do like her; she's very easy to talk with."

"You aren't thinking of her brother, are you?"

"Actually, no, I'd really like to get better acquainted with her."

"Mr. Pettigrew is hardly the most imposing person in Derbyshire."

"No, my dear, that's you. If you are going to use that standard for friendship, we shall have no friends at all."

"I mean, he is a bit crude, don't you think?"

"Perhaps he is rather unpolished; but you have to admit he is very entertaining. You're not asking me not to invite her, are you?"

"No. I have to agree with your assessment of her. I just find it hard to think of him as one of my friends."

"Is that essential?"

"No, it isn't. Are you going to invite Theresa Carleton?"

"I hadn't planned to, but I could."

"Carleton is my best friend, next to Bingley."

"She is entertaining, but she sometimes makes me feel a little uneasy."

"I think you'll like her better as you get better acquainted. Who else were you planning to invite?"

"Actually I wanted to keep the group small, so we can really get acquainted."

"And Georgiana—will she be present?"

"I see what you mean; I think I should invite Mrs. Morris and Sally."

The guest list complete, she set the date: the following week on Tuesday at 10:30 a.m. She wrote and posted invitations.

At dinner Darcy informed the ladies of an assembly to be held on Friday night in Lambton.

So the days and weeks continued. Duties and pleasures at home brought Elizabeth to a sense that this was her home and to a solid grounding in that fact. Social events instilled in her the sense that she was also becoming a part of the community.

All of the activity could not keep thoughts of the Bingley's activities from intruding frequently, but they did not dominate or detract from her enjoyment of life at Pemberley.

May 23, Tuesday

More than three weeks passed before they received a letter from Bingley. Darcy read it and handed it to Elizabeth. He and Jane had taken little more than a day to thoroughly discuss all the questions involved. Bingley had sent his offer by post to Lonsdale, who posted his acceptance soon thereafter. Bingley then journeyed again to Huntington, arriving on the 16th to complete the transaction. They would take possession on July first. They would accept Darcy's invitation to stay at Pemberley part of the time while work was being done. They would arrive Thursday, June 29 and expected Jane to stay perhaps three weeks. Bingley would arrive with her and leave the following Monday to begin supervision of necessary work.

Bingley had accepted Lonsdale's offer to examine the library and make his offer for the entire library or part of it. Once Bingley had found men to do the work and set them to the tasks, he would spend those hours in early July evaluating and deciding about the library.

Georgiana interrupted their discussion of the letter, saying, "Darcy, I want permission to spend a full morning in the kitchen once a month."

"Which morning would that be?"

"It would vary."

"When would you tell us which morning?"

"After I do it."

"This is mysterious."

"Well?"

"Do I have a choice?"

"No."

"Permission granted."

Wednesday

The Bingley's activities settled, Elizabeth turned her thoughts to her mother. The next day while riding, she disclosed to Darcy her thinking.

"I think we must invite Mama to visit us for a week in June."

"As you wish."

"I wish the decision had been so easy for me to make!"

"Have you settled on a date?"

"Perhaps the second or third week in June. I want her safely back in Meryton when Jane and Bingley arrive. If only there were something special happening in this area at that time."

"I'll mention it to Sir Humphrey at church on Sunday. He always knows the local gossip. If there are to be any special events, he'll know about it."

"Perhaps we could ride there tomorrow."

"On horseback?"

"Why not?"

"Why not, indeed."

The following day they left immediately after breakfast since it was 10 miles to the Winston estate, Georgiana riding with them.

Cirrus clouds wisped their way across the sky, a pleasant day nevertheless for a long ride.

Sir Humphrey was at home, happy to be called from his study to greet his guests. He ushered them into the sitting room where Mrs. Winston also greeted them.

"I didn't realize you were such an enthusiastic rider, Mrs. Darcy."

"It's something new; I'm becoming more venturesome."

"Mrs. Darcy has a mission today, Sir Humphrey," Darcy explained."

"Indeed? What could that be?"

"We've decided to invite my mother to visit us for a week in June. We thought it would be agreeable for her to come when there is something special happening."

"...and thought you might be aware of coming events," Darcy added.

"Like the Morrises ball, perhaps?"

"They're having a ball?" Elizabeth asked.

"Yes, Morris asked me recently who they might get for musicians. The 16th, I think. You can ask them to make sure."

"You must stay to tea," Mrs. Winston insisted.

"Thank you, that would be delightful." Elizabeth replied.

Friday

The following night was the Assembly in Gormley. Not only were the Darcy's in attendance, but the Morrises as well. They confirmed the date for the ball and indicated the Darcys should receive their invitation within days, assuring them that Elizabeth's mother and sisters would be very welcome.

Elizabeth wrote to her mother suggesting that she arrive on Tuesday the 13th and stay until the following Monday, the 19th. She mentioned the ball and suggested that she bring Kitty and Mary along.

The following day at dinner, Selbey had just finished serving the pudding when Elizabeth said, "Georgiana, I had all I could do to restrain myself from telling Mrs. Winston about your success with the steak and kidney pie."

"But you didn't, did you?"

"She's an extraordinary woman; I think she would have enjoyed hearing it, but I think you should be the one to disclose the secret."

"It wouldn't embarrass you?"

"To tell someone you've developed a new talent? Certainly not." Then she looked to Darcy, half expecting to see him scowl. What she saw was a very contented look as he ate his pudding.

"This is one of my favorite puddings," he remarked. "Mrs. Sims is really surpassing herself."

"Is she really?" Georgiana asked.

"Indeed," he replied, and then caught the smiles on the ladies' faces.

"Have you both forgotten that today is a very special day?"

"What day is it?" Darcy asked.

"It's six months since you two were married; it's an anniversary!"

"And are we perhaps celebrating with a pudding created by Miss Darcy?" Elizabeth asked.

"I am," she replied.

During the following days, Elizabeth planned with Mrs. Reynolds as far ahead as she could, for the week her mother, Kitty, and Mary would be visiting, and for the weeks later when Jane and Bingley would be staying with them. Deciding which rooms would be used, selecting foods she hoped would please, Georgiana sitting with her and Mrs. Sims, to take advantage of anything she had learned in the kitchen that would add to the pleasure of the visits.

She requested and received Darcy's approval for a dinner party the day following her mother's arrival—just inviting Sir Humphrey and his mother, Mrs. Winston. She sent a note of invitation and received a note of acceptance.

June 13, Tuesday: Mrs. Bennet

The 13th arrived, and Elizabeth was glad it was a Tuesday and not a Friday. She was concerned enough without an old superstition nagging at her.

Elizabeth and Georgiana rode in the carriage to Lambton to meet the stage at four and brought the Bennet ladies back to Pemberley. Mrs. Bennet was tired at the end of the day's travels and rather subdued. Nevertheless she was alert, and Elizabeth told her when they had entered the Pemberley estate and when she might soon see the house. She told Kitty and Mary that they would have the same room they had occupied in February and her mother that she would have the room the Bingleys had occupied.

That evening passed quietly as well as breakfast the following day. Elizabeth entrusted Kitty and Mary to Georgiana's care and invited her mother for a walk on the grounds, going first to the kitchen garden to see how the herbs and flowers were coming along, then taking a turn around the lawn. Finally they retired to the morning room. Mrs. Bennet was not fond of reading so she had brought a piece of needlework with her. Elizabeth picked up her own so they could chat. Mrs. Bennet proceeded to tell her all the news of Meryton—who had married recently or had babies and who had died—and of Mrs. Phillips' and Mrs. Gardner's activities.

While Mrs. Bennet was catching her breath, Elizabeth intervened, "Mama I must tell you, we're expecting guests for dinner today—one of Darcy's oldest friends, Sir Humphrey Winston and his mother, Mrs. Winston. You'll meet many others of our acquaintances at the ball on Friday at the Morrises, but Sir Humphrey was a friend of Darcy's father and is a friend of ours as well. I should warn you, though, his mother is rather outspoken."

"Hmmph," Mrs. Bennet responded. "And what is that to me?"

"Mama, I don't want to offend them; they're good friends. I'm sure you'll like them if only you give yourself the opportunity to get acquainted with them."

"Hmmph," she repeated. "Titles; sir this and sir that; it really is too much."

"Mama, please!"

"Oh, very well; I'll be on my good behavior. I suppose I must now you've become such a grand lady."

"Mama, you know that's not fair."

The door opened, admitting Georgiana, Kitty, and Mary. Not far behind them were Sir Humphrey and Mrs. Winston, accompanied by Darcy who had been pacing in front of the house awaiting their arrival.

Introductions were made and pleasantries exchanged during the interval before Selbey announced dinner.

When all were seated, Sir Humphrey looked to Elizabeth and said, "I suppose Darcy has told you we're trying to organize a fox hunt this fall." Seeing her assent, he continued, "I suppose you will be riding with us?"

"Perhaps; Darcy has been urging me to join the party, though I'm not so sure I'll be that confident of my riding skill. Georgiana has become a very skilled rider, though, so perhaps she and Darcy can represent our family."

"Mrs. Morris and Mrs. Howell are showing some interest."

"Is it a competition among the ladies?"

"I wouldn't say that. But I think most of the men like to see ladies joining in. Not all of them. Some of them would like to leave all the ladies at home sipping tea."

Elizabeth turned to Mrs. Winston and said, "Georgiana and I recently had occasion to take tea with a gentleman of Leicestershire who claimed he remembered you from childhood: a Mr. Lonsdale."

"Do you mean Dr. Lonsdale?"

"He didn't say he was a doctor, though I suppose he could have been. Mr. Darcy's friend Bingley—my sister Jane's husband—is purchasing Mr. Lonsdale's estate near Huntington; Thornwood, it's called."

"Amazing. It must be the same man."

"He said he hadn't seen you since childhood."

"I suppose that's true. I have rarely gone back to Huntington, though I still have a friend who visits me on occasion; actually we usually meet in London when we do see each other. You say he's planning to sell his estate. Where will he go then?"

"To Bath, possibly, but to Brighton for summers."

"Well, son, we shall have to look for him on our next summer holiday."

"You say Bingley is purchasing an estate in Leicestershire?" Sir Humphrey asked.

"They'll be taking possession in July."

"Will Miss Bingley be living with them there?"

"Part of the time, perhaps, Elizabeth replied, "but I think she really prefers London."

"But you said you visited Huntington—why was that?"

Elizabeth looked to Darcy, who replied, "Bingley asked me to inspect the property for him and report on it. Georgiana and Elizabeth rode along with me—it was just a two-day trip, a pleasant outing."

Sir Humphrey turned to Mrs. Bennet, "So another of your daughters will leave Hertfordshire."

"Yes; quite unnecessary. He could just as well have purchased Netherfield. It's a fine estate. I told them not to leave, but young people just don't want to listen. Hertfordshire is so much more agreeable."

"Perhaps you and Mr. Bennet will move also—possibly somewhere near here."

"Hmmph! Take his nose out of his books? Not likely."

Sir Humphrey turned and said, "Darcy, I've heard a rumour about Pemberley."

"What might that be?" Darcy asked.

"It concerns your kitchen. Rumour has it that your cook has been blossoming—actually becoming the envy of your neighbors. I see nothing on the table today to dispel the rumour either." Looking to Miss Darcy, he said, "Has anyone mentioned that to you, Miss Darcy?"

"No, but Mrs. Sims is a good cook, and I do think Elizabeth's suggestions have inspired her."

"So that's what you think it is, do you? Inspiration from Mrs. Darcy. Hmmm."

Mrs. Winston turned to Elizabeth, "You'll have to tell us some of your secrets, my dear."

Elizabeth responded, "Mrs. Sims was a fine cook when I arrived, and I assure you I'm entitled to little credit in that department. But I'll pass on to her your compliments."

Sir Humphrey continued his queries about the Bingleys and their new estate and the possibility that they might have an enjoyable fox hunt in their future, but at length returned to his interest in the Pemberley kitchen.

"Actually, Darcy, what I heard is that you've hired an assistant for your cook and that she's so much help that your cook has been able to concentrate on improving her culinary skills."

During Sir Humphrey's earlier comments Kitty had been looking across the table to Georgiana, but at this last comment she tried to suppress laughter and stared intensely at her plate. Sir Humphrey was as observant as most people, and he did not fail to notice Kitty's behavior.

Looking to Darcy again, he said, "Some have suggested something even more sinister—that you do have a new assistant cook, but that you don't pay her."

This was said jokingly, but Darcy's face darkened, and Elizabeth, fearing he was near real anger, felt the tension mounting within her.

Georgiana spoke now. "It's not true, Sir Humphrey. It's me. I've been spending some time in the kitchen."

"Well!" Mrs. Bennet interjected, "I never let my daughters near the kitchen!"

"Nor did my mother," Mrs. Winston added. "She made sure I was kept thoroughly ignorant of the culinary arts! After all, ignorance is the hallmark of a lady."

"What's the matter, Darcy? You're not in financial difficulty, are you? I'm surprised to hear that you'd ask Miss Darcy to cook!"

"He didn't, Sir Humphrey," Georgiana protested. She paused, not wanting to say more. But all eyes were on her, demanding further explanation. "He didn't want me working in the kitchen. I had a great deal of difficulty convincing him that I should be allowed to do so."

"How did you finally convince him?"

"I told him it didn't seem fair that I should not be allowed to do things just because I'm rich."

Everyone laughed at this except Mrs. Bennet, who continued to maintain that Miss Darcy was endangering her status as a lady, and Darcy, who merely smiled weakly in relief after suffering under the implication that he was a miser who would consign his sister to the kitchen.

On Friday all six of the Darcy party squeezed into the carriage and went to the Morris ball. As usual, on returning the young ladies were quizzed about their dancing partners but somehow endured. And, once again, no husbands were found.

Monday

Monday morning came, and Elizabeth knew that the following day her guests would depart. While no disaster had occurred, she was not pleased with the cold manner in which her mother had consistently treated Darcy. For his part, having previously observed Mrs. Bennet's willingness to make snappish and unkind remarks, he had said as little as possible and frequently stayed out of her company entirely. He spent three mornings with Woodbury visiting the tenants. In addition he often retreated to his study to review accounts and to read.

Monday after breakfast, with Darcy in his study and the young ladies engaged in their own pursuits, Elizabeth invited her mother to go for a walk.

"The day is very pleasant; then we can return to our needlework," Elizabeth said.

"Oh, very well."

They walked, absorbing the freshness of the morning and the beauty of the surroundings.

"It is very beautiful," Mrs. Bennet conceded. "I'm glad you have that at least."

"What do you mean, 'at least?'"

"Mrs. Bennet turned to her and said, "It is very hard to have to marry for money, you must admit."

"Is that what you believe, that I married for money?"

"Humph. Why else would you have married Mr. Darcy?"

"For love, Mama, for love."

"You're a dear girl to say it, but I know the truth. It's plain to see how he is—cold and proud."

"That's not how he is; he's warm and kind and generous."

"Generous? Humph!"

"Yes, generous. And the Bennets have a great deal to be grateful to Darcy for. I suppose you still believe it was Uncle Gardner who found Lydia and made Wickham marry her."

"Of course it was."

"It was not. It was Darcy. Darcy insisted the Gardners keep his part in the whole affair secret. Even Father saw through that—that Uncle Gardner didn't have that kind of money."

"That's not true."

"It is. Why else would Darcy have been at Lydia and Wickham's wedding?"

"He was not."

"He was; Lydia told me so herself. When I wrote to Aunt Gardner, she sent me a letter, revealing the truth. Darcy did it all—paid the wedding expenses, got Wickham the commission, everything. Ask Aunt Gardner. She'll tell you."

"Even if all this is true, why are you telling me now?"

"Because it pains me to see you treat Darcy like a stranger, or worse. He's my husband, Mama, and I love him very much. I want you to realize what a fine person he is."

"I'm sorry, Elizabeth," she said, taking her in her arms. "I didn't know. But why did Papa stay such a short time when he came in February?"

"Because we couldn't persuade him to stay longer. You know how he is. You said it yourself. All he wants to do is go to his study and read."

Elizabeth could see a softening in Mrs. Bennet's manner during the rest of the visit. The Bennet ladies left the next morning, and as the carriage left to take them into Lambton, Elizabeth and Darcy watched them leave. Then as they walked back into the house, Darcy said, "Your mother seems different somehow; did something happen?"

"Yes, I had a little talk with her yesterday morning. I hope you'll forgive me. I told her about your part in the affair between Lydia and Wickham."

"It certainly seems to have had a salutary effect."

The weather was fine, and, beginning to fear she would be pressured to participate in the fox hunt, every morning she possibly could Elizabeth went riding with Darcy. It would be only nine days until the Bingley's would arrive, and after they arrived she would be reluctant to leave Jane to ride.

Following dinner the day the Bennet ladies departed, the threesome gathered in the drawing room. As she picked up her needlework, Elizabeth said, "Georgiana, perhaps we should discuss the kitchen duty again."

"What do you mean?"

"I'm referring to Sir Humphrey's comments. It set Darcy in a very bad light, you know. It made him look cruel, even miserly. I realize that you did clarify the situation, but Sir Humphrey never did say where he heard the rumour. I suppose it was servants gossiping."

"I don't see how we can prevent servants from gossiping, and I don't see why I should stop. I really don't do a great deal, but what I do, I enjoy. What's the harm in it?"

Turning to Darcy, Elizabeth said, "Remember the day we went to the Pettigrews to see Midnight? They mentioned 'my mysterious ailment,' and you said, 'Perhaps we should have a ball so everyone can see that my wife does not have a mysterious ailment?'"

"Yes, I remember."

"Then in the carriage on the way home I suggested that a rumour about a ball might begin to circulate."

"Yes, you did."

"And what did you say then?"

He thought it over and finally said, "Well, let's turn rumour into reality."

Turning to Georgiana, she said, "Perhaps that would be a good way to handle this rumour."

"I don't understand."

"Consider this: Jane will be arriving soon. To celebrate her arrival, it would be entirely appropriate to invite several ladies to tea. I suggest that you and I conspire with Mrs. Sims to plan an elegant tea, that we make biscuits and cakes and lovely sandwiches—the three of us together. And when the tea is served, we can tell our guests what we have done: that Mrs. Sims is still our cook, but that you do spend some time assisting in the kitchen."

They both looked to Darcy. He had been listening while staring into the fireplace flames. When Elizabeth stopped talking, he looked up to see them waiting for his response. Finally, he said to Georgiana, "Are you ashamed of your work in the kitchen?"

"Certainly not."

"Are you proud of it?"

"Yes, I am."

"Then the tea is probably the best course to take. But, Elizabeth, are you sure you want to do it? I mean work in the kitchen. You shouldn't have to; this is not your doing."

"Yes, I am sure. I must own to being a bit envious of Georgiana's new talent. I know I'm capable of doing things, but Mrs. Winston was right. We've been kept ignorant just so we can be called ladies. But it seems to me Georgiana has proved it's possible to be a lady and be capable. Yes, I want to do it."

They proceeded to make up the guest list. In the end they limited the list to 14. Perhaps 10 would come. That should be sufficient for the rumour to be corrected.

The Bingleys would arrive on Thursday, June 29. They would have the tea on Wednesday July 5.

Together, Elizabeth and Georgiana worded an invitation and split the list, each writing part of the invitations:

"Elizabeth and Georgiana Darcy invite you to a tea in honor of Mrs. Darcy's sister, Jane Bingley, at Pemberley on Wednesday, July 5 at three-thirty p.m."

The next morning they met with Mrs. Sims and continued to meet daily until the plans were complete.

It seemed they might be able to settle into a quieter routine, but Elizabeth asked Darcy again and got his approval for alteration of the previous Mrs. Darcy's dress riding habit. The rest of her own clothing seemed entirely suitable for the demands apparent in the home and social activities for the summer. However, Georgiana's plan for an apron had been ignored. Elizabeth suggested that Mrs. Flanders might be able to make such a simple item as well.

Elizabeth wrote to her, received a reply, and they visited her the next Wednesday. She agreed to alter the riding habit. Georgiana then showed her the drawing she'd made for an apron. "Nothing could be simpler," she said. "You might be able to get fabric for it at Wilson's store."

The store carried few fabrics, but they found two cotton prints that would serve nicely. They bought enough for two aprons, brought it to Mrs. Flanders, and arranged to come back the following week on Friday.

The night before the Bingley's were to arrive Elizabeth and Darcy were about to get into bed when she said, "Darcy, I've been thinking about the library at Thornwood."

"So have I. I haven't been able to get out of my mind what Mrs. Winston said about Lonsdale being a doctor."

"My thought exactly."

"I want to look through those books and see if there's anything that can help us."

"And why would Bingley object?"

"He wouldn't, I'm sure. Besides, I think it's time I told him our secret. Would you still object?"

"No, I wouldn't. Jane wasn't entirely happy with her pregnancy. I think they'll be as eager as we are for assistance, probably moreso."

"Moreso? Do I detect a change in your thinking?"

"Yes."

"Does that mean you're ready now?"

"I'm not sure. I don't feel as desperate as I did."

"You know I call them modern inconveniences with good reason, don't you?" he said. "I'd so much rather not use them."

"I do feel more settled, but still...I really think I need more time."

"Does that mean we still need our modern inconvenience?"

She nodded her head.

He snuffed out the candle.

Thursday

With carts loaded with their possessions following their carriage the Bingleys first traveled to Thornwood where they left the carts carrying their possessions. They stayed at the inn that night at Huntington, and after Jane had made a thorough inspection of their new estate they proceeded to Pemberley, arriving the 29th as planned in the early evening.

Jane was obviously enjoying good health. The principle reasons she had not gone earlier to see Thornwood were because the description in Darcy's letter and Bingley's own descriptions were so complete and her trust in both so complete that it simply had not seemed necessary. The principle ingredient for her happiness was Bingley, and all else followed from that.

Three days of visiting followed during which Darcy disclosed to Bingley his interest in the Thornwood library and in examining it with the hope of acquiring some of the books for himself, providing Bingley himself did not want all the books. He did suggest that some of the books might be suitable for the planned library in Lambton as well. He did not disclose the more intimate reason for his interest. That he would disclose later. But all agreed that the sensible thing would be for him to go with Bingley that first week in Bingley's carriage. Both would return Saturday evening, and Bingley would go back to Huntington the Monday following to resume supervision of the redecorating.

July 2, Sunday

Sunday morning Elizabeth awoke very early. She scanned the edges of the draperies, but could see little light. She remembered the night before—Bingley and Darcy talking until near midnight, and later how quickly they had both fallen asleep. "Tomorrow morning they leave and won't be back until Saturday night. Seven months and we've never slept apart one night." The multitude of events that had transpired during those seven months flitted through her mind causing her to alternately flinch with pain and smile with pleasure. She luxuriated in the comfort of the bed and the sound of Darcy breathing. She reached to his back and ran her palm over it, feeling its warmth under her touch.

He turned over and sleepily drew her to him. Their bodies entwined as they caressed each other in mute pleasure.

"Should I get...."

"No."

He turned onto his back and pulled her over him.

"You'll be in danger of...."

"I know."

"It's all right?"

"It is more than all right."

"You're sure?"

"I'm very, very sure."

After church Sir Humphrey mentioned to Darcy that the fair committee had been approached by two businessmen from Gormley. They had heard about the planned fair at Pemberley and were requesting permission to participate as well, hoping to found a library of their own. Since Pemberley was almost the same distance from both communities, perhaps there was merit in the idea. Darcy indicated approval of the scheme and told Sir Humphrey he would meet with them the Wednesday following his return if he was able. Sir Humphrey agreed to host the meeting.

Darcy and Bingley left early Monday. Elizabeth and Georgiana took Jane to the morning room and disclosed to her details of the tea they had planned.

"Then I'll help too," Jane said.

"No, Jane; you're already showing—not a lot, but you really must be careful now not to get overtired."

"Is this what you meant when you said 'the ladies cluck-cluck like a mother hen over the mother-to-be?'"

Elizabeth conceded that she might be over-solicitous. They agreed that they all would work for an hour each morning in the kitchen, except Thursday, when only Elizabeth and Georgiana would do so.

So accustomed to each other's company over the years were the sisters that they slipped into the old habits of companionship, only making the necessary adjustments for Georgiana's participation when she joined them.

They selected the dresses they would wear for the tea, each showing the others her choice. They decided to use the drawing room for the tea since it was larger than the morning room. They gave instructions to the maid to prepare the room, adjusted the placement of chairs and other furniture, planned where the tea and delicacies would be placed, and decided that, for so many, Katie and Susan should pour the tea, leaving the hostesses free to enjoy the event. Not a little discussion revolved on the choice of which chair Jane should occupy so everyone would have easy access to her—so all the ladies would meet her, though in fact several had already met her the night of the ball. While Jane was central on the invitation, the unadvertised focus of the tea was to be the revelation of Georgiana's new interest—cooking.

The ladies began arriving just before three-thirty, and before long they had all arrived, 12 in all. One of the first was Mrs. Humphrey Winston. She found a place to sit—in the very chair they had so carefully selected for Jane. Other than that, everything went so well that years later the only way Georgiana would be able to remind Elizabeth of the event was by saying, "You remember, the time Mrs. Winston sat in the chair we'd arranged for Jane." And Elizabeth would reply, "Oh, yes, the time you first publicly displayed your culinary talents."

Saturday

Saturday came, and Darcy and Bingley arrived from Huntington in the late afternoon. Bingley had first made arrangements for workers to do the necessary redecorating. Much of the week had been spent in selecting a supervisor to direct the workers and in searching for and hiring workmen. The foreman, Smith, would arrange for materials and see that all proceeded in a satisfactory manner.

Though Bingley had spent only a few hours in the library, Darcy had spent almost the entire week culling through the books. It appeared there might be as many as 4,000 altogether. Lonsdale had apparently inherited his father's library and added to it rather enthusiastically. Lonsdale did take some books with him, but not many.

After supper, Darcy mentioned that he thought he should return with Bingley on Monday and spend another week sorting the books.

This had been the first time Darcy and Elizabeth had been parted since they married, and Elizabeth was not eager to see him leave for another week. Alone together in their bedroom, Elizabeth reminded Darcy that the fair committee was to meet on Wednesday. They debated how to handle that problem and the advantages and disadvantages of the proposed second week at Thornwood, Elizabeth raising every objection she could think of.

"Don't you think you're being rather selfish, Lizzy? If Bingley goes alone it's going to be a tiresome week for him. My being there will relieve the tedium for him as well as give me the opportunity to finish looking through the books. Besides, I noticed that the little time Bingley had to examine the books he often as not lapsed into reading one instead of just looking it over and deciding whether or not he might like to read it. He only has until September 30 to make his decisions. I jog him to move along."

"You still do take care of him, don't you?"

"Is that so bad? Moreover, with both of us gone, you can better attend to Jane's needs. Have you forgotten that you urged me to help them in any way possible?"

They still hadn't come to a satisfactory resolution of the affair when exhaustion and sleep overtook them.

Sunday had its own momentum: breakfast and then church, with the rest of the day and evening passing as if in confirmation of predestination. They were late to bed and on Monday early to rise, and Darcy did go to Thornwood with Bingley.

July 10, Monday

On Monday, Friday had seemed the distant future, but old activities and duties repeated, and new ones found, filled the time more agreeably than could have been predicted.

Elizabeth and Jane picked flowers for the dinner table Saturday and arranged them with many changes and not a little conversation.

Darcy and Bingley arrived not long before dinner. Darcy's task with the books was complete. "We decided to make an offer together to Mr. Lonsdale for the entire library—an offer we feel sure he'll accept," Darcy said. "I've selected the ones I'm interested in and Bingley will spend the coming weeks selecting what he wants to keep and which to pass on to others."

After another week at Thornwood, Bingley arrived the following Saturday with the news that enough of the rooms were completed so that Jane could leave with him on Monday. They would be gone almost six weeks and would return for the Pemberley Fair on September 2.

Darcy attended the committee meetings held during the last several weeks before the fair so he could be on hand to approve or disapprove final plans as they were made, informing Elizabeth as things progressed. For her part she behaved very cautiously when persons involved in the fair came to the house or even near her, such as after church. "Until Jane's baby is born, I want to avoid any demands others might want to make on me," she thought. She paid particular attention to any comments she made in the presence of Sir Humphrey and Mrs. Wilson, the former because of his penchant for teasing, the latter because of her tendency to press all around her to participate in her schemes.

Darcy found time to walk with her on occasion, but more often they rode, often before breakfast.

August 31, Thursday

Bingley and Jane arrived on Thursday before the fair so they would have a full day before the fair for quiet enjoyment. Jane bubbled over with comments about the servants at Thornwood that had agreed to continue and others she and Bingley had interviewed and hired or offered positions. Indeed, in six weeks she had accomplished more in establishing herself as mistress of Bingley's estate than she had in seven months at Netherfield. With no Miss Bingley, no Mrs. Hurst, and no Mrs. Bennet to impede her she felt as free as a bird—only the agreeable Bingley to consult on each question.

Her cheeks bloomed with health as her body foretold the advent of their first child.

In watching Bingley as he monitored Jane, Elizabeth was struck with the thought, "I do believe I'm viewing someone who loves his wife as much as Darcy loves me. Remarkable."

On Friday Elizabeth and Jane occasionally looked out the windows to watch the men laying out paraphernalia for the fair. It was obvious there would be many vendors and other hosts and, hopefully, many patrons as well. A few of the workers slept in a hay loft that night after being served an evening meal at a table with benches outdoors in the pleasant summer air.

September 2, Saturday: The Fair

Early in the morning vendors and concessionaires began to arrive and people the large grassy area arranged for them. By ten o'clock carriages loaded with patrons began arriving. They were taken to a field next to the Lambton road. Drivers unharnessed the horses and tethered them loosely to trees so they could graze during the day and brought buckets of water for them. Farm wagons brought fair patrons from the two towns, turned around, and returned to the towns for additional loads.

By one o'clock Elizabeth conjectured that both villages must be vacant of humans, tended only by stray dogs and cats.

No dinner would be served at Pemberley that day. Each resident was armed with coins for food and for any bargain that one could not survive without.

The weather cooperated; only feathery clouds made their slow progress across the sky, occasionally dimming the sun's bright glare.

Darcy and Bingley began circulating through the crowds soon after ten, usually together, but occasionally pulled apart by loquacious neighbors or even the entreaties of the concessionaires. As the day passed the crowd thickened, children scurried after dogs, parents after children, and the thrifty after bargains.

Just after one o'clock Elizabeth and Jane began their stroll through the fair area. Families had purchased food or brought their own and were sitting on the grass nearby enjoying the sun and their food. Elizabeth and Jane first visited the various food tables, intending to shop for bargains later. While discussing the choices, Bingley and Darcy approached and welcomed them to the fete. They selected food and made their way to some chairs and a small table that had been set up for them under the trees.

"Mrs. Winston asked for you, Elizabeth," Darcy said.

"She's here?"

"She is."

"Amazing. Perhaps we should send for more chairs in case she comes by."

Darcy beckoned for Farris, who was the nearest servant he could see and sent him to fetch two more chairs.

"I'm going to get another of those pasties," Jane said.

"You should have bought more the first time," Elizabeth teased.

"I didn't realize how good they'd be."

"Let me go; I'll get it for you," Bingley said.

"No, please, let me go; I'll be right back." She walked gingerly between the little knots of people and got the pastie. As she walked back toward the tent she bent to pick up the bun a toddler had dropped. As she crouched a large dog bounded forward and knocked her down backwards onto her buttocks. He grabbed her pastie and ran off leaving her surprised and empty handed. All eyes turned towards her as the noise of the commotion attracted their attention.

Bingley had been watching her progress through the crowd and was by her side before anyone else could collect their thoughts to help her.

"Are you all right?" he asked as he assisted her in raising her swollen body.

She whisked her hands over her skirt to tidy it, appearing dazed. Finally she said, "I don't know." They started to walk toward the chairs, but on the first step she winced with pain and stopped.

"What is it?"

"My ankle."

By this time Darcy and Elizabeth were before them. Elizabeth took her other arm and the entire party slowly moved toward the house.

Farris was just returning with the chairs, and Darcy told him to check the carriages. "If Dr. Thornton is here, find him."

"He is here, sir; I saw him."

"Then find him and bring him to the house. And ask other servants you see to look for him as well."

In the drawing room Jane sat down and, as all attended, she said, "I don't feel well. I'd like some water."

By this time Georgiana had discovered something was amiss and was entering the room.

"Georgiana," Darcy said, "Please send for a drink of water for Jane."

"What happened?"

"She twisted her ankle. She'll be fine; just get the water."

"Of course."

She pulled the door open and collided with Fenton, who was showing the doctor in. Dr. Thornton took in the situation and upon hearing the explanation for the twisted ankle, now resting on a footstool, he proceeded to examine it. "You'll need cold compresses, and you'll not take kindly my assurances that you're lucky you have broken nothing." As he twisted and turned the foot, prodding with his fingers, he was looking at her flushed, sweating face and swollen belly.

"However, I think we should make sure you don't end up with a worse problem." Looking to Elizabeth he said, "I think we should get her into bed." Looking to Jane, he said, "Then I'd like to talk with you further, Mrs. ...."

"Bingley," Elizabeth offered.

Jane sipped the water Georgiana handed her, then quietly accepted Bingley and Elizabeth's assistance to the bedroom as Georgiana followed with the glass.

Darcy poured a glass of wine for Dr. Thornton and one for himself.

In the bedroom, Bingley left Elizabeth and Georgiana to assist Jane into bed. "Georgiana," Elizabeth said, "I think you should go back to the fair and take Darcy with you, and Bingley if he'll go. People will be wondering what happened. Assure them she only twisted her ankle, that she'll be fine."

She left, but a rap at the door revealed Bingley, "How can I go back to the Fair?" he pleaded.

"Come in and see that she's fine; then you can go."

Jane was resting in bed, calm, a cool compress on her forehead. Reassured, he left saying, "Send for me if you need me."

Elizabeth nodded in assent.

"Do you really want me to go back to the fair, Elizabeth?" Georgiana asked.

"Yes, please do, but first bring Dr. Thornton up."

Dr. Thornton came into the hall after examining Jane and said, "Mrs. Darcy, she looks fine right now, but she's late in her pregnancy. I'm concerned about the fall she took. Keep her under close watch, and if there are any other symptoms, call me at once. You'd be wise also to make arrangements with a midwife to be ready on short notice. I glimpsed Mrs. Whipple at the fair. You might talk with her before she leaves."

Leaving Annie to stay with Jane, Elizabeth walked with Dr. Thornton to the door and then went to the drawing room where she found Darcy. Bingley and Georgiana had returned to the fair. Together they walked to the grassy area where festivities were still in full swing. First they noticed Mrs. Sims and then Mrs. Reynolds. Both acknowledged they knew what Mrs. Whipple looked like and said they'd look for her and send her to Darcy and Elizabeth.

"All the excitement doesn't seem to have dulled my appetite," Elizabeth said.

"Then let me get you something," Darcy replied. "What would you like?"

"I trust your judgment."

He wasn't gone long, but long enough for Mrs. Winston to appear and install herself next to Elizabeth.

"My dear, the fair is a great success; I do congratulate you."

"But I did nothing."

"Nonsense; men can never manage an event like this."

"But they did."

Mrs. Winston looked at her intently, her eyes narrowed. "Well, perhaps you are telling the truth. No matter. You'll get the credit anyway. I notice Mrs. Wilson has been very busy lately. Every time I've seen her lately she's practically running. Even today she's constantly scurrying among the stalls and concessions. Darcy approached with a sandwich and handed it to Elizabeth. "Good afternoon, Mrs. Winston. Could I get you something?"

"No, nothing; just sit beside me and flatter me that I'm looking particularly elegant today."

"Indeed you are."

"Such a dear boy—just like your father." She looked off in the distance as if conjuring up the image of the elder Mr. Darcy. "So, Mrs. Bingley took a fall."

"Yes, a dog knocked her down."

"You'd think people would have more sense than to let a dog run loose in a place like this. No consideration at all." Not waiting for a reply, she continued, "Lovely setting for the fair; very generous of you to permit them to have it here. The library committees should profit very nicely."

Her gaze now turning in the direction of the waiting horses, she remarked, "I do hope you will be riding next Saturday, Elizabeth."

As Elizabeth had accepted the sandwich she was remembering some of the comments Mrs. Winston had made in the past and considering that she might ask a question that would require an answer. Consequently, she took small bites to make the food last and chewed it thoughtfully, hoping to be able to stall until she could think of an innocuous reply. Actually, there was little danger that a response would be required.

"You should ride, Elizabeth, before you find yourself in the family way. Then you won't be able to get up on a horse. Ladies didn't ride at all when I was young; at least my parents wouldn't permit me to do so." Looking to Darcy she said, "I suppose you're eager to have a child, especially now that your best friend will soon have his own."

Darcy also was doing his best to anticipate what she might say and how he could respond. For a moment it seemed he might have to say something, but she turned again to Elizabeth and said, "Competition, you know. If there's a race, every man feels he must win, whether it's a horse race or anything else—who has the most money, the largest house, the most beautiful wife, the brightest child."

As she was talking, Sir Humphrey approached and greeted Elizabeth first and then Darcy. "Mama," he said, "let me have a word with Darcy and then I think we really should leave. I've sent Richard to harness the horses."

Mrs. Winston nodded and Sir Humphrey and Darcy walked off. Mrs. Winston addressed Elizabeth again: "Next Saturday, after the fox hunt, we'll be having dinner for several of our closest friends. You and Darcy and the Bingleys too would be most welcome."

"I'm afraid that's likely to be a very confusing day; I'm not sure we can come."

"Don't worry; come if you can. If you don't come, we'll remove your place settings from the table."

"Thank you."

The Winstons left, and Darcy and Elizabeth sat in the shade, a gentle breeze blowing. The crowd was thinning as people left, and many persons approached to introduce friends or extend thanks for the Darcy's hosting the event. Elizabeth's disclaimers that "I really did nothing," were greeted with disbelief.

"They're making me feel quite guilty," she said to Darcy during a moment when they were alone.

"Don't let that trouble you. We'll let you patch the holes in the grass when they uproot all the posts they've sunk."

"Perhaps I can find some other way to relieve my guilt."

"You might make some of that raisin bread. Mrs. Sims seems to have forgotten to make it lately."

"You—suggesting that a Darcy lady bake bread? The sun must have affected you."

"I saw rather a lot of scones being devoured in the crowd today. Where do you think they all came from?"

"I haven't the smallest idea."

"I saw Georgiana walking from the kitchen to one of the stalls this morning."

"Indeed? I spent the morning with Jane. I thought Georgiana was at the fair with you."

The crowd had dwindled so Darcy and Elizabeth started walking toward the house.

"Did you see the Blakelys?" Darcy asked.

"I do believe that I saw every Derbyshire resident I'd ever met today and most of the ones I hadn't met—even Mrs. Pettigrew."

"Ah, then it was young Harrison I saw helping Georgiana. I thought he looked familiar."

"Perhaps that was while I was still inside with Jane. I didn't see him."

"That could be."

They had only walked a short distance when a plump, middle-aged woman approached them.

"I'm Mrs. Whipple. You wanted to see me?"

"Yes, please, come into the house," Elizabeth replied.

They walked together, and in the entry explained the situation: Mrs. Bingley wasn't due to deliver for almost 6 weeks, but Dr. Thornton was concerned about her. Elizabeth took her up and introduced her to Jane, who was awake and quite comfortable except for the ankle.

Elizabeth listened to Mrs. Whipple's instructions on how to find her home in Lambton and wrote them down, in case she should need to contact her later. They left together, Elizabeth promising Jane to return shortly. She walked with Mrs. Whipple to the door and returned to the drawing room where Darcy, Bingley, and Georgiana were assembled. Bingley immediately went to keep Jane company and to hear from her directly what the doctor and midwife had said.

"They can't go back to Thornwood Monday, at least not Jane," Elizabeth said.

"Of course not."

"You must convince Bingley that she must stay."

"Is she very ill?"

"I don't know. Dr. Thornton said we must watch her carefully."

Georgiana interrupted to excuse herself. "I really must change clothes."

"You look as if you'd been running in the races with the children," Darcy said.

"It was quite warm today."

They nodded to excuse her, and she left.

"We can't leave Jane alone. We'll have to alternate sitting with her—Bingley, Georgiana, and I. She really cannot be walking up and down stairs."

"No."

Elizabeth looked up to Darcy where he was standing, grinning. "After such a tumultuous afternoon, I wish I could smile."

"I just had an amusing thought."

"Yes?"

"Those last years before Mother died she frequently had difficulty walking. The servants often carried her around in a chair."

"Like the kind they use on the streets in town?"

"Precisely." I saw that old chair in the loft of the barn when I went to get Father's old saddle for Fitzwilliam at Christmas. I suppose Jane would feel ridiculous riding in it, but if we all act serious, we may be able to convince her."

"We should at least try."

"It could be weeks before she's walking properly again. Let us ask Fenton to put a table in the picture gallery. We can take our suppers and tea there."

"And she and Bingley can have breakfast and dinner there as well."

"I don't see why not. In the evenings she can be carried to the music room as well. Those rooms are perfectly comfortable at this time of year, even without a fire."

"I'll talk to her alone, to persuade her," Elizabeth concluded. "You talk with Fenton about getting the chair from the loft."

Elizabeth ordered tea for three to be sent to Jane's bedroom and for several in the drawing room. She then went to Jane, and Bingley left them together.

Elizabeth did indeed have to use all her powers of persuasion, but in the end Jane's sweetness prevailed, and the family regimen was set for the duration. That settled, Jane confided to Elizabeth that she was worried. She had spotted after her fall, and when she told the doctor he seemed concerned about it. "And I'm getting these feelings in my lower abdomen," she added.

"What feelings?"

"Just a kind of tightness."

""When did they start? After the fall?"

"No, several days ago."

"You didn't mention it before."

"I didn't want to worry you."

"All the more reason to let us take good care of you."

That evening Bingley and Jane had their supper from a tray and spent a quiet evening alone.

September 3, Sunday

The next day, even though it was Sunday, the chair was found, cleaned, and brought to Jane's room. The table was set up in the gallery and all was set for the family to spend the next 6 weeks revolving around Jane's sprained ankle and her pending confinement.

Bingley did go back to Thornwood on Monday, hoping to find a response from Lonsdale concerning the offer for the library. In addition, he had to arrange matters with Smith and the other workers. On arriving, he found the reply from Lonsdale about the library. Bingley's letter to Lonsdale about the library had trailed the Lonsdales from one place to another over a period of weeks before it caught up with them. Finally he had sent his reply, accepting the offer.

Bingley arranged for payment and supervised the servants as they packed and loaded part of Darcy's books into the carriage.

All business complete, Bingley returned to Pemberley on Wednesday to find things much as he had left them on Monday morning.

Jane submitted to being transported from her door to the table for tea or supper and in the evenings to the music room. Georgiana played more of her repertoire that week than the family had heard altogether since Christmas.

Darcy and Bingley rode each morning, and Elizabeth sat with Jane while Georgiana continued in her kitchen duties, conspiring with Mrs. Sims to find new delicacies to tempt the "invalid."

Elizabeth, after swearing Jane to secrecy, confided to Jane the story of Mrs. Sims' "fertility festival." Jane blushed at hearing the story, but owned she must have eaten such without even realizing she had done so.

Friday

Friday came, and the fox hunt would be the next day. Elizabeth confirmed that Annie had brushed and hung her habit to be ready for the morning. She didn't want to leave Jane, but neither was she eager to involve herself in an argument she was uncertain of winning. After all, it was almost five weeks until Jane's baby was due. What could be the harm? Argument seemed futile.

The servants were instructed to alternate sitting with her: Annie, Sarah, Katie, and Fiona. Elizabeth and Georgiana had been teaching her backgammon, and she was becoming quite expert. She could teach the servants while the neighborhood went into an uproar over a silly little fox.

In the end the men had decided the hunt should begin at the Howell estate, just about two miles from Pemberley.

In their bedroom the night before the hunt Elizabeth disclosed her hesitancy to Darcy.

"I thought it was all settled—that you would ride with us?"

"You know I'm not entirely confident of my riding yet."

"You don't have to lead the pack; take your time; bring up the rear. The party at the end of the hunt usually goes on for hours. There will be plenty of food and drink even if you are the last to arrive."

"It's not just that; it's Jane. I'm really uneasy about leaving her. Besides, you don't really know which way the hunt will go, do you? It could be quite a long ride home later."

"Sleep on it then," he said, "and we'll talk again in the morning. You don't have to go, though I think you'd truly enjoy it. Come," he said, taking her in his arms. "This is not the time to argue; it's time for something very different."

September 9, Saturday: The Fox Hunt

She awoke with a start, immediately realizing she had a decision to make that lovemaking and sleep had not resolved. Her movement woke Darcy and he reached for her, tugging her into the curve of his body.

"My lovely Elizabeth."

"You do know how to turn me to jelly."

"I was hoping for something a little firmer."

And he got it.

Dressed in her habit, still uncertain how far she would go in it, she went first to see Jane. Bingley had already gone down to breakfast, and Jane was wide awake, washed, and waiting for her breakfast. Elizabeth chatted with her until the tray arrived. Satisfied that Jane was in good spirits, she joined the others in the dining room.

Conversation was lively and, not entirely aware of how it happened, Elizabeth got caught up in the spirit of the hunt. It would take less than half an hour to ride to the Howell's. She would decide there what to do.

Sims and Davy had all four horses saddled, and the gentlemen assisted the ladies onto their horses and mounted theirs. They led the way out of the stable yard in their handsome caps and red jackets, the ladies following in black.

Most of the participants had already gathered when they arrived. The few others arrived soon thereafter. It looked like about 30 riders altogether.

Servants offered each a drink, which they accepted and drank, returning glasses to the trays.

Elizabeth moved Midnight beside Darcy and said, "What am I doing here? I don't have the smallest idea of what to do."

"Just stay near the rear and follow. Ride only as fast as you feel comfortable riding. Enjoy yourself. There's no one perfect way to run in a hunt. It's a show. After the fox is caught, we'll be riding back to find the stragglers; we'll find you then."

"You're going to be at the front of the pack?"

"Possibly. One can never be sure. That's part of the enjoyment."

He reached out his hand to her; she touched it with hers, and he moved forward.

Now the dogs could be heard barking. Soon she could see them milling about.

She was trying to keep Midnight facing the other horses to be ready as they left when she heard, "Mrs. Darcy, Good morning." She looked up to see the speaker.

"Mrs. Pettigrew. Good morning. How good to see you. I suppose you'll be riding up front with the better riders."

"Not likely. I'm here for a good time—not to win anything. The men need some of us ladies riding along to prove they're better riders."

Elizabeth looked up, not knowing quite how to respond.

"Yes, I am naughty. But, they are rather like a bunch of 10-year olds, don't you think?"

"I really shouldn't be here. I should have stayed at home."

"Nonsense."

"Have you ridden in a fox hunt before?"

"No, I've never managed to attend when I have been invited, but every one of these riders went out for the first time at one time or another."

They heard the sound of the horn now and the dogs were beginning to move out. Soon they were all on the move.

"Did you see Georgiana?"

"Yes, she was talking with a Miss Bingley."

"Miss Bingley?"

"Yes, you see that woman," she said, pointing.

Elizabeth's eyes widened, and her mouth opened in amazement.

"You know her?"

"She's my brother-in-law's sister."

"She did look familiar; did she attend your ball in February?"

"Yes, she did."

"I must have seen her there then."

The whole crowd was picking up speed now, the front of the hunt already far ahead.

"If I get ahead, I'll look back from time to time to see you're all right."

"Thank you."

She looked ahead and to her right, saw two women riding together, recognized them as Mrs. Morris and Mrs. Blakely, and waved to them.

The horn sounded, and the dogs barked. How many were there—20, 30, 40? Swarming and running as they did and then scattering, there was no way to tell.

The morning was cool. Just a week ago the fair was held on a day that could only be called the peak of summer. And now hints of fall could be sensed on all sides: steam from a boggy area, frost on the grass here and there, tinges of color on leaves, and especially the cool air and a thinly overcast sky.

With no provocation from herself that she was aware of Midnight had switched into a trot. "Perhaps we only flatter ourselves that we have tamed them. Perhaps horses are as wild as they ever were and strive without direction to keep up with the herd," she thought.

The last rider she could see was some distance ahead, and she began to feel uneasy about being so far behind. Now an image returned to her:

Mrs. Pettigrew mounted on her man's saddle. "How secure she looked," Elizabeth thought, "and steady."

Glancing at the riders ahead of her every few moments, she scanned the ground ahead for obstacles and the air above for tree branches.

She could still hear the horn and the hounds, but her mind was focused on her fit with the horse—rider and horse now one unit. It was not conscious thought that motivated her to urge the horse into a gallop, but switch he did, at least for a short distance. They had been riding for some time, all the while Elizabeth concentrating on doing all the things necessary to keep steady on Midnight and still not lose sight of the other riders. She could see Mrs. Pettigrew at the top of a low hill, looking back and waiting.

Again, Elizabeth was not aware that she had signaled Midnight to slow, but slow he did.

"You waited."

"Yes, it looks like there's trouble ahead. Let's go together."

As soon as Elizabeth got to the top of the rise she could see the group. It looked like two people and three horses. As they approached she soon recognized Sir Humphrey and Miss Bingley standing near a tree with three horses. As they approached she looked at the third horse and thought she recognized the markings. She looked at the saddle. "Georgiana, where is she?"

"Don't worry, Mrs. Darcy," Sir Humphrey replied calmly. "She's resting here by the tree."

"What happened?" she asked. He held Midnight's tether as she dismounted.

"She fell off her horse."

"I can't believe it." She followed Sir Humphrey to the other side of the tree and saw Georgiana cradling her left arm with her right hand, her expression revealing the pain she felt.

"What happened, Georgiana?"

"I'm sorry, Elizabeth," she said, near tears.

"What happened?"

"I don't know. I just came over the rise of the hill and we were riding down when I saw Sir Humphrey and Miss Bingley. The next thing I knew I was on the ground, hurting."

Sir Humphrey stepped in to explain, "Miss Bingley's horse went lame, and she had stopped. I looked back and saw her. I came back and was examining the horse's leg when Georgiana came over the hill. She looked over at us, and something frightened her horse. I'm not sure what it was, but he stopped short and she flew off, landing on her wrist."

"We must get help," Elizabeth said. She stood up and looked ahead to where the riders could barely be seen. The hounds could be heard only faintly. They had waited for some time when, over the hill ahead of them they could see a rider coming—a red jacket. They all watched and waited except Georgiana, who closed her eyes and waited.

Elizabeth thought, "Will he never get here? Who is it?"

Finally he arrived. It was Mr. Harrison. He dismounted, and they explained what had happened.

"She can't ride," Elizabeth said.

"No, she can't." The road is right over there," he said, pointing. "It's really not far. If you'll ride there, Sir Humphrey, and wait at the road, I'll have our driver bring our carriage. I'll bring back something to support her arm so we can get her to the carriage. Just wait here."

"And bring a blanket," Elizabeth added.

"There's one in the carriage," he said and left.

"She's going to get chilled lying on the ground," Elizabeth said. Sir Humphrey removed his jacket and laid it over Georgiana's legs.

"You might just as well follow the hunt, Mrs. Pettigrew," Elizabeth said. "There's no point in all of us waiting."

"Perhaps you're right; I can tell Mr. Darcy if I meet him coming back. I would like to ride farther."

"Thank you for waiting for me."

"It was nothing."

"Someone must go for the doctor." Elizabeth said.

"As soon as Harrison takes Miss Darcy to the carriage, I'll go," Sir Humphrey said. He mounted his horse and went to the road to halt the carriage at the closest point.

"Why didn't I bring something along to drink?" Elizabeth complained. "Men are so clever with their little pocket flasks."

"I have one," Miss Bingley said. "It's only water."

"That's exactly what we need."

She brought it out of a concealed skirt pocket and handed it to Elizabeth who took it to Georgiana and offered it to her.

"Thank you, Miss Bingley."

"Not at all. If one observes men long enough one is sure to learn something." She moved toward Georgiana. "I am sorry, Miss Darcy."

"It's not your fault. I should have slowed at the top of the hill to see what lay beyond. I wonder what it was that frightened Dancer."

"I thought I saw a rabbit," Miss Bingley replied, "But it happened so fast, I'm not really sure. It could have been that large, pecularly shaped tree root."

"I didn't know you rode, Miss Bingley," Elizabeth said.

"I don't ride often, but I learned when I was quite young."

"Where are you staying?"

"At the Winston's."

"I didn't realize you were so well acquainted."

"We're not, really, but Sir Humphrey was very insistent. He's been talking about this hunt for months. I first heard him talk of it at the Pemberley Ball in February."

"Indeed? And you've seen him since?"

It's the most peculiar thing. Everywhere I go he keeps appearing—almost as if he'd planned it. Ridiculous, of course; why would he do such a thing? But the hunt seemed appealing, and when his mother wrote to invite the Hursts and myself, I could think of no reason to refuse."

"The Hursts came also?"

"Yes, but not to ride; just for the party following. They came with us to the Howell's this morning. They're waiting for us there."

Elizabeth heard hoof beats and looked up to see Mr. Harrison approaching. He jumped off and took two sticks and cloth ties from his pack. Elizabeth held Georgiana's arm and the splints as he tied them in place and secured a scarf over her shoulder and around her neck to support the arm. Together they assisted Georgiana to the coach.

"Sir Humphrey has said he'll go for the doctor," Elizabeth said as they began to move toward the coach.

"No," Harrison said. "I'll go; then I'll follow him back to Pemberley."

All three thanked him as they parted. Sir Humphrey returned to escort Miss Bingley back to the Howell's as she rode Dancer, with Midnight and the lame horse following.

After arriving at Pemberley, they waited for the doctor in the morning room. Elizabeth arranged pillows so Georgiana could lie down and removed her boots. She sent Fenton, who was hovering nearby, to fetch a blanket, order tea, and make sure that there would be a servant nearby for the rest of the day to attend to any immediate needs.

"I'm so sorry, Elizabeth. I've ruined your day."

"I'm the one that's sorry—that you've ruined *your* month!"

"But the hunt...your first hunt."

"It was your first also."

"I deserve to be punished for being so foolish; but you...."

Elizabeth interrupted, "If you only knew how hard I tried to persuade Darcy to let me stay at home...Oh, Lord, I completely forgot." She rose and rushed to the hall. Susan was sitting there. "Susan, how is Mrs. Bingley?"

"She's fine ma'am, I just brought her some tea."

"Thank you." She then turned her attention to Georgiana, drawing a chair near to her.

"You didn't want to go?"

"I was worried about leaving Jane, and you know I'm still far from an expert rider." The wait for the doctor seemed endless, though in fact it was less than two hours. She wanted to quiz Georgiana about Mr. Harrison, but decided that she had been present at the only events worth quizzing about and so cast about for every other topic of conversation she could, and much of the time they simply waited in silence. They had sent for more tea when Darcy and Bingley arrived. They burst in during some quiet moments.

"How is she?" Darcy demanded.

"She's hurting, but I'm sure she'll be fine," Elizabeth answered.

"I'm so sorry, Darcy. I've spoiled your day," she said, tears flowing.

"Don't be silly. My day will be just fine...but your arm, how bad is it?"

"I'm afraid it's broken. It's not so bad when I hold still, but the smallest movement is painful."

"What happened?"

"Let me tell you," Elizabeth intervened. She then related the story as it was told to her earlier.

Katie brought tea for them and served.

Darcy arranged the pillows so Georgiana could sit up and drink the tea and brought a small table for her cup.

"We should be happy it's your left arm, not the right. Or, perhaps you'd like someone to hold your cup for you. Mr. Harrison will be along soon, no doubt, to continue his attentions."

"Don't tease me, Darcy," she said, resting her head on the pillow and closing her eyes. "It hurts too much when I laugh."

Elizabeth turned to Bingley and said, "Susan tells me that Jane is well."

"Good God, I forgot...." He went to open the door left with no further comment.

"When will that doctor get here?" Darcy complained.

"I'm sure he's coming as quickly as he can. Did you go back to the Howell's after the hunt?"

"We did. When we arrived Sir Humphrey and Miss Bingley told us what had happened. We told them we would return later to get Dancer and Midnight and left immediately."

Finally Dr. Thornton arrived. Harrison had had to follow Thornton to the home of a patient to fetch him. From there they came together to Pemberley.

Greetings completed, Thornton sat down to talk with Georgiana and examine her arm. He removed the scarf and splint and gently probed the forearm with his fingers. "Well, it could have been a lot worse." Looking up to Georgiana's face, he continued, "You're doubtful, are you? Well, it seems only one bone has broken, it has not severed, and the skin is not broken." He paused to let the words take their effect. "However, if no worse fate is to befall you, we are going to have to secure that arm very carefully. I'm afraid we're going to have to cut the jacket to get it off." Seeing the alarm on her countenance, he reassured her, "We'll just expose your arm. Mrs. Darcy can cut the rest off later."

To Elizabeth he said, "Perhaps you could assist me."

"Of course."

"Mr. Darcy," he said, "I left Mr. Harrison in the entryway. He seemed rather worried; perhaps you could reassure him."

"Certainly," he replied and left.

As the doctor was finishing, Elizabeth went to the hall and sent Susan to get a shawl for Georgiana. The doctor left powders for pain, then assured them he could find his way out.

Susan returned with the shawl, and Elizabeth went to the drawing room where she found Darcy and Mr. Harrison.

"How is she, Mrs. Darcy?"

"She's going to be just fine, many thanks to you. She's ready to see you now." The three walked to the morning room, and Darcy opened the door for him. "Elizabeth," Darcy said before they entered the room, "I'd like just a moment." He closed the door and they stood in the hall. "I could be wrong, but I suspect we're likely to have some unexpected visitors today."

"Who?"

"Some of the hunters."

"What makes you think so?"

"I'm not sure, but you know how people love accidents, particularly if they're not fatal. It's really not far from the Howell's to Pemberley. They were having a very good time at the Howell's, and sometimes people like to extend a party as long as they can. I think it might be wise to alert Mrs. Sims that it could be a rather busy day. In fact, you might consider telling her to forget about dinner and start making sandwiches."

"That seems rather drastic."

"Who is going to come to the table? Jane is in her room; Bingley will eat with her. I doubt if Georgiana will want to sit up."

"You're right. You entertain Mr. Harrison and I'll go talk with Mrs. Sims."

When she returned, Darcy and Mr. Harrison were standing holding glasses of wine, watching Georgiana who was following their conversation as calmly as she could, trying to maintain her dignity while looking like a granny in her shawl.

"They'll be bringing us some sandwiches soon," Elizabeth said, canvassing the room for the best post from which to observe the other three.

"The carriage," Elizabeth said, "Mr. and Mr. Pettigrew will want it. I was so concerned about Georgiana I completely forgot...."

"William told me when I arrived; the driver took it back to the Howells."

"Oh, yes, of course."

The door opened again. This time Miss Bingley and Sir Humphrey were admitted. They approached Georgiana and extended their sympathies.

"We brought Midnight and Dancer back," Sir Humphrey said. "We wanted to thank you and assure ourselves that Miss Darcy is all right."

"I'm going to be fine, Sir Humphrey. Thank you for coming."

Katie then arrived with sandwiches and tea, and Elizabeth asked, "Will you have some sandwiches?"

"Just tea, thank you. We stopped for refreshments at the Howells," Sir Humphrey replied. "And Mama will be waiting dinner for us" he said, consulting his watch. "She's no doubt wondering what happened to us."

They left, and as she sat down, Elizabeth could feel how tired she was. "I'd better have a sandwich myself," she thought. "I'm beginning to think Darcy's right; before the day is ended, we'll see them all." She tried to sit up straight and to listen to Darcy and Mr. Harrison's conversation, but her mind kept wandering. She remembered Darcy's words about the people at the Howells, "...they were having a very good time..." Then she remembered her reluctance to ride at all. "It's a good thing I did. At least I was there to help Georgiana. Mr. Harrison did come back, though. He seems competent enough for just about any situation." This thought jarred her to consciousness and she looked to Georgiana and then to Mr. Harrison. He was standing so he and Georgiana could look directly at each other, though he seemed to look in various directions as he conversed with Darcy, his gaze always returning to Georgiana. "That look. My God, that's exactly what Darcy used to do whenever we were in the same room. Almost every time I saw him he was looking at me." Now she looked to Darcy. He had sat down and was arrayed with Georgiana and Mr. Harrison in a triangle. "And that, I'm afraid, is exactly how it is going to be—each of them pulling at her. He's not penniless like Davy or the Flanders boy, but Darcy will never consider him rich enough for her." Now she stood and saw the reflection of herself in the mirror behind Mr. Harrison. She turned toward the fireplace, but had acted out of emotion rather than reason, moving too quickly.

"Is anything wrong, Elizabeth?" Darcy asked.

"No, nothing. I think I just need some fresh air."

"Let me come with you. We'll send for Fiona to attend Georgiana."

Fiona came, and they went out through the morning room doors to avoid anyone who might be coming in the front entrance.

"You seemed upset," he said as they began to walk.

"It's been a hectic day," she dissembled, wondering if she should tell him. Perhaps she was wrong. No, she could not be mistaken. But if she told Darcy now, he'd interfere. But surely it would be worse to wait until Georgiana's feelings were also engaged. Perhaps they already were. Last Saturday at the fair...Darcy said he saw him helping her with trays from the kitchen. And Georgiana went to change her clothes because she got so warm. Where did she go then? Jane's ankle. Georgiana brought the glass of water and was it then that she excused herself or later? I'm so confused.

"Elizabeth, you really do look worried. Are you all right?"

"Yes, I'm well. It's Georgiana."

"I know; it was unfortunate, but she'll be just fine."

"I'm not referring to her arm; I'm thinking of her heart."

He stopped walking and turned towards her, waiting for an explanation.

"Didn't you see?"

"See what?"

"Georgiana and Mr. Harrison."

"Oh, Elizabeth, do be serious."

"I am serious. It's possible he hasn't won her heart yet, but he has determined to do so."

"She's just a child."

"She's almost 18 years old."

"A mere child."

"Lydia married when she was more than two years younger."

"Surely you can't believe she would be so foolish."

"Mr. Harrison is no Wickham. As nearly as I can tell he's a very honorable young man."

"But he has no fortune, no estate; she wouldn't be so foolish."

"Love makes fools of many of us. I had even less than he has, yet you married me. He at least has an education and the potential for respectable employment. Surely his position is superior to what mine was."

Now his face clouded over, and she could see she had reached him.

"What can we do?"

"I don't know. But I hope you'll be careful. You don't want to lose Georgiana's love. She's your only sister, and you have no brothers. Consider also that except for Jane, Georgiana has become more dear to me even than any of my own sisters. You could hurt me as well."

"Oh, Lord," he said. "What a day!" He wiped a tear from his eye with his fingers, and they turned toward the house. They walked to the front door. There the Carletons were just alighting from their horses. William took the horses, and the two couples entered the house together. In the hall they met Mr. and Mrs. Morris and Stephen, who had tendered their sympathies and were leaving. The Darcys greeted them and then bid them farewell as the Carletons entered the morning room.

Then they met Mr. Harrison entering the hall to leave.

"Must you leave so soon?" Elizabeth asked.

"My sister and brother-in-law will be waiting for me at the Howells. May I call on Miss Darcy in a few days?"

Elizabeth looked to Darcy. "Of course," he said. "And thank you; we're greatly indebted to you."

"Not at all," and he was gone.

Elizabeth looked up at Darcy again, and he flicked his eyebrows in that "Yes, I'm afraid you were right" expression. Then he shook his head and shrugged shoulders in that "What in the world can we do now" expression.

They entered the morning room and found that the Carletons had extended their sympathies to Georgiana and now both turned to Elizabeth and Darcy with knowing looks covering their faces.

"I believe congratulations are in order," Carleton said.

Darcy had missed their expressions as he looked for a place to sit. "Whatever for?" he replied casually.

"Don't play coy, old man," Carleton continued. Everyone was talking about Mrs. Whipple's visit here last Saturday at the Howell's after the hunt."

Darcy looked up and said, "So? Congratulate Bingley when he comes down. He should be here shortly." He scanned the room and alighted on Fiona. "Fiona, would you pour me a glass of wine?"

"Let me do it," Carleton interjected. "Bingley's here?"

"You didn't see him at the hunt?"

"It was quite a melee, and we were, I think, the last to arrive."

Elizabeth intervened, "They've been here much of the summer."

"But I thought they'd left."

"They did, but they came back for the fair last week, and she twisted her ankle. We expect them to stay until after the baby is born," Elizabeth explained.

"But Darcy, I heard someone at the hunt congratulating you."

"I thought he was remarking on Mrs. Darcy's fine appearance on Midnight. He looked at her as he said it."

"Now I think I'd like a glass of wine," Carleton said.

"I'd like one too," said Elizabeth. He brought it to her, and she sipped it, lapsing into absentmindedness as the conversation rambled on. She heard the Carletons say goodbye and herself responding, but stayed in her thoughts.

"Elizabeth, I think you need a nap. Fiona and I will attend to Georgiana."

"You're right." He opened the door and sent Susan with her to her room. She lay on the bed, pulled a quilt over herself and fell asleep. When she awoke it was dark. She looked to the window. The draperies were open, and she could see the starlit sky.

Now thoroughly awake, the room didn't seem dark enough. She sat up, and her attention was drawn to a strip of light coming from her dressing room.

"Annie?" She heard rustling.

"Yes, ma'am."

"Oh, Annie. You frightened me."

"Mr. Darcy told me to wait here 'til you awoke."

"Where is he?"

"He went to sleep in his dressing room."

She moved her legs off the bed and slid down to the floor. "Look at me. What a mess!" She shuffled into the dressing room. "Get me out of this habit," she said struggling with the buttons she could release. "I'm sorry; I don't mean to be so cross."

"It's alright, ma'am. Let me help you. Do you want me to get some hot water? I brought some earlier, but I'm afraid it's barely warm now."

"No, that's fine; I just want to sponge down with a warm cloth. If I take a real bath it will waken me too much." She sighed. She sponged herself off and handed the cloth to Annie for her back. "It's amazing I could sleep like that at all."

"You were sleeping very soundly ma'am. Just before you woke I heard you snoring, beggin' your pardon for sayin' so."

"Oh no, not that too."

"Maybe you were just overtired."

"I was, indeed." She slipped into her robe and sat down so Annie could brush her hair.

Suddenly remembering, she asked, "Have you heard anything of Mrs. Bingley?"

"She was fine just awhile ago."

"Thank you, Annie. I'll see you in the morning."

"Good night, ma'am."

She took one of the candles and, in her bedroom closed the door to the dressing room. She noticed for the first time that the door to Darcy's dressing room was ajar and tip-toed towards it. She could hear his rhythmic breathing and approached the bed. She set the candle down on the table and lifted the quilt. As she was about to get into the bed, he said, "What are you doing?"

"Oh, you startled me."

"This bed is too small." He sleepily lifted the covers and got out of bed, nudging her before him. He took his robe, picked up the candle, and gently prodded her back into their bedroom. He closed the door and got into bed beside her. He snuffed the candle and pulled and tugged to remove her nightie, then removed his own night shirt.

He pulled her into the curve of his body and began caressing her. "You smell like...what is it?"

"Nothing."

"No, it's something...it's Elizabeth scent."

"And you smell like you had a bath."

"Of course I did. After a day like that! Horses, hounds, sweat...unless you would prefer...."

A gasp of laughter escaped her. "No, I would not prefer horses, hounds, and sweat!"

"Well, then...."

Under his caresses she could feel herself getting excited. "I was just planning to go to sleep."

"You think you can sleep now after you've removed the last barrier to my pleasure? Your thinking is usually more sound."

September 10, Sunday: Benjamin

She awoke to the sound of birds. She opened her eyes and could see the draperies had not been closed. By the light she could tell it was not yet dawn. She turned over, and her movement awakened Darcy. He reached for her and moved his hands over her as if determined to examine every curve and plane of her body.

"You're going to get me excited."

"That's the object."

"I thought last night...."

"Your thinking wasn't very sound then either."

"Remember when Blakely said he'd never heard of a marriage turning a man into a humorist?"

"Yes, I remember; something new under the sun."

"The quotation says there is no thing new under the sun."

"There is now." He had lifted his torso to kiss her when they heard a loud knock at the door.

"Who is it?" Elizabeth called.

"It's me, Bingley. Come quickly, Elizabeth. It's Jane."

Darcy dropped back on the bed with a monstrous sigh, "My best friend."

Elizabeth jumped out of bed and grabbed her robe. She tied it as she ran to the door bare-footed.

"Is something wrong?"

"The baby—I'm afraid it's coming."

"Calm yourself."

"No, this is no time for calm."

"Let me get my slippers. Darcy, come along."

He sighed again, but rolled out of bed, put on his robe and slippers, and dragged himself behind them.

Bingley was nearly running, with Elizabeth not far behind.

"What happened?"

They were entering the bedroom as he explained, "I was asleep. She got out of bed and went to the stool. She told me she couldn't stand up, the pain was so bad. She finally managed to rouse me, and I helped her to stand up and get to the bed. She said that while she was on the stool, the water broke."

Jane was lying in bed, sweating and breathing hard.

"The water broke?"

"Yes."

"Run, send the carriage for the midwife and send Davy on horseback for the doctor. Then see that all the maids are wakened. I want Katie, Susan, Fiona, Annie, and Mrs. Sims and Mrs. Reynolds too. Both of you, go."

She ran to a cupboard and pulled out some towels and wash cloths. She took them back to the bed. "What happened, Jane?"

"I woke up about an hour ago. I went to pee and I couldn't stand up, just like he said." She winced with pain again, and her explanation ceased.

Elizabeth took a washcloth and mopped her brow. Then she lit several more candles. "Do you need a drink?"

"Just a sip," she said, and started heaving again in short rapid breaths.

Elizabeth poured water into the basin and brought it to a table near the bed. She lifted the covers and could see they had a bit of a mess.

"I'm so sorry."

"Don't be silly. Let's get you out of your gown. There. Now, let me lay some towels under you."

"You look like you know what you're doing."

"I haven't the smallest idea of what I'm doing. Just start praying that Mrs. Whipple gets here soon. I'll pray too."

The maids were beginning to arrive—Susan first.

"Susan, go heat some water for washing. Sarah, find more towels and a pail for these soiled linens, and get some clean linens for the bed."

"Annie, sit here by the bed and hold Mrs. Bingley's hand. Use this cloth to mop her face. All this sweat is most unladylike."

"I'm so sorry, Lizzy."

"I'm teasing you, Jane. No more apologies, absolutely none. If I hear one more apology, I'll send for the carriage and bundle you off to Thornwood."

A faint smile curved her lips until the pain began again, and she gasped and groaned. When she relaxed, Elizabeth asked, "How's the ankle?"

"As long as I don't move it, it's fine."

Mrs. Sims and Mrs. Reynolds arrived and Elizabeth brought them close to the bed and told them all she knew of what had happened. "Is there anything else you can think of that we should do?"

Mrs. Sims offered, "It looks like this baby is going to be born soon, maybe even before Mrs. Whipple comes. Is there a blanket for the wee one?"

Jane motioned to a cupboard.

"And we'll need some string or cord," Mrs. Reynolds said. "And a pair of scissors."

"Annie, go—there are scissors in Sarah's workroom, and find cord or string somewhere."

Mrs. Reynolds directed her where to look for cord.

Mrs. Sims laid her hand on Jane's forehead. "No fever."

Elizabeth directed her to continue as Annie had, holding Jane's hand and mopping her brow.

Mrs. Reynolds suggested that it might be better if she took Mrs. Sims place and ask Mrs. Sims to go to the kitchen. The whole household was roused. Everyone would be ready for breakfast early.

"I quite agree," Mrs. Sims added. Before she could leave, Elizabeth asked, "Is there anything else we've forgotten?"

"You'll need a bed for the wee one."

They all looked around. "It's at Thornwood," Jane said.

"A dresser drawer," Mrs. Reynolds suggested, until we can get something better. Later we may be able to find something proper in the store rooms."

Elizabeth opened the door and drew Katie into the room. "Katie, empty one of those drawers; put the things into the other drawers. We're going to use it for a crib."

"Mrs. Sims, what else have we forgotten?"

"Nappies."

Once again she opened the door. Sarah had returned with the linens. "Sarah, I'm afraid we're going to have to prevail on you to prepare an emergency supply of nappies. Perhaps some old sheets can be pressed into service. Whatever you have to do, do it."

"Mrs. Sims?" Elizabeth asked.

"That's all I can think of now. If I think of anything else, I'll send word," and she left.

By now Annie had returned with scissors and cord.

"Annie, I want you on that side of the bed. Let Mrs. Bingley hold onto your hand. Keep as calm as you can; Mrs. Sims says this baby may be born before Mrs. Whipple arrives."

"Mrs. Reynolds, if you think of anything we can do, please tell me."

She opened the door. "Fiona, please go down and see that someone is at the entry to greet Mrs. Whipple and Dr. Thornton when they arrive. And tell Mrs. Sims to send tea to Mr. Darcy and Mr. Bingley. They're probably in the morning room. Then come back here."

She re-entered the room and paced back and forth at the foot of the bed. She looked to Mrs. Reynolds, questioningly.

Mrs. Reynolds stated calmly, "I'm sure everything will be well."

Elizabeth clenched her hands before her and looked up. "I certainly hope you're right."

Jane seemed calmer, but her breathing if anything was more violent.

"Perhaps we should look," Mrs. Reynolds suggested.

Elizabeth lifted the bedding and Jane lifted her knees.

"Oh, my God, it's coming." I can see the top of the head."

"The door opened, and Mrs. Whipple entered, removing her coat and handing it to Elizabeth. She surveyed the scene, removed her hat, and placed it on a chair.

"How are you, Mrs. Bingley?" she asked.

"Not so well," she gasped.

"You're going to be all right. But now each time it hurts, push as hard as you can. My Lord, this is going to be the fastest birthing I've ever attended," she said as she placed her hands to support the head.

Jane rested back and sighed deeply again and again. Then with the pain she pushed and gasped and grunted, and the shoulders emerged.

"Mrs. Bingley, I am embarrassed. You've done all the work before I could even help. Well, well, look what we have here...young Master Bingley," she said as she gently moved to lay him on Jane's abdomen.

Elizabeth stood in the middle of the room and sobbed violently. Mrs. Reynolds rose and put her arms around her. Come, sit down; let me get you some tea; the battle is won; the general can rest."

Elizabeth looked up at her, puzzled. Mrs. Reynolds handed her a handkerchief, and she dabbed at her eyes.

She approached the bed and took Jane's hand. "Forgive me, Jane, I must leave. Send for me later."

To Mrs. Whipple she said, "Just ask the maids for anything you need."

She stumbled back to her own bedroom and collapsed on the bed, sobbing. She cried, allowing the thoughts of the past hour—or how long was it?—to flood over her consciousness, until she drifted into sleep.

When she awoke the light streaming through the window told her the day was far advanced. She looked at the clock: ten-fifteen. She stretched and then noticed that she had slept in her robe. She got up and confirmed that Annie was not in the dressing room. She rang for her and began washing herself in the water left in the pitcher. "That's cold!" She was half dressed when Annie arrived. Annie fastened her buttons and brushed and arranged her hair.

Elizabeth opened the door to the morning room and found it empty. She went to the dining room and rang the bell, then poured some coffee.

Selbey arrived, and she ordered a generous breakfast for herself. She walked to the window with her cup and saucer and sipped as she looked out at the beautiful view. Remembering Mrs. Reynolds's comment, she thought, "The general will have a hearty breakfast. I wonder where everyone is. No matter. After all this excitement, I do believe I'd be content to spend the entire day alone."

She was happily devouring the breakfast when Darcy and Bingley came in.

"Well?" Darcy questioned.

"You mean they didn't tell you the baby was born?"

"Of course they told us."

"Oh," she said. "Congratulations, Charles. I am sorry; by the time it was all over I was in such a state, I just went back to bed. You have seen them, haven't you? Jane and the baby, I mean."

"Yes, I've seen them. They're fine. But you. Aren't you going to tell us what happened?"

"Well, we just did everything we could think of. What Mrs. Sims and Mrs. Reynolds could think of, that is. I suppose we would have survived even if Mrs. Whipple hadn't come, but I can assure you I have never been so happy to see anyone in my whole life. Baby is all right, isn't he?"

"Yes, he is."

"Is he very small?"

"Dr. Thornton says he looks like a full-term baby. Didn't you see him?"

"I did, but I was too upset to think clearly. And Jane?"

"She's fine."

"I was so sorry, but once it was all over, I just had to leave. I was so upset. It all happened so fast." She continued her breakfast, then remembering, asked, "Where's Georgiana?"

"She's with Jane; she'll be here shortly," Bingley replied. Bingley looked intently at Elizabeth and said, "I'm not saying I doubt you, but I should tell you that I overheard one of the servants this morning refer to you as 'the general.'"

Elizabeth's brow furrowed as she chewed. "Mrs. Reynolds called me that. It's not easy to imagine a general looking so disheveled. I just kept ordering everyone around until everything we could think of had been done. I can't remember when I've been in such a state."

They sat in silence for a few minutes, drinking their tea. The door opened, and Georgiana came in. "There you are, Elizabeth; have they told you they're calling you 'the general?'"

"Yes, they told me; just so they don't call me the general who lost the battle!"

September 10, Sunday

Benjamin, as the Bingley baby was to be named, had been born early Sunday morning, and that night, finally, Elizabeth and Darcy found themselves alone together in their bedroom as they retired for the night. All the tumult had left them subdued, even thoughtful, content to complete each act slowly, deliberately.

They climbed into bed and settled down, but remained wide-eyed, examining the design of the canopy fabric.

"I've been thinking," Darcy said.

"Yes?" she responded, turning to look at him.

"Maybe having a child isn't such a good idea."

She reflected and then said, "Would you like to tell me what has brought you to that thought?"

"Well, there we were, right in the middle of a most agreeable...encounter, shall we say, and a madman starts pounding on our bedroom door—in truth, my best friend. That should tell you something right there. I mean, it has become very clear to me that infants can be thoroughly disruptive of one's life."

"Is that all?"

"No. I've been thinking: where will it all end? Think about it; if it had been just a sprained ankle last week, Jane and Bingley could have returned to Thornwood with no great difficulty. It was the pregnancy that caused them to alter their plans. They were prepared to stay an additional five weeks until the birth and who knows how much longer afterwards. You have to own that's a great deal of disruption caused by that...diminutive being."

He paused, and she kept watching him, but he didn't continue.

"So now I suppose you expect me to say something like...'Are you really serious?'"

"I wasn't really thinking about what you would say, but I would not be shocked to hear you respond in that way."

"I would."

"Why?"

"Where's your nightshirt?"

"Why do you ask?"

"Where is your nightshirt?"

"It's on the chair."

"Where is your modern inconvenience?"

"It's around here somewhere."

"Somewhere?"

"I can easily find it."

"You aren't taking much care that your actions support your new philosophical position."

They were facing each other now examining each other's expressions. She was intent on the tensions of his jaw and chin, proof positive of an attempt at secrecy or manipulation, even mendacity.

He, in turn, was waiting for the hint of a curve of a smile or possibly excessive blinking.

At length he said, "Confess it; you're pregnant."

A gasp of laughter escaped her. "Whatever gave you that idea?"

He took his time in answering, allowing her to contemplate the possibilities. "It's been a very long time since you had your period, don't you think?"

Muscles around her eyes began to twitch and scowl lines appeared on her forehead. She looked upwards, eyes darting here and there. "Is it possible?" she replied at last.

He sighed in exasperation, "We have not gone 3 days without making love for months, probably not two days—confess it."

"If there is any confessing to be done, it is you."

"For what?"

"For pretending you are no longer eager to have a child."

This broke him. "Oh, Elizabeth," he said, pulling her to him, "I'm so happy."

"Then why are there tears in your eyes?"

"I was beginning to believe we couldn't have a child."

She reached up and ran her finger over his eye to remove the tear.

"I'm happy too," she said, moving closer. They lay embracing, quiet.

"My lovely Elizabeth."

Now her eyes teared, and an intake of breath sounded suspiciously like sniffles.

"Turn around, Lizzy," he said, tugging at her.

Her back curved against his body, and they lay contemplating the new being that was now growing as a result of their union. He laid the palm of his hand over her abdomen and the thought occurred to her: "Has he ever performed any act that more surely revealed his feelings?"

"How long have you known?" he asked.

"Several weeks."

"Why didn't you tell me?"

"Have we really needed more excitement during these weeks?"

"No, I suppose not."

"How did you guess?"

"Carleton's remarks started me thinking. When he congratulated me, how did you manage not to reveal it then?"

"He wasn't looking at me; he was looking at you. If he had been looking at me he might have guessed. If you remember, it was not long after that that I asked for a glass of wine. All that tumult over Georgiana's arm—I was almost unmasked by his teasing you."

"Then later I sent you to take a nap."

"Never have I found a command more to my liking."

"But that whole uproar over Benjamin's birth—you really did act like a general, yet you were pregnant yourself."

"Several weeks."

"But it was four o'clock in the morning when Bingley came pounding at the door. That wasn't much sleep."

"But I had slept during the early evening. By four o'clock I had had a full night's sleep."

"I didn't think about that. The hunt though: weren't you taking a chance with all that bouncing around? Risking a miscarriage, I mean."

"If bouncing around could cause miscarriage there would be few unwanted children in the world."

He contemplated this thought until he had exhausted his mind's catalogue of images that could support or refute that idea until he got lost in the associations his mind conjured up.

"I do think we should celebrate this event."

"How?"

He pulled at her nightie until she was as bare as he was.

September 11, Monday

In the days that followed the tumultuous events surrounding the fox hunt and Jane's precipitate delivery, all the usual activities and emotions followed a predictable sequence: Jane and Bingley's gratitude to Elizabeth for her quick thinking and energetic leadership; the enthusiastic response of all family members, and the servants as well since almost everyone had had a part in the events; the naming of this first son of a family of wealth—Benjamin would be his name—an oblique reference to his maternal parentage; the accelerated and varied activities attendant to the introduction of a new member of the human species—frequent feeding, crying, floor pacing, and anxious looks exchanged; increased laundry; and the inevitable speculation regarding the size of the baby and how it could happen to be born a month earlier than anticipated, including counting the months back to the wedding, which everyone knew was at the same time as the Darcy's wedding—late November the preceding year.

Tuesday
This was a great deal of additional activity, but, as Darcy had so frequently reiterated, with so many servants to carry out necessary tasks, much can be accomplished. So, even though it was expected that the Bingleys would continue as guests at Pemberley for some additional weeks, Elizabeth turned to a new thought.

She and Darcy had felt little disappointment at the absence of Lady Catherine de Bourgh from their wedding. She had, because of her objections to their marriage, refused to attend the wedding. Nevertheless, some attention might now be paid to this personage.

It was the second "normal" day after the birth—Tuesday—at breakfast. Georgiana had left for the library, her broken arm now permitting few activities besides reading. Elizabeth began, "Darcy, I've been thinking about Lady Catherine." She looked up and noted his raised eyebrow. "I do think we now might make a gesture of reconciliation. She did, you must admit, entertain me at Rosings on quite a number of occasions. We might even own—at least to each other—that if it weren't for her attentions to Mr. Collins and our meetings at Rosings it is quite unlikely that we should ever have reached our current happy state."

"You're very formal this morning, aren't you?"

"Yes, I suppose I am. Perhaps it's best even in thinking of Lady Catherine to stay at that level."

"What did you have in mind?"

"Well, Jane and Bingley will likely go back to Thornwood in a few weeks. I would be reluctant to invite Lady Catherine for Christmas. I prefer to surround myself at that time of year with more soothing company. Winter will not be very agreeable for travel, so I think that early October might be a suitable time. If we do have a larger event later, like the ball, or even next year if the fair is held again, I would not want her to come. I'm sure all my thoughts would have to be spent on how everything would affect her and vice versa."

Darcy nodded each time she introduced a new aspect of the problem and stated her position, so she continued, "I've been thinking that we could have a dinner party for perhaps 10 or 12 altogether. You, Georgina and I make three; Lady Catherine and Miss de Bourgh make five. So, we would need seven more to make a dozen." More nods.

"Now, how do we flatter Lady Catherine sufficiently to induce her to come? This is my thought: I have heard a number of people lately commenting on Mrs. Wilson and how she always seems to be on hand when any community project is in progress. This is something that interests Lady Catherine. We could tell her that we are honoring Mrs. Wilson for her work in the community."

From this premise proceeded many hours of discussion spread out over two days—at meal time, while riding, and at bedtime. The guest list for the dinner party was particularly troublesome: who would not offend Lady Catherine and who would not be offended by Lady Catherine? In the end the list of guests included Mr. and Mrs. Wilson, Sir Humphrey Winston and his mother, Mrs. Winston, Vicar and Mrs. Ford, Mr. and Mrs. Pettigrew, and Mr. Harrison.

Mr. Harrison was suggested by Georgiana on one of the occasions when she was present for the discussion.

"Isn't he back at Oxford now?" Darcy queried.

"Yes, he's been accepted as an instructor; but if the dinner is going to be on Saturday he can ride here on Saturday and back to Oxford on Sunday."

"That should sufficiently exhaust him," Darcy responded. "Yes, it sounds like a good plan."

Mrs. Ford was selected on Elizabeth's recommendation. "She seems always to be attempting to calm troubled waters wherever she goes. She should be a proper counter-balance for Lady Catherine."

Darcy approved the Vicar's inclusion. "Lady Catherine is partial to the clergy. She is most at ease with one of them at her elbow."

Elizabeth had a secret reason for including Mrs. Pettigrew: She had decided she wanted to try a man's saddle, but was not yet ready to confront Darcy on the subject. Since Mrs. Pettigrew used a man's saddle, possibly her presence might be the occasion for raising the subject. Her stated reason for including Mrs. Pettigrew was that "She has the happy ability to assess a situation and find the humor in it. She should surely be an asset in Lady Catherine's presence."

Mrs. Winston found favor in Georgiana's eye. "I don't think Mrs. Winston would be frightened by Lady Catherine. In fact, Lady Catherine might at last meet her match."

Darcy modified that position. "I don't think she would carry on a verbal battle with Lady Catherine, though. If they contend, Mrs. Winston is more likely to use withering glances, or perhaps even ignore her altogether."

"I suspect you're right," Elizabeth concluded.

"But what of Miss de Bourgh?" Darcy asked. "Will she get lost in this gathering of determined individuals?"

"She might prefer being lost," Elizabeth responded, "but I think some of the ladies might take her under their wings: the mothering instinct is very strong."

After these extended discussions and building on his long acquaintance with Lady Catherine, Darcy wrote in his firm hand the following letter, to which Elizabeth then added her own signature beneath his:

"My dear Aunt Catherine,

We were sorry not to see you at our wedding last November. As our first anniversary approaches we are reminded of that absence, and are now hoping it might be possible to bridge an unseemly chasm.

To that end we now extend to you an invitation to visit us for a few days at Pemberley early next month, October 6—9, to be precise.

There is a lady living near us in Derbyshire who has distinguished herself by her sustained perseverance in good works on behalf of the community. To be specific, she has been untiring in her efforts on behalf of the Lambton infirmary and more recently on a project to found a library, also in Lambton.

Mrs. Wilson will be our honored guest along with several others at a dinner on Saturday, October 7. In considering how we might enhance the honor, we have decided that she might be interested in meeting someone of acknowledged status in the larger community—to be specific—England.

Our thoughts naturally turned to you, especially because you have distinguished yourself in a similar manner.

In short, we would be honored if you would condescend to visit Pemberley for the dates mentioned.

We shall, of course, expect Miss de Bourgh and Mrs. Jenkinson to accompany you.

Should you be unable to accept our invitation for whatever reason, we will of course understand. However, we do look forward to your acceptance.

With respect,
Fitzwilliam Darcy,
Elizabeth Darcy"

Elizabeth then composed an invitation for the other guests:

"You are invited to dinner at Pemberley on Saturday October 7 at two o'clock p.m. We do hope you will be able to join us.

—Fitzwilliam and Elizabeth Darcy"

"Should we mention that we've planned the dinner in honor of Mrs. Wilson?" Darcy asked.

"I don't think so. You can stand up at the dinner and remark on Mrs. Wilson's contributions to the community. Then we can drink a toast to her. A great many people have worked on these same projects and might feel slighted at being left out. None of those people will see the letter we're sending to Lady Catherine."

"We are being rather devious, aren't we?" Darcy suggested.

"I suppose so. It's hard to be straightforward with anyone as prickly as Lady Catherine without offending her. We could, of course, omit the mention of Mrs. Wilson. But would Lady Catherine come all this distance just for a little visit...and that at the home of that upstart, the former Miss Elizabeth Bennet?"

"You do present a very convincing case, Lizzy. I approve the entire scheme."

Given the frequent daily contact between persons who knew each other as well as Jane and Elizabeth and Darcy and Bingley, the Darcys decided that if Elizabeth's pregnancy should be suspected, they would not attempt to conceal it from the Bingleys. They hoped to be able to keep Georgiana unaware longer though, and her ignorance of the symptoms might assist them.

In the end that hope led them to the conclusion that they should take Jane and Bingley into their confidence, fearing that an unthinking comment in Georgiana's presence might lead to an untimely disclosure.

Both Jane and Bingley were delighted and not a little surprised at the timing of the news so soon after their own happy event.

September 14, Thursday

Darcy arrived at dinner with a letter from Carleton. "He's invited me to hunt with him, tomorrow if possible."

"And will you?"

"Would it be inconvenient for me to be gone for the day?"

"Not at all."

"Then I shall."

While generally Bingley enjoyed hunting, the new father was still hovering over the new mother and child and decided not to go along.

As Jane was becoming more confident in her new role of mother to a tiny infant, she accepted Elizabeth's offer to assist with Benjamin's care in Darcy's absence—timely experience for Elizabeth who was only six when Lydia, the youngest of her sisters, was born.

Saturday

Saturday morning as they were rising, Darcy said, "Elizabeth, there's something I need to discuss with you that I don't want Georgiana to hear. Could you come into my study this morning after she goes to her own activities?"

"Of course. Is something wrong?"

"Nothing to worry about. It's just some business that is a bit complicated; until it's resolved I don't want Georgiana to know."

Because her broken arm had ended the kitchen duties, at least for the time being, Georgiana was spending much of her time reading.

After breakfast this day she went to the library, and after she left, Elizabeth went to see Darcy in his study.

"I have some troubling news," Darcy began. "Carleton gave me this letter that Fitzwilliam asked him to give to me." He handed the letter to Elizabeth, and she read it.

"Dear Darcy,
I have commissioned Carleton to relay to you certain information that will no doubt trouble you but which nonetheless is true.
I was unwilling to relate the facts in a letter to you and unable to leave my duties to visit you. Nor was I willing to ask you to come to see me.
While I do not merit a positive reply to the request he will make, I nevertheless was determined to make the attempt.
Please be assured that whatever your reply, of all the persons in the world you will remain among the persons most beloved by me.
Your cousin,
Fitzwilliam"

"What does it mean?" Elizabeth asked.

"You must remember that I told you that Carleton had a sister that he hasn't heard from in years."

"I do remember."

"Carleton received a letter from his sister Margaret early this week. She told him she was living in London and asked him to visit her. He left almost immediately. When he arrived in London, she told him she was about to be married and would soon be leaving with her husband for America."

"But what does all this have to do with Fitzwilliam?"

"The man she is going to marry is Fitzwilliam."

"Fitzwilliam? I can't believe it. How did they happen to meet?"

"Their meeting was not a recent event. They've known each other for a very long time."

"How long?"

"It seems that while Fitzwilliam was visiting here when he was about 25 they met and fell in love. He went back to duty and didn't discover until a year later that she had run away from home. He found her and took her to London where she has lived since."

"This is absolutely astonishing. But why did she run away?"

"She was pregnant and frightened of how her parents would react."

"But how did he happen to find her?"

"He came back the following summer to visit and discovered she'd disappeared. He searched until he found her in Manchester. By then her baby was three months old."

"Then she's been his mistress all this time."

"That's a rather harsh way of putting it. One usually thinks of a mistress as the lover of a married man. And, of course, Fitzwilliam is not married."

"But he could have married at any time to whomever he pleased."

"There's no denying that. Margaret, however, claims that he has always sworn to her that he would not marry anyone else and that when he was able he would marry her."

"What about their child?"

"The child is being cared for in the country."

"But what if they had another child?"

"Do you remember our trip to London last January?"

"Of course."

"Well, Fitzwilliam wasn't entirely honest with me at the time. He did know a London supplier for the condoms. He'd been buying them for some time."

"But that must be more than 5 years. Were they effective all that time?"

"Not entirely."

"Then she did get pregnant."

"Yes. Carleton told me that he quizzed Fitzwilliam on this point. She was pregnant twice."

"What happened to the babies?"

"She didn't have the babies."

"What, then?"

"As we suspected, military persons develop sources of information that some of us do not. He found a doctor that was known to perform abortions."

"This is too much. No wonder he didn't want to write it in a letter. But the letter referred to a request. After all this I can't imagine him having the courage to ask you for anything."

"And I'm having a great deal of difficulty convincing myself that I should agree to his request."

"What is he asking for?"

"As I said, they have now resolved to marry. Fitzwilliam is concerned over the fact that they will be leaving soon for America and that it is possible we will never see each other again. He is asking me to attend their wedding."

"And will you?"

"I haven't decided yet."

"When will it be?"

"Thursday, the 21st."

"That's next week. Where will it be?"

"In Oxford, to make it more convenient for Carleton, and for me should I decide to attend."

This news cast a shadow over Elizabeth and Darcy, making it very difficult for them to conceal their lowered spirits from Georgiana and the Bingleys.

That night in their bedroom, Elizabeth said, "I think you must go to the wedding. If you never see Fitzwilliam again you will later regret this failure of generosity. We may regret or criticize the quality of his care for Margaret, but he has taken care of her, and the child as well. Surely he deserves some degree of forgiveness for that. For myself I shall always be grateful to him for his part in bringing us together.

"You look doubtful. If Fitzwilliam had not been at Rosings, would you have proposed to me?"

Minutes went by as he pondered her comments. "Once a person takes one pathway it is never possible to know what would have happened if one had taken a different path. In this instance, I believe that if Fitzwilliam had not gone with me to Rosings, I would not have gone alone."

The next morning he sent a message to Carleton that he would attend the wedding. He would ride Prince early on Wednesday the 20th, to Carleton's, and they would ride together in Carleton's carriage, returning on Friday the 22nd.

To Georgiana and the Bingleys he only said he would be gone those three days on business.

September 18, Monday

By the following Monday the household had settled into a somewhat livlier routine, but routine, nevertheless. However, Elizabeth joined Darcy in his study after breakfast to discuss with him a subject that had been arising in her mind repeatedly of late.

He set aside the papers he had been perusing to listen to her as she sat opposite him.

"Do you think we're overworking the servants?" she began.

"Have they been complaining?"

"I've been so wrapped up in my own concerns, I'm not sure that I would be aware."

"Perhaps you should discuss it with Mrs. Reynolds."

"What if she says we need more help?"

"Then I think we should get it. Perhaps one or more of those who helped out for the ball would be available."

"But can we afford it? You never talk about money. I don't have any sense of what we can afford."

"My lovely wife insists on clothing herself for shillings, and my sister is determined to be our assistant cook. If I am to avoid becoming as rich as Croesus, we shall have to do something."

She rose, walked around the desk, cupped his head between her palms, and kissed him. She had not yet withdrawn when a knock at the door disturbed their peace.

"It's my best friend or my sister; you can depend on it. They are determined to keep us apart."

She stood up, and he said "Come in."

Bingley and Georgiana watched as Elizabeth slowly moved back around the desk. "I didn't realize you were here," he said to Elizabeth. "Georgiana thought you might be here, Darcy. I was just wondering if you would be interested in going for a ride."

"I would. Maybe we can get a sense of where the best bird hunting is going to be."

Elizabeth found Mrs. Reynolds and discussed the staff and if there was enough help. She explained that the Bingleys might not leave until early October; then they hoped Lady Catherine would come with Miss de Bourgh and Mrs. Jenkinson for a few days. "And who knows what will happen after that? I would like to invite my friend Charlotte for a few days, and at Christmas I'll want the Gardners to come and possibly my parents, though they might go to Thornwood instead."

"I see what you mean," Mrs. Reynolds replied. "Yes, I think this would be a very good time to take on additional help. I suggest one more assistant in the kitchen and another maid to assist Katie and Susan downstairs and Sarah upstairs."

"Can you begin a search now?"

"Yes, of course. I'll take care of it. I would like to say something, though I hope you won't take offence."

"I can't imagine that I would. Please, say it."

"My remark that morning when Benjamin was born—about you being a general. I've since overheard some of the servants using it. If you've heard it, I do apologize. That birth was upsetting for all of us, and I'm afraid I spoke out of turn."

"I have heard it, but I was not and am not offended. Indeed, I considered it something of a compliment, though I'm sure I would have felt differently if we had lost the battle."

"I did not hear any complaints about the quality of your leadership."

"Thank you."

Wednesday

Wednesday arrived, and Darcy left on his three-day trip with Carleton to Oxford. With adjustments necessary for the new baby and Georgiana's immobilized arm, the days passed quickly.

Darcy arrived home on Friday in time for supper. When finally in their bedroom, Elizabeth asked about the events at Oxford. But Darcy said, "Elizabeth, I recall a conversation very early in our marriage when we had been discussing Georgiana at length; at the time I said "I hope there will not always be three of us in bed."

"I remember."

"Nothing happened in Oxford that can't wait until tomorrow."

"Of course," she said. She turned over and he pulled her body into the curve of his own.

Then she added, "But I'm afraid it's too late for your wish to be honored now."

He was sufficiently tired so that it took some time before he took her meaning. "At least so far little one is no trouble to us," he said, stretching his hand over her abdomen.

September 23, Saturday

After breakfast Darcy went to his study and Georgiana to the morning room to read, Elizabeth following. However, she soon set her needlework down and told Georgiana she remembered something she had to talk with Darcy about.

He told her the few details about the trip and the wedding worth relating, principle ones being that Fitzwilliam was very grateful that he had come with Carleton and that the bride and groom seemed as happy a couple as any he had known. Fitzwilliam told him that the only real happiness he had had during the past several years were the times he had spent with Margaret, and that when an opportunity presented itself that would make it possible to leave the army and marry her, he had seized it. While originally it appeared likely that they would leave immediately for America, it was now possible they would not leave until spring.

Elizabeth listened to Darcy's narration somberly. She sat quietly, Darcy staring out the window for some minutes. When it appeared he would say no more, she said, "I believe Fitzwilliam deserves this happiness. It's sad it has taken so long to come. They might even be happier than they otherwise would have been had they not gone through so many difficulties."

She could see he was listening carefully, but he did not comment on her remarks. Instead, he said, "The weather looks quite agreeable. Why don't we take a walk?"

They had walked some distance from the house when he said, "Something else happened in Oxford. I went and talked with the professor who seemed most likely to know something about the problem we've been working on."

"The modern inconvenience?"

"The very one."

"Was he of any help?"

"No."

"I've discovered something."

"You have?"

"Remember the two weeks you spent with Bingley at Thornwood in July?

"Yes, I do."

"We went two full weeks without making love."

"We did?"

"You came back that Saturday night and we argued about whether you should go for a second week."

"That's right; we did."

"The next night Bingley kept you up late talking, and then you fell asleep immediately. The next morning you got up early and left."

"I remember."

"Well, my period was due Friday, the day before you came back, but did not begin."

"So you're saying that that's proof that you got pregnant *before* that two-week period."

"Exactly."

"It does not prove you could not get pregnant during that two-week period."

"Correct. But there's something else. Unfortunately, to tell you I have to break a confidence. I mean, when the information was conveyed to me the teller did not say, 'Don't ever tell anyone,' but the information is of such a personal nature that even without being sworn to secrecy, I feel as if I'm breaking a confidence."

He thought this over and then said, "Might it be possible to tell me what the information is without telling me who it was that told you?"

She considered this for a time. After all, she might have gotten the information from any of several of her women friends and acquaintances, or any of her four sisters. "Yes, I think that will work."

Thus she related Georgiana's story about her abdominal pains, the frequency, regularity, etc., without saying that Georgiana was the one who had told her. She began by saying, "One of my women friends told me this...."

He thought these things over as they walked. Finally he said, "You've obviously had some time to contemplate the import of these things. I think I get the sense of what you're saying, but I'd like you to tell me what you think it all means."

"I think that the pains my friend had are not an indication she cannot have children. I believe it is an indication that she can have children."

"You said that the pain typically comes about two weeks before the period begins. And in the case of your pregnancy, that it probably happened about two weeks before your period was due."

"Exactly."

"Very interesting. Very interesting, indeed."

"There's one other thing, something I remembered recently."

"Yes?"

"I had a pain like that one time myself."

"Indeed?"

"Yes, it was just as my friend described it—in the lower abdomen, towards the side, not terribly painful, but a very decided sensation."

"Do you remember when it happened?"

"Yes, the day before our wedding."

"Remarkable."

"And there's something else."

"This is quite a pile of information you're stacking up."

"Do you remember the first period I had after we were married?"

"Early in the morning."

"On a Sunday."

"That's right. You didn't go to church. Georgiana and I went alone."

"My period was about three days late, and I decided I had been pregnant."

"You did, yes, though you didn't tell me until much later. So that period was 15 days after our wedding because we were married on a Saturday, and you did go to church with me a week after our wedding before Georgiana got back."

They walked in silence trying to digest these facts and assimilate their import.

September 25, Monday: Harrison

On arising Elizabeth said, "We will ride this morning, won't we?"

"If you don't mind, I'd rather take a long walk right after breakfast."

"As you wish."

At breakfast Georgiana was complaining about her arm. "It itches so I think I'll go mad."

"How many weeks did Dr. Thornton say you'd have to wear the cast?" Darcy asked.

"Six weeks."

"There's only one thing I can suggest," Elizabeth said. "Keep busy. Keep your mind so occupied that you don't have time to think about it."

"What can I do with only one hand?"

Elizabeth thought for a while, then suggested, "Practice the right hand portion of your piano music."

Darcy had been thinking as well. "Write a letter to any, no, all of your correspondents."

"How can I hold the paper?"

"Set a paper weight on it."

"Play backgammon with Jane."

"All right. I understand. If I only think a little I can find something to do."

She did in fact go first to the piano, while Darcy and Elizabeth set out for their walk.

"There was one other thing I didn't tell you about the trip to Oxford. Our other discussions Saturday quite distracted me, and I forgot until yesterday when we were spending the afternoon with the Bingley's."

"Yes?"

"I was leaving the professor's office and walking down the street to meet Carleton when I heard my name. I looked up and saw Harrison. He seemed as surprised to see me as I was him. After our greetings, he asked if I had time to talk with him for a few minutes. As it happened, the professor had taken little of my time, so we found a pub and talked for awhile. "

"What did he have to say?"

"You were quite right about his feelings for Georgiana. He indicated that he was very fond of her and that he hopes to be able to see her as frequently as time and opportunity permit."

"Has he told Georgiana of his intentions?"

"Apparently not, but he seems to feel that she would not discourage him."

"What did you tell him?"

"I expressed concern about his ability to provide a proper home for her."

"Oxford is some distance from Pemberley. How does he expect to be able to see her?"

"He has a friend who will loan him his horse and gig on occasion and says the trip between Oxford and Gormley is fairly easy. He seems prepared to make the trip weekends rather frequently. He asked if he could call on Saturdays without specific advance notice."

"What did you say?"

"I didn't see how I could refuse. She's almost eighteen now and if she were to marry, she would have access to her fortune with no possibility of my denying it. I didn't tell him that, but he probably understands that without my informing him."

"You don't seem very happy about his interest in her."

"He seems a decent sort. I suppose at 22 I wasn't particularly impressive either."

"My impression is that he's very intelligent, and his behavior when Georgiana broke her arm certainly revealed an impressive competence."

"Oh, my God!"

"What is it?"

"We could have a daughter."

"Of course we could."

"I guess I just naturally assumed we'd have a son."

"But why?"

"I don't know. Whenever I thought of having a child, I always envisioned a boy."

"Would you be very unhappy if we did have a girl?"

"I don't know. I never thought about it."

"You've always appeared to have a great deal of affection for Georgiana."

"I do."

"Well then...."

"You're right, of course. But this business with Harrison does set me thinking of how difficult it is to be a father to a daughter."

"And what do you suppose Mr. Harrison's parents are thinking now? Surely Mrs. Pettigrew has informed them that he's been paying particular attention to a young lady in Derbyshire. In a way, they're in an even worse position than we are—so far away they have no opportunity for direct observation. They could be imagining all sorts of terrible things."

"Yes."

"Did Harrison say he intends to declare himself to Georgiana?"

"No, he didn't. He seems prepared to let her get better acquainted with him first. At least in that regard he seems more sensible than I was when I proposed to you at Hunsford."

"Do you mind if I change the subject?"

"No, I think we've thoroughly exhausted this question."

"I've been thinking we might take a trip to London the fourth week in October. I should be thinking of some additional clothing."

"Good thought. Some plays, concerts, maybe even dancing should be enjoyable."

"You...looking forward to dancing?"

"I was thinking of Georgiana. Maybe she'll see some other young men. Who was that young fellow we saw in the restaurant? Maybe we could invite him and his parents to dinner."

"I've been thinking also about Charlotte. Perhaps we could invite them for a few days in November."

"Let me think about that." He puzzled for awhile and then said, "Ah, I have it. Does Charlotte ever visit her parents in Meryton?"

"I suppose she does."

"Well, might it be possible for us to visit your parents for a day or two on our way to London sometime when we know the Collinses will be at Meryton?"

"You don't want Mr. Collins to come here, do you?"

"It's uncomfortable enough watching him kow-tow to Lady Catherine, but when he addresses me in that way, I just want to disappear. Ah, I have it. There is another possibility. If Lady Catherine does come here, she just may invite us to Rosings later—in the spring. Then too, if they hold the fair here next summer we could invite the Collinses then. With so many people around, I may not be so conscious of his presence."

"I don't think that's a very good idea."

"Why not?"

"I can just see him following you around wherever you go in the crowd."

"Yes, you may be right, but what do you think of the Meryton idea?"

"Let me write to Mama and Papa and to Charlotte. That may be the best idea of all. At least in Meryton, the grandparents can care for baby Martha while Charlotte and I visit."

"The hunting in Hertfordshire should be good in October and November. Perhaps your father and I could go out hunting. I do think I could profit by a greater exposure to his philosophy."

Elizabeth therefore wrote as follows:

"Dear Charlotte,

Is there any possibility you could visit with your parents sometime between October 23 and November 14? We are planning to take a trip to London and would find it convenient to visit Mama and Papa if we knew we could also see you there. I shall have to write to them also, of course.

No doubt you already have heard of Jane's delivery of a fine baby boy on September 10 while they were here at Pemberley. We expect them to leave next week to go to Thornwood, their new home near Huntington in Leicestershire.

Please let me hear from you at your earliest convenience.

I do hope you are all well, as we are.
Affectionately,
Elizabeth"

To the Bennets she wrote:

"Dear Mama and Papa,

I have written to Charlotte Collins in the hopes that they might visit her parents in Meryton on an occasion when it would be convenient for you to invite Darcy and myself to spend a few days at Longbourn.

To simplify things, you might talk with the Lucases regarding dates. I have suggested to Charlotte sometime between October 23 and November 14, though a later date might be suitable.

Let me hear from you as soon as convenient.

I do hope you are all well, as we are here.
Affectionately,
Elizabeth
P.S. Miss Darcy will come with us, of course."

On the 26th a letter arrived from Lady Catherine accepting the invitation to visit Pemberley October 6—9. The primary tone of the note was of condescension, but was mercifully short, and this encouraged the Darcys to cherish a hope that the visit would not be a disaster.

October 1, Sunday: Miss Bingley

When leaving church, Sir Humphrey approached Darcy and Elizabeth as they were leaving and said, "I wonder if I might have a word with you both. Mr. Ford has said we could use his study."

There he disclosed that he and his mother were delighted with the invitation to the dinner with Lady Catherine, but that he had already invited guests for that weekend—Miss Bingley and the Hursts.

"Then bring them along," Darcy said, after consulting Elizabeth's reaction to the request.

"They would be very welcome," Elizabeth added.

"I was hoping you'd say that."

Georgiana was waiting in the carriage. As Elizabeth and Darcy seated themselves in the carriage, she asked, "What was that about?"

"Miss Bingley and the Hursts are going to be visiting at the Winstons the weekend Lady Catherine will be here. We told him to bring them along."

"Now that is interesting," Georgiana said.

"Is it indeed?" Darcy responded.

"Yes it is. You know, I began to be suspicious that day of the fox hunt. I saw them riding at the beginning of the hunt. Instead of pushing ahead with the other gentlemen, it looked as if he was trying to keep behind her. Then they got way ahead of me. Later when I fell and they helped me get up and find a place to sit by the tree, he was very attentive to her. She didn't seem to notice, but I did. It took awhile before you came along, Elizabeth, and it was very obvious."

"So, we'll have 15 at dinner if everyone comes," Darcy said.

"Sixteen," Elizabeth corrected. "I forgot that Mrs. Jenkinson will have to sit with us."

Monday

Just over three weeks old, Benjamin was ready to take his first journey to the home that was new not only to himself, but to his parents as well. It was just over four weeks since Jane had twisted her ankle and, finding it easier to walk, she was understandably eager to go to her own, new home, however much she and her sister cared for one another.

The Bingleys left Monday morning, leaving Pemberley considerably less busy than it had recently been.

Two days later, on leaving the dining room, Elizabeth found a letter from Lydia. "Lydia. Well, she could have turned up at a worse time—last week for instance."

"Dearest Elizabeth,

I do hope all is well with you. Wickham and many in his regiment are being reassigned for some months to the south of England and will be leaving October 13 by ship. Some of us wives are following and will be leaving about the same time, though we must travel by land.

I should like to visit at Pemberley on my way to Longbourn, where I will visit Mama and Papa for a few days.

If I do not hear from you before we are ready to leave, I shall go directly to Longbourn.

Please greet the Bingleys for me if you see them.
Devotedly,
Lydia"

"Dearest? Devotedly? Well, perhaps she has changed, but I shall not depend on it."

She went directly to Darcy's study to show him the letter. She stood at the window as he read it. "The view is lovely here; I should come more often," she thought.

"You are going to invite her, aren't you?"

"Do you think I should?"

"Why not? I would not agree to Wickham coming, but she's very clear that he will be otherwise engaged." He examined his calendar. I've been thinking about the books at Thornwood. Bingley said he made the rest of his selections before they arrived for the fair. This might be a good time to fetch the ones neither of us want. We've decided to take them to Manchester to a book dealer after those for the Lambton and Gormley libraries have been selected. I was talking to Wilson the morning of the fair. He says he goes up at least once a month to Manchester for stock for his store. Generally when he goes to Manchester his wagon is empty so he agreed to take the books for a very reasonable compensation."

"You're considering being absent while Lydia is here?"

"Would she be disappointed if I were gone for part of her visit?"

"I doubt if she would care much one way or the other."

"Well then...."

Thus the decision was made to invite Lydia in accordance with her request. Elizabeth therefore wrote her letter and sent it immediately:

"Dear Lydia,

Your letter arrived today, October 4. It would be convenient for us if you were to come here sometime between October 13th and the 16th, provided you do not stay longer than the 19th.

You must have heard by now that Jane and Bingley were here on September 10 when Benjamin was born. Though delivery was not expected until a month later, the doctor assured us that he looked like a full-term infant and is healthy in every way.

Let me know when you will arrive, and we will send our carriage to Lambton to meet you.
Your sister,
Elizabeth"

Final touches were made to the plans for Lady Catherine's stay and the dinner. By Wednesday all the acceptances had been received, orally or in letters, with no refusals.

October 6, 1815: Lady Catherine de Bourgh

Lady Catherine did arrive on Friday the 6th as planned. It could not be ascertained by her air that she had completely dismissed the idea that the "shades of Pemberly had been polluted" by Darcy's marriage to Elizabeth. She was not blatantly rude, but one could hardly call her gracious. That would be too much to expect, perhaps.

If she perfectly remembered her encounter at Longbourn with Elizabeth, and one must assume that she did, in view of the acuteness of her mental faculties, it apparently caused her no embarrassment now to be the guest of "that upstart, the former Miss Elizabeth Bennet."

Even that dreadful encounter had not been able to shake Elizabeth's confidence in the soundness of her own character. Now as the beloved wife of Fitzwilliam Darcy, and the respected mistress of Pemberley, Lady Catherine's imperiousness was not likely to disconcert her, and it did not.

Indeed, in private, she and Darcy speculated on what the opinions of Derbyshire residents might me as to why the Darcys had invited Lady Catherine at all. Surely this month they would be accumulating credit for supplying their neighbors with amusement. They might even be fortunate enough that someone would discover that there had at one time been speculation that Darcy might marry Miss de Bourgh.

"That mousey little thing, married to such a grand gentleman!" was the way Elizabeth put it to Darcy in one of their lighter moments.

His response was, "I certainly missed my cue on that score. Look at how rich I would have been then. Perhaps I could have gained a title. Titles do follow money, don't they?"

So, if they were to provide amusement for neighbors, they took advantage of it themselves as well.

But their original plan never envisioned the rich reward that resulted from the inclusion of Miss Bingley and company.

It was just as Georgiana had said. Later when the three of them were alone, they noted that Sir Humphrey had apparently discovered many of Miss Bingley's preferences: he was ready to secure for her additional wine, a well-placed chair; to relate an amusing anecdote; help her with her cape; or hand her into the carriage. Indeed, one would almost think by observing them that they had been companions for years.

For her part, she did not seem so disdainful as she had at dinner the day after the ball in February when she dismissed him as "that old man!" She did not reject his attentions, and, if she did not reciprocate by attention to his needs, one could wonder if such a state would be far in the future.

The other guests, while acquainted with Sir Humphrey, were not well acquainted with Miss Bingley and seemed not to notice the particularity of his attentions. Perhaps since so many years had passed since the death of his wife, they had become accustomed to Sir Humphrey's sociable nature and his attentions to the wishes of any unattached lady in the company.

It should not be surprising that Lady Catherine did not, at least so far as could be determined by observation, make any new friends on her visit to Derbyshire. It could only be hoped that she did not make any new enemies.

In short, Lady Catherine was very much as she had always been. She gave advice on any subject that arose in the conversation, though the rest of the guests, being generally reasonable and sociable creatures, did not reveal any offence if they felt it.

If Lady Catherine noticed any particularity of Mr. Harrison's attentions to Georgiana, she said nothing. Mr. Harrison had arrived from Oxford that day and was to return the next; if he was exhausted, as Darcy had predicted he might be, it was not obvious. While he was attentive to Georgiana, he enjoyed the company of the others as well and gave no indication that he believed he was already assured of her affections.

After the dinner, alone in their bedroom, Darcy commented, "This is a formidable young man—at least four years younger than I was when I first proposed to you, but giving no evidence he is likely to make a fool of himself. If this continues for another two years, I am likely to be more of a wreck than he is."

"Two years!" Elizabeth exclaimed.

"Well, it's going to take him some time to establish himself. I would expect two years to be the minimum."

"Perhaps we should now revert to our maxim that two in our bedroom is enough," Elizabeth said. "At the moment I count five."

By this time they were settled in bed. Within seconds, he took her meaning and reached over and tickled her until she begged for mercy.

"You're right, of course. We shouldn't let these nights pass without taking advantage of them: after all, you can't get pregnant now, can you?"

October 11, Wednesday

Letters arrived from both Charlotte and Mrs. Bennet. The Bennets and Lucases had conferred, so that when Charlotte's letter arrived suggesting they visit at Meryton from October 26 to the 30th both sets of parents were ready with their replies: "Yes, please come, and be prepared to dance on the 27th at the Assembly!"

A letter arrived on the 12th from Lydia that she would arrive on the 16th.

She did arrive on Monday as planned. On Tuesday after Darcy left for Thornwood, Elizabeth persuaded Lydia to go with her for a walk on the grounds. "It's too chilly out," Lydia protested.

"It should be very refreshing. Dressed warmly, we'll be fine. If we get too chill, we can finish our walk in the portrait gallery."

"Don't you get bored out here in the country?" Lydia asked.

"No, not yet; we seem always engaged in some activity or other."

"But is there any place to dance?"

"Yes, we've gone dancing several times since I arrived. Besides our ball in February and the Morrises ball in June, we've attended several assemblies."

"In Newcastle we go dancing every week, sometimes more often."

"And what else do you do?"

Lydia cast about but could think of nothing else to mention. "There is always gossip, of course. Actually, I even heard something that you might be interested in."

"Indeed."

"I don't remember who it was that told me, but I think it's true that Colonel Fitzwilliam is Darcy's cousin."

"That is true."

"Well, one of the officers that was transferred to Newcastle recently came from Colonel Fitwilliam's regiment at Portsmouth. He says that Col. Fitzwilliam has a mistress."

"You mean that he lives with a woman he is not married to?"

"Yes."

"As you lived with Wickham in London before you were married?"

"But that was just for a short time. They say he has lived with her for years."

"I hope you have not repeated this gossip to anyone but myself."

"Why not?"

"Because it's a very damaging thing to say about anyone."

"But why would someone say it if it isn't true?"

"As it happens, Colonel Fitzwilliam was married recently."

"Well. I didn't expect you to be able to supply me with gossip."

"That can hardly be called gossip."

"It is one of the best kinds of gossip. Did you go to the wedding?"

"No, I did not."

"Why not?"

"Lydia, I have no intention of explaining all my actions to you. Especially since you have never explained to my satisfaction your elopement. The note you left said you were going to Gretna Green."

"That's what Wickham told me."

"Then why didn't you go there?"

"Because he had business in London."

"What kind of business was it?"

"I don't know."

"Have you ever wondered?"

"No."

"Well, perhaps you should."

"Why?"

"Lydia, what do you suppose we were doing and thinking at Longbourn after you ran away with Wickham?"

"I don't know."

"Think about it."

"What were you thinking?"

"Mama was terrified that your father and Wickham would fight a duel."

"I don't believe it."

"Then ask her. Or ask any of your sisters."

"And what was Papa doing?"

"He was in London searching for you. And Uncle Gardner was searching as well. Lydia, do you know why Wickham married you?"

"Well, I suppose he finished his business, and then he could marry me as he said he would."

"He married you because Darcy insisted he do so."

"I don't believe it."

"Then why was Darcy at your wedding? Wickham never had anything good to say about him; why would he ask him to be there?"

"Why are you telling me all these things?"

"Because I think it's time you knew the truth. Because you need to realize that you are the one that has to do the things that will make a satisfactory life for yourself. Wickham left gambling debts wherever he went. Darcy paid them at the time of your marriage, and Papa paid his debts in Longbourn. If he runs up debts again, who will help him?"

"You don't like me very much, do you?"

"I like you enough to want you to create an agreeable life for yourself."

They walked on in silence until Elizabeth said, "Let's walk through the kitchen and ask Mrs. Sims to make some hot chocolate for us."

Lydia stayed until the 19th, accepting Elizabeth's embrace as they parted.

October 26, Thursday

The Darcy party arrived at the Bennets late in the afternoon on Thursday. Darcy let it be known that he was interested in hunting while there, indeed had brought along one of his favorite guns.

Mr. Bennet was delighted to comply for two reasons. Friday and Saturday at hunting would relieve him of the possibility of encountering Mr. Collins, the latter not being interested in hunting. The second reason was that, while he treasured his encounters with Mr. Collins and was expert in leading Mr. Collins to expose his oddities, very little time was necessary for the exercise.

In the weeks of his engagement to Elizabeth, Darcy had continued in quite a reserved manner, and the occasions now for the two men to be alone allowed him to expose his intelligence as well as his gentler qualities, the principle one being his deep affection for his wife, a quality Mr. Bennet could well appreciate.

Elizabeth and Charlotte took those mornings to visit with each other, while her father, Sir William, was instrumental in their comfort by taking Mr. Collins to his gardens, thereby giving Mr. Collins the opportunity to expound on his own horticultural triumphs as well as to display his satisfaction at his own good fortune in having such frequent and convenient access to the beautiful grounds at Rosings, the estate of his noble and condescending patroness, Lady Catherine de Bourgh.

On one of the rare occasions when she was alone with her mother, Elizabeth was subjected to an interrogation of sorts.

Mrs. Bennet began, "You're pregnant, aren't you, Elizabeth?"

"Why do you say that?"

Because you're sleepy so much of the time. Besides, you always used to drink coffee for breakfast. I saw you take tea. And you haven't eaten one strip of bacon the whole time you've been here."

"I guess I can't fool you, can I?"

"Elizabeth, you must be happy about it, aren't you...at least your first?"

"I am very happy, Mama, just short of deliriously happy."

"I only hope you don't have 11, like Mrs. Pierce."

"And I also, Mama."

But the chief delight of the visit was the Assembly at Meryton. While two years earlier, Darcy had been unwilling to dance with any of the Hertfordshire ladies, "at an assembly such as this!" this time he seemed determined to dance every dance of the evening. He did not fail to ask Elizabeth in advance for the first two dances, and during the course of the evening, Elizabeth being otherwise engaged, he danced with Mrs. Bennet, Mrs. Phillips, Mrs. Lucas and Charlotte Collins.

Elizabeth was certain that the Hertfordshire residents present would delight for weeks in the change in Mr. Darcy. When she quizzed him about it later, he admitted that it was easier to dance than to converse, noting pointedly that the other ladies did not, apparently, find conversation necessary during the dance.

For her part, Elizabeth was not a little amazed at how easy it was for her to get partners now that she could no longer be counted a potential mate. Every married and unmarried man at the dance seemed eager to stand up with her.

To the extent she was able she kept Mary at her side to "pick up the leftovers."

Miss Darcy happily attracted the attentions of several of the young men present, and Kitty had little difficulty finding partners. Indeed, one of the gentlemen seemed even rather particular in pursuit of her, a curate from a nearby community.

Nor did Mary sit out every dance. A certain young man who danced with her was a clerk in Uncle Phillips law firm and had shown more than passing interest in Mary. Mary had for some time been playing the piano in accompaniment of the church choir in rehearsals, and his joining the choir was seen as a hopeful sign.

Mrs. Bennet invited the Phillipses for dinner on Sunday night, but the largest dinner gathering of the visit was that at the Lucases on Saturday, where all the Bennets and Darcys joined the Collins and Lucases, the Lucas house being larger and better suited to such a large group.

Even in these gatherings where conversation was necessary in a way that can usually be avoided while dancing, Darcy was easy in his exchanges with everyone except on those occasions when Mr. Collins managed to participate. On these occasions as he cast his eyes around seeking escape he couldn't fail to notice Mr. Bennet's obvious enjoyment of his predicament. He would have to develop a thicker skin or a deeper level of self deprecation before he would be able to forgive Mr. Bennet for the enjoyment he took on these occasions.

Nevertheless, Elizabeth was not the only one of the threesome as they journeyed to London that considered the visit a significant success. Darcy had to concede that point himself. Georgiana had to rejoice in the fact that she had just before the trip been released from her cast and therefore could look back on this visit with considerable satisfaction, even though Mr. Harrison was not a member of the party.

October 30, Monday

The stay in London passed agreeably but with no astonishing events. Darcy visited his tailor three times, but spent much of the remaining time in new and used book stores trying to track down additional assistance with their problem, with no significant success.

Among other things, Georgiana got a new riding habit—again. Elizabeth passed up that idea for herself again, thinking, "If I had been the one with the new habit perhaps I would have been the one thrown from the horse. No, I'll wait until spring." However, now four months pregnant, she got several gowns that would accommodate a larger bulk.

They did find and invite the Price family to dinner, but Georgiana seemed rather unresponsive to James's attentions. However, as a result of that contact they were invited to a ball and met a number of other people.

In observing these various encounters, Elizabeth couldn't help observing that Georgiana looked very much as if her affections were already engaged elsewhere. Darcy did not disagree.

Their stay was filled with entertainments and other pleasures of the city, providing memories for the coming months.

November 11, Saturday: A Thornwood Ball

Upon their return to Pemberley a printed invitation from Jane and Bingley arrived for a ball to be held at Thornwood on Friday, November 24, almost precisely two years after the Netherfield ball and one year after their wedding. Penned on the invitation was Jane's suggestion that they arrive Thursday the 23rd and stay until Monday, the 27th or longer, if possible.

The decision to accept required no debate whatsoever. Elizabeth kept thinking of how much she would be confined during the coming year and that it would be delightful to enjoy the event with virtually no responsibility on her part.

November 23, Thursday

They did travel to Thornwood on the day before the ball, an easy half day's trip. While Darcy had made the trip several times, this was only the second occasion for Elizabeth and Georgiana, and they took advantage of the opportunity to see as much as could be seen on a misty, gray day.

They arrived in time for dinner, and spent the afternoon enjoying Jane and Benjamin's company while Bingley showed Darcy the results of his efforts to date and his plans for improvement of the estate.

Jane had duties supervising the servants the day of the ball, and Elizabeth and Georgiana again took advantage of the occasion to get better acquainted with baby Benjamin.

Only five months had passed since Bingley had taken possession of Thornwood, but his friendly, agreeable nature attracted people to him, and here, as in Hertfordshire, everyone loved Jane. Therefore there were about 50 people in attendance at the ball. Nevertheless, there was one too few—Mr. Harrison. Once again, though Georgiana danced and participated, it was even more apparent that her affections lay elsewhere.

Mr. and Mrs. Bennet, Kitty, and Mary also attended, arriving on the day of the ball before dinner. They had begun the trip the day before and therefore Mr. and Mrs. Bennet were refreshed and ready to observe the triumph of their beautiful daughter and her admired husband.

This, however, was not the end of the list of family members. The Hursts and Miss Bingley also arrived before dinner. As the group of diners, 14 in all, were nearly finished with their dinner, Bingley rose to announce the engagement of Miss Bingley to Sir Humphrey Winston, with the wedding planned for March.

"That explains why Mrs. Winston and Sir Humphrey are here," Elizabeth thought.

This was not the only announcement of the weekend. Another announcement was of a non-verbal nature. It was heeded nonetheless. Elizabeth's increased bulk was noticed by each of the persons who knew her, and none failed to congratulate her and Darcy on the expected event.

At the ball Elizabeth was content to sit with the other observers on this occasion, and Darcy managed to stay close at hand, talking with other guests, but exercising his excellent powers of observation to attend to Elizabeth's needs and wishes. No one argued with them when they left before midnight for an early night.

Georgiana was left under the watchful eye of the rest of the family members, though she required little watching since, obviously, her heart was in Oxford.

In bed Darcy and Elizabeth speculated on whether Caroline Bingley or Sir Humphrey was getting the best of the bargain.

"He is much older than she is," Darcy said.

"But he's a great deal more agreeable." Elizabeth contended. "In truth, I expect they shall both be as happy as they deserve to be."

More enjoyable was their enumeration of the pleasures they had found in their first year together. By their second anniversary, if all went well, their first child would be eight months old.

"Can next year possibly be as eventful as this past year? Elizabeth asked."

"Only time will tell."

"More philosophy—and very sound too, I believe."

Monday

Returned to Pemberley, Elizabeth, in contemplating the holiday season, decided that Jane's invitation to join them at Thornwood was very tempting, indeed. The Gardners were planning to spend Christmas in Meryton with the Bennets and Phillipses.

While Elizabeth might have acceded to the idea of inviting Colonel Fitzwilliam and Margaret, she was unwilling to attempt to persuade Darcy that it was a sensible idea, and she felt sure he would not raise the question. The principle difficulty might be Mr. Harrison.

However, when she raised the question of going to Thornwood at Christmas, Georgiana agreed without debate and Darcy, while generally approving the scheme, suggested they delay the final decision for awhile.

Elizabeth was no longer riding, but Darcy was frequent in his walks with her, and at other times Georgiana kept her company.

December 2, Saturday
Darcy was hunting regularly with his friends—Morris, Howell, Carleton, and Sir Humphrey, in various combinations and at various locations.

On a morning the day following a day of hunting, awake and conversing in bed before rising, Darcy told Elizabeth he'd like to talk with her in his study after breakfast.

"Is it about Fitzwilliam?"

"Why do you ask?"

"Because you hunted with Carleton yesterday."

"Yes, it is, but let's keep our two-in-the-bedroom rule."

"Agreed."

She found him by the window looking out at another rainy day, and joined him there. He put his arm around her, and hers circled him.

"Carleton and Theresa want us to come to dinner on the 29th," he said.

"But you said this was about Fitzwilliam."

"He's going to be there with Margaret."

She walked to her usual chair and sat down. "What did you tell him?"

"That I'd talk to you about it."

"When do we have to let them know?"

"He didn't give me an exact date, but we'll certainly have to tell him before the 21st when we leave for Christmas at the Bingley's."

"We are going to Thornwood then?"

"Unless you're feeling unwell, or change your mind about wanting to go."

"I do want to go, and I've certainly felt well so far, though Mama detected symptoms even I hadn't noticed."

"Did she?"

"So, since you didn't reject the idea immediately, you must be considering going—to the Carleton's, I mean. You haven't forgiven Fitzwilliam yet, have you?"

"How can I? We've practically been brothers."

"But if he had told you—a few years ago, for instance—might not your relationship have been severed then?"

"I can't decide which is worse, really. I've had his friendship during those years, but somehow his keeping the secret so long makes it even worse. I feel like I'm penned in." He paused and then said, "You've forgiven him, haven't you?"

"He wasn't concealing the truth from me for such a long time. Then too, I keep thinking of the times when I've seen him in company—at our ball, for instance. He always spread his attentions between all the ladies, never allowing any one of them to suspect he had designs on them. Maybe his pledge to Margaret was sincere. Maybe he was just trying to maintain contact with you and Georgiana. After all, he never knew if you might need his assistance with her. Let's just think about it for awhile. We have more than two weeks. After awhile it might not seem so difficult. Did Carleton say if anyone else would be there?"

"Only his parents."

"And the child?"

"No, he won't be there. They decided that would make things too complicated, at least for this visit."

"He must have included Georgiana in the invitation."

"He did, but I just don't see how I can agree to that."

"Perhaps I could talk with Mrs. Howell. They've been wanting to have her come to visit Sally. We could leave her there for dinner, go on to the Carletons and pick her up on the way home."

"That might work. But eventually Georgiana will hear about this meeting and the marriage and will wonder why she wasn't included." After reflecting awhile he concluded, "Let's just think about it for a few days."

The days passed quietly. Going to Thornwood for Christmas reduced the demands on Elizabeth's time, and being able to follow the plan from the year before for gifts to the tenants also simplified preparations. Georgiana insisted on participating in the kitchen with the preparation of fruit cake and other recipes, pleading compensation for all the days she had missed while her arm was healing.

Weeks earlier they had been invited to contribute to the bazaar, and they followed the last year's list of contributions, adding some additional breads and an item of stitchery from each of the Darcy ladies. The bazaar was on the 9th, but, though she did not feel particularly unwell, Elizabeth chose not to go, commissioning Georgiana and Darcy to purchase certain items should they be available, keeping in mind that they'd like to take gifts to the Bingleys. She wasn't eager to listen to the endless congratulations attending her now very obviously altered shape and was content to have people believe she was "in delicate health." She suggested to Darcy that if anyone asked, he should say, "She's well; she's just taking advantage of the situation."

While hunting with Howell, Darcy told Mrs. Howell that Elizabeth would be glad to receive her for tea—alone—on a morning of her choosing. She came on Thursday, the 14th. Before Georgiana arrived from her morning's activities, Elizabeth asked Mrs. Howell if she might invite Georgiana for dinner on the 29th. She indicated that she and Darcy had been invited to a small party and that there would be no other young people.

Thus was the problem resolved.

December 22, Friday: Christmas at Thornwood

Elizabeth and Georgiana delivered the gifts to the tenants on the 22nd, and they left for Thornwood on the 23rd.

If human affairs always were managed so well as they were at the Bingley household during that holiday, novels might never be written. All that can be said is that many happy memories of the event were laid up in the minds and hearts of the participants.

December 29, Friday: Dinner at the Carleton's

Darcy and Elizabeth left Georgiana at the Howell's as planned and proceeded to the Carletons. Carleton greeted them at the door, took their wraps, and ushered them into the parlor where the other guests were waiting.

He introduced them to his parents and allowed Fitzwilliam to introduce Margaret.

"I'm pleased to meet you," Elizabeth said.

"And I you," Margaret replied.

Fitzwilliam, very seriously, said, "Elizabeth, you're looking well; congratulations. I can see you're very happy." Then looking to Darcy he said, "And you too; congratulations."

Elizabeth responded, "Thank you; I am; but I still haven't heard what it is that will take you to America."

"Business. My eldest brother has a number of friends in London who have formed an import-export business and they need someone to handle the business from the colonies—The United States, I mean."

"Where will you live?"

"Boston."

"Aren't you concerned about how you'll like living there?"

"I'm more concerned about the sea voyage. Once there, I'm sure we shall manage quite nicely."

Elizabeth may have appeared to Fitzwilliam anxious about the whole scheme because he continued, "The people are quite civilized, you know. After all, most of them or their ancestors came from England. I'm told they only paint their faces and don feathers when they want to make an extremely large batch of tea."

This brought smiles to most of the faces.

During this conversation Margaret remained quiet, but listened attentively. Theresa entered the room, greeted them and invited the party to follow her to the dining room, with apologies for her absence when they arrived.

There were only eight at the table, and the elder Carletons contributed little to the conversation. With the added reticence that blanketed the gathering resulting from the return of the daughter so long estranged from her family, and with her new husband, a single conversation was followed by the entire group during the course of the dinner.

Fitzwilliam looked at Elizabeth and began "Georgiana...."

"She was invited to dine with the Howells today and their daughter Sally."

With Margaret across the table from her, Elizabeth could not fail to notice that she was concentrating her attention on her plate during this exchange.

Darcy came to the rescue asking, "Do you know what your housing accommodations in Boston will be?"

"This was one of the reasons for delaying our departure to the spring. We do have additional business here to tend to in organizing the company, but housing in Boston is short, so we expect to buy a plot of land and have a house built for us during the summer. Winter building simply is not attempted."

"Is it much colder there than here?" Theresa asked.

"In the winter, yes; very decidedly. They get quite a lot of snow, and wind as well. Fortunately they are used to it, and with so much stone for building fireplaces and wood for burning, they get along very well."

So the evening continued. Later when the party was dispersing, Fitzwilliam said privately to Darcy, "Thank you for coming; and if we can manage it somehow, I would like to see Georgiana before we leave."

All parted cordially, and Elizabeth and Darcy retraced their path to the Howells to pick up Georgiana who, it appeared, had enjoyed a much livlier and more pleasant visit than had her brother and his wife.

Saturday

The next morning Darcy and Elizabeth agreed to meet in his study after breakfast.

"What do you think?" Elizabeth began.

"I don't know. I feel torn. I'm afraid that Georgiana eventually will find out that Fitzwilliam was here, and if he never comes back from America, how can she help but resent it if I conceal his visit."

"Margaret was not what I expected."

"What did you expect?"

"I don't know. Because she ran away from home I suppose I expected someone louder, more brazen, possibly even insolent. Instead, she's very like the kind of woman I would expect to attract Fitzwilliam, except that she was so quiet. She seems very intelligent."

"How could you tell? She barely said a word."

"You couldn't see her during dinner, but I sat opposite her and could see her the whole time. She followed the conversation very carefully. And her countenance revealed understanding, but at times a critical attitude, as if questioning, wondering.

"If I had met her in London in company with strangers, knowing nothing of her life history, I believe I might have judged her the very kind of person I'd like for a friend."

"If we do arrange a meeting—invite them to tea, for example—we'll have to tell Georgiana the whole story in advance. There's too much chance she would find out the truth later. I don't want to be a position of lying to her."

"She's no child; eventually she's going to have to learn about some of the difficulties people get into—that not all young women who run away from home escape as lightly as Lydia did. I don't know if you observed Georgiana while Lydia was here, but I did."

"I did. It was almost as if she were a student trying to learn as much as she could by observing."

"I think we should concede she's a lot wiser for her age than we sometimes give her credit for."

Thus it was decided. They sent a message to invite Fitzwilliam and his bride for tea on Sunday, the next day, the day before they would return to London.

That afternoon, in order to prepare Georgiana for the meeting, they revealed the story to her, and as they hoped, while saddened by the story, Georgiana was glad to be able to see Fitzwilliam one more time before he left for America and to meet his bride.

January, 1816

January, February, and March: most agreeable months to precede a birth. The mother-to-be spent few moments bemoaning her inability to go riding when so few of the days were fine. Darcy rode with Georgiana on pleasant days, offering pointers on riding that would assist her in the future to avoid falls.

The threesome engaged in most of their other usual activities, accepting invitations to teas and dinners as they were offered and occasionally inviting friends for Sunday afternoon tea as they left church.

Four times during these months Mr. Harrison came on Saturday evening and stayed for supper. In each case a note would arrive the preceding Tuesday or Wednesday reading something like this.

"Dear Mr. and Mrs. Darcy,
 I intend to visit the Pettigrews this coming weekend and hope you will be able to receive me late Saturday afternoon. Should this be inconvenient, be kind enough to send a message to them for me.
 I hope that both you and Miss Darcy are well. I look forward to seeing you all.
Respectfully,
Stuart Harrison"

Because their social life had been restricted by Elizabeth's condition, in each case they were able to entertain him at supper. By the third time it happened Darcy began to believe Mr. Harrison was blessed with luck that few mortals enjoy, and by the fourth time it happened, he was certain of it. "Will our friends never invite us on a Saturday evening that he has selected?" Darcy complained, though not in Georgiana's presence.

"It could be worse, my love," Elizabeth replied. "He could be a boring, sycophantic, stupid oaf who has never read a book or contemplated life beyond his own village."

Early in January, following a meeting with Mrs. Whipple, Elizabeth talked with Mrs. Blakely about her impending confinement. Of the several ladies she had become acquainted with during the year at Pemberley, she was the one Elizabeth had come to look to for comfort and easy companionship. Now it was she whom she requested to assist her and Mrs. Whipple at the birth. Mrs. Blakely agreed, even seemed honored by the request. She would have liked to ask Mrs. Pettigrew, because she so admired her courage and lively manner, but was concerned that Darcy might think she was attempting to forge a closer relationship to the family of Georgiana's suitor. An added difficulty was the greater distance Mrs. Pettigrew would have to come. Then too, Mrs. Pettigrew had not had a child, and Mrs. Blakeley had.

During March, Elizabeth's walk became slower, more deliberate, attempting to avoid an unthinking movement that could result in a fall. Walks became strolls as baby pushed up against her lungs, restricting her breathing. As the weeks went by she felt ever more intensely the loving presence and assistance of the man she had come to love so dearly.

The Darcys did attend the wedding of Caroline Bingley and Sir Humphrey Winston. While observing the ceremony Elizabeth considered the gratitude she felt at being the one who now sat beside Darcy in her enlarged condition instead of Caroline, who had seemed so intent on that position. Should the situation have been otherwise, she might now have been marrying someone very like Sir Humphrey, hardly the worst fate that can befall a woman, but infinitely worse than the position she now filled.

April 10 was the expected date of delivery, and as it came and went Elizabeth began to feel an envy of her sweet, beautiful sister Jane such as she had never before experienced. "She had her baby a month early—or at least we thought it was a month early—and here I am, past due and big as a horse." For at least three weeks Elizabeth had been experiencing pains like the ones Jane had described so well. Not severe pains, but not sensations that would go unnoticed either.

"If I could only breathe like a normal human being," she would complain.

"You are very normal, Lizzy," Darcy would respond.

"You just say that because you love me."

"I stand indicted, tried, and convicted; I do love you, indeed."

April 18, Thursday: Emiline

It was late afternoon when Elizabeth asked Darcy to send for the midwife. Darcy sent Elizabeth to their bedroom with Susan while he ordered the carriage to fetch Mrs. Blakely and Mrs. Whipple. When he arrived at their bedroom, Annie had helped her undress, and she was in bed, resting comfortably. Darcy set a chair by the bed and stayed with her.

Mrs. Whipple arrived and quietly took charge. She accepted Mrs. Blakely in the bedroom, but was quietly insistent that Darcy should leave.

"I'll send someone to you at least every hour to let you know how things are progressing.

"Every hour!" Darcy objected.

"These things often take many hours; don't you worry; all will be well.

"But Mrs. Bingley...."

"A most unusual birth. In all my years I've never seen another like it. You haven't had supper yet, have you?"

"No."

"Then I suggest you go have something to eat."

"What about Mrs. Darcy?"

"We can't let her have anything to eat now. She'll be fine. The first one is always the most difficult, especially for the husband."

He left and found Georgiana still in the drawing room. They had supper, though neither ate much. They spoke even less. They returned to the drawing room for the dreary waiting. Darcy couldn't read; he kept wandering about the room, looking out the window at the chill, starlit April night. It was just past the full moon, and as the evening progressed, he marked its rise in the sky. He folded his arms, then unfolded them. He walked to the fireplace and stared at the flames; He looked at his watch again and again, despairing at the slow advance. He sat down and almost immediately stood up again and resumed his pacing.

Mrs. Whipple was as good as her word. Every hour close to the hour Sarah appeared to say that all was progressing well.

It was nearly eleven o'clock when Darcy looked at Georgiana and said, "You look very calm, Georgiana."

"I'm not. Do you think they'd let me go in to see how she is?"

"You want to?"

"Yes."

"Childbirth is serious business; you're very young."

"Women younger than I have babies."

"Yes, but...."

"Please, Darcy, if it's too difficult for me, I promise I'll come back."

"She told me she wished you could be there."

"She did? Then let me go, please."

He nodded and said, "Tell her I love her."

"She knows that."

"Tell her anyway."

She nodded and rushed out the door.

Once Mrs. Whipple realized that Elizabeth did indeed want Georgiana with her and was adamant, she admitted her. Mrs. Blakely was sitting beside Elizabeth. Georgiana brought a chair to the other side of the bed and sat down.

Mrs. Whipple sat in her chair near the window, relaxed, but seeing and hearing all—Elizabeth's breathing, her alternating restlessness and calm.

Mrs. Blakely mopped Elizabeth's brow with a soft cloth and offered her a sip of tepid tea from time to time.

Annie sat on a chair near the door, ready to respond to any command.

Near midnight Elizabeth groaned and shifted about restlessly, more agitated than previously, then called, "Mrs. Whipple, come."

Georgiana reached across the bed and took Elizabeth's hand.

Mrs. Whipple lifted the covers and commanded "Annie, bring several fresh towels; the water has broken."

Annie brought a stack of towels from a table and removed the pail of soiled linens. Mrs. Whipple skillfully stretched several fresh towels under Elizabeth and covered her again.

"There, there, Mrs. Darcy, it shouldn't be long now."

Mrs. Blakely took Elizabeth's hand, and Mrs. Whipple moved her chair near the bed.

Elizabeth moaned and grimaced, sweating, then relaxed, her eyes closed. Mrs. Blakely dabbed Elizabeth's face and neck with the cloth.

"Is she sleeping?" Georgiana asked.

"No, Miss Darcy, just resting."

"Mrs. Whipple, it feels...."

Mrs. Whipple stood up, pulled the covers back and examined Elizabeth. Then she rearranged the covers. "You're doing just fine, Mrs. Darcy; it won't be long now."

"I'm so glad you've came, Georgiana."

"Me too. Darcy told me to tell you he loves you."

She responded with a weak smile.

Now urgently, Elizabeth called, "Mrs. Whipple...."

She pulled the covers back again. "You're doing just fine; it won't be long now." But this time she didn't cover Elizabeth. "When the pain comes next time, Mrs. Darcy, push."

The pain began, and Elizabeth pushed, her face reddening. Once again she closed her eyes and lay still, breathing deeply. The cycle resumed: pain and push, then relax. Each time Mrs. Whipple urged her to push even harder. At each push she grasped the hands of her companions even tighter, so that finally she was grasping as if trying to keep herself from falling off a cliff.

"Mrs. ...."

"Push, Mrs. Darcy, push; just as if you were having a bowel movement."

"I think I am."

"No, this is something quite different," she said gently.

The pain began again and Mrs. Whipple urged Elizabeth to push.

"The head is coming; push."

And push she did 'til her face was nearly beet red.

"The head is out...look at that dark hair. Georgiana and Mrs. Blakely rose up to look.

"Now one more, big, big push!" Mrs. Whipple urged.

Elizabeth took a deep breath and strained and tightened her grip on both her companions' hands.

"Ah, here she is," Mrs. Whipple said, taking the newborn in both hands and laying her on Elizabeth's abdomen, "crying as if she already knew what life is all about!"

Tears came to Elizabeth's eyes as she sobbed and sighed in relief that it was over.

"Oh, Elizabeth, she's beautiful!" Georgiana cried.

"Annie, bring me that tray," Mrs. Whipple commanded. She took a piece of string and tied it around the umbilical cord near Baby Darcy's abdomen.

"Just a little more unfinished business here. Mrs. Darcy, you're going to need to push one more time. Push," Mrs. Whipple commanded, and Elizabeth pushed, expelling the afterbirth.

Now she took the scissors from the tray and cut the umbilical cord. She removed the afterbirth and tidied up.

She laid out the small blanket on the bed, then took a moist cloth and gently patted baby Darcy to clean her. She took baby from Elizabeth's abdomen, put her on the blanket, wrapped it snugly around her, and laid her on the bed beside her mother.

Mrs. Whipple checked to see that there was no abnormal bleeding, wrapped cloths around Elizabeth and covered her.

Mrs. Whipple turned to the door. "Annie, you can tell Mr. Darcy he's the father of a healthy baby girl."

"No, let me," Georgiana said.

"Very well, and tell him he can he can come in for just a few minutes."

Georgiana rushed to the drawing room. "Darcy, it's a beautiful baby girl!"

"And Elizabeth...?" he asked as he moved toward the door.

"She's fine—just very tired; she was wonderful. Mrs. Whipple says you can go in for just a few minutes."

"And you'd better go to bed."

She nodded.

Darcy hurried to the bedroom and found Elizabeth with her eyes closed, but awake and waiting for him, her straggling hair now brushed back from her face.

Mrs. Blakely had been taken to the bedroom prepared for her, and Mrs. Whipple had settled back into a comfortable chair. She stood up as Darcy entered.

"We've ordered tea for Mrs. Darcy," Mrs. Whipple said. "I think I'll go and take mine in the kitchen. I'll be back before long. Would you like hot chocolate instead, Mr. Darcy?"

"No, tea will be fine."

He walked quietly to Elizabeth's side, bent down and kissed her forehead. He lifted her hand and held it between both of his. He sat down and gazed at their sleeping infant, now fully clothed.

"She's so small."

"Mrs. Whipple assures me she's plenty big for a mother my size."

"Look; her tiny fists are clenched together on her chest; she looks almost as if her eyes are squeezed shut." Then, looking up, "Was it very painful?"

"Dreadfully, but mostly it was extremely hard work. I wouldn't do it for anything else in the world."

"Even for diamonds?"

"Not for all the diamonds in Africa."

The tea came and she took a sip. "When Mrs. Whipple comes back, you'll have to leave; I need to sleep. I'm so tired."

"When should I come again?"

"I'll send for you when I wake up."

"I had Bradford make up the bed in my dressing room; I'm going to sleep there."

She smiled in response, and he left as soon as Mrs. Whipple returned.

"I'm going to put baby in her crib now, Mrs. Darcy, so you can sleep. She won't sleep long. When she starts crying you'll waken, and we'll put her to breast for her first feeding."

That done, Mrs. Whipple snuffed all the candles but one and pulled a blanket over herself in the most comfortable chair.

Darcy awoke abruptly to a strange noise; not loud, but somehow frightening. The room was nearly dark, but as he looked at the draperies, he could see bright light streaming in through a narrow strip.

He flung himself out of bed, drew on his robe, and moved swiftly to their bedroom door. Hearing rustling and quiet voices, he opened the door and found Elizabeth sitting up in bed, babe at her breast with Mrs. Whipple standing beside her assisting.

"Darcy," Elizabeth whispered, "Come in."

"If you'll be here, Mr. Darcy, I'd like to leave for awhile," Mrs. Whipple said.

"Of course; I'll wait until you return."

Nodding, she left.

"Sit on the bed beside me."

He arranged the pillows and climbed up beside her. He reached over, put his thumb on baby's cheek and gently stroked it.

"She's a greedy eater."

"This is her third feeding already."

"What time is it?"

"It must be almost ten. She woke me first at just after four. I was so hungry myself that I sent Katie to get me some breakfast. Sarah and Annie went to bed when you left and got Katie out of bed to attend if I needed anything. Mrs. Sims went to bed, but left everything waiting."

"You have the servants functioning very nicely."

"They've been wonderful."

Baby released Elizabeth's nipple, and she shifted her to the other breast.

"It really looks like she's working."

"It feels like it too."

Darcy leaned back on the pillows, closing his eyes. "It seems as if my mind has been dredging up every trite phrase I've ever heard."

"Like what?"

He put his hand over baby's side and said, "...like 'the fruits of your labor.'"

"And...."

"There's no such thing as free love."

"I don't think I've heard that one."

"Maybe it's because I've thought it so often, it seems trite."

"Phrases are trite because they're true. Are there more?"

"Yes; I keep thinking: 'We pay for our pleasure.'"

"We certainly have had our pleasure."

He closed his eyes. "I'm so relieved, Lizzy."

"Me too." Propped against the pillows they rested, listening to the sounds...the breeze in the trees, distant sounds of people walking in the house, and the faint chirping of birds.

"Have you had any really useful thoughts, like a name for her?"

"Yes, I have. I'd like to call her Emiline."

"Do you know someone by that name?"

"My father's mother's name was Emily."

"It's a beautiful name. She's asleep. Would you take her to the cradle?"

"Gladly." He got off the bed, walked around and gently picked up his daughter in his beautiful hands. He lifted her up and kissed her cheek. "So soft," he whispered, as he gently laid her in the cradle. He sat down on the chair beside the bed and said, "You still haven't had much sleep, have you?"

"And I'm hungry again too."

"I'll send for something." He opened the door to the hall and found Annie had returned to her post. "Annie, please send for breakfast for Mrs. Darcy. She's very hungry."

He returned to the bedside and said, "I need to get dressed and have some breakfast myself. Mrs. Whipple will be back soon. When should I come again?"

"Let me send for you."

"I'll keep Fenton informed of where I am. As soon as you send for me, I'll come."

It was almost three-thirty when William found Darcy returning the dogs to the kennels.

Mrs. Whipple left as he entered the bedroom.

He kissed Elizabeth and sat down to watch.

"She doesn't let me sleep much. After I nursed her again about noon Annie washed me and I slept until she woke me again a little while ago."

"I wrote notes to your parents and to Jane and the Gardners."

"Oh, thank you, Darcy; I completely forgot. Did you send them already?"

"I sent Davy with them after I had breakfast. Did you have dinner?"

"Yes, I was starved. Mrs. Sims sent me a lovely tray. I ate so much she'll think you were here with me!"

"She knows Georgiana and I were in the dining room for dinner."

"Did Georgiana sleep late?"

"She came down at about 11:00 for a hearty breakfast and ate like a field worker at dinner as well. She's so proud of you! Keeps talking about how you sweated and pushed and made the most awful faces, but never cried or screamed; not a tear until it was all over."

"A pretty picture!"

"A beautiful picture; I only wish I could have been here."

She lifted baby and shifted her to the other breast, then extended her hand to him.

He caressed it as he observed mother and child. "Mrs. Blakely slept late too, and after some breakfast I sent her home in the carriage. Actually she and Georgiana ate together."

"She was just wonderful; barely said a word; just kept mopping my brow and holding my hand. And Georgiana too. I needed both of them."

"It doesn't seem to have harmed her. She seems positively exhilarated. She wants to see you again."

"Tell her I'll send for her later, after I've slept again. I feel so tired...and yet I can't sleep soundly. It's as if every tiny bit of my body is vibrating. She's quit nursing again. Will you put her in the cradle and call Mrs. Whipple? I feel sleepy again."

He picked her up and carried her to the window, examining her face and fingers, making soft clicking sounds to her with his tongue.

He put her into the cradle and returned to the bed. Sitting on the edge of the bed he drew Elizabeth towards him, embracing her, her head against his shoulders.

"I love you." he whispered.

"And I love you."

He allowed her to rest back on the pillows and caressed her cheek with his thumb. He left as Mrs. Whipple re-entered the bedroom.

He found Georgiana in the drawing room. "She's going to send for you when she awakens. Let's take a walk."

"It's really quite chill."

"Just a short one; I think we could both use some exercise."

They took a turn around the grounds and agreed to go for a ride the next morning. They walked through the kitchen on the way back to ask that hot chocolate be sent to them in the drawing room.

They both tried to read, but before long Georgiana picked up her needlework, and Darcy was leafing through a book of drawings of ancient structures—pyramids, temples, bridges, and amphitheatres.

Finally, near seven Fenton came and announced, "Mrs. Darcy would like to see both of you."

Darcy told him to tell Mrs. Sims to delay supper until they returned. "We won't be an hour."

Mother and baby were into the feeding routine again. Georgiana approached the bed, and Darcy closed the door as Mrs. Whipple left.

"Elizabeth, isn't she just wonderful? Just think! I'm an aunt! What can I get her for a birth present?"

"I think you've already given it...your presence at her birth."

Georgiana looked up at Darcy. "Come, see her, isn't she grand? Just think, the first Darcy of her generation. When...if I have children, they'll be her cousins."

"You are racing on ahead, aren't you?" said Elizabeth.

Darcy stood behind Georgiana observing the scene.

"Are you hungry?" Georgiana asked.

"Yes, Mrs. Whipple is going to have her supper and bring back a tray for me."

"Are you still tired?" Darcy asked.

"I'm feeling better. I slept more soundly this time. I still feel...heavy...and tender, she said, laying her free hand on her abdomen." She shifted baby to her other breast.

Georgiana moved to leave, but Darcy said, "No, don't leave; wait until Mrs. Whipple returns. I'll look in again before I go to bed." He bent down and kissed Elizabeth and baby and left.

When he did return at bedtime, Darcy opened the door from his dressing room and saw that only one candle burned, and all were apparently asleep. He quietly closed the door, undressed, and was himself soon asleep.

He awoke, opened the draperies, dressed, and opened the door to their bedroom. Feeding was once more in progress.

"Good morning, Darcy."

"Good morning, Elizabeth." He approached the bed, kissed her, caressed baby, and left as quietly as he had come.

Georgiana was already in the dining room, dressed to ride.

"Mother and baby are awake and busy with her feeding."

Georgiana smiled, "How proud the new father looks!"

"Almost as proud as the new aunt."

On his way to breakfast, Darcy had asked Fenton to send word that he and Georgiana would be taking Prince and Dancer for a ride and that they should be saddled. So when they arrived at the stables, David and Sims were just bringing the horses out. Darcy observed that Georgiana's greeting to David seemed very easy.

Darcy helped her mount, then mounted Prince. He led the way out of the stable yard along the Lambton road, and Dancer followed close behind. Before long, they turned into a field. The grass was sprinkled with dew, the ground firm. They walked the horses over the uneven turf until Georgiana pleaded chill. He turned and they made their way back to the stable, riding for a stretch at a gallop before nearing the stables.

He helped her dismount and they left the horses to Davy's care. Darcy stopped at Fenton's station and asked, "Any word from Mrs. Darcy?"

"Not yet, sir. I did see Annie taking bath water up."

"Good idea; Fenton, tell Bradford to prepare a bath for me. I'll go up shortly."

"Aye, sir."

He picked up mail in the hall and went to his study to look it over.

Bathed and again dressed, he looked in again and found mother and babe sleeping.

"Mr. Darcy," Mrs. Whipple whispered as she approached and beckoned him to the hall. "Mrs. Darcy says baby's nanny will arrive about noon, and I would like to go home this afternoon."

"We'll keep the carriage harnessed and ready for you to leave after Mrs. Peters arrives."

"Thank you, sir."

"And I'll leave your pay with Fenton."

"Thank you, sir. Mother and baby are doing fine."

"Many thanks to you."

Soon after Georgiana and Darcy returned to the drawing room following dinner, Fenton came in to say that Mrs. Darcy was ready to see them. Georgiana went first and came back smiling.

Mrs. Peters greeted Darcy when he arrived, and then left the room. Elizabeth was resting and baby was in her cradle.

"Progress."

"Yes, she seems content for the moment. Come, lie down beside me."

"In my clothes?"

"Yes; Bradford can tidy you up later. I need you to cuddle me."

He took off his shoes and lay beside her, caressing her hand. They had been resting for several minutes, enjoying each other's presence, when Darcy said, "It seems inevitable that Georgiana will marry Harrison. It's just a matter of time."

"Oh, I'm sure you'll find many diversions and obstacles to set in their way."

"Do you also predict whether or not I'll be successful?"

"There is something you may not be aware of."

"What is that?"

"I suspect that Georgiana has determined to learn to sew."

"Whatever makes you say that?"

"You remember how her new riding habit was ruined at the fox hunt?"

"Yes. The doctor cut the sleeve off."

"You've been hunting rather frequently lately, haven't you?"

"But you've never objected."

"No, I haven't. But those mornings have been rather long. And on some of those mornings Georgiana was ripping out the stitching on that jacket."

"Why would she do that?"

"I think she was trying to learn how it was constructed."

"But why?"

"I think she's decided she just might like to be a professor's wife. Or perhaps even a head-master's."

"Oh, Lord. Well, I do believe I shall have countless moments when I'll be grateful for the distractions Emiline will create."

"Are you forgetting our two-in-the bedroom rule?"

"I think we're going to have to change the rule to "three-in-the-bedroom."

"At least for some months." She reflected for some time and then said, "Darcy, I've been thinking about something else—about your nephew."

"Yes, so have I."

"Once they leave for America you may never see any of them again, and you've never even seen him once. Have you considered that John is Carleton's nephew also?"

"I have. Strange, isn't it? Carleton and Theresa are desperate to have a child, and Fitzwilliam and Margaret had one too soon and two pregnancies more than they could manage."

"Why do you say 'desperate?'"

"You may have been watching Margaret that day at dinner, but I keep remembering Theresa and the way she looked, especially at you. I'm sure of it—she was envious. In fact, I'm so sure that I want your permission to disclose our project to Carleton."

"You mean the modern incon..."

"Exactly."

"But how could he help?"

"If they're desperate enough, they might be willing to make a sacrifice."

"What kind of sacrifice?"

"If we tell them all we've discovered, and that we believe that conception takes place about two weeks before the period is expected, they may be willing to confine their lovemaking to those days."

"It's an interesting idea, but I'm going to have to think about it for awhile. After all, if they are desperate to have a child, they may not exactly approve of our efforts to delay having ours. It does mean, though, that we have an additional reason for remaining good friends with the Carletons. And that brings me back to my original concern—Fitzwilliam's son John. Will you ever forgive yourself if you don't see him before they leave?"

"That's what concerns me."

"We do have an opportunity before us, a small gathering."

"Emiline's baptism."

"I know you won't be sorry."

"Isn't that Georgiana's line?"